Exhumed

S.J. Patrick

Also by S.J. Patrick

Dark Matter

The Sentience

© S.J. Patrick 2024

All rights reserved. No part of this publication may be reproduced, distributed, or transmitted in any form without prior written consent of the author.

Cover art by D. Bright

ISBN: 9798870864631

Stockholm

Present Day

Prologue

Could this get any worse, wondered Cristina Grigorcea. Cristina was the head of archaeology at the Institute of Archaeology and Art History in Cluj-Napoca, Romania, and was currently located on the deeply forested slopes of a small extension of the Carpathian Mountains marking the eastern boundary of Satu Mare County.

This site had been a labour of love for Cristina since she discovered it over a decade prior, during her time as a student at the Babes-Bolyai University in Cluj-Napoca. But every single step of the process had been met with frustration and resistance. The fact that it had taken the better part of a decade for her team to be granted rights to perform the archaeological dig said enough. She often lamented that it would be easier if she simply resorted to grave robbing instead.

The cause for Cristina's latest consternation was

the fact that her team, consisting of herself and six graduate students from Cluj-Napoca University, had been robbed overnight – and not for the first time. They awoke to find precious specimens missing, artifacts that Cristina believed to date as far back as the 13th century. It was a disaster.

Following the first theft several weeks earlier, Cristina had alerted the authorities and demanded action – something she soon regretted when she found a pair of disinterested policemen tramping crudely around her meticulous site. To make matters worse, they had informed her that they'd 'keep an eye out' for the stolen material before brushing her off whenever she called to enquire. Why even bother reporting it this time …?

Cristina's students were running around in a disorganised frenzy, trying to itemise everything that remained. There was just as much at stake for each of them – this research would form the backbone of their doctoral theses and they couldn't afford to lose two months' worth of field samples.

Just the reminder that they had been in the field for two months now and potentially had nothing to show for it made Cristina want to crawl back into her sleeping bag and cry. All she could wonder was what she did to deserve such misfortune. But rather than let her emotions get in her way, she forced herself to take charge of the situation and wrangle her students.

For the past week or so, Cristina had a hunch in the deepest part of her gut that they were on the precipice of a career-defining discovery. It was this hunch alone that kept her going. Having gathered her students into a makeshift meeting and learnt the scope of their losses, she gave a pep talk that somehow surprised even herself at how positive and upbeat it was.

All of her students knew exactly what was on her mind – she could barely shut up about it in the evenings when the sun set too low for them to continue their exploration. She believed that they were on the verge of uncovering an ancient tomb. A tomb from the 13th century that would prove an invaluable discovery in the fields of archaeology and history.

In truth, it wasn't wholly a hunch. All of the signs were there – or at least they had been – before their theft in the night. They had discovered several ancient crucifixes crudely formed out of silver and buried in a suspicious layout surrounding the area Cristina was focusing on excavating. To a modern person, they might think these represented objects of worship lain around a burial site – but Cristina suspected something entirely different. She knew just how superstitious the people of this region had been back in the 13th century (and, in truth, still were to this very day). She surmised these crucifixes instead to represent 'warding' to prevent the entombed from rising once more as a *strigoi* – a vampire.

The artifacts weren't the only clues. The fact that she had to fight tooth and nail in the legal system against a group of fanatical lunatics for years of her life in order to be granted access to the site all but confirmed her suspicions. Obviously, there was no such thing as actual strigoi – but these superstitions ran deep. Cristina knew that there were oral legends passed down about this location, and she intended to find their source!

Her rousing pep talk worked wonders – initially ... However, as the days dragged on and they still had nothing to show for it, the morale of the camp once more descended to one of morose depression. Everyone (in truth, even Cristina) was pondering pulling the plug on the entire operation. It was only the sunk-cost fallacy (or was it the gambler's fallacy?) that kept them going – the desperate hope that something would reveal itself if they just persevered.

Eventually, nine days after the theft of their previously collected artifacts, they struck gold, so to speak. It was Cristina herself, dirty and bloody from her travails, who uncovered what appeared to be the lid of a coffin. This was it!

Contrary to the public perception of archaeology, where the 'scientists' would have the find unearthed in the blink of an eye – that was not how things worked in the real world. It took Cristina and her team a further six painstaking days to fully expose this buried casket. They worked with the meticulous care of a surgeon, careful not to damage the find in any way. Their care was perhaps even too meticulous, as the casket was clearly made out of a very heavy iron. If it were a wooden box, it would have rotted away centuries ago.

Over the course of the excavation, the team couldn't help but notice that the lid of the coffin appeared to be locked in place. Cristina forbade any attempt at forcing through the locks (in spite of her own burning curiosity), she knew that if there truly was a body entombed within, allowing the air into the casket would only kickstart a ticking time bomb of decay. Finds like this must be treated with the strictest of care.

It was not a popular instruction amongst her cohort. Cristina's students were less mature than she, and almost without exception they wanted to see some results for their hard work and sacrifice. Again, Cristina put her foot down and threatened expulsion from their graduate program for anyone stupid enough to disobey her instructions. Satisfied with the reaction to her very real threat, Cristina retired to her tent, eager for the following day when the transport she had already organised would arrive to deliver the casket back to her laboratory in Cluj-Napoca.

Contrary to her instructions, once Cristina drifted off to sleep, things were not destined to go as she planned. She was awoken in the dead of night to screams of abject terror. Her first instinct was to suspect that the thieves had returned to seek more plunder, but that didn't make sense. Not with how these screams sounded …

She rushed out of her tent and spotted torchlight in the direction of the casket. The same direction from which the screams had originated. Her stomach knotted at this point. Whether in fear or rage, she couldn't quite say – but either way she knew that she had been disobeyed. One of her (soon to be former) students had opened the casket under the cover of darkness.

Racing towards the casket, joined by the remainder of her students who had also received the same rude awakening, Cristina saw that two fools had indeed cracked through the brittle and aged locks and cast the lid of the coffin aside. It was still too dark to view inside from her approach, but Cristina could see that one of the fools – Tomas – had stumbled backwards and fallen to the ground with his hands pressed to his blood-soaked throat. The other fool, Zsanett was the source of the shrill screams piercing the night.

Finally arriving on the scene, the cries immediately made sense to Cristina. Unlike Zsanett (and now several other students) who were shocked into screams, Cristina reacted differently. Despite holding no religious beliefs, she made the sign of the cross as she slowly backed away from what they had unearthed.

One

Standing at the podium and delivering his seminar, Dr David Reynolds had an excellent view of the packed lecture theatre, so the late arrival of two well-dressed gentlemen did not escape his notice. David was no novice in this situation, so the distraction did nothing to throw him off his talk – however, in a subconscious stream of thought, it did make him wonder just what was the point of showing up so late, since his presentation was already nearing its conclusion.

David was 42 years old and even at this comparatively young age he had risen to the very top of his field as a clinical haematologist, with several breakthrough discoveries giving rise to his prominence. It was for this very reason that he was presenting at the International Conference on Haematology and Immunology, conveniently located in his home town of Sydney.

As his keynote presentation drew to a close, David mentally prepared himself for the onslaught of questions he knew would be waiting for him. Glancing over his shoulder at the presentation screen so that he could guide his laser pointer to help describe a series of charts on his slide, he spotted the picture of himself in the top corner of the screen and cringed a little. There was nothing wrong with it, he just always hated the way he looked in photos. David was a tall man, coming in at 192 centimetres, or around six feet three inches tall. He was thin as a rake and had a thick mop of unkempt brown hair. He was never one to go out of his way to try and look nice, considering it a waste of his time.

The final slide of the presentation flicked up onto the screen, displaying David's name and contact details. He thanked the audience for their attention and waited for the prolonged round of applause to peter out, mildly anxious to discover how his research had been received. Every presentation went the same way; the majority of the audience were content to simply listen, but there were always a number of people with questions at the ready. Some genuine, some with an agenda, and some just seeking attention.

The presentation he had just concluded was on his latest research into rare blood types, specifically 'Golden Blood'. Golden Blood was not a new discovery, first found more than 60 years earlier in an Australian Aboriginal woman. It was an extraordinarily rare subgroup of the Rh blood group system, and David had been performing groundbreaking new research into how the secrets it held could be unlocked, which could lead to a new era of treatments for various blood disorders.

'Have you considered expanding your search pool to include rhesus monkeys?' asked the first attendee. This immediately irritated David, this questioner fell into the 'attention-seeking' category right off the bat. The 'Rh' initially stood for 'Rhesus factor', as the original science from 1937 mistakenly concluded that it was the same as an antigen found in rhesus macaques – but this had long since been disproven. Unfortunately, the 'Rh', and even the term 'Rhesus factor' had become too pervasive and had stuck for all eternity.

Carefully considering his words, trying his hardest to be polite when answering the question that he thought everyone in the room should already know, David diplomatically explained why he had *not* expanded his search to include rhesus monkeys. He then waited as the session chair selected the next eager attendee with her hand raised to provide another question.

Being the keynote speaker for this conference session meant David had the longest talk and also the longest period of questioning. Giving talks was the easy part, they had long since lost any scare factor. But answering questions to a quorum of his peers never got any less nerve-racking. David had full confidence in his skills and understanding of his research, but there was always that fear of making a mistake and looking foolish.

A rush of relief ran through David's body when he heard the session chair say those magical words: 'That's all the time we've got for questions. Will everybody please thank Dr Reynolds once more for his fantastic presentation.'

Smiling awkwardly through the applause, David made his way off the stage as the session chair began the introduction to the next speaker. He would have loved to get out of the theatre and walk off some of the tension, but that was impolite, so instead he sat through the next talk before quietly making his exit as they were applauding its conclusion.

The corridor of the Sydney Exhibition Centre was almost empty in comparison to the crowded lecture theatre he had just exited; however, David's eyes were immediately drawn to the two well-dressed men who had walked into his keynote presentation towards the end – they were staring straight at him. He gave a polite half-smile and turned to walk away, but they quickly cut him off and introduced themselves with Nordic names that he was too frazzled to properly absorb. What he did absorb was that they said they were operating on behalf of the ECDC.

What the hell would the European Centre for Disease prevention and Control want with him? Obviously he could conclude that they probably wanted his advice on something related to haematology – he wasn't *that* frazzled – but why him? Why like this? Surely, they had their own expert haematologists who could handle the problem?

Snapping out of his confusion, David turned these exact questions back on his assailants – enjoying being on the other end of questions for a change. The responses he received went a long way towards piquing his interest, though they also annoyed him with how vague and secretive they were. He was told that a 'situation' had arisen and that he was identified as the 'leading expert' in his field, which was why they wanted none other than he himself. They concluded with something that gave him a sinking feeling in the pit of his stomach, saying that it was a matter of 'international concern'. Politically correct terminology that David assumed could only mean a newly discovered blood disease with some potentially nasty consequences.

David caught the sideways glances of several other conference attendees who were clearly wondering what was going on. Cornered by two men in suits, it looked more like he was being questioned under suspicion of something rather than being recruited. Before he could even begin to ask any more questions, one of the men cut him off at the pass by saying that they needed him to leave with them immediately.

This kind of tactic pissed David off; he knew it well. By putting pressure on him to make a decision right this moment, they truly had backed him into a corner. It was the oldest trick in the book, akin to a used car salesman saying 'this is our last one and several other people have been interested, better act quick!'. The reason it pissed him off was because it was working. His mind was whirring, thinking about what he might learn and subsequently be able to publish. If he gave up the opportunity, he was sure they would select another haematologist and then *they* would reap the potentially career-defining benefits that he had stupidly passed up.

Fortunately for David, he was single and had no pets. He also had the next several days free from his job at the Royal Prince Alfred Hospital in Sydney due to his presence at the conference. Hoping that he wouldn't come to regret his decision, he agreed to the terms his new European friends (abductors?) had set and no more than two hours later he was already airborne in a specially chartered flight to Stockholm by way of Dubai.

It was a surreal experience, sitting in a privately chartered 747 aircraft. Everyone knew that they were huge vehicles, but somehow that size becomes muted when there are hundreds of other people crammed in like sardines. They suddenly become cramped prison cells. But when you have one of these aerial monsters to share between only three people then they seem downright cavernous – their true size becomes easier to appreciate. David couldn't help but grimace at the obscene carbon footprint that flights like these generated. Hundreds of thousands of litres of aviation fuel being wasted on little old him. These thoughts certainly helped cement the sincerity of the situation in his mind.

Early in the flight David finally learnt the names of the suited men that he had missed when they introduced themselves earlier. Vidar Olufsen was the younger of the two; he had the stereotypical Swedish look with blond hair and blue eyes. If David were to guess, he would assume that Vidar was in his early thirties. His older compatriot was Melker Larsson. Melker's age was harder to place with his stern features and prematurely grey hair. He could be anywhere from 40 to 60 and it was clear that he was the one in charge in this assignment.

Shortly after the plane completed its take-off and reached cruising speed, flying over the continent of Australia en route to Dubai, Melker reached into a briefcase and removed a folder. He opened it and pulled out a stapled document that he then handed to David, instructing him to read it carefully and to sign it when he understood.

David was no stranger to non-disclosure agreements; he'd signed his fair share in his life as part of his research career. The first couple of pages were boiler-plate legal-speak. Needlessly complicated mumbo jumbo that could be more concisely summed up with the sentence: 'I pinky promise not to talk about anything I see'. Pushing aside his sarcasm, he took the document seriously and read it carefully, he wanted to be certain he understood absolutely everything about it.

Once past the first couple of pages, was where this NDA suddenly stood out from any others he had seen before. Where most of them would include sections outlining the consequences for breaking the agreement, usually involving the (unspoken) threat of litigation and heavy fines – this one was different. In no uncertain terms, the consequences for breaking this NDA were dire. Extensive prison time dire. *What the hell had he gotten himself into?*

David could feel their eyes on him as he turned over the final page of the document. As if reading his mind, Melker provided what he probably felt as reassurance for David – explaining that this wasn't a typical NDA for some patented intellectual property, this involved national, no, international security.

Before he signed, David turned to the last page to re-read one section, wanting to be very clear what it said. This was the section about his right to publish his research. He was allowed to publish, however anything he wrote needed to be approved by the ECDC. Fair enough. Vidar handed him a pen and he fulfilled his obligations, signing, dating, initialling, jumping through all the hoops so that he could be let into the inner circle.

After scanning the NDA to ensure it was all in order, Melker was satisfied and he passed the rest of the contents of the folder to David. Now for the interesting part, thought David. He opened the documents and found the oh-so-familiar charts containing pages upon pages of serological reports. He saw with frustration that even after completing the NDA, things were still redacted from the report. The patient's name read as: ███████ ███████ as did his DOB and several other aspects of the paperwork.

Scanning the reports, one thing became clear to David very quickly – the reason why he was selected. This patient had 'Golden Blood'. Thinking back to the talk he had given only a few hours earlier (in what felt like another lifetime entirely), he recalled the statistic that he read to the enthusiastic crowd. Only 45 people on the planet were known to have Golden Blood. Better make that 46 now.

David asked Vidar and Melker if they were aware

of what was inside the folder, and they acknowledged that they shared the same clearance level as he himself. They were authorised to know what was within the folder, however they knew nothing further and he shouldn't bother even questioning them about the redactions. David didn't care about the redactions anymore. He was excited, and he was glad that he could use these two as a sounding board for his own thoughts – he always thought best when he was explaining things to others. Without further ado, he set off on a little lecture explaining the mystique behind Golden Blood.

'Everybody knows about the ABO blood group system. Where people have either A, B, AB, or O blood types, defined by the antibodies present in the plasma. These four types are then narrowed down further into positive or negative, widening the four main blood types to a group of eight. Do you know what the positive and negative represent?' David asked his captive audience.

Vidar enthusiastically answered, excited to share his own understanding: 'The rhesus factor, right?'

This was a little trap David had set to learn more about Vidar and Melker – and it had worked exactly as he intended. It confirmed to him that neither of them was a medical professional. They obviously had a decent working knowledge pertinent to the case, but it seemed more likely that they were the military type. Good to know. David kept a poker face as he replied: 'That's right, but it's not quite that simple either. Specifically, the positive or negative assigned to a blood type relates to the existence (or lack thereof) of the RhD antigen. There are many, many other Rh antigens that can narrow blood types into far deeper categories, but RhD is the most commonly utilised.'

Melker kept his own poker face, silently watching on, however Vidar was not as adept at containing his enjoyment at what he was learning. He clearly had a curious mind, and David appreciated that. Vidar even pre-empted the next section of David's makeshift lecture with the question: 'So where does Rh_{null} come into things?'

'Rh_{null}, otherwise known as "Golden Blood", is the complete absence of an Rh factor,' David replied.

'But isn't that just Rh-negative?' questioned Vidar.

While David had already confirmed to himself earlier that his kidnappers (as he sarcastically thought of them) were not doctors, Vidar's questioning was all the proof he needed that he was right in this assumption. He replied: 'Rh-negative indicates an absence of RhD' (emphasis on the *dee*), 'Rh_{null} however, is the complete absence of any Rh antigens.'

David expected further questioning about what the big deal was behind Rh_{null} and why it was so important, but no further questions were asked. He realised that this was probably because Vidar and Melker had entered his lecture earlier in the day and already listened to him explain this very thing towards the end.

Not wanting to make a pest of himself and talk their ears off, he let the conversation draw to a close and quietly read through the rest of the serology reports, making notes and circling various intriguing aspects that were new, even for him. He was suddenly very excited to reach their destination and learn more about this mystery patient. He had no idea how somebody with Golden Blood was mysteriously a threat to 'international security', but he was certain he would find out.

Two

David was exhausted by the time he finally arrived in Stockholm. Sleeping on planes had never been his forte, and he only managed a couple of fitful hours over the Indian Ocean. The flight from Sydney to Dubai benefitted from some fortunate tailwinds and arrived in slightly less than the expected 14 hours. There, the plane was grounded for about an hour as it refuelled, before once again taking to the sky to complete the final leg of the journey to Stockholm.

Another six and a half hours in the air brought David's travels to a close. He glanced at his wristwatch that he had not yet recalibrated to the local time and noticed with tired cynicism that almost exactly 24 hours ago he was standing in front of a podium giving his keynote presentation. How quickly things can change …

After exiting Stockholm Arlanda Airport with Vidar and Melker, David was guided into a waiting vehicle that promptly delivered him to a surprisingly nice hotel overlooking a lake by the name of Brunnsviken. Melker explained that he was to meet them out the front of the hotel at 8:00am, where he would then be escorted to the ECDC. David cringed at the fact that this only allowed him a maximum of five hours rest, so he wasted no time dallying and collapsed into the king-size bed in his room.

A fortunate side effect of not being able to sleep during the flights meant that David was exhausted and therefore he completely negated jetlag by managing to sleep at what was still only lunchtime back in Sydney. Nevertheless, his body was not impressed when he awoke only several hours later to the infuriating sound of his alarm clock. There was a silver lining, however – he was now going to finally learn just what the hell he'd been whisked halfway around the world for. It surprised him how excited he found himself.

Heading downstairs, Vidar and Melker were already waiting for him in the foyer. Neither of them looked anywhere near as tired as he felt, but he kept his bitterness to himself as they guided him back to their official vehicle. The drive to the ECDC only took about 10 minutes. It took far longer than that for him to get checked into the building, but this didn't surprise him in the least.

David was thankful that most of the signs in the building had an English translation on them, because he didn't have the faintest understanding of Swedish. These translations allowed him to learn that Vidar and Melker were guiding him to the quarantine wing of the facility. He got a little pang of nerves in his stomach, but quickly repressed it. He knew it had to be something like this for him to be whisked all the way across the planet – no point acting surprised now.

Arriving at an imposing pair of double doors with the very obvious warning signs for biohazard, this was where Vidar and Melker bid their goodbyes. They ushered David inside and told him to take a seat; explaining that the Director of the ECDC would be along any time now. After thanking them, David stepped through the doors and found himself in a room with a group of people who appeared to be as equally mystified as he himself. All of their heads turned towards him, likely expecting *him* to be the person they were waiting on, but when it became clear he was just another clueless ring-in they returned to whatever it was they were doing.

The nerves in David's stomach began to reappear. Everything was just so damn surreal. *What the hell was going on here?* He barely had a chance to ponder these thoughts when an older gentleman approached him, introducing himself as Janik Schuler. As was the case with many Europeans, Janik's English was impeccable, so David wouldn't have had any chance guessing where he was from if not for Janik offering the information himself. He was a linguistics professor at the University of Bern in Switzerland, specialising in Balkan Romance languages.

As if on autopilot, David returned the introduction while his subconscious worked in overdrive to figure out just what the hell he could possibly have in common with Janik – or in other words, what someone like Janik would be doing at the ECDC in the first place. Surely they had their own translators, right? Then again, surely they had their own haematologists too …

Janik was clearly a very extroverted person. He had barely stopped talking since David walked into the room, and David realised about halfway through that he had not been paying attention to a word that was said – his mind was very much elsewhere. Being honest, David admitted as much and Janik laughed a friendly laugh, saying he understood completely. He cycled back on his verbal onslaught and began telling David the story of how he had come to be here – a story, David realised, that paralleled his own almost identically.

David asked whether anyone here had any clue why they were here. He kept the serology reports about the patient with the Golden Blood to himself for now simply because he wasn't sure if he was permitted to bring it up in present company under the NDA he had signed. The last thing he wanted was to get himself into trouble immediately. The sentiment seemed to be shared throughout the room, as nobody had anything else to say on the matter.

Janik continued his ceaseless chattering, beginning to introduce David to others in the room. He began with the handsome woman with mousy blonde hair in the back corner named Barbara Wood. She looked about David's age and was a research microbiologist from the CDC in America. Hearing her name being mentioned, she met David's eyes with a half-smile before returning her attention to her phone. Internally David was thinking that it certainly made more sense for her to be here than Janik, but as he would soon learn – perhaps Janik wasn't the odd one out after all.

Before any further introductions could be made, two people – a man and a woman – walked through the door with an undeniable air of authority. It was clear to everybody waiting that these individuals were in charge, so the room fell silent as all eyes watched in eager anticipation. The man was wearing the black coat of Swedish military dress, and his lapel was adorned with an array of medals, while the woman was his inverse, wearing a pristine white lab coat hanging down over her stylish clothes.

The man was the first to speak. His voice was gruff and accented, but he spoke in English and everybody in the room appeared to be comfortable with that. David felt a pang of guilt that he was likely one of the few people in the room who wasn't bilingual – but he let it pass quickly, not wanting to miss anything that was said.

'My name is Colonel Elias Sandberg. I am here to remind you of the NDA that you all signed. Absolutely *nothing* you see or hear is to be repeated beyond the walls of this building – understood ...'

David found himself nodding like a meek schoolboy, even though he was aware the question was rhetorical.

'Now now Eli, let's not scare everyone too soon,' the woman cut in, mildly amused at his tone and the reaction of the room. 'My name is Dr Maja Nilsson; I am the Director of the ECDC. I'm sure you are all very curious why you are here.'

Murmurs of agreement filled the room as they all watched on, entranced.

'My surly friend here is right, however – this is a matter of strictest confidentiality, I must request that anybody uncomfortable with that to leave now.'

Heads turned around the room, but nobody took Dr Nilsson up on her offer.

'Okay then, good,' she continued. 'I must warn you that what you are about to learn is very ... how do you say ... bizarre ... and there is a reason why each and every one of you has been selected to be here today. With that in mind, I would request you all to please introduce yourselves.'

Wasting no time, Janik leapt at the opportunity to hear himself speak and introduced himself to the room. Next was Dr Barbara Wood, who David had already been introduced to before Dr Nilsson and Colonel Sandberg walked into the room. David wasn't sure what exactly he expected, but the next introduction most certainly wasn't it. He was taken aback to hear the thick French accent of the youngest individual in the room, who said in mixed English and French: 'I am called Denis Blanc, et I am un occultiste'.

David's brows furrowed very deeply and all he could think was *what the fuck* ..., but he didn't have time to dwell on it before the next individual took over and introduced himself as Jürgen Albrecht, an anthropologist from Germany.

Including himself there were nine people who played their part in this ritual of introduction. The remaining four members of the room were Dr Eva Björklund, a middle-aged general practitioner from right here in Stockholm; Dr Nancy Miller, another middle-aged woman, who was a world-renowned psychologist; Ms Ana Vida, an older historian specialising in Eastern Europe; and finally, Bishop Enzo de Luca, from the Vatican.

David was the last to speak, doing his best to absorb as much of the information he was hearing, and knowing he would certainly forget people's names. It was his turn to introduce himself after the Bishop, and he felt foolish as he stuttered a bland biography for himself. His mind was still trying to make sense of this ridiculous assortment of people, and what they could possibly have in common here at the ECDC.

Dr Nilsson finally put David out of his misery by thanking the room. What she said next was like she was reading his mind:

'I am sure you all must be wondering the cause behind this eclectic group of experts. Thus far, each of you have been provided with information relevant to your specialties' – the patient with the Golden Blood, David thought – 'but there is far more to this picture. If you will be so kind as to follow me.'

With that, Dr Nilsson, who insisted to simply be called Maja, led the group down the corridor and through another door with biohazard warnings plastered all over it. Trailing behind Maja like a gaggle of geese reminded David of his time as a med student doing rounds. They eventually made it to what was very obviously a quarantine zone, where Maja stood before a thick glass viewing pane and ushered everyone to look inside with a wave of her hand.

'This – gentlemen, ladies – is Csanád Farkas. He was buried in the Carpathian Mountains in the 13th century and exhumed just six days ago.'

Like a show-woman, Maja let her statement end right there while an incredulous murmur erupted from the congregation staring through the window. This was clearly some kind of a stupid joke. There was no corpse in this room. Staring back at them from within his quarantined cell was a man whose age was near impossible to guess. He was extremely tall, even by David's standard – probably somewhere around 210 centimetres, or nearing seven feet tall. He had the complexion of somebody with olive skin who had not seen sunlight in a very long time, but it was his face that really stood out above all else.

Ignoring the escalating tension in the group as they each said their piece, mostly to the tune of anger at having their time wasted – David remained silent and found himself locked in eye contact with the man behind the glass. The man – Csanád – had eyes that evoked the deepest, darkest of wells. It was like they had no colour in their irises at all, just pits of black gazing back at him. With no small effort of will, David dragged his eyes from the mesmerising gaze of Csanád and took in the rest of his features. He had naturally slick black hair that hung down, framing his face. His bone structure was very angular, with extraordinarily pronounced cheekbones and jawline that was only emphasised further by the fact that he looked as if he were half starved and emaciated. David shuddered at the idea of how intimidating this man would be with a bit of meat on his bones.

Finally drawing his attention away from Csanád, David came back to reality to hear Maja saying: 'I must assure you that this is no joke. Everything you have been told is correct. The man you see behind the glass is at least 800 years old.'

More outbursts immediately followed from the group. At this point however, after having remained silent up until now, Colonel Sandberg boomed 'ENOUGH!', which immediately intimidated the group into silence. He then continued, 'If you are unhappy. Leave. But utter one single word to break your NDA and you'll be dealing with me.'

The group remained silent – and nobody turned to leave, so Sandberg continued: 'Good. Now pay Dr Nilsson the respect she deserves and listen to what she has to say.'

The friendly, almost playful aura that Maja had been expressing was dropped and in a flat tone she said: 'Thank you Colonel. Now, Eli is correct. This is not a joke. We do not "pull pranks" here at the ECDC. Allow me to provide you the rest of the details, and I will request that you hold your questions until the end.'

With that, Maja began detailing a story that

sounded like it belonged in some kind of fiction novel. But the tone and absolute sincerity of her voice more than convinced David that she was telling the truth, or at the very least – what she believed to be the truth.

The story began with a group of archaeologists excavating a 13th-century dig site in the Carpathian Mountains in Romania. One of the members of the dig had dialled 112 (which David knew to be the European phone number for emergency services) in a panic, requesting urgent medical assistance. At this point Maja pulled out her phone and played the recording. David didn't understand the words in Romanian so he could only watch as a few of the group who understood the language reacted. What was clear regardless of whether he could understand the words was the unadulterated panic in the voice.

Maja then continued, explaining that the panicked archaeologists were screaming about a 'strigoi' that had gravely wounded one of their cohort. David glanced towards the French occultist as he audibly gasped, and Maja continued by explaining that one of Romania's most well-known myths is that of the strigoi – more commonly known in Western culture as 'vampire'.

At this point, nobody took the archaeologists' ravings seriously – however emergency services were still dispatched. Unfortunately, due to the remoteness of their location, they did not arrive in time and the injured archaeologist was found dead at the scene with a violent gash spreading across his throat. Tensions rose, with the emergency crew assuming one of the archaeologists to be responsible for the brutal murder – but with shaking hands and gibbering voices they were eventually able to communicate for the emergency services to check the coffin that they had exhumed.

Maja now pulled out a manilla folder containing what she explained to be the sworn statement of the emergency services personnel. It was in Romanian, so she paraphrased a translation for the group. The paramedics had seen the near skeletal remains of a body bound with heavy silver chains within the coffin, splashed with the blood of the dead archaeologist. When they inspected the scene more closely however, they noticed that the 'remains' were very much alive. Deep, black eyes were surveying them, and they only narrowly escaped the bony, clawed fingers of its free hand as it made a violent attempt to grab at them.

'Since this moment,' Maja said, 'Csanád has not been out of sight. The man you see behind the glass is the same "near-skeletal remains" that the archaeologists dug out of the side of the Carpathian Mountains in Romania.'

Three

Maja paused for a short time to allow this bombshell to sink in. David's mind was numb with shock as he simply stared towards her and waited for her to continue – it was clear that she had a wealth of additional evidence to support her wild claims.

After a few moments, Maja continued: 'Believe me when I tell you that this is just as incredulous to me as it is to all of you. As a doctor and a scientist, I would need to return my qualifications if I was not sceptical – however the truth of the matter is simply undeniable.'

Maja went on to explain that the Romanian emergency services contacted the ECDC almost immediately in the aftermath of the discovery. Their superstition led them into a frantic panic about the possibility of a 'vampiric contagion'. Understandably this was met with the scepticism that it deserved – however protocol dictated that any concern of contagion within Europe must be investigated, which was how the ECDC made it onto the scene.

The team dispatched by the ECDC arrived at the site the following day to a very odd sight. Only the leader of the archaeological dig – Professor Cristina Grigorcea – remained; the rest of her team had immediately taken the chance to return to their homes and put as much distance between themselves and this 'cursed' mountainside. The area was understandably cordoned off as the crime scene that it was, but the most bizarre sight to see was the tent erected over the coffin, draped with thick blankets and sleeping bags.

'Mr Farkas, you see, suffers from the most severe case of xeroderma pigmentosum that we have ever seen,' Maja said.

David and the other medical professionals in the room understood the implications of this immediately, while the other members of their esoteric group looked around waiting for somebody to fill them in. Since the pause dragged on uncomfortably, David himself filled the silence by explaining to those without medical degrees that xeroderma pigmentosum was an allergic reaction to UV light – sunlight.

Dr Wood questioned now: 'Does it present as urticaria?', to which Maja immediately responded:

'It is not a typical physical urticaria response with Mr Farkas. His skin quite literally burns away as if he is being subjected to intense heat.'

The medical lingo being utilised was again going

over the head of most of the room, but David felt that Maja's final statement made things very clear. The patient's skin reacts violently to the UV rays present within sunlight.

With the minds in the room now slightly more open, and having explained the allergic reaction to sunlight, Maja now connected her phone to the display monitor in their viewing room and brought some pictures onto the big screen. The pictures provided a stop-motion montage of the story that Maja continued to unfold for them. They saw the densely wooded mountainside in Romania; some evidence of the archaeological site, including ornately carved silver crosses (must be why the Bishop is here, David thought); and finally, the tent with sleeping apparel draped over the top.

Maja took this moment to pause, warning the room that the next photographs were rather graphic and that they should prepare themselves. Giving her warning a couple of seconds to sink in, she flicked to the next picture, which showed what appeared to be a skeletal corpse with papery skin that had been severely burnt. If not for the living, breathing (?) specimen in the adjacent room then they would have been certain that they were looking at a corpse – but there was one thing in the photograph that displayed life. Those eyes …

David glanced back into the quarantined room and was met with those staring black eyes and he knew with complete certainty that they belonged to the same person as the charred 'corpse' in the photo. Once more, it took all of David's mental fortitude to drag his eyes away from Csanád, and by the time he managed to bring himself back to Maja's demonstration he realised that he must have somehow missed the conclusion of her slideshow of photographs. She was now talking about Mr Farkas's unprecedented (her word) recovery.

'Following ECDC protocol, Csanád was rushed straight to this very room and—', Maja began, before being interrupted by Ana Vida, the historian specialising in Eastern European history, who asked: 'How do you know his name is Csanád?'

Maja nodded, acknowledging her own oversight and explained that an epitaph was found engraved on the lid of his coffin. With this, she scrolled through her phone and zoomed into one of the pictures they had already seen. From here, Janik took over, translating the archaic (pre-)Romanian for the room:

'Here lies Csanád Farkas. May the Old Wolf rot.'

Janik chuckled at a joke that only he seemed to understand. All eyes were on him as he went on to explain that the surname 'Farkas' was Hungarian for 'wolf'. Even Maja seemed surprised by this revelation – and it more than justified to David just why the ECDC had reached out to such an odd grouping of specialists. It all made sense now. Even the occultist and the Bishop being here was enough evidence for David to conclude that the ECDC genuinely believed that Csanád actually was a vampire.

Picking up where she was cut off earlier, Maja explained that Csanád had been in their custody for four days now. Initially, of course, they did not believe that there was anything supernatural about him. He simply suffered an allergic reaction to the UV rays of the sun, which had driven him mad and caused him to lash out violently. But when they realised the strange, undying vitality with which he clung to life it began to make them all question their medical knowledge.

On the flight back to Sweden – still heavily bound – Csanád was hooked up to an IV drip. Fluids and antibiotics were pumped through his veins to stem infection from the broken and shrivelled skin caused by his exposure to the sun, along with a sedative to help alleviate the agony he was experiencing from his burns. The fluids were also the first attempt at helping him with his starvation and dehydration. Little did they believe that he had *truly* gone over 800 years without any sustenance whatsoever.

Eventually, as the plane was halfway over continental Europe – one of the ECDC doctors proposed that they simply couldn't wait any longer – their patient needed a blood transfusion or else he wasn't going to make it. David's brows furrowed at this, and out of the corner of his eye he noticed the other doctors in the room also seemed a little confused. Being the expert in blood here, he interjected to question why the transfusion was indicated.

Maja nodded knowingly and replied: 'That, Dr Reynolds, is an excellent question. There was no medical basis for the treatment to be justified – the doctor in question said that he operated on a "hunch". However, this hunch proved fruitful. With a fresh bag of O-negative coursing through his veins the change in Mr Farkas here was near instantaneous.'

After flicking through her phone once more, two photographs appeared side-by-side on the display screen. On the left was Csanád, charred and burned; and on the right his skin was freshly healed. He even looked a little more fleshed out than the pile of bones draped with skin on the left.

'These photographs were taken 90 minutes apart …' Maja said to the stunned room.

The implications were obvious; they didn't need to be occultists like the Frenchman to understand that blood had acted like a miracle cure for this individual under suspicion of being a vampire.

Speaking of the occultist, Denis now spoke for the first time since his gasp at hearing the word 'strigoi' earlier. He asked ''ave you, ehhh, been feeding him …?'

Again, the implications of his question were very clear, and all eyes turned towards Maja. She grew visibly uncomfortable as she tried to frame her reply: 'The patient, uh, Csanád, has refused almost all food …'

'Almost all?' asked Denis.

'You have to understand …' Maja began, 'when a patient presents with starvation it is not indicated for them to simply be fed whatever they want. They must carefully build up the caloric intake.'

David and the other medical professionals understood this to be true, but he could sense the 'but' tacked onto the end of Maja's statement. After a few beats she continued: 'After two days of refusing all of his meals, Mr Farkas suddenly spoke his first word. He tossed his tray against this here window and screamed "Kött!"'

'Meat ...' said Janik. 'But how does he know Swedish?'

'We do not know,' replied Maja.

'But you've been communicating with him!?' burst in Nancy Miller – the psychiatrist making her presence heard for the first time.

'I wouldn't call it communication,' Maja responded. 'He bellowed for meat, and after a great deal of deliberation from our medical staff we acquiesced to his request. He hadn't eaten for days; despite what he'd done, we couldn't just starve him ...'

This was an odd way to phrase things, David thought. There was something more to this story that Maja was holding back ...

Maja continued by recounting how Csanád was delivered a steak cooked medium-rare – and that despite looking at it with disgust and barking 'Förstörd!' (translated by Janik to mean 'ruined' or 'destroyed'), Csanád devoured his meal – bone and all. Some murmurs spread around the room at the images this description evoked. Since this time, Maja explained, Csanád had been fed steak of increasing rarity for every meal for the past two days, which incidentally explained why he looked somewhat healthier now than he did in the most recent photographs they had seen of him.

Whether it was a coincidence or planned, it was now time for Csanád's lunchtime meal. David watched as a man in a lab coat carried what looked to be nothing more than a plate of raw meat. He was visibly nervous, and flanked by no less than three armed men in Swedish military garb. All of the armed escort had weapons drawn, two of them holding pistols pointed to the floor and the third holding a bright yellow gun-like weapon that David correctly surmised to be a taser.

All eyes turned towards the spectacle, and David felt a little pang of guilt that it was almost like they were treating Csanád as an exhibit at the zoo. As the group approached the airlocked outer doors of the quarantine room in which Csanád was imprisoned, they saw him stand from his bed for the first time. His height was truly overwhelming, and even with his relative emaciation he still moved with a deft grace as he made his way to the interior door of the airlock.

The military personnel all raised their weapons and began barking orders in Swedish that David didn't understand, but he didn't need to know the words to realise that they were quite frankly terrified of him and wanted him to move away from the doors. Csanád obliged, turning instead to face directly towards the gaggle of people staring at him through the glass window. David was cautious this time to avoid his mesmeric eyes and within a few short seconds the food delivery was completed and the relieved doctor and his guards locked the external airlock doors.

With the external doors locked, they remotely unlocked the internal doors which granted Csanád access to the food – and then everyone watched on as he ignored the cheap plastic cutlery entirely and began tearing at the red, dripping meat with his hands and gaping maw alike. It almost felt voyeuristic to watch this spectacle, but nobody spoke a word for at least a minute before the German anthropologist finally broke the silence to ask: 'Why were zey so afraid of him?'

Maja's mood became sombre now and David realised that there was something that she clearly hadn't told them yet. Uncomfortably trying to find the right words, Maja eventually explained that Csanád was responsible for the murder of one of their doctors and the maiming of another.

It was within hours of arriving at the facility. Until this point the silver chains wrapping him tightly had been left in place. Nobody believed the superstition at this time, of course, but under the assumption that he was a starving human with severe burns to his body – there was too great of a risk of infection to justify removing them until they reached their medical facilities.

It was explained to them that shortly after the silver chains were removed – Csanád lashed out. Maja explained that as the chains were lifted, so too was what appeared to be a wooden stake. It was difficult for her to find the right words to explain the attack from here, but her broken attempts at describing the event painted a vibrant, gory picture. Swift as a viper, Csanád had grabbed the wooden stake and used it to puncture a crude hole into the side of one of the doctor's throats. The other doctor watched in abject horror, hiding in the corner of the room, as Csanád then put his mouth to the gushing wound and appeared to drink …

Everyone reacted differently to this revelation. The Frenchman muttered 'Mon dieu'; the Bishop performed the sign of the cross; the historian Ana turned away with her hand to her mouth looking like she was stifling vomit. Without exception, everyone was shocked to their core. Unable to help himself, David felt his eyes dragged away from the group and through the glass where they were once more met by those empty wells belonging to Csanád. There was a twisted, toothy smile on his face and David could've sworn he saw a hint of a flash in those eyes. Without knowing how he was so sure; David was certain that Csanád knew *exactly* what they were talking about – and he was thrilled.

Janik tugged at David's sleeve and asked him if he was alright, which served to break David free from his trance and turn his attention back towards the end of the story from Maja. He missed the part about the second doctor also receiving a deep gash to his throat and instead heard Maja explaining that it was only at this point that security personnel had arrived and subdued Csanád using their tasers set to maximum voltage.

'What 'appened to the doctors?' the French occultist asked with something akin to enthusiasm in his voice. Now that he had grown to accept that he wasn't being pranked there was almost a perverted grin on his face to realise that his life's dedication was proven true – the supernatural *did* exist. The implication of this question was clear – in popular myth, vampires were undead … had anything happened after the doctor had died? Or to the one who survived?

Maja clearly did not appreciate Denis's enthusiasm and her reply was very curt as she explained that *no*, her deceased colleague did not return from the dead as a vampire. Her gravely wounded colleague, however, *was* kept in his own quarantine containment cell in an abundance of caution.

'We have no idea if this is a contagion. We have no idea if it is even possible to spread "vampirism". Now you can understand why we have gathered you all here. We need answers, and you are at the top of your respective fields.'

Four

At this point – with everybody both sufficiently convinced and spooked – Maja requested for the group to split. The social scientists (including the occultist and Bishop) were to join one group and begin brainstorming everything they knew about the history of the region, vampiric lore, and any potential way to learn more from Csanád himself. Meanwhile the medical experts would branch off and go over the science (if that word even applied for a vampire …) of the phenomenon.

The two groups were escorted to separate rooms, and each provided every shred of evidence relevant to their skillsets. Maja's protracted recounting of events notwithstanding, it was clear that there was still far more that they had yet to learn. For instance: when David, the biologist Dr Wood, the GP Dr Björklund, and the psychiatrist Dr Miller were seated around an office table, Maja provided a laptop computer and bulky folder containing rather extensive medical tests for Csanád.

As it turned out, the ECDC had made the most of Csanád's unconsciousness after he was tasered. They injected the already unconscious patient with methohexital to ensure he would remain that way and used this opportunity to subject him to a battery of tests – most comprehensive of which was the full-body CT scan. Dr Björklund, who, like Maja, preferred her peers to refer to her by her given name – Eva – began navigating the CT imagery on the laptop. Being a Swede herself, it only made sense since the language on the laptop was, of course, Swedish.

The collective noticed many small irregularities as Eva scrolled through the CT imagery, none more so than David himself. One of the first things he picked out was that Csanád suffered (was that really the right word in this case?) from the most severe case of vasculitis he had ever seen; his blood vessels were incredibly enlarged. From what David had seen of Csanád in his quarantine room though, he certainly didn't look like he was suffering. Vasculitis of this severity should be debilitatingly painful, but perhaps this was somehow beneficial for his alien physiology. These were the exact mysteries that the ECDC had recruited them to solve. Eva also noted his enlarged adrenal glands as they progressed through the scans.

Jotting the disorders on a notepad as topics of future of discussion, David turned his attention back towards the CT scan as Eva continued scrolling through the imagery. Dr Wood, the microbiologist from the

American CDC gasped when the scans progressed to Csanád's thorax. His sternum and left lateral third rib were very violently cracked as if something had punctured straight through them. However, the heart underneath was a picture of good health (well, except for the enlarged blood vessels, David thought).

It didn't take long for the room to reach a hypothesis for what they were seeing. They didn't need to be occultists to know that staking the heart of a vampire was part of almost all vampire myths – and these myths evidently dated back through the centuries. Clearly though – the myth was wrong. The stake may have incapacitated Csanád centuries ago, but it had not killed him – and as his body wasted away it had likely come loose and dislodged. The fact that his soft tissues were completely healed though – that held the most frightening of implications … David noted the injuries on his pad and Eva continued flicking through the scans.

Csanád's emaciation was also clearly detected within his full-body CT scan. A severe lack of fatty tissue and muscle density. However, the group agreed this was most likely as a result of his starvation (was that even the right word?) and lack of mobility. David mentioned that somebody with the skeletal structure of Csanád would likely strike an imposing figure at full health – which everybody very much agreed with.

Emaciation aside, no other major abnormalities were detected by the scan, so the group took this opportunity to begin discussing what they had learnt thus far. All of their thoughts were focused primarily on the puncture through the chest; it was far more interesting than a case of enlarged blood vessels or endocrine glands. The concept that any creature could survive a violently punctured heart – much less heal naturally and show no signs of scarring – was the most frightening aspect. But if they could understand it … harness it … imagine the advances in medicine!

Dr Wood – who now joined Eva and Maja by requesting that the group call her by her given name, Barbara – cautioned the room from getting ahead of themselves. As a microbiologist specialising in communicable diseases, she was highly cautious about the concept of trying to harness something from a newly discovered species. It would need decades of testing and they would need to understand if there was any risk of 'catching' vampirism. This only highlighted the deep end into which they had been thrown. Nobody had any clue what they were dealing with – it was simultaneously frustrating and exhilarating.

Dr Miller – Nancy – finally broke her silence. Nancy was a psychologist, so despite having completed medical school (almost 30 years ago), she was a little out of her depth compared to the rest of the medical/clinical physicians in the room. She posed the question: 'If his soft tissue has healed so completely, why then are his bones still broken?'

It was a good question, but David chimed in to remind everybody that the scan was performed two days ago – for all they knew, his bones were now fully healed. If they worked under the assumption that ingesting blood had a healing effect for a vampire, then …? David ended his sentence with a pronounced shrug of his shoulders, leaving the implications to speak for themselves. Miraculous healing wasn't unheard of in the animal world, but for higher lifeforms like Mammalia it was most certainly unprecedented.

David reached into the manilla folder and pulled out the serological reports that he had already examined on his flight from Australia. Given everything else he had learnt over the past several hours, his memory was triggered for something he'd noticed but paid very little attention to previously. Csanád, whose name was redacted on the forms, suffered (again, was that the right word?) from a rare disorder called polycythemia vera – an overabundance of red blood cells. For normal people it caused somewhat benign feelings of discomfort – but there was clearly nothing normal about Csanád.

What if – David proposed – the polycythemia vera actually stimulated healing in a vampire's anatomy? It was no medical secret that red blood cells help create collagen and promote healing. What if there was something in a vampire's physiology that took this healing to the next level?

Having assessed all of the medical data present for Csanád, the group now had all of their (available) cards on the table. In addition to his xeroderma pigmentosum, they had diagnosed him with severe vasculitis, enlarged adrenal glands, polycythemia vera, and David had also explained his Golden Blood to the group (not that it was a symptom of anything – more a medical curiosity). For what must have been hours, the conversation went around in circles trying to determine what all of this had in common and how it could conceivably account for the facts at hand. The facts being: his seeming immortality, miraculous healing, and his insatiable urge for raw meat — or more likely — blood.

The only thing that became clear from this conversation was that they needed far more data. They knew this wasn't like a movie where you could plop a few smart people in a room and play a montage until somebody comes up with a definitive answer. Science simply didn't work that way. As the sun started its dip towards the horizon outside of the facility, Maja stepped back into the room, having left shortly after the group got settled.

She asked the group to outline all of their insights, which they did, and she also asked whether they required any further testing. Unanimously, a follow-up CT scan was requested. Csanád clearly possessed far more flesh on his bones now than two days ago, it would be important for them to view how his physiology had changed. Maja simply nodded and said it would be done. David was curious how they would manage it, given how dangerous Csanád was, but he rightly assumed that they would have to resort to sedatives once more.

Maja escorted the group back towards the foyer of the facility where they were joined by the social science contingent led by Colonel Sandberg. She explained that everybody would be escorted back to their hotels for the evening before being picked up again at 8:00am sharp the following morning. Tomorrow, Maja said, each member could decide if they were willing to stay and join a taskforce – or return to their lives. If they stayed, then the ECDC would complete all arrangements on their behalf with their employers. It was a hell of a lot to think about, thought David.

Maja encouraged the medical and social science groups to discuss their various findings this evening – but to recall their NDA and to be extremely careful about being overheard. Colonel Sandberg was standing menacingly by her side, which punctuated her point. With this, they were ushered into a series of vehicles and each delivered back to the hotel on the banks of Brunnsviken lake. They agreed to meet for drinks at 9:00pm, and with that they dispersed to their various rooms.

David collapsed onto his bed as soon as he made it into his room. He wasn't the most extroverted person, so spending the entire day in such intense close contact with people was a very stressful experience. This stress was only exacerbated by the utter insanity of everything that he'd learnt. His whole world had been turned upside-down in an instant and he could scarcely comprehend the fact that vampires actually existed.

Well – maybe he was still getting ahead of himself here. Yes, they were treating Csanád as a vampire and for good reason – but that didn't mean that some entirely other species of humanoid creature existed. Csanád could simply be a medical marvel – a one-of-a-kind mutation. This was the kind of thing that they really needed to learn more about, and it was where the social science cohort came into play. Hopefully they might have learnt the answer to this very question.

David had a long, hot shower where he did more thinking than actual washing. After about 30 minutes under the steaming water, he climbed out and ordered room service for dinner. By this point he had sufficiently unwound and was now actually excited to meet up with the rest of the contingent. He wanted to know more. He *needed* to know more. That was a curse most scientists bore – an insatiable lust to learn.

Sitting down for drinks in a secluded booth of the hotel bar, eight of the nine members of the eclectic group (the Bishop wanted nothing to do with them) began to discuss the events of the day. David happily sat back and allowed Eva to explain all that the medical contingent had discovered. She had a real talent for simplifying the complicated disorders, and this bore immediate fruit.

At the mention of the enlarged adrenal glands, the occultist – Denis – showed a deeper understanding of human anatomy than David would have expected from a regular person. He asked whether the adrenal glands were related to sweating. A perplexing question on its surface, but when Eva confirmed that yes, the adrenal glands were part of the endocrine system and certainly had at least a tangential connection to sweating, then Denis explained the purpose of his question.

Common vampiric lore suggested that they were capable of generating mists. Was it possible for this to be related? All David could think was that they'd entered the realm of fantasy at this point – but who was he to deny it in the face of everything else they had discovered. None of the medical professionals were willing to outright say that Denis could be right – many years of experience had trained them against leaping to such conclusions – but it was certainly an intriguing concept nonetheless.

At this point the psychologist Nancy turned the conversation back to Denis and the rest of the social science contingent and requested that they share all that they had learnt. Denis began to speak, but his English was clearly the weakest of the group and he struggled to form his narrative cohesively, so the enthusiastic Swiss linguist Janik leapt at the opportunity to take the lead. Janik was a genuinely nice person, which made David feel guilty for his sarcastic thoughts earlier in the day about how much he liked the sound of his own voice.

Putting these thoughts aside, David sat back and finished his second beer as Janik spoke. Unlike the medical contingent who had quantitative data in the form of extensive testing, everything was far more qualitative on the other side of the fence. They had spent all afternoon discussing the history of the region and general vampiric lore ranging from ancient myths to modern fictions.

The 'allergy' to the sun was one piece of the lore that spanned all eras of vampire superstition, but as he refilled his glass from the pitcher of beer David listened to a list of other superstitions. It was often said that vampires did not cast a reflection, but this myth was quickly and easily disproven with Csanád. Likewise, it was said that they feared the cross, but Csanád did not appear to care whatsoever.

The list continued, but what it eventually boiled down to was that just like the medical contingent had requested further CT scans, so too had the esoteric contingent requested tests of their own. They had requested to see how Csanád reacted to the presence of garlic, of holy water, and of silver – three of the most commonly attributed weaknesses of vampires through the centuries of superstition.

The psychologist, Nancy, who in truth bridged the divide between medical and social sciences mentioned that they could only get so far by running their tests. What they really needed was for somebody (namely herself) to actually engage directly with Csanád. Put simply – they needed to speak to him, to interview him. It was the only way they were going to truly learn about what he was and what he was capable of. Beyond that they were simply fumbling in the dark. It was a good idea, but not as simple as it sounded. It would require a concerted effort between herself and Janik as translator, as well as Jürgen the anthropologist and Ana the historian.

David sat in contemplative silence as the group excitedly discussed ideas and plans for the following day. He noticed himself feeling a little lightheaded, which he realised was because he was tipsy – he'd already drained his third beer in relatively short order. It must be the complete surrealness of the situation that had driven him to drink, he thought. Ordinarily he wasn't much of a drinker. He pushed his cup away in a gesture that he was done for the night, but by the time the group disbanded and everybody went back to their rooms he had reneged on this intention and downed two further glasses.

Lying in bed, David's head was spinning. Without even bothering to undress he quickly fell into a deep slumber. After his whirlwind plane trip to the other side of the planet and the frankly insane day he had experienced, he hoped for a long and restful night of sleep to help recover – but this was not to be. His dreams were plagued by those deep black eyes – as if they were staring into his soul. The difference was that in his dreams, he was the prisoner and the owner of those eyes was the one with all the power.

David awoke with a start to the sound of his alarm clock violently ringing in the new day. Part of him was thankful to be freed from his litany of nightmares, but the other part desired nothing more than to go back to sleep – he still felt so exhausted! It was only understandable to have these vivid dreams after having his entire reality shattered the previous day, he thought. The booze certainly didn't help. He had a quick shower to splash some life back into his body and clear the cobwebs from his mind and then he made his way downstairs to begin another day of discovery.

Five

David reunited once more with his minders Vidar and Melker as they escorted him back to the ECDC. True to character, Melker was quiet and probably wouldn't have said a word if not for his more jovial compatriot Vidar prompting conversation out of him. David was too tired to share Vidar's enthusiasm for conversation at this time of the morning, and in truth what was there to say? In just 24 hours he had learnt some of the most fantastical things imaginable, but he was bound by law to keep them to himself.

As he exited the vehicle to be further escorted into the building by his polar opposite Swedish guards, something caught David's attention out of the corner of his eye. Parked across the road from the large government facility was a little Dacia Sandero. The reason it caught David's attention was because it was a car that was heavily mocked on his favourite TV show,

Top Gear. Cars like these simply didn't exist in his home country of Australia, so seeing the iconically shaped Romanian car is what caught his eye – but then he noticed something else … There were people in the car with binoculars, and they appeared to be looked straight at him …

As soon as these strange observers noticed David's attention turn towards them, the car immediately drove away and disappeared from sight. Understanding the gravity of the situation, David reported this to his escorts as they made it through the large doors of the ECDC facility. Melker, ever so serious, left Vidar to escort David inside while he went to examine where the Dacia was parked. David heard him barking something in Swedish into a walkie talkie before he turned a corner and lost contact with the big man.

Unlike the previous day, today David was one of the first people to arrive and this time he had to wait for the rest of the group to trickle in over the following 10 or so minutes. The German anthropologist Jürgen Albrecht was the only one waiting in the room when David arrived. He was a very quiet person and David hadn't spoken more than a few words to him since their introduction yesterday. He decided to take this time to try and strike up a bit more of a conversation.

Their conversation didn't go far, but what it boiled down to was that Jürgen felt somewhat out of place here and he was likely going to decline the offer to stay on the taskforce. He felt that he would be able to provide any anthropological expertise remotely. His logic made sense and David wondered whether Maja and Colonel Sandberg would accept that proposal or instead try to replace him with another anthropologist that they could keep on site. Jürgen was right though, it's not like he was able to provide real-time translation, or knowledge of the occult, or medical advice like the rest of the team – he was a little bit of the odd one out in this situation.

At 8:15am on the dot, Maja and the Colonel walked through the door and greeted everybody with the same friendly enthusiasm as the day before (before she had dropped the act in frustration at the group's disbelief). Without any ado she began detailing the results of the many tests that the group had requested before departing the prior day, but she was very quickly interrupted by Janik who mentioned that the Bishop wasn't present and that she should wait until he arrived.

Maja, with no small amount of sarcasm in her voice, said: 'The good Bishop has declined taking any part of this "ungodly" affair. We will be continuing without him. Frankly I was opposed to his inclusion in the first place.'

She used air quotes to punctuate her dripping sarcasm when she said the word 'ungodly'. A few chuckles quietly spread around the room, mainly from the medical specialists who agreed with her that he clearly had no place here and that his absence would not be missed.

Continuing now where she was cut off by Janik, Maja began detailing the results of their testing overnight.

She explained that Csanád, with no less than eight armed soldiers patrolling him at point-blank range with both guns and tasers, had allowed himself to be sedated. After this, he was subjected to another full-body CT scan, the results of which could be viewed at their leisure on the same laptop that was provided yesterday. But for now, Maja wanted to talk about some of the slightly less scientific tests – namely the scratch test for allergies.

After being requested yesterday to test Csanád's sensitivity to three substances – garlic, holy water, and silver – they had thought of no better way to perform this test than using the stock standard allergy test, the scratch test. What this involved, she explained to the non-medical members of the group, was a series of small scratches to Csanád's skin – into which was administered a small amount of each prospective allergen.

'Now, before I explain the results of these tests, there was something else that we discovered at this moment …' Maja began, 'Csanád's skin was far tougher than we had previously experienced. It bore almost a leathery texture and required more force than should be expected to penetrate the epidermis.'

'But you've drawn blood from him before, didn't you notice then?' David asked.

'You must remember, Dr Reynolds, that the only time we drew blood previously was when the patient was nothing more than a bag of skin and bones. Now – not so much …'

It was no secret in vampire mythology that they were supposed to have advanced durability, this just may be one way it presents, thought David.

'Nonetheless …' Maja started again, 'the results of the allergen tests are as follows: 1) Garlic – minor response; 2) Holy Water – no response; 3) Silver – extreme response.'

Now it was the occultist Denis's turn to get excited. These were obviously rather surprising results for him. He remarked in his somewhat broken English that he was surprised at the fact that both garlic and holy water showed minimal or no response, those two were clearly mainstays in the superstition. Even the response to silver piqued his interest, as silver was more typically associated with werewolves.

Denis then gasped, remembering the epitaph on Csanád's coffin referring to him as 'The Old Wolf'. Confused murmurs spread throughout the room as everybody processed this information, wondering if perhaps they were too quick to diagnose Csanád with vampirism when perhaps it may be something quite different, albeit equally supernatural. However, this line of thought was very circumstantial and when considering the aversion to sunlight and proclivity for blood then it seemed far more likely that vampirism was the correct diagnosis.

The historian Ana chimed in at this point with an insightful remark: 'I am no occultist like Mr Blanc, but these superstitions are unavoidable when studying Eastern European history. Perhaps the vampire myth and werewolf myth both stem from the same source …?'

It was as good a hypothesis as anybody could

muster at this moment. Maja let the room brainstorm for a little while longer before she once again took control of proceedings and set events into motion for the day.

She suggested everybody split into the same groups as yesterday and pick up where they left off. The social science cohort could continue to build on their research with their increased understanding of Csanád's weaknesses, while the medical cohort could view the latest CT scans to assess for any differences now that Csanád had three more days of healing under his belt.

At this point the psychologist Nancy spoke up, explaining to Maja what she had already discussed with the group over drinks the previous night. She wanted to join the social science group and begin to develop a plan for initiating communication with Csanád. Maja and Colonel Sandberg shared concerned looks at this idea, but they allowed it for now. It was clear that there was an abundance of caution where any contact with Csanád was involved. Understandable, thought David. He'd only been freed from his tomb for about a week at this point and he'd already killed two people and maimed another – he was clearly an entity that was not to be trifled with.

Unlike the day before, this time Maja joined the medical cohort of David, her Swedish compatriot Eva, and the American microbiologist Barbara. This time Maja guided the virtual tour through Csanád's anatomy with the updated CT scans and the differences were like night and day. David could scarcely believe just how much Csanád's soft tissues had rebounded in such a short amount of time. His muscular system was far more developed than before, and based on how emaciated he still looked when David saw him through the viewing window the previous day it was clear he still had a lot of room to continue growing.

The extra muscle mass was not the only thing that the group saw when viewing these updated CT scans. Two features stood out most clearly – firstly, Csanád's adrenal glands. Even when he was still a pile of skin and bones these glands had looked enlarged, but now – now they looked downright cancerous. Clearly this played some beneficial role for the ancient vampire, but if David had seen this on a normal patient, he would have told them to draft a will. Well, not really, but he would have been thinking it …

The other major difference that was very clear with this scan was the injury from the stake through Csanád's chest. Where previously the sternum and third left lateral rib were both cracked – now they were both completely healed. In the span of no more than three days these bones had reknitted themselves and David was sure they were stronger than ever before. All from just some rare meat and blood? It was absurd! The group of doctors sat in stunned disbelief as they toggled between the old and new CT scans to see the world of difference. Absurd was right – this was pure fantasy. Nothing in the class of Mammalia should be remotely capable of this.

Excusing himself to use the restroom, David exited the room for some fresh air. He was feeling flushed and cooped up in there and mainly just wanted to stretch his legs. He began walking to the bathroom, but for reasons he could not say, he walked past the restrooms. As if on autopilot, his feet delivered him back to the viewing room in which the group saw Csanád for the first time the day before.

Walking to the large glass window, David stared into the room to see Csanád sitting on the side of his bed – looking straight back at him. Once more those deep black pits that plagued his nightmares locked onto his eyes, and once more David felt helpless to avert his gaze. Csanád rose to his feet and began a slow, almost cocky walk towards the window, stopping a couple of paces away to continue staring straight at David.

At this point, feeling weak and scared, David began to question his own eyesight (and sanity?). It looked to him like a flash of electricity flitted across Csanád's irises, but before David could make anything more of the strange phenomenon his trance was broken by an angry military guard who roughly grabbed him by the arm and turned him away from the staring eyes of the vampire.

Despite being chastised like he was back in primary school, David felt a deep rush of gratitude to the guard for freeing him from the hypnotic gaze of the unearthly vampire. It was at this point that the decision cemented in David's mind – when Maja asked who was going to stay and form the taskforce, he would politely decline.

David was escorted back to the room with Maja and the fellow medical personnel, and he blushed deeply as the guard tattled on him while the other doctors stared at him with looks of confusion in their eyes. In truth he had no defence for himself, it wasn't something that he had set out with the intention of doing. It just ... happened ... All he could think was that his curiosity got the better of his common sense, though nothing like that had ever happened before ...

After the guard departed, David did ask Maja whether anybody had noticed anything strange with Csanád's eyes. He couldn't come out and straight up say that he thought they were hypnotic. Regardless of the realm of fantasy he had been drawn into, this still seemed too out there and he did not want his credibility to be lessened. When Maja responded that no, nothing strange had been noticed about his eyes other than their dark colour, then David let it go. He concluded that it all must be in his head and that he would only look foolish by bringing it up.

After another hour or so the two groups got back together to discuss their various findings over lunch. The medical contingent learnt from the psychologist Nancy that they were now prepared to make 'first contact' with Csanád – provided they were permitted to do so. Colonel Sandberg, as their chaperone, was opposed to the idea, but Maja was able to sway him.

Given the number of unknowns on the medical side of the fence, it really was imperative that they managed to learn more from Csanád himself. Maja was also cognisant of the fallout regarding 'human rights violations' that they would open themselves up to if they simply kept Csanád as nothing more than what amounted to a caged animal. Whether he was actually human or not, the bleeding hearts would have a field day.

The plan that Nancy had devised was remarkably simple. To begin with, she only wanted to establish a rapport with Csanád. In essence, with the help of Janik as a translator, they wanted to find common ground with him. With this groundwork laid, then they could go on to bigger and better things, learning about his history and physiology and filling in all the gaps. It all sounded so simple on paper, but somehow David doubted it would actually work as planned.

Nonetheless, immediately following lunch, the group set about enacting their plans. Everybody returned to the viewing room where David was so recently chided, but this time Nancy and Janik were shown how to use the communicator so that Csanád could hear them. David was careful to pay close attention to his colleagues, keeping his eyes far away from the caged vampire. Whether he continued denying it or not, he was afraid. Genuinely terrified of the man (or monster?) just behind the glass.

Through the communicator, Nancy said: 'Hello Csanád, my name is Dr Nancy Miller, it is a pleasure to meet you' – which Janik then repeated in both Romanian and Swedish. All eyes (except David's) were on Csanád; you could hear a pin drop in the room as people watched with bated breath to see if – or how – he would respond. Csanád arose from his bed and paced towards the glass, much as he had done with David earlier. He stood before Nancy and Janik, dwarfing both of them in height, and when he responded it sent shivers down pretty much everybody's spines.

'Sânge!' he bellowed deeply.

'That means blood in Romanian,' Janik translated. 'But ... that's modern Romanian ... It wasn't even created until centuries after he was entombed ...'

Without missing a beat, and ignoring the fresh mystery for now, Nancy replied to him asking: 'Would you like some blood?', which was translated this time only into Romanian by Janik.

'Da!' came the response. It needed no translation.

'If we provide you with blood, will you agree to communicate with us?' asked Nancy.

'Sânge!' was all the reply that he deigned.

Nancy turned to face the room and explained what was clear to her. She said that Csanád was clearly a very proud person and was not one to beg or strike bargains. Orders were all that he was willing to use. But she thought that if they showed a sign of good faith and gave him what he was after, at least just this once, then he might soften and allow for further discourse.

Maja and Colonel Sandberg dispensed with their usual conversation in English and began conversing rapidly in Swedish about whether they should acquiesce. David did not need to be a linguist to realise that they were clearly arguing. Based on their personalities David assumed that Colonel Sandberg was against the idea while Maja thought it might prove to be fruitful.

After several long minutes of deliberation, Maja turned and spoke to one of the ECDC staff doctors who then scurried away out of sight. She then explained to the group who couldn't understand the Swedish argument that they would give him what he wanted just this once. It could prove a useful bargaining chip to get more knowledge out of him in future.

David's nerves were on a knife's edge when the staff doctor returned from some back room carrying a bag of donated blood. He couldn't help but glimpse through the glass to see how Csanád was reacting. For the first time, those black pits of eyes were not boring through his own. This time they only cared about one thing. As the doctor, with his armed escort, placed the bag of blood into the airlock chamber and then scurried back out to lock it – Csanád paced impatiently waiting for the internal airlock to be opened.

With the door now unlocked, Csanád rushed to the bag. He used the sharpened point of one of his fingernails to slash one corner of the bag and then held it over his mouth like a drunk teenager downing bagged wine. The spectacle was abhorrent, and David wasn't alone when he turned away, not wanting to bear witness any further.

Six

Despite trying to avert his gaze, David's scientific curiosity quickly got the better of him. As he turned his attention back towards the gorging vampire, he was blown away by the effect that something as simple as a bag of O-negative blood could possibly have. Csanád, who just moments ago looked borderline anorexic, now absolutely radiated as the seven-foot-tall monster he was. The complexion of his olive skin, the natural oiliness of his dark hair, and the imposing figure of his deeply muscular body all appearing far more refined.

As Csanád drained the bag of blood completely dry, he bellowed a loud roar of what … triumph? … before finally deigning to turn his attention back towards the peanut gallery staring at him nervously through a hardened glass viewing window that suddenly didn't feel like it offered anywhere near enough protection.

Everything was completely surreal for David. Being a haematologist, blood was his bread and butter — but he had never once imagined that *drinking* blood could even remotely provide such sustenance or vitality.

Between the archaeologist that Csanád had killed for a mere splash of blood, the ECDC staff doctor he had killed and drained, and now this bag of blood — he had managed to undo the horrors of almost a millennium of starvation. How were you supposed to kill one of these monsters, David thought? Almost as if in response to the thoughts passing through David's mind, Csanád's eyes once more sought him out. He paid no attention to the fact that Nancy was trying to communicate with him once more, instead simply staring intently towards David.

Not wanting to be caught in the quicksand of that glare again, David quickly turned to look at the ground. As he did so he could have sworn he heard a snort of derisive contempt. He glanced around the room to determine its origin, but all eyes were focused on Csanád. Now the snort of contempt turned to a harsh laughter. David continued looking around until his strange behaviour caught the attention of Janik, who managed to bring him back to a semblance of reality. To say David was spooked would be an understatement, he was now counting down the seconds until the day drew to a close so that he could put this crazy place behind him.

Mercifully, only several minutes later, Maja pulled the plug on any further discourse with Csanád for the day. He was showing no desire to communicate and, if anything, it was like he was openly mocking them.

Exhumed

Standing around like a gaggle of fools was not helping their cause, so it was best for them to regroup and determine their options. As Maja led everyone away from the viewing window, David went out of his way to keep his eyes averted. He would be perfectly content never to look at that *thing* again.

Even though the afternoon was still young, as soon as the group made it back to their 'common' area Maja decided that now was the time for people to decide whether they wanted to stay and take part in the 'vampire taskforce' (what an awful name, thought David). Immediately there were two people who wanted nothing more than to stay. The occultist Denis, and so too the psychologist Nancy. On the other side of the fence were those like David. Jürgen, the anthropologist and Barbara the microbiologist each indicated their desire to leave the facility.

David already knew that Jürgen felt out of place here, but Barbara took him by surprise. It seemed she just kept a great poker face and managed to hide the fact that this disturbed her far better than David himself felt like he was doing. Now was his turn to speak up and join the exodus, but … his mouth wouldn't form the words … there was something holding back his tongue …

As he was trying to find the words to declare his exit, he overheard the linguist Janik, GP Eva, and historian Ana each declare that they wished to stay. For Janik it was the mystery of how Csanád was able to speak modern Romanian that had piqued his interest, and for Eva the chance to learn about history right from the source.

David was the only one who had not responded. *No – just say no, god damn it*, were the thoughts playing through his head as he replied, 'I'll stay too'. *What the hell, you moron*, his inner monologue chided him.

'Okay. Would those of you who have chosen to stay please follow me. Eli will escort Mr Albrecht and Dr Wood from the facility.'

There was an undeniable note of judgement from Maja as she would not even use Jürgen and Barbara's first names. David barely had time to say a hurried goodbye before he exited the room in tow with Maja and the five other remaining specialists.

Until this point David had only seen a tiny portion of the ECDC buildings. He knew that it was a big facility, but it took him a little by surprise just how large it truly was as Maja led the group to what would be their new sleeping quarters right here on site. She explained that it would be organised for their personal effects to be transported from the hotel, but for now they should make themselves at home and begin devising a plan for further communication with Csanád. The only caveat to their stay was that they were in essence 'confined' to the living quarters and would not have clearance to enter other parts of the facility without escorts. This made sense, as the ECDC couldn't have random people wandering around, given the massive security risk it posed.

While Csanád only spoke two words to them today, this was as much as he had spoken in the entire week that he had been at the facility. The medical tests were not really getting them anywhere, and considering he was such a dangerous 'patient', it was preferable to stay as safely away from him as possible. Engaging a discourse would be the desired path that they were to follow in the immediate future. With these instructions, Maja scurried away and left the now-dwindled team to explore their utilitarian rooms and to discuss between themselves how they wanted to move forward.

At this stage, David was still in a very introspective mood. He sat with the group as they discussed various methods for convincing Csanád to talk, but for the most part the words went in one ear and out the other. Instead, all he could wonder was *why* he was still here. Was it his subconscious that refused to let him leave? He obviously knew the magnitude of a discovery such as this and perhaps his brain refused to let his silly superstitious fears get in the way of not only the advancement of his career, but possibly the advancement of medical science as a whole …

Evening rolled around and David this time chose to stay alone in his room. He didn't want a repeat of the previous night where he had too much to drink (did they even have alcohol at the ECDC?), which he assumed would lead to further nightmares. Mercifully, it seemed his theory held weight when he managed to sleep through the night uninterrupted and awaken feeling the most fresh he had felt in days. Even the worries that niggled in his mind seemed to have lessened and he thought that perhaps it was just his over-tiredness that was making him so spooked before.

He joined the remainder of the group at the common breakfast hall where he ate a hearty meal as they discussed their plans for the day. The psychologist Nancy helmed the discussion, and her plan was essentially unchanged from yesterday. They would engage with Csanád, but only if he willingly gave them a little more in return would they allow him to have more blood. If he proved difficult then instead, they would give him cooked steak as 'punishment'.

It felt very much like animal training to David, which immediately sparked an ethical dilemma in his mind, but considering the 'patient' at hand he managed to suppress these qualms quite easily. When the plans were outlined to Maja and Colonel Sandberg, Maja immediately provided the green light, no such ethical concerns apparent in her demeanour. Colonel Sandberg on the other hand had a look of deep discomfort in his eyes. David didn't think he cared one bit about the ethics of the situation, it was more like he was concerned at how strong and revitalised it was making Csanád – a perfectly valid concern in his opinion.

Unlike the previous day, this time only Nancy and Janik approached the viewing window to engage in conversation with Csanád. The rest of the group watched on through a series of display monitors linked to the cameras plastered within the quarantine cell. It was Nancy's idea that they do it this way, she believed that having a room full of people watching on would only put Csanád on the defensive, whereas a little woman and an old man (as she described herself and Janik) would come across as far less threatening.

Back home in Australia, David didn't have the highest opinion of psych as a 'medical' science – but given Nancy's insights here and the way she had basically taken charge of the operation he realised he might have to change his way of thinking. This sentiment was only boosted when it appeared to show immediate results.

Csanád approached the viewing window, and just like the previous day he bellowed: 'Sânge!'.

It immediately evoked the image of Pavlov's Dog for David, where the test subject is trained to recognise stimulus. In the original experiment, Pavlov noticed that dogs would salivate at the sight of meat. An elementary discovery with wide-ranging implications. Here, Csanád was figuratively salivating at the sight of Nancy and Janik because he associated them with being given blood.

'Soon, Mr Farkas. First, I would like to ask you some questions,' Nancy said.

With this perceived insult, Csanád turned away from Nancy and paced across his quarantined room. He then did something that surprised everybody. He turned to look directly into the lens of the security camera in the corner of his room and with his gaze fixed and unmoving he once more bellowed 'Sânge!'.

How the hell did someone from the 13th century even know what a security camera was? This was just one of the mysteries plaguing David ... Goosebumps prickled all over his skin at the sight of those menacing black eyes staring daggers through his soul right through the display monitors. It seemed he was not the only person affected by this piecing stare – Denis quietly muttered something in French that David didn't understand and looked like he was almost in physical discomfort.

'Mr Farkas, please. We are trying to help you, but we need your help in return,' the voice of Nancy came through the speakers.

Mercifully it served to draw those black eyes away from the camera and free the group from the hold of their glare as Csanád paced once more towards the window to loom over Nancy and Janik.

He looked them up and down disdainfully before finally saying something different: 'Slab!'.

David heard Janik's translation through the microphone. Csanád had called them 'weak'. While this perplexed David – Nancy immediately seized the opportunity and replied: 'Yes – and you are very strong. I understand your frustration, Mr Farkas. Please, let us work together, we just want a tiny bit of information – then we will leave you in peace to enjoy your meal' (nodding towards a bag of blood in the back of the room).

Csanád remained silent for a time, considering his options. It was clear that this was a deeply frustrating situation for him, at the whim of people he considered so far beneath him. He turned those monstrous eyes back towards the security camera and for the first time he spoke a complete sentence rather than a single barked word.

'O să vorbesc doar cu francezul!' Before Janik

could provide his translation, the Hungarian historian Ana turned her head questioningly towards Denis. She evidently understood Romanian also, so she was the first to realise what Csanád had said. Janik provided the translation: 'I will only speak to the Frenchman'.

All eyes soon followed those of Ana as everybody was left wondering just what on earth this could mean. It even put the unflappable psychologist Nancy on the back foot, trapping her between a rock and a hard place. This was exactly the opening that she desired, and she needed to be careful how she responded as it might be the only chance they were to get. As a spur of the moment decision, she acquiesced to Csanád's request (demand) and as a sign of good faith she motioned for the security guards watching on from just outside the room to enter and provide Csanád with his 'meal'.

Nobody much wanted to watch the vampire partake in downing the bag of blood again, and Nancy and Janik took this opportunity to make their way back to the viewing room to discuss their options with Maja and the rest of the group. The French occultist Denis was just as perplexed as everybody else as to why he had been singled out. Nancy had to step in on more than one occasion to nullify feelings of suspicion being cast towards him, especially by Colonel Sandberg. It was Nancy's speculation – which she apologised to Denis for – that he had been singled out because he was the least qualified in the room. Everyone else was a seasoned academic expert whereas Denis … well … wasn't …

Not wanting to risk Csanád having a change of

mind, it was decided that Denis (accompanied by Janik as a translator) would return and begin communication with Csanád within the hour. This left Nancy a very short time to try and prepare him for the task at hand. The main thing she put emphasis on was that it was imperative for him to avoid confrontation. He needed Csanád to see him as a harmless medium through which he could provide the information that they required.

On the topic of the information they required – there was a veritable shopping list of unknowns. They needed to prioritise. Most importantly, they wanted to learn how vampirism worked, notably if it were contagious. This information took precedence over all else, but if Csanád were to open up then they would also like to know his age and whether there are other vampires in the world. That should suffice for an opening salvo. If it went well, then they could return for more and delve deeper into all of the mysteries.

Through all of this, Denis looked like a confused child. His psyche was clearly fighting two simultaneous urges. On the one side he was obviously very frightened, and on the other he was inquisitive and wanted to know all there was to know. If anyone could understand these feelings, it was David who felt very much the same way. Denis and Janik were escorted back to the viewing window and left alone once more by the guards while everybody watched with bated breath through the monitors, wondering what would unfold before them.

Speaking in his stuttery English, Denis said 'I am called Denis, you wanted to—' before he was interrupted by Csanád, pointing at Janik by Denis's side and speaking in flawless French: 'Pars, vieil homme!'

All of their plans were immediately thrown into disarray. Not only had Csanád suddenly revealed fluency in French, but he had ordered the 'old man' Janik to leave the room. Denis looked at Janik who returned his confused gaze. This same confused scene was playing out in the viewing room.

David merely watched as Nancy and Maja burst into a rapid-fire discussion that resulted in a guard being sent to escort Janik out of the room. Moments later Janik appeared into the room with everybody else, just in time to begin translating the French into English.

Nancy cursed as Denis immediately went off script. His surprise at being able to speak his mother-tongue had made him ask Csanád how he knew French. The reply, as translated by Janik was that Csanád could 'speak all languages'. But Janik in particular was confused by this reply. Obviously, it was meant to be taken as a boast, but even if Csanád could speak French centuries ago, the language had evolved drastically since that time – so why did Csanád's vernacular sound so modern? It didn't make sense …

Janik voiced this for the second time now, still perplexed about the fact that Csanád's Romanian was highly modern also – but neither he nor anybody else had any time to dwell on it as the conversation between Denis and Csanád resumed once more. It was almost unbelievable how much they were actually getting out of Csanád at this point. After limiting his responses to single words for the past week he was now engaged in a full-blown conversation.

Denis eventually returned to the script by asking Csanád whether there were any other vampires in the world. Janik translated the reply by Csanád stating 'how should he know', though he did mention he sensed a degree of evasion in the tone of the reply. A near identical response was provided when Denis questioned whether vampirism was contagious. The conversation continued with Janik translating that Csanád was born in Dacia, but whether in secrecy or lack of his own understanding he would provide no answers with regards to Denis's questions about how he became a vampire. The historian Ana quietly marvelled at the prospect of being able to question a living Dacian about history from more than 1600 years prior.

After several minutes Denis reached the end of his scripted questions and suddenly went silent. He was just sitting there as if in a trance, staring straight into those black pits of Csanád's eyes. Nancy and Maja alike both reacted quickly and ordered for him to be removed from the scene since it seemed he had completely blanked and had no idea what to say next. They had made such overwhelming progress today that they didn't want to risk losing it.

Something felt off to David. He had been entranced by those eyes himself, and while he'd been trying to pretend it was all in his mind, he was certain that there had to be more to it … The thing that really piqued David's interest was that Denis turned as if he was spooked to look towards the door *before* the guards even entered to escort him out. *How could he know they were coming …?*

While David's mind was awhirl trying to get to the bottom of these thoughts, he largely ignored all of the discussion taking place in the room around him. He had nothing to contribute anyway, he wasn't a linguist, a historian, an occultist. His medical skills held no credence in this conversation. Ironically, it was his medical credentials that prevented David from drawing a conclusion that may have seemed more obvious to others without such strict adherence to the scientific method. The conclusion that Csanád possessed extrasensory abilities and could be using these covertly without anybody knowing a thing.

As David lay in bed late that evening, still mulling over the events of the day and trying to make sense of things in his mind – he became aware of somebody walking through the corridor outside his room. Little could he know at this moment that the footsteps belonged to Denis, deeply entranced by Csanád and making his way towards the airlock doors – armed with the codes required to escape their living quarters and subsequently unlock the vampire from his captivity.

Seven

Something didn't feel right to David and he couldn't even say why. Of course, he was fully aware that he was staying in what was usually a busy facility, yet those footsteps outside his room kept playing on his mind. There was genuinely no reason for him to fixate on them, but in the back of his mind there was just something that felt wrong. It reminded him of his youth when he suffered from OCD and struggled with the compulsion to get up and make sure that all doors were locked and appliances were turned off – even though he knew they already were.

Knowing he'd never be able to get to sleep without satisfying the infuriating itch in the back of his mind, he climbed out of bed and made his way to the door. Stepping into the brightly lit hallway, it took his eyes a couple of seconds to adjust from the darkness of his own room, but upon doing so he immediately noticed something. Denis's room was directly across from his and his door was fractionally ajar – like someone had made a cursory effort of closing it but hadn't made sure that it clicked in place.

David pushed the door open a fraction and poked his head inside, calling out to Denis in a hushed whisper and trying not to wake any of their other immediate neighbours. After a couple of attempts and no reply, David opened the door further to let some more light in and very quickly realised the reason that Denis was not replying to him. Quite simply – because he was not in his room at all.

David figured he must have been unable to sleep and gone for a walk around the sleeping quarters, perhaps to the cafeteria. It's not like he could get far, given that only authorised ECDC personnel had the security codes to access the biohazard areas. He turned and made to go back into his room, but his long-repressed OCD had chosen this moment to really rear its ugly head. Just like it is impossible to get back to sleep when you are bursting to use the bathroom, David knew the same would hold true until he managed to find Denis and scratch that damn itch in his mind. For this reason, he too began to quietly walk down the corridor to search the living quarters for the missing Frenchman.

The bright lights in most of the corridors made it so you couldn't tell whether it was night or day, but it was still a very surreal feeling walking through the facility at this time of the day due to how deserted it was. The isolation he felt at that moment gave rise to goosebumps all over his arms – at least, he blamed the isolation for them …

David was 'following his nose', so to speak. He had no idea where Denis had walked off to other than the general direction that he had heard the footsteps recede earlier. This direction, he quickly realised, was leading him towards the furthest extent of the sleeping quarters – the exit into the ECDC proper that would lead towards Csanád's quarantined room. Upon seeing the security door that was intended to keep them penned into the sleeping quarters standing ajar, David realised that something was seriously wrong.

How the hell had Denis managed to escape? David thought as he scurried through the door to try and either find him or report him to the first staff member he stumbled across.

Surely Denis wouldn't do something so stupid as attempt to talk to Csanád in private, would he? But David remembered how entranced Denis had been at the end of their conversation earlier today – *was it possible he wasn't entirely in control of his own faculties?*

After traversing the several corridors it took to reach the imposing quarantine doors through which David had stepped on his first day at the facility, his heart sank when he realised that much like Denis's bedroom and the exit to the sleeping quarters, they too were ajar. *How the hell had Denis gotten through them?* They needed a keycard or a PIN override … David now found himself with a very uncomfortable decision. He hadn't encountered any ECDC staff on his way to this point and he knew that he should seek out the nearest military personnel in the facility and tell them what had happened, but if he did that then Denis would likely find himself in rather deep trouble. Hoping he wouldn't come to regret it (and very quickly lamenting his decision), David sighed and stepped through the doors to try and track Denis down.

A couple of rooms later, David finally found his quarry. Denis was standing before the outer airlock door to Csanád's quarantined room – and it, too, was open … Too shocked to conceal his presence, David called out in horror to Denis, half asking, half screaming: 'What are you doing!?'

Denis turned back to face him with a dull look of incomprehension in his eyes, before turning back towards the interior airlock doors of the quarantined room and fiddling with the keypad. David's heart sank to the floor as he heard the pneumatic hiss that signified the seal to the door breaking.

Time stood still for David – but not for Csanád. With his feet planted to the spot in terror, David could not convince himself to turn and flee – or even to scream. He wanted to. He knew it was the right thing to do. But … *what the hell was wrong with him …?* Was Csanád doing this to him? David could only watch as the brutally powerful hands of the ancient vampire grasped Denis and dragged him off his feet. Csanád then bit through Denis's throat, severing his carotid artery – based on the amount of blood it produced – before he placed his mouth over the wound and savoured as much of Denis's fading lifeforce as he had to offer.

Throughout this whole atrocious ordeal, Denis remained as silent as a church mouse. Much like David, it was like he was compelled to not make a noise. David was almost certain now (scientific method be damned) that Csanád possessed some kind of extrasensory abilities, a way to dominate the minds of others. It explained everything, including how badly he had felt trapped by those deep black pits of eyes on more than one occasion.

With Denis now very much dead, and his body looking completely pale from the loss of blood – only then did Csanád turn his attention towards David. Never more than at this very moment had David felt the urge to scream, to run, to shit his pants and cry. Csanád's face was the embodiment of a nightmare, with a gawking toothy grin showing what had to be far too many teeth that were stained deep red from his latest meal. He even had a red equivalent of a 'milk moustache'.

Csanád began walking towards David and as soon as their eyes locked together then David understood that his earlier speculations were correct. He could literally 'hear' the fiend's 'voice' in his own mind. He had to blink to make certain that Csanád was not talking aloud, but it was clear that he most certainly was not. Something that also took David by surprise – despite the brutal murder he had just witnessed and his own imminent demise – was the fact that the 'voice' penetrating his mind was speaking in perfect English.

Csanád, seizing on this latest thought from David,

produced a monstrous chuckle as he said (thought?) *'You insignificant fools all thought you were so smart, so in control. I have been in control since the moment the lid was lifted off of my tomb!'*

David tried to reply and found that he was still deprived of the use of his mouth, but his thoughts clearly made it through to Csanád nonetheless – and he was punished for them. In his mind, without even intending to, he had thought about how Csanád was burnt by the sun after his 'tomb' was opened, which meant he really wasn't in control.

Unable to describe the sensation, aside from perhaps fingering a raw nerve, David experienced an agonising pain shooting through his head. 'Punishment' for his insubordination against Csanád. Despite his fear, knowing that he would soon find himself drained and dead like Denis, David had never responded well to bullies throughout his life. As soon as the pain subsided, he shot back his defiance into Csanád's mind – questioning him what he was waiting for, telling him to get it over with, trying to do anything to downplay the smug satisfaction of his torturer.

'You have a special role to play, Doctor *Reynolds—'* Csanád's sonorous mental voice replied, placing biting sarcasm on the word 'Doctor' before he continued: *'—do you think it is mere coincidence that you are here right now? FOOL! You have been mine since we first locked eyes.'*

David's mind reeled at this revelation. Did this explain why he had recklessly wandered through the facility in pursuit of Denis? He knew that something was wrong when he found himself trapped in the glare of those eyes. It was his own stupid fault for keeping quiet about it out of fear of looking stupid. Hell – it could have even been Csanád that had subconsciously convinced him to remain quiet about it. It was a tremendously helpless feeling not even knowing which thoughts in his mind even belonged to him. Even so, the scientist in him was burdened with unceasing curiosity, causing him to ask: 'How are you doing this …? *Why* are you doing this …?'

Once more he was met with the sonorous chuckle of Csanád's thoughts, and to his surprise he was granted an answer to both of his questions.

'In my time it was called "mysticism", however I believe in your time it would be called "extrasensory perception" – or to be more precise: telepathy and hypnotism. It was child's play controlling yourself and Denis, and easier still to pluck the security codes from the dull minds of the guards.

'And why, Doctor Reynolds? *Why indeed! It quickly became clear to me that this new world is not the same as the world I once knew. Frightened little serfs with nothing more than pitchforks make for easy sustenance, but this new world is different! You will serve me as my thrall, Doctor – and you will serve as my source of a limitless supply of blood!'*

David was unsure as to the appropriate response in this moment. On the one hand he had learnt that Csanád did not plan to kill him – but on the other … Life enslaved to a vampire sounded much, much worse. Once more, that ungodly chuckle began ringing in his mind, but this time it was cut short. Distracted by gloating and tormenting David, Csanád had not noticed the two

Exhumed

guards performing their regularly scheduled check of the facility. It was only when one of them screamed out 'Hallå!' (*Hey!*) in Swedish that their presence at the open doorway was noticed.

The mental bind that had imprisoned David until this moment dropped in an instant, it was clear that Csanád needed to maintain his concentration in order to dominate someone's mind – but David turned in a panic towards the guards expecting to see them freeze to the spot when their minds too were subjugated. To his surprise though, this never happened. He filed this information into the back of his own mind, the abilities and limitations of the vile creature, but for now he could only watch the scene unfold before his eyes.

He saw both Swedish military guards reaching for the sidearms holstered on their hips. There must have been about 10 metres between them and Csanád so they had the complete advantage – no way could he cross that distance before they managed to put him down … That was where David's assumptions were wrong. Moving in a fluid motion with all the grace of a gymnast, David couldn't believe his eyes as the seven-foot monster crossed the room in a flash. Neither of the Swedish soldiers had managed to even begin raising their weapons before Csanád was on top of them.

The first man was punched in the throat with such force that David could hear the sickening crunch from across the room. The terrible sounds of the man then choking for breath through his collapsed windpipe made David want to shrivel up and hide, but instead his attention was drawn to the conflict between Csanád and the second soldier. There was no contest. The man – a model of physical fitness – was overpowered by Csanád as if he were a small child. With one hand around his throat and the other holding his wrist to prevent him from levelling the gun – Csanád lifted him bodily from the ground and rammed his head into the wall with so much force that the man fell immediately limp – his skull crushed like an eggshell.

Despite the sheer speed and violence of what he had seen – David was not idle. With his newly regained mobility, he rushed towards the first soldier who was still choking for breath – destined for a slow and terrifying death. His natural instinct was to drop everything and try to help this poor man, but David knew it was futile and he had to get his priorities straight. He grabbed the man's gun from where it had fallen and levelled it at Csanád's back while he was in the process of crushing the other soldier's skull. He pulled the trigger and he did not stop firing until the clip was empty.

Thank fuck, he was thinking. He couldn't believe how lucky he'd gotten to escape this situation … but his thoughts were entirely too premature. Despite taking no less than 10 bullets to his back, Csanád turned with a look of raw fury in his eyes and began storming towards David. His grace and agility were barely even stunted. Clearly, he was in a lot of pain – but he still possessed more than enough strength to lift David by the throat and hold him off the ground.

'DO IT!' screamed David – ever defiant in the

face of a bully. In response, he felt the vice-like grip of that clawed hand bear down on his throat and knew that this would be the end. In his white-hot rage, Csanád had obviously put aside all of his schemes; he was driven now by revenge. But before he could satisfy his lust for retribution he was once more interrupted. The sound of David blasting the weapon had awoken the entire facility. Soldiers began streaming into the room to find the bloody scene filled with bodies, Csanád still holding David by the throat.

Csanád lowered David and instead held him in front of himself, a human shield. David could only watch as the weapons of the soldiers began to rise and point straight at him – or more accurately, straight at Csanád who happened to be behind him. He could hear a litany of shouts in Swedish, but he didn't understand a word. All he knew was that whether he lived or died in this moment – there was no way out of this for Csanád, he was completely trapped …

'I wouldn't be so sure of that!' gurgled Csanád quietly to David, he had picked the thought straight out of his mind.

Not waiting even a second to explain himself, David felt the clawed finger of the vampire press across his throat. It was so fast that it didn't even hurt, but the heavy warmth that he felt gushing down his torso told him something was very wrong. His mind quickly became fuzzy … *what the hell just happened* … the blood loss was making him sleepy, the sounds of the screaming Swedes seemed so very far way – but the sound of the first gunshot jolted a small piece of consciousness back into David, at least momentarily.

The shot had come from behind. Colonel Sandberg had snuck into the room through the emergency exit behind the monster, and the single bullet he fired must have hit the mark because David immediately felt much of the strength leave his captor – at least momentarily. An animalistic roar filled the room from the wounded monster that was Csanád. In his lightheaded state, David then became conscious of himself being lifted like a ragdoll and tossed unceremoniously across the room towards the soldiers. He crashed bodily into several of the men and there he lay, capable of nothing more than listening to the frenzied roar of gunshots all around him.

Somewhere on the fringes of his consciousness, David became aware that the gunshots had ceased. Everything was a blur, even his thoughts as he lay on the ground with the life draining out of him. The last sensation before his world faded to black was the feel of hands once more around his throat …

Eight

David's eyes shot open and he reached for his throat to pry the away claws of the vampire – but … there were no claws to speak of … Instead, he found only what appeared to be a thick, padded bandage. It took several moments for his eyes to focus on the room around him, and longer still for his mind to settle. Without any comprehension of how he had gotten to where he was, he recognised that he was in the very familiar setting of a public hospital – however usually he wasn't the one laying on one of the awfully uncomfortable beds.

As clarity settled back into his mind, David did not need to understand the Swedish words plastered on the walls to realise that he was in the intensive care unit of whichever hospital this was – probably Stockholm. He glanced down at his wrist and spotted the reason for the sharp pain in his hand when he thrashed it at his throat upon waking, it was connected to an IV that fed back to a bag of saline solution.

    A minute or so later, a nurse rushed to approach him and showed visible relief to see him awake and staring around the room. His jerky movements had disconnected the pulse oximeter from his finger, which had made it look like his heart had stopped on the unthinking machine behind him. No alarms went off – for him at least – but something must have been triggered in the nurse's station. His familiarity with the setting of hospitals provided David a sense of calm as the nurse slowed her approach and applied a trained smile as she reached for his hand and reconnected the device to his finger.

    David blurted a litany of questions for the nurse, hoping that she understood English. Unfortunately, she was the first European that he had encountered since his journey to the other side of the world that *didn't* appear to understand him. She made the universal gesture that everybody makes when they don't understand, and David could read from her body language that she was going to get somebody who could understand him – then she scurried away.

    While he lay waiting, David took this opportunity to perform a self-assessment of his injuries. Obviously, there was his throat. Csanád had raked his chitinous nail across it and opened one of his blood vessels. It was unlikely to have been his carotid artery, as he would have died within minutes back at the ECDC – so therefore it must have been his jugular vein. Even still, for him to have survived long enough to be here now, actually feeling somewhat fine, meant that he must have received first aid very quickly.

The hands on his throat as he lost consciousness! Of course! In his delirious state he had assumed it was Csanád having returned to finish the job, but it must have been somebody applying pressure to the wound and stemming the flow of his blood. If it were safe for someone to do that, then surely that meant Csanád had to be dead, right?

Before he had the chance to ponder any further, he saw the nurse returning with a familiar face. It was Maja from the ECDC – she must be the one who saved him! The nurse performed one last check of David's IV and vitals, then spoke in quickfire Swedish to Maja before departing. Maja immediately translated for David saying that the nurse couldn't believe how strong his vital signs were, and that the staff doctor should be by to see him within the hour.

Her role as translator completed, Maja was then able to fill David in with some of the other questions that interested him much more. He asked her how they had managed to take care of Csanád, and he saw her face contort into a picture of discomfort. She recovered and told him that they hadn't. A pit formed in David's stomach as he learnt that Csanád had managed to escape the facility and was now loose on the world.

'But, how …?' he finally managed to ask.

David watched Maja's face drop once again as she recounted the sheer toll of bodies that Csanád had racked up. David knew about several of them from when he was still conscious. Denis and the two guards for example, but he assumed that Csanád had been overwhelmed when he was surrounded by Colonel Sandberg and his men ... From the story he was told, this evidently was not the case. *Just how bloody durable was he?* David had shot him 10+ times, Sandberg had shot him at least once – yet he still managed to overpower them?

Maja paraphrased what had happened, which she knew from watching the security footage after the fact. Csanád had thrown David like a ragdoll across the room and into the converging soldiers. The confusion and havoc bought him time to race back towards Colonel Sandberg (Eli, as Maja affectionately called him), moving with an almost preternatural speed and grace even carrying such injuries. Sandberg had fired the remainder of his clip at Csanád, though how many of these bullets connected with the frantically moving monster are unknown.

Csanád then grabbed Sandberg and pulled him into the emergency exit through which he had emerged – and that was where his pale, drained corpse was later found ... What made it worse though, was that Csanád had somehow figured out how to reload Sandberg's weapon and began returning fire on the approaching soldiers. Three were shot down before they appeared to be getting the upper hand, and only at this point was he forced to flee into the bowels of the building.

David had witnessed the scary speed and grace of Csanád's motion first-hand, so he realised just how difficult a target he made himself and also why the soldiers had been unable to catch him when he set about fleeing the facility. Looking at Maja, seeing her downcast face, he realised that she still held one last unpleasant surprise.

He learnt that the psychologist Nancy had also been killed during the escape. Even while being hounded through the facility, Csanád still managed to find the time for one last 'meal'. Or perhaps he needed to do so to recover from his injuries? Either way – the final death toll of the chaotic night stood at eight, with three (including David) hospitalised.

At this point David had recovered enough of his senses to question Maja about how the public were reacting to the news of a vampire on the loose. She hushed him quickly and corrected him like a child.

'A *terrorist*, David, a terrorist did this.'

Sitting quietly, taking this in, David realised that it was actually the perfect cover story. Far more plausible than reality. Fear of extremist attacks was on the rise in Europe. Hell, if they told the truth then they'd be thrown into the loony bin. Meanwhile, Maja had already coordinated with Colonel Sandberg's superiors to create a taskforce for covertly capturing the escaped vampire.

'But where are the police then?' he finally asked. Maja explained that he wasn't expected to recover anywhere near as quickly as he had, the police and probably even INTERPOL would be by for his statement tomorrow.

'What time even is it?' David asked. He learnt that it was still only 9:00am on the same day of the attack. This had all only happened about eight hours ago. *But ... there's no way he should be recovered this quickly ...*

Now it was Maja's turn to read David's expression and she explained that, frankly – it was a miracle that he was so cognisant right now. He had lost over two litres of blood. Throughout his unconsciousness he had had two units of blood transfused and they had planned on a third, but given his recovery this may not be necessary. For now, he just needed to keep his fluids up and let his body recover the blood naturally. He may have been the most qualified individual in the entire hospital on the topic of blood, but David didn't comment and let Maja explain what he already knew.

At this point, David wanted to be alone with his thoughts. He thanked Maja for everything and promised he would tow the company line with the 'terrorist' excuse when he was questioned by the police. Hell, Csanád *was* a terrorist, so he wouldn't even be lying. Maja touched David's arm softly and smiled, telling him to get some rest.

As she was walking away, David burst out with one final question: 'The soldier that Csanád injured when he first arrived at the ECDC – he hasn't ... you know ... uhm ... turned or anything?'

Maja smiled reassuringly and affirmed that no, he was perfectly human, David could rest easy.

Rest was the last thing David wanted. He had too much on his mind. Everybody knew that doctors make the worst patients – David was about to live up to that stereotype. He slowly, excruciatingly removed his catheter before sliding his legs over the side of his bed. He left the pulse oximeter connected to his finger so as not to send a nurse running back towards him, but he dragged the whole IV stand and monitor along with him as he rose to his feet and made his way to the bathroom. He wanted to maintain his dignity rather than pissing through a tube in bed.

He was again surprised by how ably he had managed to cross the room. If he'd really lost two litres of blood then he shouldn't have the energy for that kind of exertion. Not this soon, that's for sure. They must be mistaken; it was the only answer. An educated guess or a rounding error.

As he made his way back to his bed, he was surprised to see a pretty girl with dark hair and olive skin waiting in the room. He stopped and stared as he exited the bathroom, but her smile set his nerves at ease and he felt almost an aura of comfort wash over him. Before they had even been introduced, she helped him back into his bed and when he was finally comfortable again, he managed to ask who she was. In a soft voice, speaking English with a hint of something from Eastern Europe in her accent, she replied that her name was Gabriela Albescu.

It was a pretty name, but David quickly came to learn that the reason for her visit was anything but pretty.

She said: 'We know about Csanád. We know he is free. And you are deeply unsafe here …'

It was a lot to take in from somebody he had only just met, but then something triggered deep in his subconscious memory. *Had he seen her somewhere before?* The Sandero! She was the one watching him as he entered the ECDC the other day …

In his shock, he ignored everything she said and instead replied: 'You were watching me … why?'

'We were not watching you specifically Dr Reynolds, we have been watching the ECDC since they first took custody of that *bastard thing*,' she replied with a level of venom in her voice that did not seem possible from someone so lovely. 'Please, you have to listen to me. You are not safe here. He will come back for you …'

This threat was enough to break through David's shock and grasp his attention. In a small, childlike voice, he replied: 'B-but why? I'm nobody …'

'You're a liability,' she replied.

'But how!?' queried David, not comprehending.

'Strigoi have an aversion to progenerating. None more than Csanád. We fear he may see you as a threat …' Gabriela stated bluntly.

'But he only cut my throat … and the other soldier he injured did not, uhh, change?' David said nervously.

'That is not how a strigoi progenerates Dr Reynolds—'

'Please call me David.'

Gabriela smiled, despite the morbid conversation, and said: 'Okay, David. Strigoi can only be created by the transfer of cerebrospinal fluid. The necessity for CSF is why they are not a plague on the world, as it causes the progenitor great pain.'

David sat there just blinking in confusion at everything he had learnt. He finally regained enough sense to say: 'But none of that happened to me …'

'You are on strong medication, and the wound on your throat is dominating your senses. But concentrate, David, feel your back …' she replied.

David did as instructed, and quickly came to realise that she was right, he *did* have another injury that he hadn't even realised until this moment.

'A bullet passed through Csanád and entered shallowly into your flesh. The blood transfer alone is insufficient, but we fear that if it passed through his spine then it could have inadvertently triggered the change …' said Gabriela, dropping a bombshell on David.

'But … wouldn't that have crippled him if it went through his spine …? Doesn't that mean it didn't and I'm fine?' he asked hopefully.

'I'm afraid not. These creatures are not made like anything you know. Their durability verges on the invincible. The only way to incapacitate one is with a stake through the heart. And further, the only way to kill one is to remove the head and burn the body. They are *monsters*, David.'

Still trying to cling to any sense of sanity, David said: 'But that still doesn't explain why Csanád would want to come after me. Even if he thought I might be infected (is that the right word?), why should he care?'

'You have a lot to learn, and we are your only hope. We can explain everything to you, and if you show any signs of "the change" then we have medicines to prevent it. Please, David, I know it is a lot to take on faith, but you have to believe me …' Gabriela said.

'Okay, okay, I believe you, and I'm sorry for all the questions, but please humour me just a little longer … Assuming all you have said is the truth, what's in it for you? Why do you want to help me? And who is this "we" you keep talking about?'

David could tell that Gabriela was struggling to maintain her patience at this moment. Getting exasperated, she replied: 'We are the ones who put Csanád into the ground almost 800 years ago. And he is not the only one. We need to make sure you do not join their ranks, and we think that someone of your skills who *actually knows* what we're fighting would prove invaluable.'

There it was again. Just like Csanád, Gabriela and her mysterious group wanted him because of his expertise. It all came back to blood in this crazy world just under the surface of reality. As David was considering everything he was told, he saw Gabriela scurry to the other side of his hospital room and unfold a wheelchair.

'Quickly, please trust me,' she said as she then reached into a vibrantly woven bag and handed him clothes matching her own. 'The sun is nearing its zenith, now is the time for us to get you out of here – he will be hiding during the day.'

Almost akin to how he acted back at the ECDC, when his actions were guided by the will of Csanád, David now found himself doing exactly what the pretty Romanian girl asked of him. He wasn't sure what it was that made him trust her, but she was just so earnest with everything she was saying. How else would she know everything that she did if she wasn't speaking the truth? And if she and her group were the only ones who had some mystical medicine to protect him on the small chance that he was infected – then he'd be a fool to stay and take his chances with conventional medicine that scoffed in the face of the idea of 'vampires'.

Gabriela unclipped the pulse oximeter from his finger and applied it to her own, allowing for him to get changed without causing one of the nurses to come and check up on him. David realised he may have overestimated how much he had recovered – with the whirlwind conversation and sudden decision to flee with this mysterious stranger, he found himself experiencing the light-headedness that was customary to someone who had so recently experienced as much blood loss as he had.

He slumped into the wheelchair, now dressed just like his abductor, and without missing a beat Gabriela set off. It was obvious to David that she wasn't simply flying by the seat of her pants – she made a deliberate detour in the opposite direction of the nurse's station and within minutes they were exiting the front doors of the hospital completely unaccosted. David was vaguely conscious of messages flying over the PA system in Swedish – it was likely that they translated to 'Code Grey', which (among other things) was the code for a missing patient. Nonetheless, within minutes David found himself hustled into the same Dacia Sandero that he had seen spying at the ECDC and was whisked away.

Gabriela joined him in the back seat and spoke in rapid Romanian to her two male compatriots in the front. At this point all of the excitement and exertion coupled with being disconnected from the IV fluids in the hospital finally overcame David. He faded once more into unconsciousness and was not destined to awaken until night had long since fallen.

When he finally did return to consciousness, David found himself laid out in what appeared to be a cheap hotel room. He had another IV in his wrist connected to a bag of saline that was jerry-rigged to hang from a coat rack. Too late for second thoughts now, he told himself sarcastically — though he couldn't help questioning the series of crazy choices he had made.

Gabriela quickly noticed his return to consciousness; she had been attending his side ever since they had arrived ... wherever the hell they were ... She smiled that pretty, reassuring smile of hers, which helped David calm down slightly from his growing concerns. As he relaxed, he saw the two men from the car walk into his field of view. They both shared the same olive-skinned complexion as Gabriela. One looked slightly younger, probably early twenties, and the other a little older, probably late forties. Gabriela introduced them as Istvan Popa (the young one nodded brusquely) and Marius Stoica (the old one raised his hand and said 'Hello' in thickly accented English).

Gabriela lifted her mobile phone and handed it to David. The article, time-stamped from only 45 minutes earlier, read: 'Six dead in terrorist attack at Stockholm hospital'.

'It was exactly as we feared,' she said to him.

'Why didn't you warn them!?' David suddenly blurted.

'We tried!' Gabriela replied sadly. 'We called in an anonymous bomb threat so that they would heighten security. Who do you think the six dead people were? The police who tried to get in that creature's way ...'

'He's unstoppable then ...' David simply said.

'No – he has been taken down before, and it can happen again,' she replied.

Finally, David needed to understand just what the hell kind of underworld he had fallen into. He said that it was time they filled him in and brought him up to speed. It was a fair request and obviously one that they expected. Gabriela was the most accomplished English speaker, so she performed the brunt of the talking – however Istvan and Marius also chimed in here and there.

What followed was a tale that seemed too unbelievable to be true – starting in Romania in the year 1220.

Interlude 1
ECDC Check-Ins

Dr David Reynolds

Age: 42
Nationality: Australian
Occupation: Haematologist

EUROPEAN CENTRE FOR
DISEASE PREVENTION
AND CONTROL

Dr Maja Nilsson

Age: 41
Nationality: Swedish
Occupation: Director of the ECDC

EUROPEAN CENTRE FOR
DISEASE PREVENTION
AND CONTROL

Colonel Elias Sandberg

Age: 53
Nationality: Swedish
Occupation: Swedish Armed Services

EUROPEAN CENTRE FOR
DISEASE PREVENTION
AND CONTROL

Dr Eva Bjorklund

Age: 54
Nationality: Swedish
Occupation: General Practitioner

EUROPEAN CENTRE FOR
DISEASE PREVENTION
AND CONTROL

Jürgen Albrecht (PhD)

Age: 69
Nationality: German
Occupation: Anthropologist

EUROPEAN CENTRE FOR
DISEASE PREVENTION
AND CONTROL

Dr Barbara Wood

Age: 47
Nationality: American
Occupation: Research Microbiologist

EUROPEAN CENTRE FOR
DISEASE PREVENTION
AND CONTROL

Denis Blanc

Age: 32
Nationality: French
Occupation: Occultist

EUROPEAN CENTRE FOR
DISEASE PREVENTION
AND CONTROL

Dr Nancy Miller

Age: 50
Nationality: British
Occupation: Psychologist

EUROPEAN CENTRE FOR
DISEASE PREVENTION
AND CONTROL

Ana Vida (PhD)

Age: 63
Nationality: Hungarian
Occupation: Historian

EUROPEAN CENTRE FOR
DISEASE PREVENTION
AND CONTROL

Enzo De Luca

Age: 74
Nationality: Italian
Occupation: Bishop

EUROPEAN CENTRE FOR
DISEASE PREVENTION
AND CONTROL

Janik Schuler

Age: 66
Nationality: Swiss
Occupation: Linguist

EUROPEAN CENTRE FOR
DISEASE PREVENTION
AND CONTROL

Szatmár

AD 1220

Nine

The ambient sounds of what was otherwise a tranquil summer day were shattered by the cries of the young boy as he ran across the green grass field. He was streaked with blood, with sweat and tears rolling down his face as he fled for his life. Looking back over his shoulder, he saw that the wolves had stopped chasing him as soon as he cleared the tree cover and made it out into the bright sunshine of the field – but this wasn't reprieve enough to stop him from racing across the countryside.

The year was 1220 and the boy was fleeing from the Boyar's castle back to his family's hovel of a farmhouse. Earlier that morning he had set out with his younger sister, each breaking their father's strict orders, in their curiosity to see the 'Castle of the Wolf'. To the children it was all a big magical mystery. They had lived peaceful lives, albeit in relative poverty, and the story of the rich Boyar seemed like nothing more than a tale woven by parents to keep a tight leash on their children.

The boy now understood how wrong he was.

His name was Andrei Albescu and he was 11 years old at the time. After running through the blazing summer heat for what felt like an eternity to a child in panic, he finally arrived back to the small wooden farmhouse where he raced through the door, still screaming. He was lucky to arrive at a time when both of his parents were actually at the homestead. His father Florin toiled long hours in the field to provide for his family, and his mother Alina would often be found crossing the many miles to the river to provide fresh water.

Andrei stumbled to the floor in front of his parents, a picture of distress. His arms and legs were both bloodied from his frenzied escape from the wolves in the dense forest near the Boyar's castle. His feet were filthy, his clothes were damp with perspiration and shredded even more than they were to begin with. He was met with a firm slap to the face by his father, bringing him out of his panic in an instant.

His father was a hard man. Life in the (then) Hungarian countryside was not a place for weak people, and his father would broker no weakness in his son – the only way he knew to turn him into a strong man was through strict discipline. After the slap brought Andrei's cries to a swift halt, he was then asked in a barked voice from his father just what he was acting like a woman about — and where was Daniela?

This last question made Andrei cower into himself. Daniela was his sister. He had dragged her along on this fun little adventure ... and now she was ... Another hard slap from his brute of a father finally managed to provoke Andrei into spilling what had happened. How he and Daniela had gone for a walk to look at the Boyar's castle in the hills. He told them that they could barely see anything because of all the trees, so they quietly began sneaking through them to get closer — and that was when they were ambushed by the wolves ...

Andrei expected to be beaten within an inch of his life from his brutish father — hell, he almost *wanted* to be — he deserved it ... But when he finally gained the courage to raise his eyes and look towards his parents, only then did he see something that surprised him more than anything else. His mother was weeping quiet tears — trained to keep her emotions quiet by her abusive husband — but his father was the real surprise. The man that had dominated every aspect of Andrei's life had dropped to his knees and was visibly trembling. Seeing him look so positively terrified had the same effect on Andrei, who was still too young to understand exactly what was going on.

After what was an eternity for Andrei, waiting for his father to recover and surely punish him severely — he was surprised once again when his father muttered something very softly.

'It's over …'

These ominous words would stick in Andrei's mind for the rest of his life, especially because the man who predicted them was correct – it was over, he would be dead shortly after nightfall.

Andrei's father Florin rose to his feet and slowly stepped out of the front door of the house to gaze at the sun in the sky. After being born and raised on the land, he was perfectly accurate in his assessment that the sun would sink behind the horizon within three hours. Nowhere near enough time to get away. Hell, he had heard tales of people fleeing at the first rays of the sun and still being hunted down mercilessly. The damned Boyar refused to let any of his 'subjects' escape his domain. They were little more than free-range livestock for that monster.

'Boy – come to me,' said Florin in a strange tone that Andrei was not used to hearing from his father. He almost sensed sentiment in those words as he left his mother to quietly weep indoors and walked outside to his father.

'You must listen, and you must listen well. And you must never forget that the last time you failed to heed my words you got your sister killed,' he said.

These words stung more than any of the backhanded slaps Andrei had received at the hand of his father – he would have preferred a beating than to hear those words spoken again.

'The Boyar in his castle – the Old Wolf – is called

Exhumed

Csanád Farkas, and he has lorded over Szatmár for more than two centuries …' began Florin.

Andrei remained quiet, he knew that it was not a wise move to interrupt his father, or generally to even speak in his presence. Now was the time to listen, and listen well.

☆ ☆ ☆

His father wove a tale that spanned centuries. It told of a noble lord who rode into town one evening with deep black eyes and a deeper booming voice. This lord was dressed in the finest silks and rode the most majestic horse. Andrei's ancestor was present that evening and watched as the silver tongue of the 'lord' washed over the petty serfs in the town. While it would take them longer to realise the truth of the matter – he possessed a mysticism that allowed him to exert his control over their meek little minds. This control was something he performed subtly, and only when needed. His primary desire at that time was to settle and build a realm to rule over as its 'benevolent' leader.

There were some in town who were not as completely cowed by this 'so called' Boyar. They were pig-headed enough to speak their minds, even over the mysticism he exerted. Why should they bow and scrape to some 'Boyar' who just rode into town …? The Boyar used them as examples, dismounting from his beast and approaching the dissenters in the crowd. At this point they thought he was just some pompous shit of a 'lord' – but after they witnessed the acts of inhuman brutality that he performed on those who dissented then the town was firmly, and forevermore, under his dominion.

Not only did he butcher these dissenters right there in town, but he lifted their lifeless, bloody corpses and placed his mouth to their ragged wounds – draining them until they were pale and white. It was the first sign the town had of the true nature of their new master, the strigoi, Csanád Farkas.

In those early days – having witnessed the monster in their midst, many people had been frightened enough to overcome the mysticism that Csanád held over them and attempted to flee – but not a single one made it out of Transylvania alive. In an abhorrent display of power, Csanád captured and subsequently impaled each and every one of them on spikes that he then raised in the town centre – an act that a certain Wallachian warlord would replicate centuries later. There, the bodies remained until they rotted from the poles, and for the two centuries following this act of barbarism – the dominion of 'The Old Wolf' Csanád had remained uncontested in this region.

★★★

Florin stopped to regather his thoughts as he was telling this tale to Andrei. The fact that it was his father relaying such a nightmarish history to him was more than sufficient to confirm that what he was being told was the truth. His father didn't have a funny bone in his body, nor much of an imagination, so there was no way this was a joke or a fabrication. Andrei wondered why he hadn't been told this story any sooner, and despite his youth, the answer came to him and shocked him to his core. His father, the bullying brute, had been protecting him – allowing him to have a childhood without the dreaded reality constantly hanging over his head. He almost broke into tears at the realisation.

By now – Florin was ready to continue his story and Andrei listened intently as the sun began to lower towards the horizon.

✯ ✯ ✯

Using slave labour, comprised of unfortunate travellers passing through greater Szatmár – Csanád commissioned the construction of his castle within the wooded hills of the Carpathian Mountains. The construction spanned over a decade, and upon its completion the slaves were summarily executed by the monstrous Boyar – burying the secrets of his domain with them. He decreed to his 'loyal' subjects that the region around his castle was to be off limits under punishment of death. Nobody knew why – and nobody was stupid enough to press their luck and find out.

After a tumultuous 13 years following Csanád's arrival in Szatmár, life actually began to return to a semblance of normality – despite the monster in the mountains. He seemed content to simply play at being a prince and cared very little for the goings-on of the petty subjects beneath him. He did not even make a habit of feeding off the town, instead seeming to prefer to hunt travellers passing through wider Transylvania. It appeared to the townsfolk that the primary goal of his feigned aristocracy was wealth.

As long as the townsfolk paid him their taxes and stayed out of his way – he was content to stay out of theirs in return. He would make the occasional example out of people who fell behind or tried to cheat his taxes – but for the most part he kept to himself. As the decades progressed, rumours were whispered through the town that many wagons containing scrolls and books were seen heading in the direction of the Old Wolf's castle. What he wanted with them; nobody knew – nobody in town could read a book to begin with.

Generations of human lifetimes came and went, and with each passing generation the town became more deeply imprisoned by the Old Wolf. Their lives belonged to him – whether they liked it or not (and who would like it?). Attempts to flee became fewer and farther between, and every time they were met with the same brutal punishment to deter any further members of the town from such notions. Their lot was to simply live their small lives, to provide the Boyar the perfect cover to live in plain sight.

★ ★ ★

The sun was setting as Florin concluded his tale to the overwhelmed Andrei. The boy was instructed to return inside, quickly, and to take care of his mother.

'Go!' instructed Florin as Andrei tarried, struggling to come to terms with everything he had been told.

Exhumed

This conversation with his father was more than the old bully had spoken to him in his entire life. Finally returning to his senses, he obeyed his father's instructions and rushed inside. As he was closing the door behind him, that was when he first heard the sound of wolves howling in the distance.

What followed next was a memory that Andrei would never forget. He witnessed a pack of what must have been 20 giant grey wolves approach and circle his father in a formation that looked choreographed enough to be part of a circus act. They growled menacingly and snapped their slavering jaws in his direction, keeping him pinned to his spot as the imposing figure of Csanád – the Old Wolf himself – slowly approached from the distance. Despite his mother's fearful protests, Andrei was still wilful enough to peer through the cracked window and watch what was unfolding before his very eyes.

The description his father provided of the Boyar was very accurate. A giant, pompously outfitted monster of a man with deep black eyes and a sonorously deep voice. Andrei could hear the words as if he were standing right beside them as Csanád said: 'Your children ventured to my castle today, peasant. You know the rules … Present the boy and let's be done with this …', before turning to look right into the eyes of Andrei through the window.

Florin proceeded to beg the princely strigoi for his son's life at this moment. Andrei could never have imagined seeing his father stooped so low, grovelling so pathetically. He didn't even think the old man liked him until he witnessed this display. Csanád was not one to bow to sentiment or emotion – he couldn't care less about Florin, Andrei, or any of these plebeian fools – but this did not stop him from possessing a twisted sense of humour.

Unsheathing a dagger from his belt and tossing it to the dirt in front of Andrei, Csanád told him that he had three choices.

'You could pick up that blade and try your chances with me – in which case your whole family will be dead this fine night; you can use this same blade to slice your impetuous boy's throat – then live to create more ill-behaved children; or finally you can slice your own throat. Choose.'

Florin bent to pick the dagger from the dirt and Andrei watched through the window nervously. As an 11-year-old child he was too young, too naïve to understand his father's choice as he watched the dagger raise to his father's throat and rake the flesh in one smooth motion. Unable to watch any further, Andrei slumped away from the windowsill and wept into his mother's arms.

From outside the window the sound of howling wolves pierced the night, but even that was drowned out by the sadistic gurgling laughter of the Old Wolf himself. He had taken his fill of amusement for the night and set about retiring back to his castle in the hills. Those laughs triggered something in Andrei's mind. The helplessness he felt; the blame that would stick to him for his entire life; the rage at the injustice. He would not soon forget what had happened this day – and the anger he felt at this moment would echo through the centuries.

Ten

Andrei's entire world had been turned upside down over the course of one fateful day. When he awoke, he had a doting younger sister who looked up to him like he was her hero ... and he had gotten her killed. He also had a harsh, domineering father who had shown unexpected tenderness at the end of his life, sacrificing himself to save Andrei. It was a lot to take in for a child of eleven. The scars on his arms and legs served as a constant reminder of these harsh truths, never allowing him to escape from the guilt – but also never allowing him to forget the rage he felt in his heart for the accursed strigoi beast in his distant castle.

The years passed with startling rapidity after this day of horrors. Following the untimely death of his mother Alina shortly after his 16th birthday, Andrei abandoned his life of solitude in the countryside and moved into the township proper. Szatmár was located on the banks of the Someş River, and it took him no time at all to find a new living as an apprentice blacksmith. The years of hard labour he had performed in the fields to provide for himself and his mother after the death of his father had crafted him into a wildly strong, burly individual.

It was difficult initially for Andrei to adjust to life in the town. The majority of his existence in the countryside was secluded – but he persevered and after the completion of his apprenticeship he became a well-respected member of the village. One factor that bolstered his popularity was the tragedy of his past, especially among the younger members of the town. To them, he was almost as much of a living legend as the Old Wolf himself – simply because he had seen the castle and seen the reclusive Boyar in the flesh.

Andrei had become a hard individual himself. Not like his father, he wouldn't abuse anybody with his physical strength (except for one whoreson of a strigoi), but he was hard emotionally. It was this fortitude that allowed him to provide an accurate recounting of the traumatic events to anybody who would listen. The biggest difference between Andrei and any of his forebears, however, was the fact that this experience had emboldened him with the desire to take action – where previously the violent actions of the Old Wolf had only ever served to cow the simple peasants into submission.

Throughout the years of quiet, brewing rebellion,

Andrei had developed a small network of likeminded individuals. Folks who wanted to escape from under the thumb of their overlord and see more of the world than the tiny, impoverished corner to which they had been cursed to stay simply through the act of their birth. These rebellious undertones were kept as secretive as imaginable, only shared between individuals that could be trusted – simply because they knew that if the Boyar heard about them then he was bound to make examples of them.

The quiet preparations of Andrei and his growing network of dissenters took a hit in the year 1239, only days before Andrei would celebrate his 30th birthday. Rumours of the Mongol horde sweeping across Europe preceded them – causing the town to drop all else and prepare for a potential invasion. Not that they could do anything to stop this irresistible force if it set its eyes on Szatmár …

Fortunately for Andrei and his town – the Mongols, led by Batu Khan, grandson of the great Genghis Khan – had far bigger ambitions than the pillaging of some backwoods little town in Transylvania. They were marching into the heart of the Hungarian Kingdom. It seemed Szatmár would somehow avoid the conflict entirely, until one horrific night in the year 1241 when everything would change.

★★★

The moon was hiding, leaving the night sky a portrait of perfect darkness as the strange, almost sentient mist began to flow through the township. It was like no mist anybody had ever seen before, with wisping tendrils creeping their way through windows and under doors, perfectly enshrouding the town in a veiled discomfort. Andrei was still awake, ever a child of the night, and he saw these wisps as the mist flowed past his window like a slow milky wave.

From somewhere out in the obscured darkness he then heard a sound that sent chills down his veins. The sound of wolves howling for their missing lunar goddess. Despite the many years that had passed since his childhood trauma; despite his bravado and bulky muscular physique; despite the finely crafted sword he had spirited away from his work as blacksmith – still these howls sent chills down his spine and made him question his entire life of rebellion against the Old Wolf.

The wolves were not the only wild creatures breaking the silence of the night to torment the town. An almost deafening cacophony of chittering from what must have been an ungodly horde of bats assaulted his ears. It could only mean one thing – this had to be the Old Wolf, the Boyar – Csanád Farkas.

It was the sound of a woman screaming somewhere in the mist-shrouded town that finally galvanised Andrei into action. The scream reminded him of the terrible sounds his sister had made when those damned wolves had torn her small, innocent body to shreds. Grabbing his blade, he rushed out into the blurry night air and hurried towards the sounds of the crying.

He couldn't bear to do nothing, even if his actions resulted in his death at the hands of the Old Wolf.

Despite his best intentions, it became obvious to Andrei just how insignificant a player he was in the grander scheme of things. He found the source of the initial screams – a poor pretty girl that he was very fond of. Her arms shared many of the same wounds as his own – only hers were fresh and bloody. But her neck was the real nightmare. Something brutal had torn half of her throat away in one sickening motion – and he knew exactly why ... The pale, white hue of her flesh within the milky misted air displayed the true nature of her death. The strigoi had feasted upon her.

Similar screams and scenes were playing out all over the small town. The sadistic wolves were tearing people apart indiscriminately; the bats were providing a chorus of nightmarish music as they swooped to claw at the faces of anything that moved; and somewhere in the misty obscurity of the night – the bastard creature was feasting ... But why? Why now? Was this all Andrei's fault? He stumbled through the night in terrified disorientation, holding his sword before him as he witnessed scene after scene of brutality.

The growls of an approaching wolf managed to snap Andrei back into reality. The jaws of the beast were blood red, and with its hackles raised, it clearly wanted more. Finally faced with a foe through which Andrei could expend some of his pent-up rage, he pivoted as the wolf lunged at his back. His swinging blade caught the beast across the side of its massive head and generated catastrophic damage – dropping the animal in its tracks.

Andrei let loose an adrenaline-fuelled whoop of exhilaration, but it was only then that he realised that the sounds of the howling wolves and screeching bats had disappeared in an instant. The only sounds breaking the silence of the night were the sobbing cries and screams of pain from his fellow countrymen. This silence, he quickly learnt, was fuelled by the rage of the Old Wolf for having lost one of his familiar creatures.

In the blurry, misty distance, Andrei heard an almost inhuman roar of fury. Turning his head and trembling, he then saw the outline of the giant seven-foot-tall monster looming, staring straight in his direction, before suddenly disappearing into the mist. For reasons Andrei couldn't even begin to comprehend – the assault on the town was evidently over ... The strigoi himself, with his wolves and bats in tow, suddenly disappeared from sight. The milky, living mist took longer to dissipate – but as the night passed then it too disappeared, leaving Andrei and his town to take toll of the brutal attack in the light of the new day.

Familiar scenes were witnessed under the healing glow of the sun. Tens of people – almost exclusively women – were torn to shreds by the vicious lupine familiars of the Old Wolf. And not only that, many were pale and drained of their blood. For whatever reason, after centuries of moderately benign rule over the region – the Boyar had partaken in a mighty feast, leaving his 'subjects' to pick up the pieces of their shattered lives.

This simple act of barbarism served to stir the town into a frenzy. The same rage that Andrei had been carrying through his life, ever since the moment his sister and father had been killed all those years ago, was now stirring among many others. Even many who were not privy to Andrei's quietly rebellious group of townsfolk. The simple fact that the monster had targeted their women, their sisters and wives and daughters – it was an unbearable burden to carry.

Word quickly leaked and Andrei found himself surrounded by a great deal of people who had been galvanised into action. It had all happened so fast that he could scarcely believe his eyes, but within hours he found himself leading a group of men driven by their emotion-filled rage as they crossed the countryside to the castle in the hills of the Carpathian Mountains.

Andrei was the only one who had ever been there before, and he knew all too well that a great pack of wolves patrolled the wooded region surrounding the castle. For this, he had planned ahead. Each member of the mob carried weapons, ranging from blades to clubs to bows. It was a different story this time to when two innocent children tried to peek through the mystical forest at the hidden prince.

Crossing through the deep woods unaccosted by the Old Wolf's pack, Andrei led his mob of around 30 men from the town to the walls of the mighty stone structure built into the hillside. For peasants who lived in tiny wood and mud hovels, the scale of this castle beggared belief – but they were there with a singular mission. Many torches were lit, and using these flames the angry mob set about burning down the dense wooden door to the castle. The hunters, adept with bows, also fired waves of flaming arrows in long arching flights through all of the many windows – taking great pleasure at the dancing light emanating from within the dark confines of the imposing stone structure.

The attention of the Old Wolf was finally roused from the confines of his stronghold. A single roar echoed through the hillside, startling birds from their perches and working to lower the bravado of the angry mob in an instant. The fabled mysticism of the beast radiated through all of their minds as they 'witnessed' the sickeningly violent deaths that each and every one of them had in store for themselves once night fell. This mysticism wasn't simply limited to verbal assaults in their minds; they could see vibrant images of themselves being torn asunder in slow, torturous ways.

These mental threats, followed by further roars from within the confines of the castle were enough to unsettle and disorganise the mob. The group that had traipsed through the forest unmolested began to scatter in fear, and as the herd thinned – the predators emerged from the shadows.

Unlike the previous night, a good deal more wolves were either killed or beaten back in self-defence, but the town suffered even worse losses. Accompanying

Andrei in retreat were no more than half of the original mob that had set out in their bravado to put an end to the tyranny of their vampiric overlord.

Standing clear from the dense forest in bright sunlight, Andrei stopped to look back at the castle on the hillside. Despite their losses – he was cautiously optimistic. The flames had clearly taken hold of the lush interior of the castle and it was very evident that they were burning brightly within. Their only hope was that the bastard inside found himself trapped between a rock and a hard place – unable to flee into the sunlight and cornered by the flames …

'Don't get your hopes up, you peasant scum!' the poisonous voice entered Andrei's mind. *'You yet live through my good graces – and this is how you repay me? Enjoy the sunlight while you can, boy …'*

Andrei's heart sank, but out loud he fired back in rebellion: 'Burn, you whoreson!'

Several of his surviving friends looked in his direction, unaware of the reason for his outburst. They were torn between celebrating and mourning, thinking that they had successfully emancipated themselves from the grip of their master. Andrei could only hope that they were correct …

Eleven

Csanád became aware of the mob marching towards his castle the moment they crossed through the perimeters of his forest. His mind was telepathically linked to his pack of wolves, and if he flexed his mysticism he could even see through the eyes of his beasts. There was no fear in his mind upon seeing such a pitiful 'force' approaching his castle, it amused him more than anything else. Especially seeing the face of Andrei leading the pack like a gallant leader. He remembered Andrei fondly, the experience that they had shared.

Despite being creatures of malice, completely lacking empathy for their human prey, strigoi treat their familiars with high regard, so for this reason Csanád issued the mental command for his wolves to keep their distance, skulking in the dark underbrush of the woods.

He didn't view these peasants as any threat to himself. Let them have their fun while the sun still shone – he would take great pleasure in punishing their insolence under the cover of the night. So violent would his retribution be that the people of Szatmár would not dare rebel for generations to come.

After centuries unopposed, the Old Wolf had grown complacent. It was obvious that he was the strongest force in the countryside. If the blasted sun wasn't shining, he could ravage all 30 of these fools without breaking a sweat – however, what he *didn't* expect was the fire with which they attacked. His castle was a massive stone structure; however, within its walls Csanád had crafted a refined mansion with the finest silk curtains and foreign carpets. In short – the perfect ingredients to turn his unassailable refuge into a giant oven.

His problem was compounded by his extensive collection of literature in the form of dusty books and scrolls. A lifetime of research into his own condition – up in flames. If the impetuous – unprovoked – attack on his castle was not enough to enrage Csanád, the massive loss of his wealth and research sufficed to send him over the edge into a fit of pure incomprehensible rage. The emotions, as with all other senses, are heightened drastically within a strigoi – so the roar of fury that Andrei and his mob heard radiating through the castle was one unrivalled throughout history.

Csanád suddenly had to act fast. The flames

ravaging his stronghold were no longer merely threatening his belongings and his life's work – they were beginning to threaten him too. He knew all too well that flames were one of the only ways to bring an end to the otherwise ceaseless life of one of his species. Rushing to his study, ensuring he rescued a few special tomes from his collection, Csanád then descended into the bowels of his castle. These fools may have thought that they had him trapped – but he had planned for all contingencies when constructing his fortress centuries earlier.

From the safety of a dank and moist basement free of flames, Csanád could only sit and fume. In his fury, he had earlier forgone his concern for his familiar wolves and mentally ordered them to lay attack to the mob. Now he could only sit and use his mentalism to scry through their eyes at the satisfying sights of peasants being torn asunder within the ravaging maws of his children. It was not a one-way fight. Many of his familiars met their end at the hands of this worthless band of scum, but in the end the assault of his wolves served to drive all of the remaining (ambulant) mob out of his forest in retreat.

Despite being 'granted' limitless years and near limitless strength, still Csanád cursed the vicissitudes of his condition. To be banished from the light of day for all eternity was a frustrating limitation, one which he had dedicated decades of his long life to research in a desperate attempt to skirt the curse. Due to his failures in this endeavour, Csanád could only simmer in his fury from within the basement of his castle as he cast his seething mind out to meet the leader of the doomed mob of humans.

The only consolation for Csanád at this moment came via his thoughts for retribution in only a few short hours when the sun fulfilled its arc through the sky and sank below the horizon. He allowed his mysticism to wash over the escaping peasants and forced them each to witness the gurgling pits of his twisted mind – the ungodly tortures that they, and their families, were due to suffer. It was a very satisfying feeling for him to experience the fear and regret in their souls at this moment, and he knew he would have a merry hunt this evening with many of them bound to try and flee his domain.

Finally withdrawing his mysticism from the minds of the fleeing peasants, he was left to take stock of what remained of his castle. The intense flames that had ravaged within were fuelled by his lush assortment of luxuries that centuries of riches allowed. However, once their limited fuel had burnt out then the flames were snuffed by the unyielding stone frame of the building. Csanád tentatively emerged from his pit and into his castle to examine the damage – and he smiled at what he saw before him.

His familiar wolves had dragged the still living bodies of two peasants through the now gaping front door of his castle. These were no ordinary wolves. After centuries of subservience and contact with the mysticism of the strigoi, they had developed a degree of intelligence never before seen in their ilk. With this intelligence, they were aware of their master's limitations – his aversion to the sun. This same aversion had become ingrained in their own minds also, which incidentally was the reason that unless absolutely necessary they did not leave the shade of the wooded region surrounding their master's castle.

Conscious of the sunlight streaming through the doorway to the castle, these wolves had dragged their prisoners through the smouldering remains of the castle foyer and into a room unblemished by the harmful rays of the burning sun – and there they waited, terrorising the frightened peasants until their master arrived. The hideous, toothy grin that spread across his face told a singular story. He would not have to wait until the setting of the sun to begin the extraction of his revenge.

It was child's play for Csanád to extract the names of these petty diversions from their minds using his mysticism. Cowering before him were Mihai Stoica and Daniel Albu. He looked like a literal giant from their perspective on the floor, and as he reached to grab Daniel by the throat, Mihai could only watch in awed silence as his friend was lifted into the air like a ragdoll. Even if Mihai had the courage within him to try and save his friend at this moment, the injuries inflicted by the wolves eliminated the possibility. His Achilles tendon was severed from the jagged maws of one of the wolves and his body was weeping blood from a thousand tooth marks and scratches all over.

    Daniel screamed, but this scream was silenced by Csanád's tightening grip around his throat. Mihai thought he would simply continue to squeeze until Daniel's head popped clean off – but that would be too quick, too painless, Csanád had better ideas for these insolent fools. Carrying Daniel by the throat, Csanád walked to a nearby wall and Mihai cringed and closed his eyes so that he could only hear the awful rending of flesh as Csanád slowly pressed Daniel's body against a protruding metal rod that once held some kind of luxury before the flashfire raged through the room.

    In moments it was over, and Csanád stepped back to examine his handiwork. Daniel was impaled to the wall of the castle, feet flapping around above the ground as the metal rod held his entire body weight. With Csanád's hand released from his throat, the screams that escaped his mouth were deafening with the acoustics of the rock-walled room – however these screams quickly turned to coughs as blood filled his punctured lung.

    Sitting on the floor guarded by wolves, Mihai had tears streaming down his face. He was a lifelong hunter and a very hard man in his own right – but the utter inhumanity of what he was forced to witness was more than he could stand. He squeezed his eyes shut and tried to cover his ears like a frightened child, but he was still conscious of the abomination that was taking place just across the room. The torture that he knew would be his lot to bear as soon as Daniel finally – mercifully – faded away and died.

Suddenly, Csanád's attention was drawn away from the enjoyment he was taking ravaging the flesh of this worthless pest. His neck snapped 90 degrees as he heard the sound of booming laughter. For a creature with mysticism such as him, it only took him a short time to realise that this laughter was limited to within his own mind.

'Reveal yourself!' Csanád demanded silently. This demand was met with further coarse laughter before finally, a (mental) voice as deep and dreadful as his own responded in kind:

'Don't you recognise me, Father? I'm hurt ...'

It can't be, thought Csanád carelessly, not intending to share this thought with his mental interloper – not used to being on the receiving end of mysticism for once. The voice in his head heard this thought and responded with further hideous laughter, before finally replying: *'Oh but it is true. I have waited a long time for this reunion, Father.'*

★ ★ ★

Mihai allowed his eyes to open, confused by the sudden silence from across the room. He also sensed a change in the demeanour of the wolves guarding him. The hackles on their spines had flattened and their tails had drooped – it looked like they were frightened of something ... Casting his eyes around the room, Mihai saw that his friend Daniel was very much now dead. His corpse was so disfigured that it resembled the carcases of beasts that he himself had captured and skinned for consumption.

But why was Csanád staring off into the distance, unmoving? Why were the wolves seemingly scared all of a sudden? He cursed his injuries, but nonetheless he began the slow and quiet crawl towards the exit – trying to make the most of his tormentor's distraction.

✦ ✦ ✦

Mihai did not even register on Csanád's radar. For the first time in centuries, the Old Wolf felt a pang of the same fear and lack of understanding that his human subjects felt under him. This time, he didn't make the amateur mistake of allowing his thoughts to be plucked clean from his mind – instead, with a façade of bravado he projected thoughts back to his distant mental foe:

'So you survived, this gladdens me greatly, my errant son.'

Even as a feigned pretext, the sheer idea of what he had just said filled Csanád with bile. He had killed his 'son' centuries ago – or so he thought – and for a very good reason. That he had somehow survived and tracked him down now was problematic.

The sound of spitting radiated through the mental ether, followed by: *'You always were a brute, Father. Your inability to grasp reality does not surprise me.'*

This taunt was enough to finally send Csanád over the edge, provoking a physical outburst from the furious strigoi. Thrusting his clawed hand straight into the already shredded chest of the now long-deceased Daniel, Csanád tore his heart from his body. Mihai was almost out of the room and watched in morbid horror as he saw the Boyar raise the heart to his mouth and take a large

Exhumed

bite, almost as if it were a juicy red apple.

Through the disgusting sounds of chewing, Csanád screamed the words out loud: 'YOU WILL REGRET YOUR ACTIONS, IULIU!'

The sudden outburst made Mihai cringe into himself as he continued his slow and excruciating escape from the distracted monster. Meanwhile, floating across the mystic wavelengths and privy only to Csanád was the reply from his errant son, Iuliu:

'You should be thanking me, Father. My thralls have already cleaned up your mess today. I have killed many of your former subjects as they attempted to flee from your realm. Tut tut, you must not have ruled well for them to attack you during the day like this,' followed by his trademark gurgling cackle.

It was only now, after a day of confusion, that Csanád finally pieced together the puzzle. Iuliu had attacked Szatmár the previous night – intentionally killing only the women in a heinous attack to provoke the peasants into unprecedented action against the only strigoi they knew. Once more, Iuliu held the upper hand in this mental battle and pried these thoughts straight out of Csanád's mind as he came to grips with the situation.

'I will kill the rest tonight, Father, unless you care to stop me …'

It was an obvious bait, an attempt to draw Csanád out – and Csanád was perfectly okay with that. He couldn't care less about the petty toll on human life, the people meant nothing to him. But what *did* mean a great deal to him was his pride. After a humiliation such as this he could not bear to see his errant 'son' live for so much as another day. He would finish the job that he had thought completed over 300 years earlier …

Having successfully completed his game of goading Csanád into conflict after sunset, Iuliu severed the mental connection shared by the two monsters, allowing his cackle to fade off into the distance. The minds of strigoi were impenetrable to mysticism unless such mental links were already established, which left Csanád further enraged as he tried to sense out Iuliu's location. Iuliu had evidently managed a great mastery of the mystic arts since the last time that Csanád had seen him … staked to the ground to await the rising sun …

Not willing to admit a mental defeat, Csanád continued to scry far into the distant countryside. Iuliu may have outshone him just now – an act that he would live to regret – but Csanád still had a few tricks up his sleeve. Centuries of residence in his little realm had allowed him to generate a wide net of familiars; he did not simply limit himself to the wolves in his forest. Casting his mind into the eyes of an eagle perched in its eyrie on the mountainside, he commanded it to fly a great survey of the verdant country. In so doing, he quickly discovered the lair of his errant 'son', Iuliu.

The bastard son of a whore was hiding in no other place than the former farmhouse of the most problematic peasant in his realm – Andrei Albescu. There was no way it was a coincidence. Iuliu must have pried not only the location, but his history of the location right out from under his nose – he was mocking him. This only made Csanád rage even harder. He cared not at all about the fact that Iuliu had a contingent of human thralls guarding him during the daylight hours. More meat for his larder. That impetuous child would learn his place as soon as the sun set behind the mountains …

✶ ✶ ✶

When almost clear of the gaping wound marking where the front door of the castle once stood, Mihai came to a halt. It was at this moment that Csanád set into action after having frozen in place for what seemed like an eternity. Mihai thought that it was amazing for him to have made it as far as he had, but now his life was finally forfeit. But he was wrong once again. Csanád did not seem to even notice he was there, or if he did notice, he simply no longer cared. The monstrous Old Wolf was last seen descending back into the basement levels of his castle as Mihai – now outside in the soft dirt, sped up his escape to a rapid crawl and disappeared into the dense overgrowth of the forest.

✶ ✶ ✶

Csanád smiled to himself. He had let Mihai escape. This peasant would serve as the perfect pawn to spread the much-desired fear and legend of the monstrous 'Old Wolf'. Csanád was already planning ahead for after his victory against his foolish 'son'. To accomplish this feat, he kicked open the door in his deepest sub-basement, and as his gaze passed over what lay within, his smile only widened.

Twelve

After the Old Wolf disconnected his mystical link from Andrei's mind, Andrei was a pile of nerves. Deep down he knew that their attack had failed and that there would be severe repercussions as soon as the life-giving sun set below the horizon. It was clear that all of the other survivors of his misguided mob felt the exact same way, especially after viewing the torturous scenes of their own violent futures projected into their minds courtesy of the strigoi's mysticism.

A frantic, panicked discussion broke out as they rushed to make it back to Szatmár. The prevailing sentiment was that the only recourse left was for them to flee. Andrei was heavily opposed to this idea. Fleeing would leave the defences of the town completely gutted, and the centuries of oppression by the Old Wolf had shown time and time again that fleeing his domain was futile. The monster *always* caught up after nightfall and he *always* made those who fled suffer an unbearable torture before their inevitable death.

The twitchy replies of those who had already made up their minds to flee made a decent argument in response – the fact that they'd rather have a chance on the road than to wait as a sitting duck right there in Szatmár. Nothing Andrei could say or do was able to convince several members of his group to stay and help him form a defence in town, and after a few short minutes of argument they broke off from the group. Those who fled at this moment were never seen again, their fates unknown for all eternity. Nobody from Szatmár would learn that they had been waylaid by Iuliu's thralls and killed unceremoniously, left to rot as carrion in the Transylvanian countryside.

After having set out from Szatmár with a band of 31 men, Andrei now took toll of how many remained as they skulked back into town. Including himself, there were only a grand total of 12 men left. Five had fled on the return journey from the Old Wolf's castle, which meant that 14 had been captured or killed by the vicious wolves in that awful forest. After the toll of life lost the previous night – the poor, innocent women and children – this extra loss of life was the worst outcome imaginable for Szatmár.

By the time Andrei and his remaining cohort made it back into town, the sun was well progressed on its downward trajectory towards the horizon. He knew that they had less than two hours to prepare for what was almost bound to be their final night. But despite the hopelessness of the situation – Andrei was not willing to give in to his fears.

He glanced down at his forearms, running his fingertips across the raised, keloidal scars that had followed him throughout life, and this served to ignite a spark within him. The rage of losing his sister to the monstrous Boyar all those years earlier provided him the impetus to rally and set about getting the able-bodied men prepared for the night ahead. If it was to be their last night, he was going to ensure that they did not go down without a mighty fight.

The condition of strigoi was not something that was well known. Common superstitions suggested that the monsters feared the Holy Cross, so Andrei set about ordering each individual in town to carry one upon their person. He further ordered all of the remaining women to plunder the towns larders and liberate all of the garlic, which they would then cut and distribute to the men who were planning to stand and fight. Far too few men …

Andrei glanced around at the meagre group of 'fighters' by his side. Their number counted over 50, but less than half of these could be considered able-bodied. The ranks were swelled with children quaking in their boots and the elderly well beyond their prime. Each member of the town's feeble defensive force was armed with whatever they could find nearby, only a few carried real weapons. Andrei had his sword, some hunters carried bows, and some makeshift spears were wielded by others. The rest simply carried pitchforks or lumps of wood. They weren't soldiers, they were just simple peasants who eked out impoverished lives off the land. And here they were, preparing to take a stand against a centuries-old strigoi who was almost certainly going to tear them to shreds regardless of what weapon they held.

The light began to fade from the sky at a startling pace, and as afternoon made its way through dusk and into the dark of night – the blood-curdling sound of howling wolves began to resonate through the air. Something was wrong though … Andrei realised that there seemed to be two packs of wolves, the howls of which were clashing in the air. Had the Old Wolf split his pack into two to serve as a pincer attack?

Until this point, Andrei had positioned his group of ragtag 'fighters' on the outskirts of the town nearest to the castle of the Old Wolf – but the sound of the second pack of wolves coming from another direction caused him to re-evaluate his plan. He ordered everybody to retreat to the centre of town so that they wouldn't find themselves ambushed from behind. As one of the only members that wasn't completely quaking in fear at the sound of the horrendous howling of wolves, Andrei positioned himself at the front of the group and was therefore the first to notice the spreading white tendrils of mist that floated through the town, just as they had done the previous night.

Much like the howls of the wolves – this mist

appeared to have two separate origins. It was spreading from the direction of the Old Wolf's castle – as expected, but it was also spreading from the location of the sound of the second pack of wolves to the east. How on Earth was that possible? Didn't it radiate from the strigoi himself? He couldn't be in two places at once ... The peasants of Szatmár were soon to learn the truth of the situation. The fact that the Old Wolf – Csanád – was not the only strigoi present. That they were merely pawns in a bitter rivalry that had been burning for centuries before they were even born into this cruel world.

Much like the previous night, the tendrils of white mist spread through the town, almost washing through the streets like a slow-moving tide. What happened next took Andrei by complete surprise. He had expected to be waging battle against wolves and bats and one bastard strigoi – but suddenly out of the mist to the east roared the battle-cry of a group of men. Iuliu's human thralls had been thrust into the battle with the instruction to kill everyone in town – leaving Andrei and his sorry group no choice but to engage the better trained and better prepared attacking group.

Andrei led the charge, racing towards the marauders with his sword raised and screaming a battle-cry of his own. His bulk, and the adrenaline-fuelled rage flowing through his veins allowed him to slay two men in short order, and this act of bravado sufficed to spur the remaining townsfolk into action in a battle to save their own lives. While this entirely human fight was waging, another, completely inhuman battle was simmering and about to explode.

*　*　*

Csanád surveyed the scenes of Szatmár, embroiled in the most bitter battle of its existence. His mysticism was not simply limited to mentalism – he was capable of sensing, of feeling all that went on within the creeping tendrils of his mist. It was like an extension of his nervous system – but the competing mist of his errant 'son' was serving to interfere with his senses. Yet another act of insolence for which Csanád would make his fledgling progeny pay dearly.

Issuing the mental command, Csanád's wolves began to move as a concerted force through the deep mist – his vanguard in the battle against Iuliu. These wolves were met in kind by the opposing pack, which marked the beginning of the real battle here in Szatmár. Csanád was perfectly aware that the members of his town were being attacked (and killed) by Iuliu's thralls. He did not care. While he would have preferred to punish them himself for their insolence earlier in the day – right now they were serving as a lovely diversion. If his foolish son had ordered his human thralls to attack Csanád then this move might have helped turn the battle in his favour. Csanád chuckled to himself at the pathetic battle-sense his 'son' was displaying.

From overhead, Csanád became aware of a swooping colony of Iuliu's bats. Their infuriating screeches served to dull the senses, and they bombarded him in a seemingly suicidal attack, scratching and beating at his face. The rage that Csanád had felt for the better part of the day had been simmering within him, but this latest insult was more than he could bear. He let loose a bellowing roar of fury that was so loud it caused the bats to literally fall to the ground. Their overly sensitive hearing completely overwhelmed by the sheer volume of the verbal assault.

It was not only the bats that reacted to this roar. Every single living being within Szatmár quaked at the sound – including even Iuliu. The humans engaged in their battle in the centre of town were all stricken still, their heads turning towards the horrifying sound momentarily, before once again resuming their life-or-death battle. The wolves who were similarly engaged also cowered at the sound – but it served to bolster those enthralled to Csanád and allowed them to gain an upper hand. Until this moment, Csanád's wolves were falling behind in the battle due to the loss of many of their pack earlier in the day as they attacked the mob in the forest.

Finally, there was Iuliu. Until now everything had been going perfectly to his plan. Through the tendrils of his mist, he could sense that his human thralls were overpowering the townsfolk – though not without significant losses; and he could also sense that his wolves, too, had the upper hand. This was exactly why he had ordered his bats into the battle – to distract Csanád until it was too late, until his 'armies' were spent, which would leave him vulnerable. Unfortunately for Iuliu, this plan

Exhumed

had backfired dramatically. All of his bats were dead or dying, his wolves were now on the retreat, and even his human thralls were beginning to lose ground. The only way for him to turn the tide back into his favour would be to enter the battle himself …

Sensing Iuliu spur into action, Csanád quickly followed suit. Opening his mind to mysticism, he cast a string of insults towards Iuliu that were amplified and carried along the mist. After centuries of preparation, Iuliu was not ready to be cowed into silence and he, too, cast insults and visions of destruction back towards Csanád. This mental battle continued until the pair of seven-foot-tall monsters stood face-to-face, separated only by the swirling mist, and bathed in the howls of wolves and screams of men.

'Before I kill you once more, "my child", you must explain to me how it is that you survived!' bellowed Csanád in his trademark baritone voice.

'You are too stupid to understand, "Father". You always were a brute,' Iuliu parried back.

For the first time in this long day, Csanád was able to stifle his rage at the insult. He understood that it was a ploy to try and put him off his guard. He merely leered a sardonic grin and locked eyes with his errant 'son' – recalling the last time he had seen that face, a whole 314 years earlier. Iuliu had rebelled against Csanád, ever bitter about being granted the gift of eternal life, and had tried to flee from him. He was far too weak, and the battle had resulted in Csanád pinning him to the ground with a sword through the heart. There, he had left him, immobile, to await the rising sun and suffer the worst fate imaginable for any strigoi.

As Csanád had taken refuge from the same burning rays of the sun, he had felt the pain and the terror from Iuliu radiating through the mental ether – and he had *known* that the deed was done. But evidently he had been fooled… Iuliu was standing right in front of him. He needed to know how this was possible. Iuliu let loose with another of his gurgling cackles of laughter – the same that he had taunted Csanád with so much in the prelude to this final showdown, and he said:

'I already told you, "Father", you are too stupid to understand. You never once considered that my aptitude for mysticism outshone even yours. It was as simple as projecting what you expected to hear and feel into your dull mind, before shielding my own after my poor untimely "death".'

Csanád bridled now at the insolence. He finally at least understood how this was possible. He wasn't staring down a revenant of his deceased 'child', he was staring down the real thing – and this time he would make sure that his death was permanent. Smiling a sick smile at the thoughts of tearing Iuliu's head clean off his shoulders and drinking from the ensuing rush of blood – Csanád closed the distance and prepared to engage in combat, drawing a familiar pure silver sword from its sheath on his hip.

Unlike the previous time the pair had engaged,

Iuliu was far more prepared, and he too drew a gleaming silver sword. While strigoi were exceptionally rare in the world, they were also exceptionally possessive of their power and they almost exclusively hated one another. For this reason, possessing weapons made of the very material most deadly to themselves was commonplace in the event of attack. These silver blades clashed in gleaming arcs, illuminated by the starlight overhead. The strigoi did not need any such illumination – the black pits of their eyes had unrivalled night vision.

Despite all of his training and preparation – Iuliu very quickly found himself on the back foot in this battle. An unassailable reality of the nature of strigoi dictated that as they grew older – so too did they grow stronger. Csanád was 600 years Iuliu's senior, and this differential in age and power became evident as Iuliu was forced to scurry in retreat from the relentless attack by his father. Csanád smiled malevolently, knowing that this would soon be over and he would get his revenge for all of the insults that he had suffered this day. However, his smile turned sour when suddenly Iuliu dropped his feigned pretence of fear and grinned in return.

While Csanád was most certainly more powerful than Iuliu – it was no bluff when Iuliu mentioned that he held the greater intelligence. He knew he would not be able to defeat his 'father' in open combat – so he had planned ahead. As he allowed himself to be forced back in the clash of silver blades, he had drawn the fight into position for one of his human thralls to fire a silver-tipped arrow towards Csanád. The arrow connected with his blade arm, causing him to bellow in pain and fury and forcing him to drop his silver sword to the ground.

Csanád too, was not completely unprepared. He had commanded the leader of his pack of wolves to shadow his battle as an insurance policy – just in case the tide somehow turned against him. This wolf now leapt into action, racing across the street like a torpedo and barrelling into the thrall with the bow before he could so much as nock another accursed silver-tipped arrow. Csanád had to act quickly, the gurgling of his assailant drowning in his own blood as his wolf rended the flesh of his throat gave him the strength to snap the arrow impaled in his arm and tear it out – but he was unable to bend and recapture his dropped sword as Iuliu was standing on the blade.

Iuliu swung his silver sword in a triumphant arc with the intent of removing Csanád's head from his shoulders. Moving like lightning, Csanád blocked the blade with the brass forearm guard strapped to the back of his arm. The reverberation from the clattering impact caused Iuliu to reel in surprise, and Csanád leapt upon him, closing the distance and knocking the sword out of Iuliu's hand with a brutal blow to his wrist. The two monsters stood before each other – both fuming that their plans had not gone as expected, but their battle was still far from over.

Csanád leapt at Iuliu, perfectly content with hand-to-hand combat, knowing his superior strength would carry him to victory. He had also prepared for exactly this eventuality as he scoured for weapons in the dungeon of his castle. Wrapped around his non-dominant hand was a battle gauntlet with specially designed silver spikes. Using this malicious weapon, he inflicted grievous damage to Iuliu and knocked him off his feet, before he then pounced on top of his 'son', pinning him to the ground and raising his armoured hand to deliver a series of brutal blows to his face.

'Is this how you expected things to end, foolish child!?' cackled Csanád in triumph as he leered at the beaten and bloody face of Iuliu beneath him.

Even if Iuliu were inclined to reply at this moment, his jaw was broken and Csanád did not intend to let him survive long enough for this minor injury (for a strigoi) to heal. He slipped a short silver dagger from his waistband and lined it up with Iuliu's heart. This time he would ensure his 'son' was immobilised. This time, he would be certain that Iuliu experienced the ungodly pain of the sun's rays as they melted the flesh from his bones.

Suddenly, Iuliu began to laugh. It unsettled Csanád and stayed his hand.

'DO YOU FIND THIS FUNNY, BOY!?' he roared in question.

He received two answers. The first was Iuliu's continued laughter; and the second was the tip of a wooden spear helmed by Andrei as it passed through his heart and caused him to collapse to the ground, immobilised in agony.

Thirteen

While the two monsters were keeping each other occupied, there were many other battles waging throughout the town of Szatmár. The bizarrely organised war between the two factions of wolves served to provide a soundtrack for the bloody night, with their barks and growls and whimpers echoing through the mist as the entirely human battle waged on.

Iuliu's small force of men that he had so completely captured using his mysticism were nothing more than slaves for him to command, and they set about their task of pillaging the village. If it was human and not part of their marauding contingent, then they attacked it mercilessly. For this reason, it was fortunate that Andrei was leading the feeble band of defenders from Szatmár. He had ordered that the women and children to all hide and lay low in the church – located in the north-western quadrant of town, furthest from the invading horde.

As is always the case, there were some who were too stubborn to follow good advice and who chose to stay in their homes, and many of these were found brutally slain in the aftermath of the bloody battle. Meanwhile, Andrei's plan also served its purpose of funnelling the attackers straight to himself and his mob of unlikely fighters. They had the advantage in numbers, but the marauders had the advantage in every other way. For starters, they seemingly had no fear – a product of their enthralment – but additionally they carried better weaponry and they were also all burly men like Andrei himself.

Once the conflict kicked into full force it was pandemonium. Despite not being a trained soldier, Andrei led Szatmár very gainfully and personally cut down far more than his share of marauding slaves. The hunters with their bows, who he had positioned on rooftops nearby, were also responsible for their fair share of bodies. However, aside from this – the townsfolk of Szatmár were carved through like butter. For every marauder killed, so too were three harmless peasants. The toll on human life was abhorrent.

Seeing his friends being cut down only spurred Andrei into further rage, however, not everything went his way on the battlefield. The perfectly weighted sword that he was carrying (something that he had crafted himself) was knocked from his hand in a scene that closely paralleled what was happening to Csanád nearby.

However, unlike Csanád who had been shot in the arm by a lucky arrow that had missed his centre of mass entirely – instead Andrei was caught unawares by a spear wielded by one of the remaining marauders.

The spear plunged into the shoulder of his sword arm, making him bellow in pain – but just like Csanád, he too was very quick to react, not allowing himself to fall victim to despondency and get killed. He twisted his body away from the spear and with his uninjured arm he pushed it aside as he raced towards his assailant to tackle him to the ground. Spears are terrible weapons for close combat and by closing the distance as he had, he effectively rendered his enemy to be unarmed.

What followed was something that Andrei took no pleasure in doing. He had already killed many men, but killing this one was different. It was so up close and personal. He could see into those poor enslaved eyes, smell the fetid breath as he struggled beneath him – but it was simply something that their fates had predetermined. Andrei brought the only weapon he had available to him down to bear on the marauder's face – his own head. A series of rapid headbutts quickly incapacitated the man and based on the awful way his limbs were twitching, Andrei suspected that he would not live until morning.

As he stood from this gruesome life-or-death duel, Andrei finally caught a glimpse of the Old Wolf. It was also the first time that he had come to realise the true nature of what was happening here in Szatmár. This was not something so banal as the Boyar exacting revenge, no, even the Old Wolf was engaged in a brutal battle with another strigoi.

Andrei grimaced from the wound in his shoulder, but he stooped to pick up the wooden spear and quietly stalked the fierce battle between the two monsters. He was so enraptured by the otherworldly nature of their fight that it was almost like he became enthralled simply by watching it. The howls of the wolves and screams of the men emanating from elsewhere in town stopped penetrating his consciousness – his singular focus became the accursed strigoi locked in mortal combat.

Nobody else in the town would have been able to distinguish the two giant monsters. Only Andrei had ever actually seen Csanád in the flesh, and even though it was two decades earlier, he knew that face immediately. Whoever this other strigoi was seemed to have made a fatal mistake by attacking Csanád. Andrei watched as the Old Wolf pinned the other monster to the ground and began beating him brutally in the face with a gauntleted fist. Was now his chance …?

Andrei spurred himself into motion. He would never get a chance like this again. The Old Wolf was distracted, his evil mind completely focused upon his singular task of taunting and beating the mysterious strigoi beneath him. Quiet as a mouse, Andrei emerged from behind a shed with the spear poised. He buried his own discomfort from the wound in his shoulder, and he crept towards the monster's back.

'DO YOU FIND THIS FUNNY, BOY!?' Csanád roared at his immobilised foe who had witnessed Andrei's creeping approach and begun laughing.

Before the Old Wolf could say or do another thing – Andrei carefully aimed the tip of his spear and thrust it with all his strength. It passed through the Old Wolf's back and emerged again from his chest, piercing his heart completely. With his heart pierced, it was like all of the life went out of the monster. He was not dead, but he was completely immobilised, paralysed as he collapsed to the ground in silent rage.

Andrei could only stare at the scenes that followed. He looked on as the strigoi that Csanád held pinned to the ground rolled the immobile body of the Old Wolf off of him and climbed to his feet to tower over Andrei. His face was a nightmare to look upon. All of his facial bones were shattered, with a sunken nose, collapsed eye-socket, and disfigured jaw.

Despite these wounds, Andrei still knew that this creature possessed a power far greater than his own – and now he was unarmed, his only weapon piercing through the other monster on the ground. Was this cruel twist of fate going to be how he died? After a lifetime desperate for revenge against Csanád in particular, he had finally achieved his goal yet now another beast loomed before him.

The giant strigoi did not seem to be interested in Andrei, instead he leant down and rose once more holding the Old Wolf like a ragdoll in one monstrously strong hand and the silver dagger in his other. Andrei was frozen to the spot as he watched this new monster slice the silver blade across the throat of the Old Wolf and then bury his shattered face in the surge of spurting blood. The change that followed was remarkable. Andrei watched as the wounds on the monster's face began to heal before his eyes, and after several long moments of consuming the Old Wolf's blood the new threat cast him aside and bellowed a triumphant roar. To a strigoi there is no finer delicacy than the blood of one of their own kind.

Iuliu then finally turned towards Andrei, who remained rooted to the spot. While the wounds on his face were now healed, he was still a living nightmare to look upon – caked with his own blood as well as Csanád's. Suddenly he spoke, shattering the stunned silence that had prevailed until this moment: 'You have my gratitude, Andrei.'

Andrei was momentarily confused as to how this creature knew his name, but he quickly caught up with the fact that it shared the same mysticism that the Old Wolf possessed. This was not the only realisation that gelled in Andrei's mind. He also began to put all of the pieces together that led to this horrific moment. The Old Wolf had had no idea why the town had attacked him. That could only mean that ... Iuliu had manipulated them into doing so ...

The same lifelong rage flooded back into Andrei at this realisation, and he glimpsed around the area for a weapon to blindly attack the new monster in his rage. His eyes landed on one of the silver swords, but before he could even think to make a move the monster bellowed to him: 'DO NOT PUSH YOUR LUCK!', then in a softer, but equally menacing tone, 'I have achieved what I came here to do. The lives of those who yet live are now in your hands. If you act against me, then I will kill them all – slowly. Or … you can help me … and in return you have my word that I will leave this petty town to its affairs …'

Andrei hated the predicament that he found himself in. He wanted nothing more than to kill this new monster. Despite the Old Wolf's brutal centuries-long reign, this new fiend had been responsible for more death and despair in the course of two short days. But Andrei knew that there was only one decision that he could make. He had no choice but to acquiesce … but how could he help this monster …?

Iuliu picked the thought out of his mind and answered it without being asked.

'Csanád – or as you refer to him, "the Old Wolf" – is my father. Your hatred for him spans mere decades. Mine spans *centuries*. He made me into the "monster" that you keep thinking of me. We could kill him right now; remove the head and burn the corpse … but that would be too fast, too easy … he needs to suffer, wouldn't you agree?'

In spite of his hatred for this new creature, Andrei found himself nodding, almost entranced by the timbre of his baritone voice.

Iuliu continued: 'For strigoi – there is no worse death than being staked out and forced to meet the cruel rays of the sun. No worse *death*. But there is one fate that is worse than even death. Eternal living entombment. Bury him alive! Leave him to wither and rot, with only his mad thoughts to torment him for the remainder of his years. I can think of no more fitting fate for my dear "father"'.

Iuliu spat into the dirt with venom in his voice as he spoke the final word – *father*.

Finally able to free his mind from the entrancement that Iuliu held him under during this proposal, Andrei had a million questions, largely to do with the logistics of the operation. Somehow, without him even noticing, his rage towards Iuliu had all-but disappeared. The mysticism of the monster played a strong role in manipulating his feelings in this moment. The rage would return in time, but for now, all Andrei was considering was how he could carry out the final punishment on the Old Wolf.

★ ★ ★

Lying in the dirt as his errant 'son' detailed his twisted plan for his eternal torture, Csanád began to feel a hopeless sense of desperation like no other. In his panic, he cast his mysticism into the mental ether and called for all of his remaining wolves to converge on the location – to protect him. To his dismay, only a handful of the majestic creatures raced towards him – their fur matted with the blood of their battles. So few creatures posed no threat at all to one such as his 'son', and Csanád let loose a howl of frustration and loss as the final members of his pack were slain there and then by Iuliu. All was now truly lost; his fate was sealed …

★★★

With this final hurdle cleared, Iuliu beamed in satisfaction. Unbeknownst to Andrei, Iuliu held one final exchange with Csanád using his mysticism.

'One last humiliation, "Father". It is not I who shall entomb you to your fate. I will allow this peasant his petty revenge. Such a lowly creature sealing you for eternity – ah, what an exquisite thought!'

He cackled that hideous laugh before out loud detailing to Andrei what he was to do. He explained that all would be clear once Andrei visited 'the place of his birth'.

Following this mysterious remark, Iuliu withdrew from Szatmár, taking his familiars, his thralls, and his mist with him – leaving Andrei to stand over the immobilised Old Wolf. For the remainder of the night, Iuliu remained in the vicinity, watching the events unfold. He wanted the humans to deal with his 'father' to add insult to injury – but he most certainly did not trust them. If they made an error and allowed Csanád his freedom then Iuliu would swoop in and deal the finishing blow before his 'father' could recover his strength. To his delight – this was not needed. The human Andrei was singular in his desire to see the Old Wolf suffer, and he did not falter in the

Exhumed

execution of the task Iuliu had set for him.

* * *

After the sudden disappearance of Iuliu, Andrei finally regained the fire that had burned inside of him his entire life. Iuliu's mysticism had rendered him briefly docile, but now he was left to celebrate his victory over the accursed Boyar lying on the ground before him. Slowly, a number of the remaining townsfolk converged on his location, many sporting injuries from the violent battle that they had just fought. They could not believe what they were seeing. Not privy to everything that had unfolded, it seemed to them that Andrei had singlehandedly defeated the monstrous strigoi – they viewed him as a great hero.

Now was not the time for Andrei to provide all the details of what had unfolded, that could come later. For now, he quickly ordered a horse-drawn cart to be brought to the scene. The mighty battle had felt like it had taken an eternity, but in reality, it lasted less than an hour. This left almost the entirety of the night for them to complete their task, and Andrei did not want to waste a second. He had the Old Wolf carefully lifted into the back of the cart, never once letting his hands fall free from the spear and ensuring it remained firmly in place through the monster's heart.

With Csanád loaded as cargo, Andrei began to explain very briefly what 'he' had planned for the creature. He explained that they would bury him alive to suffer throughout eternity and that their first stop was to be his long-abandoned farmhouse. There were some questions for him, but after the valour he had shown in not only saving the town but also capturing the strigoi – the simple-minded peasants complied with everything he said. Accompanying Andrei on this task were four of his most trusted friends – all members of his quiet 'rebellion' that he had been fostering for many years.

Upon arriving at the abandoned farmhouse – the location that had seeded his hatred for the Old Wolf over two decades earlier – Andrei finally pieced the mystery together as to why Iuliu had sent him to 'the place of his birth'. Waiting for them outside of the dilapidated shack was a massive, sturdily constructed casket. Andrei lifted the lid and within he found a great length of glimmering silver chain. He simply smiled, turning to look back towards the Old Wolf in smug satisfaction. Shortly thereafter, Andrei had personally wrapped the chains tightly around the Old Wolf, pinning his arms to his side and taking a perverse pleasure from the knowledge that he was silently suffering a great agony from the touch of silver to his flesh – a pain that would follow him for all eternity.

With the monster now sufficiently bound, Andrei commenced the most delicate part of the operation. He snapped the spear, leaving only its tip to penetrate the Old Wolf's heart as a wooden stake. With this completed, he was bundled into the coffin. The last sight that Csanád would see for 780 long years was the satisfied grin of Andrei as the lid slowly closed. This grin, as well as one almost identical from his 'son' back in Szatmár would

Exhumed

curse his dreams during his long, torturous entombment.

Fourteen

Despite having successfully imprisoned the Old Wolf in the coffin that would become his resting place for almost 800 years – the job was only half completed for Andrei. He knew that he couldn't simply just dig a hole and inter the box to the ground – he needed to think this through and find a place that would last throughout the ages, somewhere that was not likely to be stumbled upon and disturbed.

The first thought that crossed his mind was the Boyar's castle in the heavily forested hilly offshoot of the Carpathian Mountains – but no, a castle would draw too much attention. Instead, he thought, what if they transported the coffin into the larger mountains to the east of the Old Wolf's castle? The terrain in the area was notoriously difficult to navigate. If they could find a natural cave in the mountainside then they could seal the coffin within, making it look like the cave never existed. There he could rot for all eternity!

With the idea formed in his mind, Andrei turned to two of his compatriots and detailed his plans. He requested that they travel into the mountainside and search for just such a location. Meanwhile, Andrei would remain here at his former residence with his two remaining compatriots to guard over the casket until such time as they found a place to entomb it. The two men that he entrusted to finding the location were named Anton Popa and Iosif Balan.

Leaving with horses and supplies enough to last for several days, the two men left the farmhouse. Andrei sorely wished he could have gone with them, but his task of watching over the casket took primary importance – he would not let it out of his sight until the moment he sealed it into the earth. Time slowed to a crawl as the days crept by, waiting for the return of his friends from the east. When finally they did return, to his surprise their number had increased by one.

Andrei was delighted when he realised that the third man was none other than his close friend Mihai Stoica. Andrei had thought Mihai had been killed during the failed attack on the Old Wolf's castle several days earlier. He was bloodied and bruised, with a debilitating wound to one of his lower legs from the ravenous jaws of one of Csanád's wolves – but he had miraculously managed to escape with his life. Anton and Iosif had found him on their return journey, having literally crawled many kilometres from the Old Wolf's forest before collapsing in the baking sun heavily dehydrated.

Having been provided with life-saving water just in time, Mihai would miraculously live to tell the tale of how he had survived – providing an insight into events that even Andrei was not yet privy to know. But this was for the future. After ensuring that Mihai was safely resting in the shade of his former home, he turned his questions to Anton and Iosif, asking whether they achieved the goal for which they had set out on the expedition. The pair both enthusiastically nodded, explaining that they had found the perfect location deep in the mountainside.

Over the following several days, this group of six men from Szatmár, including a revitalised Mihai on horseback, toiled to accomplish their task. They grunted in exertion as they hefted the occupied casket into the back of the horse-drawn cart and transported it as far as the cart could take it into the woods bordering the mountainside. They then had to expend every last scrap of their energy as, over the course of days, they bore the weight of the casket up the mountain and to its final resting place.

When Andrei finally laid eyes on the location that Anton and Iosif had scouted he smiled broadly. His compatriots had done a fantastic job – this place would be perfect! Upon completion of their task, after what amounted to several long weeks of hard labour – Andrei stepped back to examine the site. They had enclosed the casket behind packed stones and dirt, and by the time they were finished with their labour it looked like the most natural scenery in the world. Nobody would even begin to guess at what secrets the mountainside held for almost 800 years until a certain intrepid archaeologist stumbled into the area, initially discovering one of many silver crosses that the group had hidden in the area to provide warding for the monster's mysticism.

Unbeknownst to Andrei at this time – the silver crosses were futile – strigoi had no aversion to such things. However, the silver binding him in his box and the stake through his heart were the true deterrents that prevented the Old Wolf from organising a mystical escape. By the time he became so emaciated that the stake through his heart dislodged – the Old Wolf was too weak to cast his mystical mind any further than his immediate vicinity.

* * *

The years marched on in Szatmár. Andrei and his fellow compatriots who bore the secret of what they had done in the Transylvanian mountainside bore families, and these six families carried forth their supernatural secret into the future. For many years, Andrei kept his ear to the ground as his children grew tall. He still harboured hatred in his heart for Iuliu – the strigoi who had escaped after causing so much damage to Szatmár. However, true to his word, the monster never once set foot within the town again.

The castle formerly belonging to the Old Wolf was systematically dismantled, a labour that spanned many years. It was an act of spite by Andrei, wanting to raze to the ground everything that his former adversary had built in his life. However, this act born of spite resulted in a great discovery. The Old Wolf had secreted several tomes in his basement dungeon. Books that Csanád had both collected and written alike, as he studied his own affliction. His attempt at seeking a means of overcoming the dreaded aversion to sunlight.

Andrei lived a long life and died at the age of 74. Despite his unceasing obsession with strigoi, he never again encountered so much as a hint of any other monster. His children told him that he should be happy with this fact, but he was ever resentful of the creatures and wanted nothing more than to track down and exterminate all of their ilk – especially now that he was armed with all the additional information he had learnt from the Old Wolf's books.

Andrei's children, as well as the children of his five compatriots who had interred the Old Wolf to the ground continued the legacy of their fathers, as did their children after them for centuries to come. They guarded the tomb in the mountain, perennially watching over it, while also listening for any news of Iuliu reappearing. This inherited calling superseded all else for these family lines, who opted to maintain the legacy of their great forebears through history.

★★★

In the year 1459, 176 years after the death of Andrei, there finally emerged a hint that perhaps Iuliu had resurfaced. The exploits of a violent Wallachian Voivode named Vlad Dracul III washed over the Transylvanian countryside. In particular, the cruel method with which he tortured and killed his enemies – impaling them on spikes and raising them to die brutal deaths. The descendants of Andrei and his compatriots knew that the Old Wolf Csanád had used this same barbarous means of torture during his conquest of Szatmár.

In secrecy, several members of the group that labelled themselves simply as 'The Watchers', rode south to Wallachia to covertly spy on the Voivode. They wore heavy silver jewellery in an attempt to ward their minds from any prying mysticism. It was an idea that they drew from one of the Old Wolf's tomes – however its efficacy was untested. Nonetheless, having arrived in Wallachia these Watchers bore witness to the Voivode himself. Vlad Dracul III was no strigoi, this became immediately evident as he was often witnessed under the burning rays of the sun. Satisfied, the Watchers returned to Szatmár with relief in their hearts.

★ ★ ★

In the absence of the monstrous Boyar, Szatmár happily revelled in its freedom from being reigned over by pompous elites. The city remained royal free for almost 300 years, until the ruthless Báthory family took possession of the town in 1526.

Life became difficult for not only the Watchers, but all members of the town – and this difficulty only compounded as the years progressed, until such a point that the Watchers chose to uproot and move their families elsewhere. Their destination was Cluj-Napoca to the south-east. Cluj-Napoca was slightly further away from the tomb of the Old Wolf in the Carpathian Mountains – but this extra distance was a happy price to pay to escape from the tyranny of the Báthory family's reign.

    Whether through coincidence or a strange quirk of fate, the Watchers soon found themselves investigating a member of the Báthory family under suspicion of being a strigoi. One Countess Elizabeth Báthory. She was born in the year 1560, and by 1602 her reputation preceded her. She would go down in history as the most prolific serial killer to ever live, with a body count purportedly over 600. The rumours circulating the countryside were what caught the attention of the Watchers: the fact that she had an affinity for killing young girls and bathing in their blood.

    Once more, as with their investigation into the Wallachian Voivode, the Countess proved to be a dead end, at least insofar as there was nothing supernatural about her. She was witnessed countless times during daylight hours, marking her as nothing more than just a deranged human – outside the purview of the Watchers' mission. Sighing in relief, the Watchers returned from their voyage to investigate Elizabeth and simply allowed the laws of men to bring her to justice.

★ ★ ★

And so, as the decades turned to centuries, time marched

on. All the while, the Watchers kept their covert vigil over the secret burial site of the Old Wolf. Due to the highly superstitious nature of the Transylvanian population – there were countless other investigations into strigoi activity, however not a single instance bore fruit. Iuliu (they did not even know his last name) had disappeared without a trace. They could only hope that some misfortune had befallen him over the years and that he had somehow gotten himself killed – however, nobody in the many generations of Watchers truly believed this to be the case.

Interlude 2

Szatmár ca. 1241

Szatmár (Satu Mare) circa 1241

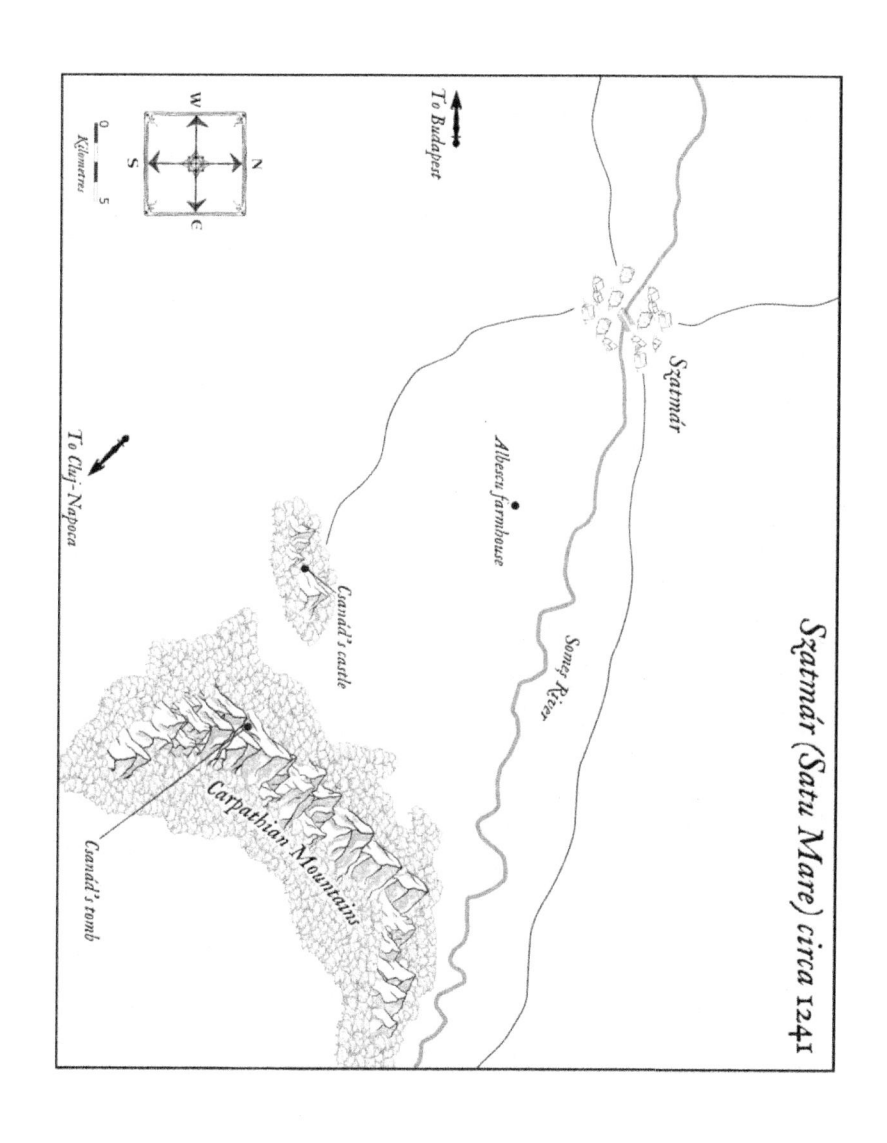

Cluj-Napoca

Present Day

Fifteen

Despite all that he had seen and experienced over the past several days, it was still difficult for David to come to terms with the sheer lunacy of everything that Gabriela, Istvan and Marius – this new generation of 'Watchers' – had just explained to him. It was not lost on him that they each shared surnames with members of the group who had fought against not only Csanád, but another strigoi all the way back in the 13th century. Given all they knew, coupled with his own near-fatal experience with the monster that he still considered in modern terms as a 'vampire', he was convinced that they must be telling the truth – whether he could fathom it or not.

✶ ✶ ✶

It was nighttime when he initially awoke in the dingy hotel room with the makeshift IV replenishing his lost fluids. He was faring far better than expected for somebody who had suffered the injuries and blood loss that he had, but he was still very exhausted. He was only able to listen to the crazy tale about Gabriela's ancestor 'Andrei' for a short while before he found himself inexorably drifting back off to sleep.

Awakening the following morning feeling refreshed, he was now finally able to eat and drink of his own accord, without requiring the sustenance to be pumped through his veins in the form of an IV. No sooner could he keep substances down than he was handed an ungodly concoction and encouraged to drink every last drop. It looked like a green and brown pasty sludge and the taste was enough to make him retch – but Gabriela stressed its importance and he managed to choke it down.

'What the hell was that?' he asked.

'Burdock, yarrow, houndstongue and hogweed,' replied Gabriela matter-of-factly – leaving David to ponder why they might have given him such an awful drink under the guise of 'medicine'. Burdock, he knew, had a moderate healing effect; yarrow had anti-inflammatory and antiseptic properties; houndstongue had been tested as an antihemorrhagic in the past; and hogweed was highly lauded in the alternative medicine community for its 'vitalisation' properties – but all of this seemed very farfetched … He sure hoped that they had more than this to help prevent 'the change'.

As soon as the Watchers, particularly the twitchy younger one Istvan, saw that he was in what appeared to be a fit state – they immediately began the preparations to get out of Stockholm. They had a long drive ahead of them and the last thing that they wanted was to still be present in the city after sundown – not with Csanád now back to full strength and roaming free.

Even though they were among the only people in the world that actually knew who and what the creature was, and even though they had packed some of their anti-strigoi arsenal of weaponry and deterrents – they knew that they'd stand no chance. Their failure was in allowing him to be exhumed in the first place – they were watchers, not fighters. Plus – they needed to get David back to their base of operations so that they could ensure they did all in their power to prevent him from undergoing 'the change'.

For now, their only hope was that the police or military with their modern weapons could take care of Csanád when he invariably made himself noticed. David didn't feel that this was likely, not after what he had witnessed and even had a role in back at the ECDC facility. Csanád had been shot tens of times. The bullets seemed to be nothing more than bug bites to him – annoying, but ultimately of no concern.

It was a 27-hour drive south from Stockholm to Cluj-Napoca. Before they even left the outskirts of Stockholm the four people crammed into the tiny Dacia Sandero stopped briefly at a pharmacy. Only Gabriela got out, and she quickly returned and tossed David a bottle of vitamin supplements. He gazed at the label, written in Swedish, but he quickly realised that what Gabriela had provided him was a bottle of vitamin D supplements.

'You're the doctor – take as much of that as you safely can …' she said.

David did not need to be a doctor to understand the implication of the pills. Vitamin D was generated in humans by the photochemical reaction to UV rays in the skin courtesy of direct sunlight. These supplements were obviously intended to turbocharge the production of vitamin D and – what? – slow or stop him from changing into a vampire? He saw that the pills in the bottle had a strength of 1000 IU, and he knew from his medical experience that it was possible to consume as much as 50,000 IU per day – however it was certain to make him sick.

The bottle contained 100 pills, over the course of about an hour he downed half of it – grimacing at the awful aftertaste that washed back up his throat. At some point while he was forcing himself to down the disgusting pills, he heard Gabriela talking, she said:

'We still use many natural medicines, but vitamin D supplements should be far more effective than anything in the Solanaceae family, so they are your best bet to start with.'

Almost ironically, given his medical background, David didn't so much care about the herbal remedies at this point in time. He was far too interested in the history that they were explaining to him and wanted Gabriela to return to her story. There were occasions when he interrupted to ask questions – notably towards the end when he heard about the silver weaponry utilised by Csanád and Iuliu. He asked them whether they had any such weaponry, for example, silver bullets.

Istvan seemed to be in a bad mood, David didn't think the young Romanian liked him. His olive-skinned face was always furrowed and his brown eyes were suspicious. He turned to David and said: 'Do you think we are incompetent?' with a level of spite in his voice that surprised David since it seemed to come out of nowhere.

Gabriela gave Istvan a hard look, silencing him with: 'Istvan ...' before turning to David with those kind eyes of hers and answering his question properly:

'Yes, we have manufactured silver bullets – but you must understand, they are only a deterrent. It's not like the movies where one shot of the magic bullet puts down the wild beast. At best they will weaken the strigoi. Staking the heart or removing the head – these are the only ways to stop him ...'

David quietly mulled this over. *Surely these things had to have their limits? Surely they couldn't regenerate forever ...? Pump enough bullets into them and they had to go down eventually, right? It was simple entropy; they could only heal for so long ...* His mind drifted for a short while, the doctor within him once more rising to the surface to try and make some kind of medical or scientific sense out of all of this, but it defied all medical science – at least, all *known* medical science.

As the afternoon sun began to fall towards the horizon, David found himself growing too tired to continue with the story he was hearing from Gabriela. He had just heard about the interment of Csanád in the Carpathian Mountains – the story was almost lined up with modern times in his head, but he would have to wait to hear the rest. His body needed more time to recover, and his head lolled to his chest in exhaustion.

After several hours of sleep, David was awoken when the vehicle pulled to a halt. His disorientation was absolute. The dark of the night was only broken by the flimsy neon sign identifying a cheap roadside motel. Gabriela informed him that they were in the outskirts of Berlin and that they'd be spending the night there before finishing the trip to Cluj-Napoca the following day.

To say David was hungry was an understatement. He had barely eaten anything for a couple of days now – only a small breakfast and even smaller lunch after a couple of days on fluids. He knew that he should pace himself, but he rationalised eating a large steak for dinner to settle his stomach from the huge vitamin D overdose he had taken earlier in the day. David abstained from alcohol, but the three Watchers seemed to have an affinity for it. They drank and made merry, their moods palpably higher now that they had put distance between themselves and Stockholm.

Marius, who had barely spoken two words all day, suddenly became a bit of a chatterbox and wouldn't stop talking David's ear off about his familial relation to Mihai Stoica, the individual who had managed to escape from the maws of Csanád's castle. Gabriela seemed almost competitive in a fun kind of way, sitting with her arm around both David and Marius and teasing that the exploits of her ancestor were far more meritorious. Even Istvan loosened up, though David occasionally still caught him staring sourly out of the corner of his eyes. He understood: it was possible he had been 'changed' and this kid was scared, that's all – David was scared too …

David did not receive any more of the history of the Watchers this evening, outside of the occasional titbits as Gabriela and Marius bragged about their 'famous' ancestors. They grew too inebriated to tell the story properly, so he resigned himself to waiting for the following morning when they continued their drive south to Romania. Slumping into his bed, David found his mind going backward and forward on his own potential affliction.

On the scary side, he had healed remarkably quickly from his rather grievous wounds. But on the other side, he had been out in the sun all day, *surely that had to mean something, right?* And so, on and on his mind wrestled with concerns that he was not equipped to solve. He needed more information and was determined to ask the right questions the following day.

David might have expected the Watchers to be hungover from their festivities the previous night, but none of them showed any signs of discomfort. Gabriela was her same vivaciously friendly self; Marius lived up to his surname and was stoically silent; and Istvan was back to his side-eyeing sour self. Their drive commenced at sunrise and was destined to take them beyond sundown before they finally arrived at their destination. Plenty of time for David to hear the rest of the fantastical history that these mystery Watchers held.

Before Gabriela could so much as pick up where

she had left off the previous day when David had fallen asleep in the backseat of the tiny Dacia – he prompted her with a question that he needed to know the answer to.

'What do you know about "the change"?' – followed immediately by: 'And how do you know it?'

Maintaining her cool, as ever, Gabriela answered simply, explaining that the 'how' of it was from the books that their ancestors had found in Csanád's castle as they pillaged it and tore it to the ground. The Old Wolf was extremely curious about his own condition and had spent centuries of his long lifetime studying not only himself, but also other innocent victims along the way. His studies were actually surprisingly detailed and comprehensive … But that was a story for another time, David was welcome to inspect copies of his notes once they arrived in Cluj-Napoca. As for 'what':

'We know that "the change" takes about 10 days on average. Sometimes more, sometimes less. We know that heavy doses of Solanaceae shortly after exposure proved sufficient on their own to stem the tide of "the change" entirely – so you should finish those vitamin D pills today. And that concoction of herbs you loved so much – it was also apparently shown to slow the change in Csanád's notes.'

'You must understand, this is the first time we have tested any of this information … I'm also very hopeful that your blood loss and resulting transfusions might have flushed any potential affliction straight out of your system. But, beyond all that I have told you – we are flying blind here …'

David gave a wry smile and replied with a sarcastic: 'Great …' before allowing the conversation to turn back to the remainder of the Watchers' tale throughout the past 800 years.

He learnt of the various suspected vampires throughout history, and how they all turned out to be false flags – nothing more than people so brutal that they evoked comparison to the supernatural.

Finally, the story made its way to modern times. Gabriela explained that she and her fellow Watchers would take turns periodically keeping their eyes on the side of the Carpathian Mountains – ensuring that they would know immediately if anybody poked their nose too close to the Old Wolf's tomb. About a decade ago was when all of their problems began. People had hiked through the mountains hundreds, thousands of times over the years – but one nosy archaeologist had spotted something that would set everything into motion.

Her name was Cristina Grigorcea and she had discovered one of the silver crosses that Andrei and his companions had buried around the site before they realised that crosses actually had no effect on the entombed strigoi. This particular cross must have weathered into view over time and ever since the moment she laid eyes on it, this accursed archaeologist had latched onto the site and never let go.

She was no grave robber, she did everything by the book – so this allowed the Watchers to covertly fight her in the legal system in what proved to be a vain attempt at having the area proclaimed a natural heritage site, which would have prevented any digging. The Romanian legal system is not known for its expediency, so this battle dragged on for the better part of a full decade before, ultimately, Cristina prevailed and was granted access to the site.

What were they to do? They couldn't exactly go and tell the truth to this woman. They'd be scorned as superstitious bumpkins and unceremoniously ignored. Nor could they just outright kill her to prevent her access either – they weren't murderers ... And even if they did, this would only generate press and more archaeologists would be crawling over the site in no time. Instead, they simply tried to make her life as hard as possible and hoped beyond hope that she would give up before finding the tomb.

Gabriela and the other Watchers knew those mountains like the back of their hands. They had been raised there and could move about in those wooded hills as if they were their own backyard. They kept a close watch on the archaeological team and twice in the evenings one of them would creep into camp and pillage all of the historical finds that they uncovered.

'It almost worked too!' Gabriela said. 'I was there, I saw her sobbing and listened as she was talking to somebody on the phone about wanting to quit. But she told whoever she was talking to about "one last hunch" – and as it turned out, this "hunch" led to the Old Wolf's discovery ... We think it may have been more than a hunch ... it was probably the bastard strigoi's mysticism leading her right to him …'

Gabriela continued, her story now beginning to overlap what David had learnt from Maja at the ECDC. He knew already that the ever-professional archaeologist Cristina wanted to preserve the find and refused to allow the casket to be opened. Gabriela explained that this gave her one small chance … that she rushed down the mountain to her vehicle to grab a small can of fuel … she was going to sneak in at night and burn the monster to a crisp before this nightmare could get any further … but ultimately, she was too late.

By the time Gabriela made her way back to the location of the now exposed coffin, it was pandemonium. People were screaming, one of the student archaeologists was lying on the ground with a deep gash to his throat, the rest were standing nearby holding anything that they could find as weapons. They were understandably spooked and if she emerged from the dark like a crazy person then it would have only served to get her killed in the panic. She could only look on in horror as everything fell to pieces on her watch …

Sixteen

Gabriela explained to David the profound feeling of shock and distress she felt when she saw the man with his throat slashed. It shouldn't have been possible ... the Old Wolf was staked through the heart and bound with silver chains – he should be completely immobilised. But she quickly came to realise her oversight. The fact that centuries of starvation had emaciated the fiend to the point that the stake had fallen free, allowing him to move and extricate at least one arm from his now loosened bondage.

At this point, David's mind was fixating upon the whole immobilisation aspect. *Was it magic?* Some mystical supernatural curse that limited vampires (he didn't think he would ever be able to adjust to calling them strigoi)? Shaking his head for even considering something so crazy, he focused on more mundane – scientific – possibilities. The heart pumped blood. It was the engine that kept living creatures running. He supposed that simply stopping the flow of blood was the cause behind the immobilisation. *Could he use that to his advantage?* Some poisons could turn blood to a thick sludge — *would that immobilise a vampire too?*

Realising that his mind had drifted off on its own tangent, David refocused and gave his attention back to Gabriela where he learnt the final aspects of her tale. How she continued surveying the scene through the night as emergency services arrived. She watched an argument break out, but the emergency rescue team needed only one look into the still-open casket to realise the truth of the situation. She still held one ray of hope at this point. The sun was due to rise any minute now. If there was any justice in this world then its cleansing rays would take care of the problem for her …

Excitedly, she watched as dawn broke and in almost no time at all she began to hear a deep bellowing roar coming from within the still opened casket. *It's happening!* she thought, full of relief — but to her deepest chagrin — the damned emergency services crew were too fast to react. The superstition of strigoi ran deep in this region, so they immediately understood what was happening and they replaced the lid on the casket before the sun could finish removing the bastard thing within.

She wasn't sure *why* they had acted to save it. Was it just instinct? Or did the Old Wolf manipulate them to do so using his mysticism? She didn't think she'd ever know the answer to that question — but nevertheless, her hopes were quashed. She had to face the reality of the situation now. The Old Wolf was back. He was still alive, and her Watchers were the only ones who knew the true gravity of the situation.

Over the course of the morning a tent was erected around the casket, which was then draped over with blankets and sleeping bags to block the sun. She could only assume their morbid curiosity drove them to do so, wanting to once more lift the lid of the casket and examine the thing within.

Eventually the ECDC arrived – they were very easy to identify, and from there the rest was history. The casket was transported back to Stockholm, and Gabriela, accompanied by Marius and Istvan followed closely behind. She had no idea what exactly their plan was, but they simply had to be there – it was their lifelong duty …

The mood in the car had lowered significantly by the time Gabriela reached the end of her recounting of events. Left with no options – short of the ultra-extremist route of straight up murdering the archaeologists – each of the Watchers felt like they had let down centuries of their forebears. The fact that something as horrendous as this could happen on their watch was perceived to be the ultimate failure.

Silence reigned within the cramped car for a good while. David pulled out the bottle of vitamin D supplements and seeing this, Gabriela provided him with a fresh batch of herbal sludge to wash the pills down with. He didn't even know when she had found the time to make such an awful thing after all the drinking that she had done the previous night. For the next half hour, the only sounds in the car were David's slurps and gags providing a soundtrack for his consumption of the 'medicine' that was supposed to stop him from 'changing'.

His mind circled back around to that same old roundabout argument. The chances of him being infected (afflicted? changed?) in the first place had to be super low, right? What kind of hateful cosmic coincidence would it be for a *bullet* to be the delivery mechanism for a vampire's cerebrospinal fluid into his body? It was almost too absurd to even consider. But then, as ever, his mind refused to let him grasp on what should be the obvious and pragmatic answer, by reminding him that he had been healing at a completely unrealistic rate ... He reached up to finger the wound on his throat and he grimaced at the touch – *but did it hurt as much as it should?*

Having finally learnt all of the long history of Gabriela and the Watchers, the conversation turned away from 'business' and simply became more casual. Gabriela in particular was fascinated by David's profession, finding it tangentially related to her own. Even more so, she was intrigued by the concept of Golden Blood, which evidently Csanád possessed. It made David realise that the Golden Blood was, frankly, the only reason he was in all of this mess. If not for that medical curiosity, then Maja and the ECDC would surely have just gone with a staff haematologist from Sweden rather than whisking him all the way across the world and into the claws of a monster.

David flipped the question on Gabriela and asked

what exactly she and the Watchers did for a living? Obviously watching over an ancient vampire did not pay the rent. To his surprise, he was met with a cheeky smile when she told him that it did, in fact, pay the rent. When her ancestor Andrei and his contemporaries had torn down the Old Wolf's castle, they had uncovered a veritable hoard of wealth.

Csanád's wealth extended far beyond just that of what he was taxing from the town. It was clear that he possessed the spoils from what was almost certainly centuries of looting and plundering. In a comparison that surprised David, Gabriela asked him if he had seen *The Hobbit*, and when he said yes, she then told him to picture the hoard that Smaug the dragon guarded jealously. The flash of laughter across her face was enough for David to realise she was (at least partially) joking – the dragon's hoard was beyond comprehension – but it conveyed the point she intended. They had discovered a treasure trove.

'As you can imagine, there have been dozens of generations since my great ancestor Andrei. The wealth from this treasure is only used by those who choose to be Watchers. Any who abandon the Watch forfeit claim to the money,' Gabriela said.

This statement finally made David realise just how many hundreds – *thousands* – of ancestors must have descended from the six original Watchers. He asked Gabriela how many remained now and was stunned to hear that, after all these years, the number remained at six.

'Can you blame them?' Gabriela said. 'Who would

want to live this life? The Old Wolf's wealth has dwindled and with it, so too have our numbers. Five cowards fled at the first sign of his awakening. *Pizdă* who were only ever in it for the easy life, who never expected to actually face a situation such as this …'

David had no idea what '*Pizdă*' translated to, but from the venom with which Gabriela had enunciated the word it was clear that it must be a choice Romanian insult.

The sun had set over an hour ago and after a long drive through the Romanian countryside, David finally began to witness the signs of a major town approaching. From the excitement within the car, he knew that they were finally arriving in Cluj-Napoca after two torturously long days crammed inside this awful Romanian car. Driving south through the northern part of the city, David watched through the windows as they crossed a bridge over a river that sliced the town in half. Continuing south, a large sporting arena arose on his left, before the tiny Sandero turned off and entered the small side streets. They had finally arrived at their destination.

David was escorted inside with Gabriela holding her arm around his waist for support. He actually felt strong enough to make this journey on his own, but the close contact with Gabriela was nice, so he didn't make a fuss. Once inside he was introduced to three more individuals, all looking very similar to the Watchers he had already become intimately familiar with. They shared the same olive skin and dark features, and for good reason – two of the three were related to Istvan and

Marius, with the final member descending from one of the other previously unnamed companions of Andrei all those years back.

Never one to miss her moment, Gabriela got David seated and like a show-woman began to introduce the fresh faces.

'This dashing rogue here is Decebal Popa, young Istvan's cousin twice removed,' gesturing to a man who looked to be around the same age as Gabriela herself.

Drawing his attention to the only other woman of the group, she continued: 'Here is Larisa Ciobanu – you better keep your wits about you around her, she has a bit of a thing for Australians …'

The last part was whispered conspiratorially, and she received a playful punch to the shoulder for her troubles.

'Lastly is Radu Stoica, dear Marius's pride and joy,' she said, gesturing towards a boy no older than 16 and clearly related to Marius.

David said his hellos and engaged in small talk with the fresh faces for a short while, but he soon excused himself and mentioned that he needed some rest. Gabriela guided him towards what would become his room as long as he stayed with the Watchers and made to leave him alone to get some rest. Just before she disappeared, he remembered to ask her if she had something he could use to charge his phone … He wanted to connect to the modern world again …

Gabriela paused for a split second, not entirely sure if she should allow him to do so, but she quickly made up her mind and returned with a universal charger for his phone. She left him with one warning, however. She reminded him of Csanád's attack on the hospital where he was staying and warned him against doing anything that would reveal his location. He was safe to trawl the internet – but he must not make any calls or send any messages – at least until they managed to confirm he was safe from 'the change', in which case he could return to his normal old life and forget all about the crazy fantasy world that he had stumbled into unwittingly.

David agreed to Gabriela's terms and at that moment something bizarre happened. She made prolonged eye contact with him, seemingly to gauge whether he was telling the truth when he answered that he would comply with her wishes. As their eyes were locked, he suddenly experienced a moment of clarity, he was able to read her body language like never before. The subtle expressions on her face, the movement of her hips, the throb of her pulse … This moment was broken almost immediately when she smiled her unflappable smile and closed the door, leaving him suddenly alone with his thoughts.

What the hell was that all about? He thought to himself. He'd always been pretty good at reading body language and gauging how people were feeling – but this had felt completely different. *Was it something he should be worried about?* But nothing happened … Hating his own tumultuous mind for continually turning things over and over in endless circles, he eventually broke free from his reverie of thoughts and brought his attention to his mobile phone, which had finally received its first charge since – when? – since he was at the hotel before being moved into the ECDC?

Shortly after the screen flashed to life and his carrier found a signal, the phone started to buzz like crazy with several days of missed calls, messages and emails. Most recently there were literally dozens from Maja. He could sense the mood shifting from anger in the beginning: 'How dare you flee the hospital?' to concern after the alleged terrorist attack on the building: 'Are you alright?' to near despondency: 'Please, David, let me know you are alright …'.

He felt terrible that his absence had caused such distress for Maja, and instinctively began typing a reply before stopping himself after remembering his promise to Gabriela. *Could he be traced to his location by a text message?* He had no idea the answer to that, but it was probably yes … Not wanting to let down the person who had rescued him from the vampire's assault on the hospital and who was actively harbouring him in an attempt to prevent him from turning into just such a monster – he deleted what he had written and made a mental promise to himself that he would reply to Maja just as soon as he was clear from this whole mess … Hell, he'd probably need her help to get home to Australia since his passport was still back at the ECDC …

Turning his attention to the web browser on his phone, he instead keyed in a series of searches that he knew would provide him information on the 'terrorist' attacks at the ECDC and Stockholm hospital. Through these searches, he learnt that not only was there no suspicion of the supernatural (why would there be?), there was even an extremist group that had already claimed responsibility for the attacks. David wondered if they were simply lowlife opportunists, or whether perhaps the late Colonel Sandberg's colleagues had something to do with manipulating the narrative in such a way.

The hospital attack was the most perplexing for David. The fact that one 'man' had managed to storm in and cause as much damage as he had before escaping into the dark of the night. He read every story he could find on the topic but was frustrated by the fact that they all contained the same information and lacked any real details. It was clear that information was being withheld ... The most he could learn was that 'One highly trained individual brandishing a bladed weapon' had managed to somehow tear through the poor unprepared Swedish police and hospital staff.

He turned to social media to see if he could learn any more that way, but quickly gave up hope since it was just a cesspool of jokes and wild conspiracy theories. These theorists proposed crazy ideas left and right, but none of them managed to actually get close to what had really happened – which was frankly stranger than fiction to begin with ...

David was on the verge of abandoning his search for information on the 'terrorist' attacks when one small headline at the bottom of the page caught his attention.

'Norrköping Man found dead – drained of blood'.

A quick map search informed David that Norrköping was a city about 160 kilometres southwest of Stockholm. Nobody had drawn any connection between this and the 'terrorism' in Sweden's capital – why would they? But it stood out to David immediately. He wondered if Gabriela already knew about this …

The story detailed a homeless man who was found with his throat slit – but curiously there was minimal blood at the scene. Local police were very confused and thought that they had a deranged killer on their hands. To be fair, they were kind of right … However, David was almost certain that there was more to this … He checked the date of the story and found that it occurred yesterday. Was Csanád somehow following his trail south? How could that even be possible?

David spent the next hour performing every manner of searches that he could think of trying to turn up any similar stories. Nothing popped. So far it was only the one isolated incident. He felt a great deal of relief at this, and as the adrenaline faded from his system, he found himself beginning to crash in exhaustion. He initially planned to get up and point out the news story to Gabriela, but as he drifted off into a troubled sleep, he decided that it could wait until the following morning.

★★★

Csanád's bipolar mood flitted between one of rage and one of delight almost at the drop of a hat. To be free amongst the world once more after almost eight centuries entombed in that accursed box; to experience the ecstasy of blood gushing through his lips, and the revitalising strength it granted – these were what provided him joy unmeasured. However, the eternity spent with no company but his own in the infernal darkness of the tomb – this had unhinged his mind even further than it already was.

For centuries he had vowed he would have his revenge not only on his bastard of a 'son' Iuliu – but also on anybody sharing the bloodline of Andrei Albescu – the insolent rat who was responsible for staking him and sealing him into the ground ... Now though, he had another person causing him rage. The blood doctor, David Reynolds. Not only had the accursed doctor foiled his plans back at the ECDC – but now ... no ... he couldn't let that happen ... he already had one errant child, allowing another to grow into power in this world was not an option ...

Courtesy of the relative torrent of blood that he had consumed in recent days, Csanád was now back to full health. His revitalisation was complete and even the rain of bullets that he had weathered both at the ECDC and the hospital produced no lasting effect on his immaculate body. He had quickly found clothing for himself – which was easier in Sweden than most places due to their notably tall population – and he had begun the long journey south, back to his old homeland in modern-day Romania.

Everything was so easy in this new world. Hiding from the hateful sun during the daylight hours was the simplest thing in the world compared to when he last roamed free. He marvelled at the development of humanity around him compared to the comparative hovels of his own time.

Travelling long distances was also very simple. Using his mysticism, he had quickly learnt how a great deal of modern technology operated by pilfering the information from the unsuspecting minds of those around him. All it took then was the theft of a vehicle and he was free to drive south throughout the night, finding shelter long before the first signs of the rising sun.

It was his mysticism that drew him south. Shining like a flaming beacon in the distance, his mind touched upon another's just like his own. It was Iuliu – he was sure of it … That whoreson clearly didn't bother shielding his presence like he had done centuries earlier. Csanád would enjoy the look of surprise on his face when Iuliu realised that he was free … As he grinned with this malicious thought, his brow furrowed just slightly … He was careful to shield his own mind though, he didn't want to give away the surprise too soon!

Csanád could sense something else disturbing the mystical frequencies. It was faint … but when he concentrated, it was there … the blood doctor … He probably didn't even realise it yet – but his mind was changing, developing mysticism … Csanád released a litany of curse words, but these only cemented his purpose. The blood doctor could wait. He was young – weak … the real threat was Iuliu. He could take care of 'David' in due course …

★ ★ ★

Exhumed

As Csanád's twisted mind was concentrating on David and he was cackling with the warped plans rolling through his mind – David was awoken by a vivid nightmare. It fell from his mind almost immediately, but even after waking he retained the sense of dread that it had imbued in him. Most strangely of all – the sense of dread had *directionality*. He turned his head and stared at the wall of his bedroom; his gaze drawn inexorably north …

Seventeen

David awoke the following morning feeling very flat. It was difficult for him to properly describe the feeling. On the surface he should feel excellent. His recovery was progressing in leaps and bounds – the wound on his throat felt markedly better than just the previous night before he went to sleep. Checking his phone, he realised he also somehow managed to sleep for almost nine hours. He should feel great … but he didn't …

Those nine hours of rest were plagued by nightmares, and while he couldn't remember any specific details after awakening, he was still left with a feeling of dread in the pit of his stomach. Whatever was toying with his unconscious mind as he slept continued to pry away at his *sub*conscious mind even though he was wide awake. More than once, he jumped at shadows, twisting his head around, certain that he would see the monstrous vampire

Exhumed

hidden in the dark recesses of the room.

There was something else about the way that he was feeling too … He really didn't feel like himself at the moment. The previous night when he had found all of those texts from Maja, he had felt a large amount of empathy for her, knowing that she was worrying for him and wanting to allay her fears. This morning it was like the empathy had faded away. He understood how she felt on a theoretical level – but it just didn't seem important anymore, it was trivial.

All of this combined to the feeling he ascribed as 'flat' when he finally exited his room and was greeted with Gabriela's trademark boisterous 'Hiya! How do you feel?'

He could smell the familiar scent of eggs cooking on the stove and sat down at the kitchen bench, hoping that they could break this malady that was plaguing his mind. While Gabriela was cooking, he finally remembered what seemed so important for him to bring up the previous night before he fell asleep – the person who was drained of all their blood in Sweden …

'You noticed that too, huh?' she replied without breaking her step. David wasn't overly surprised that she already knew, this kind of thing had been running in her family for 800 years. He was the newcomer here … Gabriela's bubbly mood lowered a little as she continued: 'There was another one this morning in Bratislava …'

Ordinarily David would have blushed as he was forced to admit he did not know where Bratislava was, but this morning he felt nothing as he asked her where it was.

Gabriela smiled playfully at the silly Westerner with his poor European geography skills. She told him that in addition to being the capital of Slovakia, Bratislava was one of its westernmost cities and that they had driven through it themselves only yesterday. David looked to Gabriela with concern as the realisation dawned on him that Csanád was closing the distance between them. This was one of the only things capable of piercing the flatness he was feeling. Was Csanád's approach why he felt such an overwhelming dread coursing through his veins? He questioned Gabriela whether she felt anything herself – and he immediately realised the mistake he had made.

Her pretty face turned towards him as he sat in the kitchen, but the near-permanent smile was no longer present. Just like had happened the previous night before he went to bed, David locked eyes with Gabriela and was once more able to read her emotions like a book. She was worried. Deeply worried … He felt like he could almost pick the thoughts straight from her head before she wrenched her gaze away from his and turned back to stare at the stove.

'Don't tell anybody else what you just said to me …' Gabriela said after a few seconds of thought.

'Why not?' questioned David flatly.

'JUST LISTEN AND DO WHAT I SAY!' she suddenly snapped with a level of tension that David would not have thought possible from someone such as her.

The vehemence of her words and the worried look on her face managed to pierce through the veil shrouding David's emotions and for the first time since waking up he actually felt something. His self-concern was one thing, but he hated to see Gabriela looking as stressed as she was.

Gabriela practically tossed the plate of eggs in front of David before busying herself rapidly in the preparation of another awful concoction of herbal medicine. As he ate the eggs (which tasted far worse than they looked), he began to grasp what was going through her mind. This 'feeling of dread' that he was experiencing must be related to 'the change', and Gabriela knew that. It explained why she was freaking out and also why she had so suddenly spurred into motion to make another terrible remedy for him to drink.

David remembered now that they had told him he could examine Csanád's notes regarding 'the change' and asked Gabriela if she could provide them for him. He figured that if anybody here could make sense out of this, it was him. He was the trained doctor after all, and despite the history of the Watchers' families, they were just backwoods hicks …

Wait – *where the hell did that come from?* – David thought, admonishing himself immediately. He had never thought negatively of Gabriela or the Watchers before – nor was he one to dismiss people with different lifestyles than himself. *So why was he so dismissive of them just now …?* Between the dread he could still feel – ever present to the northwest – and the strange muting of his emotions, he knew that something was wrong with him. *But why now?* Was it because more time had passed since his exposure to Csanád's bodily fluids? Was it because the vampire was getting closer and closer? He needed answers …

After finishing making David another vile herbal remedy – somehow even more disgusting than the ones he'd had previously – Gabriela disappeared into another room and several minutes later returned with a laptop computer. She sat the machine in front of David and he could see that it was already opened to a folder containing photographs of one of Csanád's notebooks, then a file containing translations for the old pre-Romanian script.

Gabriela sat across the bench, boring holes through David's head with her unwavering stare as he began perusing the documents that he had been provided. He didn't need to read her body language to understand that she was watching him to gauge his reaction to what he read. It angered him. *If she wanted to know something she should just bloody ask*, he thought. Again, he caught himself in this moment. *Why was he taking it out on her?* Gabriela had been nothing but a sweetheart to him. Something was wrong …

David read through Csanád's notes back to front several times over. While they obviously couldn't compare to the scientific method of modern times, he was still somewhat impressed by how detailed the vampire had been with his studies. From what David could gather, Csanád had experimented on a number of poor victims, using a bone syringe to extract his own cerebrospinal fluid and inject it into their systems. From there he had kept them imprisoned and studied 'the change', as well as if and how it could be prevented. As to why he cared so much, David did not know nor particularly care – he just wanted to know the science behind it.

His frustration grew in leaps and bounds. Everything was so nebulous, and it seemed to be missing some pages. He read that the first signs of 'the change' presented with rapid healing from wounds. It seemed to be an important part of the process, given how violent these creatures were. It made sense from an evolutionary standpoint – if the victim being converted did not possess the ability to quickly heal then they were likely to die from the process. *Was this happening with him?* He could no longer keep fooling himself – it had to be. Nobody could be as healthy as he was after having their throat slit and losing half their blood. Not after only several days …

It was what came next though, that really caught his eye. The next major symptom of the change was the development of mysticism, notably a close connection with the mind of the master who had orchestrated the change. *Was that what was going on?* The dread he was feeling … He glanced in Gabriela's direction and she kept a straight face as she stared back at him – but as he focused his attention on her eyes, he suddenly began to feel almost a pulse of electricity flowing through his mind. He caught flashes of Romanian and realised that he was detecting some of her thoughts – but she was thinking in her native tongue, so he didn't understand the words. He could understand her feelings perfectly clearly though – she was growing more and more worried by the moment.

The notes continued, outlining a gradual aversion to the sun, culminating in a deeply ingrained fear, and … and a loss of all humanity … *Oh fuck* … It made sense to him now. That was how he was feeling … There was no doubt in his mind that he was most certainly afflicted, which caused him to flick though the notes in desperation to try and find more about the cure.

It was exactly as Gabriela had already told him. No more, no less. The old herbal medicine and vitamin D. According to the monster's notes it had a fairly high effectiveness if administered early … *So why the fuck wasn't it working now!?* He pushed the laptop away in his heightened feeling of frustration and anger. Gabriela now rose and strode to his side, putting her arm around him – not needing 'mysticism' to sense his emotions.

'We'll figure this out, I promise,' she said.

Before David could reply with what would certainly have been a bitter, angry response – the door to the Watchers' abode opened and the remaining members of the group strode inside. The sunlight that streamed in with them made David squint his eyes. Only Istvan noticed David's reaction at this moment, and David immediately sensed his heightened degree of paranoia from across the room. *Why the hell was this happening so quickly …?*

Istvan started saying something in Romanian, which caused all of the other Watchers to turn their gaze towards David and Gabriela. She reassured him that it was nothing (lied to him) and left him alone in the kitchen with the laptop as she went to join the conversation in the other room. They thought they were being so quiet, but he could hear every word they said. He flatly realised that it must just be another symptom of his rapidly developing condition. But what could he do about it …?

★ ★ ★

From the safety of an abandoned tunnel system in Bratislava, Csanád was resting underground out of the glare of the burning sun above. He had just fed again the previous night and still felt the exhilaration coursing through his veins. In his youth he could feed as he saw fit and he often sated his gluttony to the point that it became almost banal. But after such a long and forced abstinence, each and every last drop was like heaven.

There was something else that was buoying his deranged mind. He could sense the turmoil that the blood doctor was experiencing at that very moment. His mysticism was not strong enough that he could understand his thoughts, but the bond they shared linked their minds and he was able to feel the dread and panic rolling through David's mind. The lack of comprehension was the emotion that Csanád enjoyed the most. For someone as educated as the blood doctor to be completely out of the loop, not understanding what was happening to him. The Germans had a word for how he was feeling: *schadenfreude* – taking pleasure from somebody else's misfortune.

He recalled fondly the experiments that he had carried out on countless peasants over the centuries. Iuliu had been the first person he had changed. He had such grandiose ideas about an eternal slave, bound to follow his commands — but it had ended so poorly that Csanád was forced to kill his own 'son'. At least he thought he had, until Iuliu reappeared ... He did not dwell on Iuliu long, knowing it would spur him into an uncontrollable rage, instead he focused his thoughts on the other experiments. He had wanted to understand the process. After Iuliu, he held no intention of creating any further progeny — but if he ever encountered other strigoi he wanted to be armed with as much knowledge as possible.

The change was slow, and after a great deal of experimentation with all kinds of medicinal herbs local to Transylvania, he found that it could indeed be prevented. He had no medical or scientific comprehension about why the herbal remedy worked, it just did. Ripping their heads off was another sure-fire way to prevent the change, he thought as a smirk broke across his face.

However, there was one thing that sealed the deal ... One irreversible aspect of the change that could not be undone. The second the progeny consumed a drop of blood — they could not be cured. For a strigoi in the wild, this was inevitable. The change warped their minds, they would become insatiable and eventually they would act on their urges. But it was different for the blood doctor.

Csanád gurgled an ugly laugh. Having absorbed a great deal from the minds of the doctors during his time as a prisoner at the ECDC, he knew that blood transfusions were common practice in this magical new age. He also knew that the only way the blood doctor could possibly have survived the wound that Csanád had inflicted upon him was to receive just such a treatment. Fresh blood pumped into his veins had sealed the deal more surely than draining an entire village. This was exactly why Csanád had acted so quickly to try and eliminate him as he recovered in the hospital.

He had raged long into the night after discovering the blood doctor missing from the hospital. The thought of another errant child running free in the world caused him to experience the nearest approximation to fear that he was capable of feeling. The mind of his older, much stronger 'son' far to the south served as all the warning he needed against allowing David to grow to power. But he had time, it would take David years – decades – to pose any real threat. He could wait ... Iuliu was the number one priority.

Even after calming himself about his failure to eradicate the blood doctor right there in Sweden, something continued to trouble Csanád's mind. *How had he known to flee?*

Back in Stockholm, David's mind was still far too weak to lock onto. However, with the three additional days having passed since then his mind was very easy to locate. The location Csanád could sense was one he was intimately familiar with. The blood doctor had fled to Transylvania – modern-day Romania ... *But why ...? Was he seeking Iuliu to form an alliance?* No. It was too soon for him to know anything about Iuliu. Besides, he had stopped moving and there was still a great distance between them ...

Csanád's ever-temperamental mind quickly forgot

the pleasure he was experiencing at David's misfortune and turned to rage at his own lack of comprehension. If he had known that David was rescued by the ancestors of Andrei and his companions, then he would have gone out of his way to pay them a special visit – but for now he could only burn in fury, unaware, as he set his plans for how he would take care of his firstborn (first-changed) son, Iuliu.

Eighteen

The situation grew very tense in the cramped abode of the Watchers over the following couple of days. It had finally become obvious to David that his reason for being there wasn't merely out of the goodness of their hearts – it was so they could keep an eye on him. Their joviality with him in the immediate aftermath of his 'escape' from Stockholm hospital could simply be put down to the fact that it appeared like he was free and clear from any affliction. But as his symptoms began rushing in like an avalanche, so too did the sideways glances and nervous actions of the Watchers.

This explained why Istvan had always been so distant and distrusting of him. Whether he had good reason to suspect or was simply youthful and paranoid – his suspicions appeared to be correct. Gabriela was the only one who continued to treat David like a person, and it was her good nature that kept David tethered to his humanity as the change wreaked havoc with his mind and body alike. Deep down she abhorred the idea that they might have to 'take care' of him, and she would do anything that she could to try and help him to fight the nature of his affliction.

David passed the majority of his time alone in his dark room, only emerging to eat meals that tasted bland and left him feeling empty inside. He didn't need to be an occultist to understand the implications of what this meant, nor the fact that he began to fully understand why Csanád had complained about his steak being 'ruined' when it was cooked back at the ECDC. Simply thinking about the ECDC at all felt like climbing into a time machine for him. It was, quite literally, another lifetime ago.

During the time spent alone, all David could think about was *why* this was all happening. He understood the sheer dumb luck that had caused him to be afflicted, and he understood now that it was far too late to do anything about it – but what he didn't understand was why his case presented so atypically compared to everything documented in Csanád's notes. He suspected he knew the answer, but he would have loved for some kind of data to confirm his thoughts.

The fact that all of his symptoms had begun presenting in a great surge as soon as Csanád had drawn closer to him was not lost on David. Between the occasional reports of drained bodies and David's ever-present beacon of dread, he could feel the distance closing between them.

As night fell on the day David and Gabriela had discussed the drained corpse in Bratislava, he could feel Csanád on the move once more, and he appeared to be heading straight for them. It concerned him so much that he broke his solitude and went to awaken Gabriela from her sleep, who in turn had awoken the remainder of the household. Just earlier in the day she had snapped at him for even mentioning such a thing as the 'dread' he felt, ordering him to keep it secret. But it was obviously futile – the change in him had become so evident that denying it was pointless.

Each member of the Watchers had armed themselves and the nervous tension was palpable as David informed them on the movements of Csanád from the awful beacon in his head. The monster had gotten unbearably close that night, but for reasons unknown he had passed them by, continuing east in the direction of Bucharest. While everybody – none more-so than David – felt the adrenaline ebbing out of their bodies in relief as the creature passed them by, it was still this moment that had effectively condemned him in the minds of the Watchers, particularly Istvan.

Each time he left his room he didn't need his burgeoning extrasensory perception (he didn't think in archaic terms such as mysticism) to sense the shift in mood for everyone around him. They all suddenly became guarded, they watched what they would say – they watched *him*. David laughed an ugly laugh internally. These indoctrinated fools had lived their whole lives under the shadow of a mighty buried vampire – and now they had one in their own home and they were too weak to do anything about it.

There was still enough of the old David left inside him to force him to admonish himself for such thoughts, especially when he saw sweet Gabriela's smiling face. Nothing seemed capable of dampening her mood. As David sat down for the thousandth time with the laptop containing Csanád's centuries-old handwritten notes, Gabriela sat by his side on the couch. In her typical way, she sat right up beside him so that the warmth of her smooth legs pressed against his own. She wasn't flirting – that was just the kind of person she was – a lover of life, of affection for affection's sake. If not for Gabriela, David did not even want to think where he would be right now ...

As David continued to flick through the images of Csanád's notes, he no longer required the English translations for the old pre-Romanian script. Probably the most useful part of his growing ESP was an affinity for linguistics – it explained why Csanád was capable of understanding so many languages during his time in captivity at the ECDC. David was still a scientist at his core, and he suspected that it was simply because he had been hearing the thoughts of the Watchers for the past couple of days now. Thoughts, he quickly learnt, convey far more than simply words on a page. They convey a complex vista of imagery that allows for translation across the language barrier.

Gabriela sensed David's growing frustration

through the tightening of his muscles and she asked him what was the problem. He finally thought to ask a question that had been on the edge of his mind ever since he first viewed Csanád's notes.

'Is this everything you have?'

David would later ponder on the concept known as 'chaos theory' where even one seemingly insignificant action could create massive ramifications. The classic example was a butterfly flapping its wings in Mexico resulting in a hurricane occurring in China. His simple question to Gabriela at this moment was just such a butterfly.

The close bodily contact that Gabriela had used to read David's emotions was a two-way street. At this point, *he* felt a marked tensing of her muscles and realised that there was something that she had been hiding from him. Until this time David had done all in his power to stay out of Gabriela's mind with his ESP. He didn't really care about listening to the foul thoughts of Istvan or the concerned thoughts of the other Watchers. They helped him hone his skills – but Gabriela had been off limits – a sanctity he did not want to break.

'David …' she said.

But in the short time it took for her to fumble for words, her thoughts had betrayed her. Like an open book, he could see in her mind that there was indeed more documentation that had been kept from him …

David suddenly exploded in a loud and uncharacteristically aggressive tone. Uncharacteristic to his old life at least.

'WHY WOULD YOU KEEP THIS FROM ME! ARE YOU FOOLS? I MIGHT HAVE BEEN ABLE TO DO SOMETHING IF I HAD ALL THE INFORMATION!'

His conscience wrestled between satisfaction and shame as he saw Gabriela leap to her feet to get away from him in fear. Meanwhile, all of the remaining Watchers who were milling around the house raced into the room. The buzz of fear radiating from their thoughts was palpable and soon the room filled with an explosion of rapid Romanian speech:

Marius was yelling for Gabriela to get away from David.

Istvan was pointing a handgun at David and yelling for him to stay where he was.

Gabriela was pleading for calmer heads to prevail.

David was simply laughing from the sheer lunacy of the whole situation.

Eventually the weapon carried by Istvan won the day. Gabriela had been dragged to the other side of the room by Marius and the others, and Istvan became their vanguard. He held the gun trained on David's chest and set off on a tirade about how he *knew* they should have killed David back in Stockholm, he *knew* that Gabriela was too weak to lead them – why should *she* be in charge just because her surname was Albescu? After he took care of David then he would track down Csanád and do the same to him!

It was all juvenile bravado, and it only served to anger David further with the way he was treating

Gabriela. The tiny peashooter in Istvan's hand had made him act like he was the hero in an action movie, he even gave David the option to: 'Walk outside and burn, or I will plug you with silver bullets right now!'

Even when he was fully human, David never reacted well to bullying – and the way Istvan was acting right now was on the verge of sending him into a full-blown fury. He focused his eyes on the little shit in an attempt to control him the same way Csanád had done to him back at the ECDC, but it was a skill he had not yet learnt how to use. The threat of the sun enraged him even further, even more so because he knew that Istvan had caught onto his rapidly growing heliophobia. All of these thoughts flashed through his mind in the span of a microsecond, before he replied: 'Just try it, you grimy little fuck!'

In the periphery of his mind, David heard Gabriela's desperate pleading – but it was all drowned out by the explosive ringing of a gunshot in the enclosed room. His ultra-sensitive hearing was buzzing, but it paled in comparison to the fire radiating through his shoulder from the feel of the silver slug lodged into his arm. The bullet was aimed at his heart, but as he was privy to Istvan's thoughts he knew when to expect the trigger to be pulled and had used some of his newly discovered vampiric grace to move to the side just in the nick of time.

Once more following Csanád's template, David acted extremely quickly, muting the roaring pain in his arm and racing towards Istvan to close the distance before he could even think to pull the trigger again. With a swipe of his powerful uninjured arm, he sent the gun clattering to the corner of the room and grabbed the whimpering, frightened boy by the throat, dragging him to use as a human shield in the event anyone else in the room possessed a weapon.

Squeezing tightly to mute the whimpers of Istvan, David looked up and surveyed the room before him. The frantic and panicked faces of the five remaining Watchers painted a vista in front of him, before his attention finally settled upon Gabriela herself. At some point during the commotion, she had gathered Istvan's weapon, which she was holding aimed towards the floor. Tears were streaming through her eyes as she begged him to let Istvan go.

David's vision blurred and he wasn't sure if it was caused by his own eyes watering with tears at the sheer injustice of it all, or whether it was a symptom of the ungodly pain that he felt radiating down his entire left side from the silver bullet lodged in his flesh. Somewhere in the back of his mind he was conscious of the fact that he needed to remove it quickly before it could cause him to weaken, but he had other things on his hands at this moment.

'YOU SHOULD HAVE TRUSTED ME! I COULD HAVE HELPED! THIS IS YOUR FAULT!' he roared to Gabriela, watching her wince from the accusation.

Desperately pleading, Gabriela tried saying: 'Please David – don't do anything you will regret! I know the kind of person you are. You can fight this! You don't have to be a monster!'

Scarcely even concentrating on her words, David found himself distracted. Holding Istvan in front of him, crouching behind his body, David's eyes had to look past the young fool's neck to see the rest of the room. He could sense the blood throbbing through Istvan's veins – his elevated heart rate beating a furious percussion as he was held in helpless panic. *How easy would it be to slice one of those veins, to drink ...?*

Before he could contemplate these warped thoughts any further it was Gabriela once again who captured his attention, and for whatever reason a sense of sanity returned to him – if only fleetingly. He experienced what could be described as an out-of-body experience as he took in the sequence of events that had unfolded. A scared little voice inside his conscience was asking him why he was holding Istvan hostage – why he was even contemplating the taste of his blood ...

Knowing that all bridges had been burnt with the Watchers, regardless of Gabriela's sweet nature – David did the only thing that could come to his mind at this moment. He tossed Istvan across the room in the direction of Gabriela and her companions, and he fled out into the late afternoon sun ...

* * *

Csanád had arrived at his final destination and was hunkered down once more out of the deadly rays of the burning sun as he felt the turmoil coursing through the blood doctor. It had become something of a sport for him to keep a metaphysical eye on David, even as he set much larger plans in motion.

Without knowing exactly where he was heading, Csanád had allowed his mysticism to guide him and eventually he found the place where his greatest enemy – his *first* son, Iuliu had made a home for himself. Careful to keep his mysticism in check, having learnt the trick from Iuliu hundreds of years earlier – he shielded his mind as best he could. Iuliu had been free in the world for centuries, Csanád had no idea just how much he had prepared and consolidated his strength over this time.

He was unfamiliar with the location from his own time – Bucharest had become the capital of Romania in the ensuing years following his entombment. The city had experienced meteoric growth since it was founded more than 200 years after Csanád was confined to what was supposed to be an eternity of imprisonment, and it was now home to almost two million people. These kinds of numbers were things that Csanád still struggled to comprehend. His 'son' must have been living like a God, drowning in torrents of fresh, warm, salty blood.

As was ever the case, his mind swung violently from one extreme to the other. The bitterness and hatred that consumed him at the thought of the life Iuliu must have lived was quickly replaced by a twisted form of entertainment that he was experiencing vicariously through his second 'son', David.

The fact that his 'change' had completed was clear beyond any doubt in Csanád's mind. The mystical bond shared by a master and his progeny allowed for a near perverse insight into the mind of the converted –

especially in the early days before they too learnt to master their mysticism. The emotions emanating from David due to his sheer agony from the silver bullet lodged in his shoulder reached Csanád loud and clear. His entertainment soured, turning to concern in an instant.

Silver. What kind of human would know to use silver in this modern age when strigoi were nothing but fairy tales to scare children? Unless ... No ... Not after all these years, it couldn't be ... Pictured clearly in Csanád's mind was his recollection of the bastard Andrei Albescu closing the lid on his coffin. Andrei was obviously long dead by now, it was one of the only solaces that he had carried through his long entombment. But ... *What if his legacy lived on?*

David was running outside into the scalding rays of the sun at this very moment, but Csanád could no longer savour his pain. He absently hoped that the sun would take care of the blood doctor for him as he made his first big mistake since awakening ... Forgetting about Iuliu entirely, he boosted his metaphysical mysticism, casting it far over the land and using his connection to David as a guide. In so doing, he was able to pinpoint the location from which he had just fled and latch onto one of the weak minds, through which he witnessed the face of the Romanian girl raising her weapon and aiming it at David's back as he fled ...

No ... it couldn't be ... She looked just like Andrei ...

Nineteen

Gabriela's mind was in a turmoil. Istvan was screaming at her: 'Shoot him! Do it now!'

Standing in the open doorway watching David flee into the sunlight, her arm instinctively began to rise and train the weapon towards his back. That was her job, wasn't it? The legacy she had been carrying, passed down through 30 generations from her great ancestor Andrei. But ... it just didn't feel right ... Why should David deserve such an ignominious fate as being shot in the back while he ran for his life? He hadn't actually done anything wrong ... Even after being shot and having the perfect opportunity to reap a bloody revenge on his aggressor, he had still chosen to flee into the sunlight that was certain to cause him intense physical pain rather than doing the unthinkable ...

Her hand began to shake as she watched David's obvious discomfort and uncertainty. The change was still extremely fresh for him — meaning the sun wouldn't be as deadly as it was for the likes of a centuries-old monster like the Old Wolf — still it was clear that he was experiencing great difficulty. Being Australian, David knew absolutely nothing about Romania, much less the city of Cluj-Napoca. He seemed to have just picked a direction and started running.

With the screaming voice of Istvan occurring somewhere in the periphery of her mind, Gabriela dropped to her knees and barely even realised the fact that the gun had been wrenched out of her hand. Gunshots rang out, which made her snap her head up to look, but David had already disappeared out of sight — she didn't think he had been hit again, and she was grateful for this small fact. Her guilt was already far greater than she could bear.

Why hadn't they been more upfront with him? The thought plagued her mind. She knew the answer of course — they had not wanted his mind to latch onto the idea of any possible connection to the Old Wolf. If he maintained his own mind, then the hope was that even if he did change, he wouldn't be inherently evil. But it was obviously a silly and naïvely misguided notion. The nature of a strigoi was unavoidable ...

★★★

The gunshots ringing behind him were the least of David's concerns. The toxic rays from the burning sun were weakening his constitution, physically radiating against his flesh and blistering it before his eyes. He knew he wouldn't last for long out there, and he was frantically scanning for a reprieve to his situation.

There was one very obvious solution. He could break into any house nearby and kill whoever had the misfortune of being inside – drain their blood to rejuvenate his wounded body ... But this was not an option he would allow himself to entertain. For starters, it would be unsafe, and he was bound to be discovered by the trailing Watchers, but that was not the reason he chose against it.

He understood that his own conscience had fallen victim to the change coursing through his body, but that did not mean he had to become the monster everyone thought he was. He was still himself, damn it. If his own conscience was missing then Gabriela could serve as the angel on his shoulder – and it was obvious that Gabriela would not condone such actions.

David did not have a lot of time to act. Between the silver bullet lodged in his flesh and the deadly UV radiation bathing him from the sky, he needed to do something – fast. As he raced around the block he began to panic slightly. *Was this how it would all end for him?* Maybe that was a good thing, a merciful end considering what he had become ... But no, his survival instincts were too strong. His eyes glanced what would be his salvation under his very feet and he skidded to a halt to stare at the large, metal manhole cover.

It was clear that this thing was not designed to be lifted by a human, the sheer weight of it looked immense – but as he bent to hook a finger into its groove he was astounded by the magnitude of his own strength, even as injured and distressed as he was. Flipping the circular plate of metal out of place, he scurried into the hole in the ground before replacing the cover and finally escaping from the terrible burning glow of the late afternoon sun. *Would he have made it this far if the sun was at its zenith?*

That was one problem being taken care of, but there was still another imminent concern for David. As the adrenaline from his frantic flight began to wear off then so returned the violent bite of malicious agony emanating from his left shoulder. A bullet wound would be painful enough on its own, but he understood that this pain was multiplied a thousandfold by his system's reaction to the silver slug. It was a poison to his vampiric body and if left unchecked then he didn't know what would happen.

He tore away the vibrant shirt that had been given to him by the colourful Watchers and examined the wound, gasping from what he saw. The bullet had entered the front of his deltoid muscle and displayed the trademark pitted hole of a bullet wound, but what had shocked him was the violent spread of discolouration in his blood vessels radiating from the location. Trademark blood poisoning …

Looking around in the filthy underground tunnel, it became immediately clear that the only tools at his disposal for this 'operation' were his own filthy hands. He also knew that removing bullets immediately was a trope that Hollywood got wrong all the time, as they would often form a natural plug and prevent further bleeding –

but in this instance he simply had no choice, the bullet had to go. He clenched his teeth firmly in place as the fingers from his right hand reached across his chest and began to probe the wound in search of the poisonous pellet lodged inside of him.

In a process that took him several agonising minutes and sent him to the verge of passing out from the pain, David eventually managed to tear the heinous silver slug from his body, and he tossed it angrily to the squalid floor of the tunnel. The relief coursing through his system was instantaneous. Still looking at the gruesome (and now gaping) wound, David almost willed it to begin its magical healing. If he had to be a monster then at least there should be an associated benefit to such an affliction – but to his chagrin the wound simply continued seeping blood, refusing to perform its miraculous healing.

Now what the fuck is the problem? He didn't have to think long to land on the obvious conclusion … He had seen it with his own eyes back at the ECDC … For creatures such as himself, blood was the elixir of life. Csanád had remained emaciated for the better part of a week after his exhumation until he began to obtain a steady supply of blood to 'reward' his behaviour. This blood had brought him back to strength very quickly.

David was unsure just what to do … The conscience of Gabriela guiding his actions would obviously not allow for him to drain an innocent victim of their blood – and he didn't exactly think he could come across pre-packaged snack packs of blood like they had delivered to Csanád in his quarantined cell. All he knew was that he would need to act quickly. *What about if he found an animal to feed from instead?* The idea simultaneously excited and repulsed him, with his human sensibilities still finding the idea sickening while his burgeoning vampiric urges encouraged him to do whatever he could to feed.

Freedom from the shooting pain allowed David to finally gaze around at this subterranean world and assess his situation. He was amazed at how clearly he could see, even in the near stygian darkness. Eventually, he would have to stop being surprised by his enhanced senses and abilities, but it wasn't going to happen any time soon. In the distance he spotted movement, which turned out to be a pair of giant sewer rats. They were filthy with grime and he almost threw up at the idea of using them for nourishment, but if Gabriela was an angel on one shoulder, then his affliction was a giant hungry devil on the other.

Putting aside his urges – at least for now – David began exploring the tunnel system in which he had taken refuge. He passed by an open street drain and had to restrain himself from bursting out into ugly laughter as he drew the comparison between himself and Pennywise the clown from Stephen King's *IT*. Glancing out at the world above his head, David saw that the sun had set further towards the horizon since he had escaped through the manhole – he decided he could wait a little longer until it went down completely before emerging in a search for something to eat (*drink* …).

David allowed a few hours to pass before he climbed out of the same manhole through which he had fled earlier in the day. It was much heavier to lift this time, which he took as a sign that he was weakening. It should come as no surprise given the gaping wound that was still showing no signs of healing. His skin was also very burnt giving him the look of a flaming red demon emerging from the pits of hell. The comparison wasn't too far off the truth ...

The region of town that David was wandering was called Plopilor and it was obvious to him fairly quickly that it was not what he would consider a wealthy area based on his standards in Australia. He walked aimlessly, sticking to the riverside of the Canalul Someșul Mic. People were walking the streets here and there, and nobody paid him much mind, despite his frightening condition. He must have looked like a junkie tweaked out on too much meth, and nobody wanted to deal with a crazy person like that.

As David approached a large bridge spanning the canal, he heard (or sensed?) a small gathering beneath its span, and his growing hunger guided him to investigate. The angel of Gabriela rang alarm bells in his mind, but he found himself carried inexorably towards whatever was happening under the bridge. As he arrived, he finally witnessed the scene that was occurring.

A homeless man was being beaten up by two young men who seemed to be doing it for no better reason than for laughs. One had his mobile phone camera recording as his violent friend tormented the poor older man. Whether it was a remnant of his human sensibilities or simply a new penchant for violence, David was unsure, but his feet carried him to the conflict in a heartbeat.

The thug with the camera turned to film David's approach and started spouting the typical tough-guy bullshit in Romanian – David understood perfectly. With a brutal backhanded blow, he caught the filming thug and sent him tumbling into the canal where he floundered to stay afloat and hold his battered face at the same time. The other thug turned towards David and thrust a small switchblade knife towards his chest. David cackled one of those monstrous vampiric laughs that he had learnt so well from Csanád and grasped the youth's wrist, halting the thrust.

Tightening his grip like a vice, he felt the bones snap in the thug's wrist and the sounds of his screams were almost melodious to his ears. Working almost fully out of instinct, David dragged the boy's neck close to his face and prepared to lean in to tear through his pulsing blood vessels – but the screams of the homeless man served to snap him back to reality before he did the unthinkable.

'Diavol! Diavol!' screamed the homeless man on repeat.

Despite that David had saved him from his beating, his appearance and the fact that he was about to bite into the throat of one of the youths evidently frightened the old man more than a few punches or kicks. 'Devil! Devil!', he was screaming. And David knew he was right …

Horrified at his own actions, David released the youth from his grasp and rushed away from the scene of what was very nearly a violent murder. Something about the fear in the old man's eyes had snapped a semblance of humanity back into him. The angel of Gabriela on his shoulder had regained ascendency and was dictating his conscience. For now, as hungry as he was, David did not trust himself being above ground with people – he scurried towards the nearest manhole he could find and laboriously climbed back into his underground refuge.

In what turned out to be far simpler a task than he expected, David's flowing vampiric motions allowed him to capture one of the large filthy rats that were scurrying around in his underground lair. He swiftly ended the beast's life, not wanting to cause any suffering, before somehow forcing himself to gorge on its still warm blood. The result was remarkable ... Before his very eyes he witnessed the blistered red hue of his skin begin to revitalise, and he felt the angry throbbing ache in his shoulder ease dramatically.

Glancing towards the wound on his arm, David saw that it while it was not fully healed, the process towards healing had well and truly begun. Something else that had begun was his intoxication for the taste of flowing blood – and by the time he found and consumed two more of the filthy rodents, he was almost drunk from the sensation coursing through his body.

What a fucked-up piece of evolution! David thought as he sat, examining his fully healed body in the aftermath of his first taste of blood. Vampirism was the purist definition of survival of the fittest. The only balm required for seemingly any wound was nothing more than the lifeblood of another living creature. The inkling of his human conscience found it completely appalling, but he was gladdened that he had managed to (just barely) restrain himself from killing the youth.

David knew his situation was untenable. He couldn't just live forever in the tunnels under a random city in Romania like a gremlin for the rest of his life. Nor could he exactly surface and be a functioning member of society. *He could kill himself right here ... he was a monster after all, nobody would mourn him ...* But something in his mind would not let him take such an easy way out. Not yet at least. He had unfinished business with the real monster that had (albeit inadvertently) done this to him. He owed it to Gabriela and the others – he would find a way to take care of Csanád before allowing them to finish him off for good ...

✶ ✶ ✶

As soon as the wave of fury at discovering the living ancestors of one of his oldest enemies waned, Csanád immediately understood he had made a mistake. Opening and casting his mind so far, beyond just the intrinsic connection he held with the blood doctor, had caused him to register his own location in the mental ether. He was not even allowed a small moment of vain hope that he had somehow gone unnoticed before a voice entered his mind, guided by the powerful mysticism of his 'son', Iuliu:

'*FATHER!?*'

Csanád grimaced at his own stupidity – he had gotten so close without Iuliu detecting him, yet here at the final hurdle he had betrayed his own presence. That filthy woman would suffer for this! He flexed his own mysticism now, understanding it was futile and would only make him look cowardly if he tried to hide once again, replying:

'Iuliu, "my child" – I have waited almost 800 long years to see you! You can only imagine the plans I have in store ...'

Csanád hoped that this threat would intimidate Iuliu and that he would sense fear radiating back towards him, but he was met with only laughter. That same infuriating laughter from Szatmár when he watched Andrei pierce his heart with a spear. Csanád almost haemorrhaged in his righteous indignation at the insult, but before he could retort with any further curses towards his hated 'son', Iuliu finished with:

'I will be seeing you, "Father".'

Iuliu severed the mystical mental connection between the pair of monsters and left Csanád alone with his 'plans', more than mildly distracted by his thoughts of 'the blood doctor' and 'the Albescu' never far from the forefront of his mind.

Twenty

The remainder of the night passed very quickly for David. He dedicated the entirety of his time to familiarising himself with his own anatomy and seemingly supernatural abilities. He loathed that word – supernatural – he knew there was nothing supernatural about it in the slightest. With enough time to study, the causes would be found to be perfectly natural – however he doubted any vampire would allow themselves to be studied as such. *Maybe he could donate his body to science?* Maybe … but not until he took care of Csanád first – that thing couldn't be left alone to roam free in this world.

The first thoughts that crossed David's mind helped to ground him back in reality, to allow his more human nature to rise to the fore. These thoughts were about what he and his fellow medical peers had learnt from their short time studying Csanád at the ECDC:

Xeroderma pigmentosum – the violent aversion to

sunlight. He had experienced this one firsthand.

Polycythemia vera – the overabundance of red blood cells. In his previous lifetime – only a little more than a week before – he had speculated that this 'disease' played a pivotal role in the vampire's healing. He had no way of knowing whether this was an accurate assumption without further study, but he suspected that he was indeed correct.

Vasculitis – the enlargement of blood vessels. As with polycythemia vera, David suspected that this condition aided a vampire's healing by allowing for the delivery of more blood throughout the body. He began a small self-assessment for any of the typical human symptoms of vasculitis, such as fever, fatigue, and joint pain – but he was free from any such problems. It was clear that vasculitis was not a 'disease' for a vampire, but simply an advancement in their physiology.

Enlarged adrenal glands – the name spoke for itself. Again, he performed a self-assessment for the symptoms. He felt no discomfort and he was not sweating – however, he most certainly experienced mood swings. He pondered further about the adrenal glands, especially after recalling the tale told by Gabriela about the warring 'strigoi' in Szatmár back in the 13th century. Specifically, the 'living mist' that they had seemingly secreted from their bodies. *Could he do that?* He had no worldly idea how to do so, and after many frustrating minutes trying to simply will his body into action, he finally abandoned the notion, and hoped that it would come to him later.

Unnaturally rapid healing – this one he could attest

to himself, especially as he fingered the now fully healed wound across his throat and the former location of the bullet wound in his shoulder. Neither of them so much as left a scar ...

Having reached the end of the list of 'symptoms' of vampirism, David cursed the fact that he did not have any further data to study. He briefly considered the idea of rising once more to the surface to steal a mobile phone but abandoned the notion out of fear of losing control again. He would love to be able to contact Maja and request more of the data that they had acquired during their time with Csanád. Even something as simple as his pulse rate and blood pressure.

On this topic, David checked his pulse and gasped at his resting heartrate of about 120 beats per minute. He was almost glad that he did not have a sphygmomanometer present to check his blood pressure, as he was certain that it would be off the charts. However, he needed to stop thinking in human terms. Who cares if his pulse and blood pressure were off the charts – his affliction obviously more than accounted for it. Csanád was – what? – at least 1100 years old, based on what he had learnt from Gabriela. Clearly, the unusual behaviour of his own heart was not a major concern.

It was all well and good for him to have created a shopping list of 'symptoms' and abilities – but before David could even consider stepping back into the surface world he needed to ensure that he more fully understood just how to control himself. Not just the bloodlust, but also the most useful ability in a vampire's arsenal – his extrasensory perception.

During the time he spent with Gabriela and the Watchers over the past couple of days, especially since the rapid progression of his 'change', David had gotten flashes of his telepathic ability. He could hear stray thoughts and translate across the language barrier – but for the most part he had tried to avoid doing so, fearing the burgeoning ability. Now – he needed to learn to master it. He walked through the tunnels, guided by his hyper-sensitive hearing, until he found himself located directly beneath people going about their lives blissfully unaware of the snooping vampire under their feet.

He almost laughed at the absurdity of it all, but in no time he had managed to master his ability at entering the minds of others and reading their thoughts like a book. A picture book, since thoughts conveyed far more than simply words – they were a complex portrait of imagery and emotions.

Recalling the control that Csanád was able to hold over unsuspecting victims using nothing other than the power of his mind, David made a mental note that this was something he would need to experiment with once he trusted himself to return to the surface. It was hypnotism, he supposed. He was no stranger to the theory of hypnotism, having both enjoyed entertainment with hypnotists and studied its use in psychology – however this would be the first time he had ever attempted to use it himself. He promised the angel of Gabriela on his shoulder that he would not abuse the power, but would use it only when necessary, as a 'nonlethal' weapon in his arsenal.

A side effect of his enhanced understanding and practise with his ESP was that David was also able to more accurately locate Csanád in the distance. What's more, he believed he could also sense another like mind in the same vicinity as the Old Wolf. *Could that be Iuliu?* It would make sense to be his 'brother', and it would also provide an answer to David why Csanád had come so close to him only a couple of days earlier to simply pass him by. He had bigger fish to fry ... But if there were two of these centuries-old monsters roaming the world then that only made David's goal more difficult. He had no idea how he could conceivably take care of Csanád alone ...

Recalling the direction of the setting sun, David oriented himself and got his bearings. The two hateful minds that he could sense in the distance were both located southeast of him. He had no way to gauge distance, his proficiency with his ESP was nowhere near at that level just yet – but he forced his mind to try and picture a map of Eastern Europe. As he struggled with the geography he thought of Gabriela and her good-natured taunts at the 'silly Westerner', but he smiled to himself for the first time in a long while when he managed to recall a map of Romania that Gabriela had shown him.

Cluj-Napoca was located in the northwest of the country. Southeast from his current location was the Romanian capital of Bucharest, or beyond that, Bulgaria. Based purely on an educated assumption – David correctly guessed that the two vampires were most likely situated in Bucharest. He would need to somehow find a way to travel there himself eventually. *How had Csanád done it?* Given how quickly he was travelling it could only have been by vehicle. Again, David felt a burst of levity at the thought of the seven-foot giant cramped into a tiny European car. Though he was more than accustomed to spending time in small, enclosed boxes …

The outburst of laughter from David caused him to ponder just what the cause of his sudden change of mood could be. It was clear that these were temperamental creatures, but he thought it was more than that. Something that he innately seemed to understand was that a vampire became all the more monstrous when they were wounded and in need of sustenance for healing. When fed, they possessed greater control over their emotions and their impulses. This revelation was highly important – he needed a clear head, his *human* head – if he ever intended to even make it close to Csanád in his fool's errand.

However, this revelation did not come without its inherent problem. To retain his sense of humanity, he needed to feed. To feed, he needed to consume blood. It was a contradiction … Thankfully the blood from the rats was sufficient to restore his body – if he continued to limit himself to animals, preferably vermin, then he might just be able to manage with this affliction far better than he initially had thought.

Feeling a wave of relief, more like himself than he had in days, David then began to turn his brilliant mind towards potential solutions to the problem of Csanád and Iuliu. *How would they be killed?* From Gabriela he knew that decapitation worked; he knew that prolonged exposure to the sun (or just any flames) worked – and probably far quicker for them than for him; he knew that a stake through the heart would incapacitate them and allow for one of the aforementioned methods to finish the job.

What else? There was silver, of course, but much like the stake it only seemed to serve the purpose of incapacitation. *What about if a machine gun or nail bomb pumped silver into them?* David didn't know the answer to this violent idea – nor did he particularly think he could get his hands on such equipment, and even if he somehow could – how could he use them without collateral damage?

He put a pin in the idea that would effectively turn him into a terrorist, and instead focused his mind on more refined methods. He recalled his thoughts about the poisons that could cause blood to congeal and whether they could be used as a weapon. But again he ran into the same hurdle as before – how could he magically get his hands on such a thing?

How about the Russell's Pit Viper? Another idea that looked good on paper, with their venom carrying very much the same properties as the poisons he had already considered – but as the snake was endemic to the Indian subcontinent, he very much doubted he would be able to find a research facility containing it here in Romania.

Despite never quite reaching a satisfactory solution to his problem – David enjoyed the sheer act of *thinking*. He felt like *himself* again, rather than the violent and evil facsimile he had become. He would keep the angel of Gabriela on his shoulder in times where his conscience wavered, but now that he was back to full health and had managed to stave off his hunger, he felt almost normal again. As normal as possible for somebody hunkered down in the filthy sewers as they hid from the world above their head at least.

Growing a little frustrated at the repeated dead ends, David rose to his feet and went for a short walk through the tunnels. He noticed with grim, sardonic humour that the rats raced away from him at the first sign of his movement. He knew they were conditioned to run from anything, but after having drained three of their innumerable ilk, the idea of his legend spreading amongst them made him laugh.

His mirth was broken as he passed the storm drain once more and he realised that the morning sun had arisen. He had spent the better part of the night lost in his own thoughts – he didn't even feel tired. *Did vampires need sleep?* There was just so much he didn't know about himself. In some fiction he had seen, vampires grew weak and had to sleep during daylight hours – but he figured this was just another silly fabrication for entertainment value, he felt no such weakness or compulsion to rest. He would gladly pass the rest of the daylight hours down here lost in thought as he attempted to learn more about himself and discern a solution to taking care of Csanád and Iuliu once and for all.

The time passed quickly, and it was not entirely

wasted. David finally managed to come up with some possible solutions. His mind had been thinking about the awful herbal remedy that Gabriela had fed him, and it set his mind on thinking about alternative medicines. One path that his thoughts travelled down was that of colloidal silver – basically, tiny silver particles suspended in water. As a medical treatment it was ridiculous, it held precisely zero merit – but what if he could trick the vampires into drinking it?

He had no idea how he would remotely accomplish such a task, nor did he know how exactly it would react to their systems – but he suspected that the ingestion of silver in such a way would certainly cause debilitating pain at the very least. Perhaps it might even incapacitate them or cause weakness as the bullet lodged in his shoulder had done to him … It was food for thought …

The bullet … His mind was on a roll now, joining the dots and making connections. If he could track down a dart gun then he could replace the traditional tranquiliser with colloidal silver and inject it into their systems from a distance. *For that matter – would a tranquiliser work?* He knew that they had used heavy sedatives on Csanád back at the ECDC, but that was when he was in an extremely weakened state, it would be a dangerous gamble to assume they would work when his body was operating – healing – at full capacity. Same with the stun guns …

So much of what he knew as weaknesses for these creatures was based either on stories passed down for centuries or data pertaining to a starved, pale shadow of a creature. He simply had no idea how well it would translate to something as strong and as old as Csanád. Hell, he had taken dozens of bullets – even one through the spine – and still managed to overpower a team of soldiers …

Night fell once again and having fed on several more of the filthy rats, David was content to emerge back onto the surface world with only minimal concern about his self-control around people. He had several immediate priorities. Firstly, he needed to find some fresh clothing so that he could look presentable, rather than the muddy, shitty, bloody rags that he had been wearing for the past couple of days. This was a simple enough task – many people left their clothes hanging to dry and he eventually found a set that were almost his size. *Had he grown?* It wouldn't surprise David to find out that he had indeed grown from his already tall six foot three – but for now he would still look short compared to the two seven-foot vampires in Bucharest.

Now looking presentable, the next item on David's list was to acquire some money. To do so, he managed to kill two birds with one stone. A man approached, nonchalantly walking down the street, and for the first time David put his hypnotism to the test. It was remarkably easy and now he was able to forgive himself for falling prey to Csanád back at the ECDC. As long as he maintained eye contact with the man, then he could easily hold him in his sway.

The human side of David felt a little bad, stealing

this man's wallet and the cash therein — but all things considered he felt it was a small sin compared to what the likes of any other vampire would certainly have done had they been in need. He pictured Gabriela's face condemning his action but he put it out of his mind. The angel on his shoulder could come out when truly required — but for something so trivial she could stay tucked away.

The final facet of David's plan was to find passage towards Bucharest. He didn't really want to steal a car and drive there himself. Obviously, it was not a moral objection — instead he would simply rather close his eyes and concentrate on his thoughts, his plans for what would follow after his arrival. Practicing his hypnotism on another individual, he learnt that the best way to travel between Cluj-Napoca and Bucharest overnight was by bus. The trains had a tendency to arrive after sunrise which was an obvious limiter in his situation. He then picked the location of the bus terminal out of his unwitting accomplice's mind before setting off in that direction.

David smiled. It was like fate was on his side. The next bus to Bucharest was leaving in less than 30 minutes and would travel from 9:00pm until 5:00am. He could safely ride through the night, arriving well before the rise of the sun and with enough time to find shelter in the morning. He climbed aboard the bus, chose his seat in the very back corner, and closed his eyes to begin turning over the litany of thoughts in his mind once more.

Apparently, vampires did get tired and sleep,

eventually. After almost two days awake, David soon nodded off into a deep, dark sleep. Despite his protestations about vampirism being perfectly natural, he would have a difficult time explaining all that happened as he slept.

★ ★ ★

Csanád sensed the moment David fell into his slumber immediately. He, probably more than any other being on the planet, understood what was happening. It was a moment that he knew was coming and had been dreading. The sleep of Ancestral Memories …

Interlude 3

Albescu Family Tree

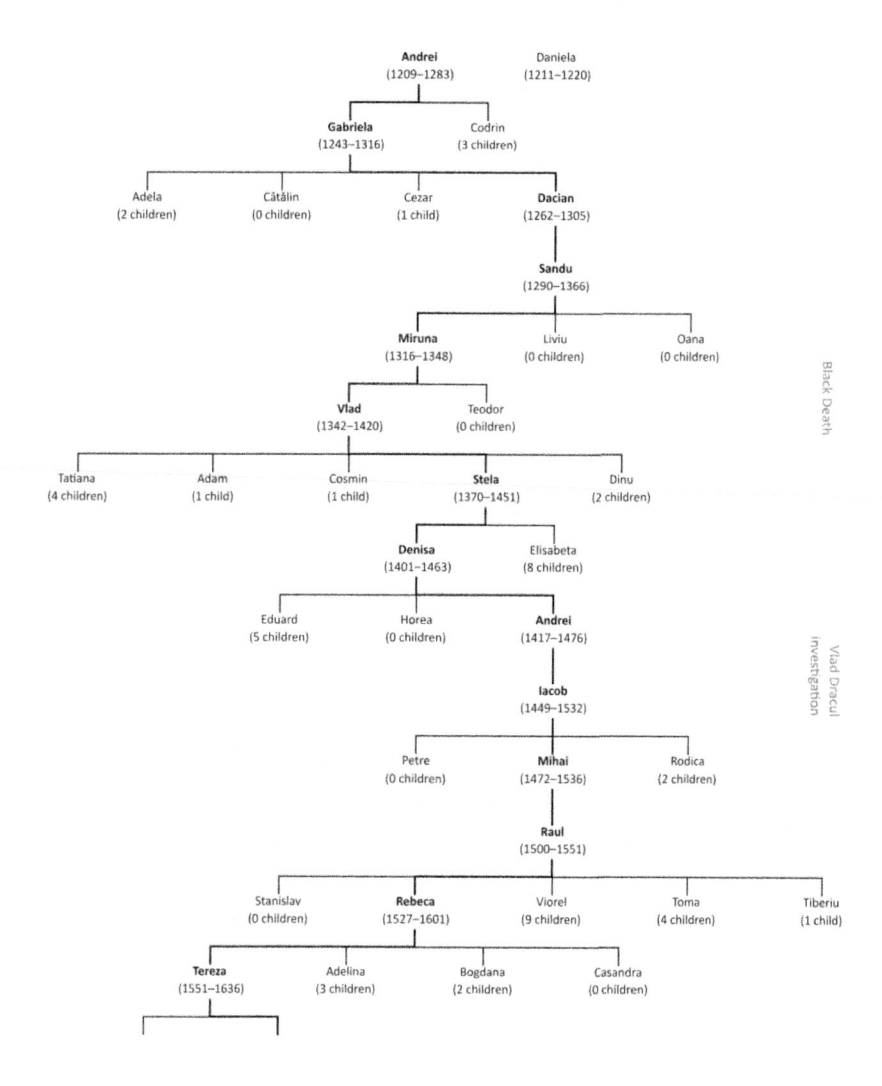

```
                          Andrei          Daniela
                        (1209–1283)     (1211–1220)
                              │
                  ┌───────────┴───────────┐
               Gabriela                 Codrin
              (1243–1316)             (3 children)
                  │
    ┌─────────┬───┴───┬─────────┐
  Adela    Cătălin   Cezar    Dacian
(2 children)(0 children)(1 child)(1262–1305)
                                 │
                              Sandu
                           (1290–1366)
                                 │
                  ┌──────────────┼──────────────┐
               Miruna          Liviu          Oana
             (1316–1348)    (0 children)   (0 children)
                  │
            ┌─────┴─────┐
          Vlad        Teodor
        (1342–1420)  (0 children)
             │
  ┌──────┬───┴───┬──────┬──────┐
Tatiana  Adam  Cosmin  Stela   Dinu
(4 children)(1 child)(1 child)(1370–1451)(2 children)
                         │
                  ┌──────┴──────┐
               Denisa        Elisabeta
             (1401–1463)    (8 children)
                  │
        ┌─────────┼─────────┐
     Eduard     Horea     Andrei
   (5 children)(0 children)(1417–1476)
                              │
                            Iacob
                         (1449–1532)
                              │
                  ┌───────────┼───────────┐
                Petre        Mihai       Rodica
             (0 children) (1472–1536)  (2 children)
                              │
                            Raul
                         (1500–1551)
                              │
    ┌──────────┬──────────┬──────────┬──────────┐
Stanislav   Rebeca      Viorel      Toma      Tiberiu
(0 children)(1527–1601)(9 children)(4 children)(1 child)
                │
    ┌───────┬───┴───┬────────┐
 Tereza  Adelina  Bogdana  Casandra
(1551–1636)(3 children)(2 children)(0 children)
```

Black Death

Vlad Dracul investigation

Elizabeth Bathory investigation

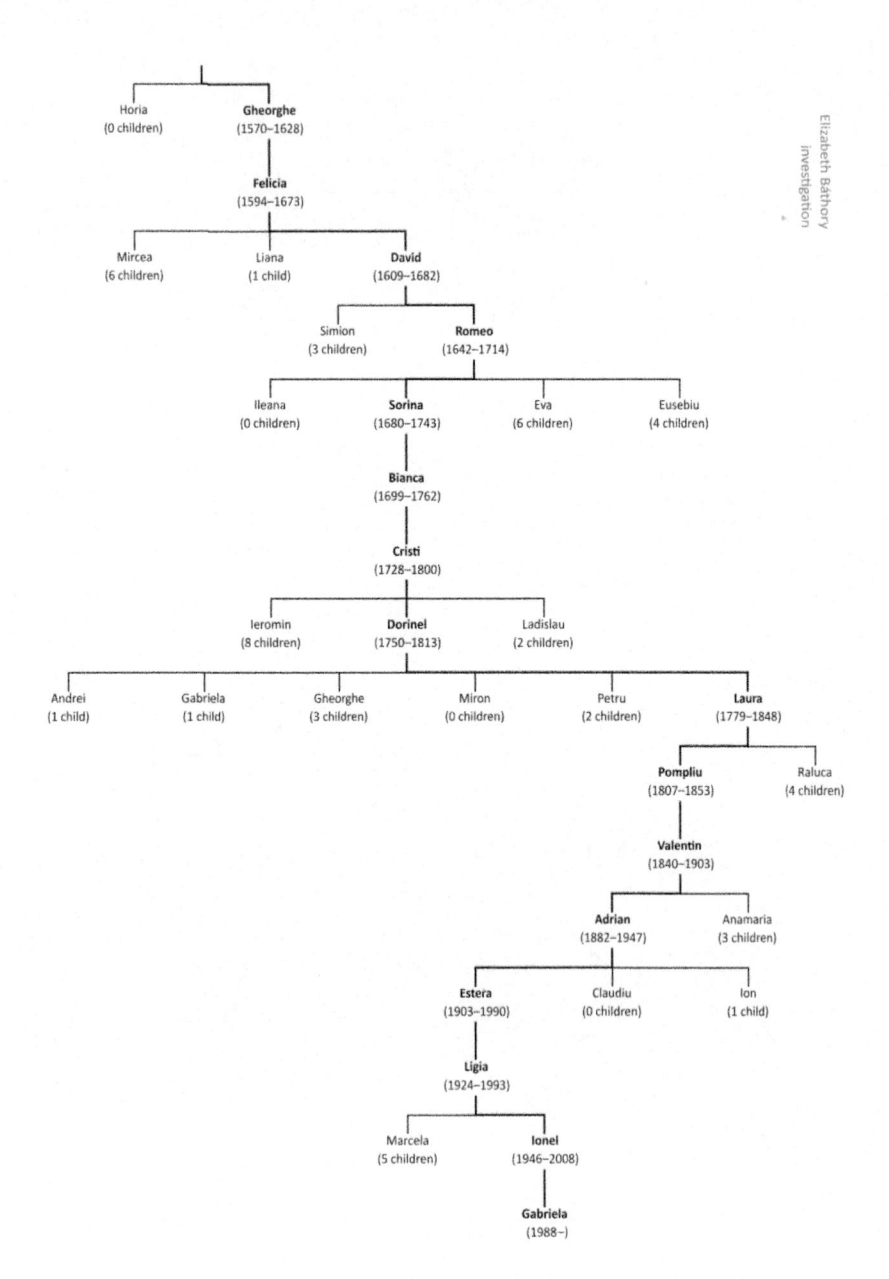

- Horia (0 children)
- **Gheorghe** (1570–1628)
  - **Felicia** (1594–1673)
    - Mircea (6 children)
    - Liana (1 child)
    - **David** (1609–1682)
      - Simion (3 children)
      - **Romeo** (1642–1714)
        - Ileana (0 children)
        - **Sorina** (1680–1743)
          - **Bianca** (1699–1762)
            - **Cristi** (1728–1800)
              - Ieromin (8 children)
              - **Dorinel** (1750–1813)
                - Andrei (1 child)
                - Gabriela (1 child)
                - Gheorghe (3 children)
                - Miron (0 children)
                - Petru (2 children)
                - **Laura** (1779–1848)
                  - **Pompliu** (1807–1853)
                    - **Valentin** (1840–1903)
                      - **Adrian** (1882–1947)
                        - **Estera** (1903–1990)
                          - **Ligia** (1924–1993)
                            - Marcela (5 children)
                            - **Ionel** (1946–2008)
                              - **Gabriela** (1988–)
                        - Claudiu (0 children)
                        - Ion (1 child)
                      - Anamaria (3 children)
                  - Raluca (4 children)
              - Ladislau (2 children)
        - Eva (6 children)
        - Eusebiu (4 children)

Ratiaria

AD 363

Twenty-One

'Well done!' exclaimed Blasius, as the spear tossed by his companion took down the fleeing wild boar. It was an impossible throw and he could not understand how anybody could be so accurate over such a distance, much less provide the necessary power to fell the large beast.

Csanád beamed in pride. Despite being an outsider to Ratiaria, his skills as a huntsman typically raised him in higher regard than his lowly birth would otherwise allow. He was no stranger to the bitter barbs of discrimination and classism. Ratiaria was located in the ancient province of Dacia in the region known as Dacia Ripensis. It was situated near the banks of the Danube River and hemmed in by the massive mountain ranges of the Carpathians to the north and the Balkans to the south.

Dacia, and by proxy Ratiaria, was at this time part

of the Roman Empire, making Csanád, with his Visigoth descent and slightly darker skin, inherently an outlier. He was a free man; however, he was highly cognisant that many of his countrymen had been captured and forced into lives of slavery by the Romans – so he was ever distrustful.

Blasius was the one person in this world that Csanád considered a true friend. After Csanád's parents had died at a young age, murdered by bandits as they travelled through Ratiaria, he was left an orphan, and if not for the atypical kindness displayed by Blasius and his family at the time then Csanád may have never lived past the age of twelve. As it was now, he was 30 years old and Blasius was one year his junior. They both made a very good living in the town as hunters – although in fairness, Csanád was more of the hunter and Blasius was more of the merchant.

'Wait until Calvus lays his eyes on this catch!' exclaimed Blasius as the two closed the distance and Csanád sliced the beast's throat to put it out of its misery. Calvus was a pompous noble from Ratiaria who favoured Blasius's wares. Csanád hated him, largely because he seemingly went out of his way to call them 'Blasius's' wares – as if Csanád's contributions didn't exist. But that wasn't all, Csanád had had more than his fair share of run-ins with Calvus over the years. It was fair to say that the two held each other in a deep disdain.

'The boar reminds me of Calvus …' Csanád replied, pleasantly enjoying the mental image of running his spear through the bloated 'noble'. Blasius was no stranger to Csanád's hatred for Calvus, and much of the rest of the town in general for that matter. He knew that Csanád had experienced a difficult upbringing and that even despite the fact that he was the best hunter in all of Dacia Ripensis, he was viewed as 'lesser than' simply because he was from a foreign land and had a slightly darker shade of olive touching his skin. Blasius was one of the very few Romans of this era who could be considered 'progressive' simply through his lack of ingrained sense of superiority earnt by nothing more than being born a Roman.

 Csanád and Blasius set to work lashing the legs of the boar to the spear, and once complete they each lifted an end and began the walk back into Ratiaria. The boar must have weighed around 450 libra, so naturally their progress was slow. It was a source of endless frustration for Csanád – the fact that Blasius was so weak, so soft – if the individual carrying the other end of the spear were as strong as he himself then they would have made it home in no time at all. However, the inverse was also true. Csanád was an awful merchant and if he were in charge of trying to make a living from selling his hunts then his antisocial behaviour would isolate him from potential buyers immediately.

 Csanád and Blasius trudged towards Ratiaria, taking frequent breaks to allow for Blasius to recover his strength. What was a vibrant and sunny afternoon quickly became a chill and dark evening. It was fortunate that Csanád had an excellent sense of direction, because the night was so black and the fog rising from the ground was so thick that if Blasius was alone, he would almost certainly have gotten lost and not found his way back into town before the sun rose on the following day.

'Did you hear that?' Blasius asked nervously – talking about the loud howl of a wolf in the distance.

Csanád bit his tongue to avoid taking his frustration out on his only real friend. *Of course he heard that. He wasn't deaf, was he* … He simply grunted his reply in the affirmative, becoming a little anxious about how vulnerable they were as they carried the boar. It may even attract the wolves to their position.

Csanád took stock of his own weaponry. He couldn't use his spear as a weapon anymore, given the boar was lashed to it, so his only means of defending himself if forced into action was the small blade on his hip that he had used to slice the boar's throat. Not a thrilling prospect if they should be attacked … He supposed that he could quickly slice the lashings that held the boar and free his spear if worst came to worst.

The pair continued their trudge into town and as they grew closer, visibility dwindled even further. The fog on the ground looked almost sentient as it was swished around by the breeze and by their movements. Csanád had never seen anything like it before. Eventually, when they finally made it within several minutes of Ratiaria – that was when another sound came to the fore even above the howls of the wolves that had been ongoing since they were first heard. This was the sound of screaming – human screaming …

Was Ratiaria under attack? Surely it couldn't be

the Gauls this far east ... Blasius and Csanád each experienced different reactions to this thought. While Csanád would have been content to simply watch from afar and let the shits in town suffer whatever fate was befalling them – Blasius was cut from a different cloth. His wife and family were back in Ratiaria, and he held a far closer kinship to the town in general. Blasius instinctively dropped his end of the spear, causing Csanád to stumble and lash out with his words at Blasius's stupidity, but his words were not absorbed.

Instead, Blasius turned towards him and begged him to help. He knew that on his own he was weak, but Csanád was one of the strongest people in town – he had to help. Csanád was not so easily swayed. Self-preservation was a strong motivator for him, and even if he would never admit it to anybody else, he was also thinking about his friend. He knew that Blasius was more likely to run in and get himself killed needlessly than he was to 'help' in any way.

Csanád was taken completely by surprise by what Blasius said to him next: 'You are a coward!', before turning on his heel and rushing towards the town that he called home.

The words stung Csanád. He was not a coward – he just saw the bigger picture and couldn't care less what happened to the rest of the scum in Ratiaria. He would be fine on his own ... But Blasius wouldn't ...

Watching his only friend disappear into the deep mist and rush towards the flickering lights that marked the beset town of Ratiaria, Csanád cursed the whole situation. He cared about Blasius – and the fool was running off to get himself killed ... They didn't even know what was happening back in town. In a grumble, Csanád used the blade on his hip to slice the lashings binding the boar to his spear, dropping it unceremoniously to the ground, before lifting his weapon and racing after his stupid friend.

He was too late ...

By the time Csanád stumbled out of the darkness and into the intermittent flickering torchlight of Ratiaria, all he could see was carnage. Corpses littered the streets, many with deep bloody wounds to their throats, many others showing evidence of vicious animal attacks. *What the hell had happened here ...?* The most bizarre thing for Csanád as he cautiously made his way through the town, following the path of chaos, was the absolute lack of fallen enemy soldiers. Even in an ambush attack you would still expect at least one enemy to fall ...

It was the ungodly panicked scream of Blasius that broke Csanád from his contemplation. He raced in the direction from which it had come, taking the path towards the centre of town that led to Blasius's villa – and that was where he finally came face to face with the cause of all of the chaos and bloodshed. He could see Blasius in the grip of a giant of a man. It looked almost like he was being lifted off the ground by his throat, but it must have been a trick of the flickering shadows – nobody was that strong ... right?

Before Csanád could get close enough to confirm that his eyes truly were not deceiving him – he was waylaid by a pair of massive snarling wolves that seemed to have simply materialised out of the swirling mist. Their fur was a flecked white and grey, so the mist had served as a perfect camouflage that had allowed them to stalk their prey until the decisive moment of attack – however, Csanád was no normal man himself.

He had encountered wild wolves in his hunts before, and while he showed them a great deal of respect, knowing what they were capable of doing – especially in a pack – he did not fear them. Rather than turning to flee, as the wolves would typically expect, he roared a loud incomprehensible cry and raced to close the distance between them, leading with the point of his spear. One of the wolves was not fast enough to react and the spear tore through the flesh of its muscular body, causing it to whine from the pain and sending its companion scurrying for safety.

This action drew the attention of the giant that was holding Blasius. Csanád watched as his head snapped in his direction and he saw the look of animal fury burning in those eyes. The wolves were clearly its pets, even though Csanád had no idea how it was even possible to tame such beasts – and this giant did not take kindly to his pet being wounded.

'You wounded one of mine. Now I wound one of yours!' Csanád was extremely confused at this moment. The words were spoken softly, almost as if they were whispered into his ear from behind. But it wasn't possible, the giant was much too far away and Csanád was certain that he hadn't spoken out loud … The

mysticism with which the giant had cast his thoughts into Csanád's mind was not something he would have time to think deeply upon – as at that moment he watched the giant grasp the still whimpering Blasius under the chin and wrench so powerfully that his head was rent from his body, leaving trailing strings of red flesh and a torrent of gushing blood in its wake.

The sight defied all logic. Csanád thought that he simply must be dreaming. Nobody, no *thing* was capable of this ... But when he witnessed what came next then Csanád finally managed to piece something together. He witnessed the giant placing its mouth to the torrents of blood pouring from his now very dead friend Blasius's neck and drinking it as if it were a fountain.

Strix ... The word leapt into Csanád's mind. He was never a believer in the supernatural, despite how superstitious the largely Christian population of Ratiaria tended to be. But what else could explain what was happening ...? Snapping free of his initial shock, Csanád replaced the feeling with outrage. He didn't care whether this monster was a man, a strix, or Mars himself – he would avenge Blasius if it was the last thing he did ...

Grasping his spear tightly, keeping a watchful eye on his periphery for any other wolves lurking in the mist, Csanád began a swift approach towards the monster that was still gorging itself on the blood of his decapitated friend. Nothing stood in Csanád's way and he soon found himself standing under the looming height of the thing that was barely paying him any mind.

Csanád thrust his spear, its sharpened tip destined

to meet with the centre of the monster's chest – but finally the strix reacted. It tossed the now drained corpse of Blasius to the ground like trash and in a motion that defied all belief it pirouetted around the thrust of the spear and grabbed the shaft, roughly yanking and dragging Csanád off balance towards it.

Csanád lost his footing and fell to his face before the giant strix, and from a mountaintop above he heard the creature laughing a deep and ugly laugh at his pitiful attempt at resistance. For the first time in his life – a life of strength – Csanád felt completely weak, despondent. *How could he possibly fight such a thing?* Nonetheless, he would not go down meekly … He grasped the blade on his hip and swung it in an arc attempting to slash the foot of the beast above him. Using that same preternatural speed, the strix simply lifted his foot and brought it crashing down on the blade, pinning it to the ground and disarming Csanád in the process.

In horror, Csanád began scurrying away, crab crawling backwards as he looked up at the terrifying grin on the blood-soaked face of the *thing* that had singlehandedly gutted Ratiaria. He kept scurrying until his back pressed up against the wall of Blasius's home. Blasius's wife had left a torch burning outside for her husband when night had fallen, and its light flickered brightly beside Csanád as he watched the monster approach, knowing that his life would soon be over. He briefly wondered what had happened to Blasius's wife, but the answer seemed painfully clear to him …

The strix reached down with a long muscular arm.

Its clawed hand grabbed Csanád by the clothes and dragged him from the ground. *Was he to suffer the same fate as Blasius?* In a last-ditch effort for survival, Csanád grabbed hold of the flaming torch and swung it towards the strix – and this time, finally, he managed to catch the beast by surprise.

The flaming brand made contact with the creature's face, causing it to drop Csanád to the ground as it roared in pain. Csanád immediately looked around for his blade. If he had managed to blind the thing then he could plunge his knife through its heart without it being able to see him and defend itself – but within seconds the strix was laughing at his naivety. Csanád turned his head at the sound of the laughter and before his eyes he now saw the face of the beast. It was completely unblemished … *How was that possible?* He was certain that he had made contact with the torch – even if it wasn't blinded then it should still be scorched …

'You think a little flame can hurt me!?' bellowed the strix in a booming voice. 'I will show you the meaning of what it is to burn!'

It would be some time before Csanád understood the meaning of this threat. He initially expected the beast to snatch the torch and burn him alive, but what came next was something he could never have imagined.

The strix made eye contact with Csanád and flexed its mysticism, holding him entranced and unable to so much as consider fighting back. Until now it had been toying with him for its own sick entertainment – but now it had something else on its mind. Csanád was able to do nothing other than stare motionlessly. He witnessed the beast pick up his small, sharp blade from the ground and hold it in the air. He then did something Csanád would never have expected in a thousand lifetimes ... he plunged it deep into his own neck ...

What on earth ... was all that Csanád could think. The knife obviously caused a great deal of discomfort to the strix and it roared in pain as it stabbed itself, but it very quickly removed the blade and right before his eyes Csanád witnessed the wound beginning to close over and the flesh to reknit. The roar of pain from the process was replaced with a sick and twisted grin as he glanced at the blade and began closing the distance towards the still entranced and immobilised Csanád. The strix lifted the bloodied blade before Csanád's eyes, as if to show him something, before it struck like a viper and sunk the blade all the way to the hilt into his chest.

The last thought that crossed through Csanád's mind before he lost consciousness did not belong to him. In truth it wasn't a thought at all – it was the cackle of the strix as it left him to bleed out and die on the street in front of his deceased best friend's home.

Twenty-Two

Csanád did not die. He awoke in a dazed and disorientated confusion almost three days after the vicious attack left the city of Ratiaria reeling from the incomprehensible loss of human life. Before he could sit up and tear the crude stitches sealing the wound on his chest, a frail old hand pressed firmly against him and made the presence of its owner known to him. Csanád blinked rapidly, trying to clear his vision and focus his fuzzy mind, but before he could figure out what was going on the voice of the man spoke: 'You must rest.'

Minutes passed and Csanád finally managed to regain a sense of clarity in his mind – he even recognised the kindly face of the old man that had spoken to him. His name was Nonus and he was the medicus of the town. However, medicus in this sense was most commonly limited to the prescription of herbal balms for fevers – it was not often that he would find himself sewing the flesh closed on a knife wound. It was even less common for such a patient of his to survive if they were afflicted as such.

Before long, Csanád began to sense the urges within his body. Most noticeably, his hunger. He learnt that he had been in an uneasy, fevered sleep for three days now, and as a result he had not eaten in all this time. Nonus had provided him fluids by cautiously sponging water into his unconscious mouth, extremely careful to ensure that it did not pool and drown his patient as he lay asleep. It was this treatment that had managed to keep Csanád alive – but now … now he needed some real sustenance!

When Nonus saw how vitalised Csanád appeared, he sighed with relief. Never in his many years of practicing medicine would he have expected a patient to awaken from such a wound with the vigour that Csanád was displaying. He retrieved a skin of spiced wine and handed it to Csanád, trying to caution him to drink slowly and restrain himself, but his warnings fell on deaf ears as the skin was emptied in mere moments. Nonus knew that he should not be surprised by such an overwhelming thirst, but somehow, he still was. Or at least, he was surprised at the vigour with which it was quenched so shortly after awakening from his injury.

The medicus left Csanád briefly and retrieved some dense, stale bread from his pantry. Csanád snatched it from his hands with nary a 'thank you' and began to shovel it into his mouth. The timid medicus watched on in amazement as Csanád ate the entire brick. For Csanád, the wine and bread alike tasted awful – but there was something instinctive within him that drove his actions. It was as if his body knew that it needed sustenance and he was simply fulfilling its biological imperative.

After finishing the bread, he glanced down and examined the crudely bandaged wound on his chest. He could see the green paste of a herbal treatment smeared to the sides of the bandage, and in his curiosity (and much to the medicus's annoyance) he tore free the bandage like a large scab so that he could examine the wound. It looked terrible. A nasty red scar on the right-hand side of his chest. It was surrounded by an angry red glow, which ordinarily should have suggested diseased flesh – but unbeknownst to either himself or the medicus, here it represented enhanced blood flow to the site, a sign of his body rapidly healing the wound.

While the wound looked (and felt) horrendous to Csanád – the medicus was momentarily taken aback by how good it looked compared to just the previous day when he had changed the dressing. He initially didn't think that Csanád was going to survive at all, he had lost a lot of blood, but for whatever reason the noble Calvus had instructed him to do all in his power to ensure that he did. For reasons Nonus did not understand, Calvus had some questions he wanted to ask of Csanád relating to the attack on Ratiaria, and he did not want 'the foreigner' to die before he could ask them.

The timid medicus finally managed to convince Csanád to lay back down so that he could treat the wound once more. As he allowed the wound on his chest to be covered, Csanád began to question the little man about what had happened in the aftermath of the attack. He said that the last thing he remembered was 'the strix' stabbing him in the chest before he finally awoke here today.

Nonus recoiled almost as if he had been slapped when Csanád mentioned the word 'strix'. Ratiaria was a deeply superstitious location and even the most educated of its folks were terrified of the supernatural. The mention of a blood-sucking ghoul, so casually, was enough for the medicus to break out in goosebumps all over his flesh.

Csanád asked again, impatient now and demanding an answer to his question. The most he was able to get out of the frightened little man was that it was a bloodbath and that over 30 townsfolk had been killed. When he was asked whether the strix was captured or if it managed to flee (in his heart he already knew the answer to this question) he was confused by the incomprehensible mumblings of the medicus who quickly excused himself and left Csanád alone on his uncomfortable wooden slab of a 'bed'.

Senile old goat, thought Csanád. It was a simple bloody question and he couldn't even answer it; it was a small wonder someone as incompetent as him had managed to save his life! Nonus, in truth, had very quickly grown scared of Csanád. Despite that he had been discovered with his own blade through his chest, the noble Calvus suspected that he was an accomplice to the attack on the town. Calvus wished to question him, and it was highly likely that he would be found guilty and nailed to a cross for his 'sins'.

Initially, Nonus was comfortable working on Csanád simply because he was unconscious and even when he awoke then he would be weak and pose no threat. But he was showing such strength already, and talking about a strix ... He had to report this to Calvus right away!

The mysticism associated with his affliction chose this very moment of frustration to spur into action for Csanád. As the medicus closed the door and made his hasty exit, leaving Csanád alone – Nonus's thoughts betrayed him and swam across the mystical channels and into his mind. Initially he thought he was simply hearing the medicus's voice through the walls, but after straining his ears he realised that what he was hearing was not a physical sound. It reminded him of something ...the way the strix had spoken into his mind as he held Blasius, right before he tore off his head. *Was the medicus a strix too!?* No – that wouldn't make any sense. From what he now knew, these creatures were huge. Monstrous and powerful. In short, absolutely nothing like the scrawny little man that had fled from the room. *So how was this possible?* Had the strix's power somehow transferred to him? Had it made him into one of its kind? He was vaguely familiar with the folklore that suggested such monsters were made, not born. But if that were the case ...

Before he could continue pondering these thoughts, Csanád recalled something that had passed through the medicus's mind – something important pertaining to his own future survival. The fact that the pompous shit Calvus suspected him of involvement in the attack on Ratiaria ... It should be obvious to anybody that he wasn't. Hell, he was stabbed in the chest by the real assailant for God's sake. But in a place like this he knew he couldn't count on a fair and unbiased trial. Calvus hated him just as much as he hated Calvus, and he knew that the cruel slob of a man would rejoice at the opportunity to punish Csanád for sins that did not belong to him.

In addition to the now-faded thoughts of the medicus that had drifted into his mind – he also sensed something foreboding in the distance. He would not discover the source of this feeling for some time yet, but it was the ever-present connection that bound him to the strix that had turned him. His 'father', whose name he did not even know.

Still lying on his back, Csanád tested out his strength. He rolled to his side and slung his legs to the floor. Considering the fact that he had been stabbed through the chest and lost a lot of blood only three days prior, he was shocked at the vitality coursing through him – however he was very aware that he was still far from full strength. He thought briefly about fleeing the medicus's villa, but worry crept through him when he realised that the door to his private room was locked from the outside – he was a prisoner.

He had very little time to dwell on this information – to fume angrily, more like it – before the sounds of approaching footsteps traced their way down the hall towards him. He returned to his uncomfortable bed, lying down and closing his eyes as the door was opened and in walked Nonus, accompanied by the garishly dressed noble, Calvus. The prat was also accompanied by two soldiers – his own personal bodyguard service.

Calvus cruelly pressed his finger against the wound on Csanád's chest, causing him to sit bolt upright and roar in pain. He reacted so quickly that Calvus slumped to the floor and the soldiers quickly moved in to restrain him, pinning him back to the bed. In an attempt to save face, Calvus smiled a shit-eating grin and said:

'Now that we've got the animalistic growls out of the way, let's get down to business. Tell me why you did it …'

There was no question of culpability – Csanád's guilt was already decided. The question was 'why'. Csanád spit on the floor at his side, growling his reply:

'It was a strix – *you fool*. You should be grateful – I alone stood and fought the creature!'

A nervous laughter emanated from the two soldiers as they held Csanád, but neither Calvus nor Nonus joined them. To the soldiers, Csanád was just the crazy foreign hunter who had gone berserk and attacked the town – but the noble and the medicus clearly knew better.

'Watch your tongue, peasant,' began Calvus, before continuing: 'There are no such things as striges …'

The venom in his reaction to being called a fool morphed into an immediate childlike uncertainty as he tried to convince Csanád (and himself alike) that such monsters did not exist. But it was evident that the ages-old superstition ran deep through his veins, as he clearly shivered at the thought.

Csanád now was able to utilise his newfound mysticism intentionally, and he sifted through the noble's mind. His fate was already sealed. The prat was only here to gloat over him, to await his return to consciousness before he would be publicly tortured and executed for his 'crimes' in front of the whole town. He was turning his grudge into a political stunt, trying to assuage the fears and grief of the town by feeding them the story of a traitor in their midst. With Csanád taken care of – *by him* – then he would be a hero in the aftermath of this bloody affair.

Calvus spent some time in Csanád's room, ostensibly to 'question' him about any accomplices, to ask him why he had tried to 'kill himself', among other nonsensical banalities. But in reality, he was there to gloat. Csanád more than anyone understood this fact, and he refused to bite any further – instead, he held his tongue and refused to answer any questions asked of him, even as the petty shit of a noble tortured him by poking and prodding the wound on his chest.

Burning inside of Csanád was an indignant rage, but he would not give Calvus the satisfaction of breaking him. He would find a way out of this, and he would make the rich bastard pay for how he was treating him. Mercifully, the charade drew to a close. Nonus was as quiet as a church mouse in the back corner of the room, watching the awful spectacle. He was far too cowardly to protest the fact that they were undoing all of the good that he had done to restore Csanád's health. Not that it really mattered since Calvus happily proclaimed that his crucifixion was scheduled for first light the following day …

Feigning his own weakness by laying back down before Calvus arrived proved to be the decisive action that would save Csanád's life. They felt comfortable leaving him in the 'care' of the medicus until such time as his execution the following morning. He was too weak to be a threat, after all. Their hubris would be their downfall.

Calvus and his soldiers exited the room, leaving Nonus to scurry towards Csanád and examine the re-opened wound on his chest. Using his cunning and guile, Csanád continued to play weak as he allowed the medicus to resew the stitches on his chest. The pain was agonising, but he forced himself to bear it, knowing it was important that he get whatever treatment possible now – because he wouldn't get another chance later. When the medicus had completed his procedure, Csanád softly 'begged' him for some more food and drink, and the timid old man scurried off to acquiesce to his requests – it was only fair.

What Nonus did not know was that Csanád was far stronger than he let on. He rose to his feet the second the medicus left the room to fetch his food, hiding behind the locked door. Using the mysticism that he still did not fully comprehend, he waited until he detected the thoughts of Nonus returning, and when the door opened, he seized his opportunity and pounced on the frail little man.

Even in his weakened state, he was far too powerful for the medicus, and he pressed his hand over the old man's mouth as he held him pinned to the floor. *Why not just snap his neck?* The thought of simply killing him crossed his mind, but his affliction was not progressed so far just yet that he was a mindlessly indiscriminate monster. Instead, he offered a stern warning to the medicus to remain quiet – or else he *would* kill him. Finally, he gathered the skin of wine and the brick of bread and exited into the hallway, locking the medicus in behind him.

In a manner that didn't seem possible for a large man such as himself, Csanád skulked quietly out of the medicus's villa and into the streets of Ratiaria. His skills as a huntsman had provided him the ability to move about soundlessly. He was wearing nothing more than a subligaria, but his modesty was the least of his concerns as he scurried between buildings, seeking the outskirts of town. He needed to escape Ratiaria before the medicus raised an alarm – he was too weak to fight back … yet …

Twenty-Three

Csanád managed to escape from Ratiaria with minimal concern. He was seen by a few people who gasped audibly at the state of him – but it was clear that his status as a fugitive was not yet common knowledge. Who could blame them for their gasps? He was filthy, his chest was an uncleaned bloody mess, and the only clothing on his body was a filthy subligaria.

He was not a modest man and was actually very proud of his powerful, toned body – but he knew that if he were to survive alone in the wilderness then he would need more protection from the elements. As part of his flight from Ratiaria, Csanád finally *did* commit a crime that the pompous shit Calvus could actually pin on him – he stole a wet robe that had been left out to dry. He was already sentenced to death for a crime he did not commit. Thievery could also warrant the death penalty – but somehow this was the least of his concerns.

As Csanád made it beyond the city limits, he used his well-honed sense of direction to guide him back towards the area where he and Blasius had been hunting before the strix had swooped in and turned the town upside down. At the thought of his now-deceased best friend, Csanád would have expected to feel a pang of guilt or at least grief – but it was like he was now incapable of feeling any emotions at all. He put this feeling down to the rage that was boiling inside him at the injustice delivered by Calvus.

How dare that fat little shit think he could torture him … Kill him … Csanád's mind was a seething viper's nest. There was one thing that gladdened him at this time and it was the fact that he had thought to steal the robe before leaving town. Its moisture was providing a great cooling effect under the rays of the sun that felt unnaturally hot on his bare skin.

Despite his injury and ensuing weakness, Csanád refused to let himself stop moving and shortly arrived back at the carcass of the boar he had dropped three nights ago. He was starving and if he could avoid it, he would rather not eat anymore of the awful bread that the medicus had given him before he manufactured his escape from Ratiaria. Unfortunately, the boar was picked clean. It was like an entire pack of wild animals had discovered and ravaged it. An entire pack … wolves … *Had the strix come this way?*

This thought toyed with Csanád's emotions. There was the sudden fear at the fact that he was now alone in the wilderness when such monsters existed – but there was also a bubbling fury and almost excitement at the opportunity to try and track him down and kill him for good. Csanád grumbled as he was forced to satisfy his hunger with the atrocious bread, but once it was gone, he still felt much stronger. He also downed the skin of spiced wine before setting off in the direction of one of his favourite hunting locations.

With all of his supplies gone, Csanád knew that he needed to act fast to survive. He found a tree branch that would serve as a spear, and he spent a long while under the shade of a tree removing all twigs and leaves and sharpening its end into a fine point using rocks he'd found nearby. It was nowhere near as good as his spear that had taken down the boar, and it would not fly as straight and true when thrown – but with this weapon he would never go hungry.

He knew that the sensible thing to do next would be the construction of shelter – but his wounded body was craving nourishment, and he intended to deliver on these cravings. As the sun began to set, he smiled in grim satisfaction as the point of his spear entered the side of a small rabbit that he had used his hunting skills to track. The little creature was killed immediately from the force of the impact. He collected his spoils and made his way back towards the thatch of trees under which he had crafted the spear in the first place. That would serve as his shelter for the night.

Csanád was not a stupid man. He knew that he was still in fairly close proximity to Ratiaria, so at least while he remained weak then he couldn't afford to send up any signs of his location. For this reason, he was unable to craft a fire to cook his kill. He had eaten raw meat before, and it was not a memory he recalled fondly – but there was just something about this rabbit that looked so enticing to him that eating it raw suddenly seemed like the best idea in the world.

Grabbing one of the sharp rocks that he had used to refine the point of his spear, Csanád set about gutting his catch, and after its entrails had been properly discarded (buried to avoid attracting scavengers – or wolves) – he examined the raw meat under the shadows of the night. He struggled to fathom as to how he could see so clearly, and he initially thought that it must be a vibrant full moon, but when he craned his neck to look around the sky there was no moon to be found at all. It was simply the rapidly progressing change surging through his body that allowed him his enhanced vision at night. A change that would grow more rapid still as he gorged himself on the raw meat – and blood – of his catch, as the strix that created him spied on from nearby with a sadistic smile on his face.

With a rapidity that defied all understanding, Csanád suddenly realised that the wound on his chest was no longer the constant throbbing pain that it had been since he had awoken that morning. He tore free the herbal balm that the medicus had applied and examined the wound. He was stunned to see that it appeared to be almost fully healed. The stitches threading either side of the puncture now served no purpose other than a ridiculous cosmetic patchwork, and he tore them free with a short grunt of pain.

He couldn't remember the last time he had felt this good. He was like an entirely new man; however, this would be the last night that Csanád spent under the belief that he was still actually a man. The change had performed a sprint through his system, it was faster than he would experience ever again in his lifetime of experimentation. It was not simply the fact that he had consumed fresh blood and that the strix who created him remained in close proximity – it was the sheer, unadulterated hatred that was flowing through his mind that sped up the process. Calvus …

With his newly discovered enhanced eyesight, Csanád realised that he did not have to simply waste the night sitting under a tree. He could put the time to good use, and he did. Before even midnight rolled around, he had crafted a shelter for himself using the bounty of the treefall around him. Using sticks as a framework, he used his skills to craft a paste out of mud from a nearby watering hole, which he mixed with leaves and long grass. In so doing, he made a crude form of shelter that would give him a 'roof' over his head for the remainder of the night.

In truth, Csanád was not sure if the shelter would serve any purpose at all. He felt great and he only crafted it out of old human habits – but since he was not tired, he instead grasped his spear and set off into the darkness to search for another kill. Despite his newfound night sight, finding another kill actually proved harder than he expected. It was almost like the critters could sense his approach and knew to hide. Nevertheless, as the sun was beginning to crest the eastern horizon, he finally managed to spear another rabbit.

He bent to lift the creature from the ground, and as he did, he felt a sharp bite against his skin. He reacted immediately, turning to discover the culprit – but there was nothing there… The pain from the bite was radiating over all of his body now… His mind took far longer than it should have to realise that the creature biting him was no bug or animal – it was the sun…

Given the rapid progression of his change, and the consumption of the warm rabbit blood the previous day – his body had now already reached the stage where the bite of the sun could prove highly agonising, even deadly if he were trapped under its rays for long enough. The strix that turned him would be dead in minutes at its age, but for a baby like Csanád it would take longer to burn through his system. Suddenly a rumbling, rolling laughter began to race through Csanád's tumultuous mind.

'Did I not tell you that I would show you the meaning of what it was to burn!' laughed the strix in his mind.

It was this taunt that finally snapped all of the pieces of the puzzle together for Csanád. Of course… The folklore suggested that these were creatures of the night… And now he was one of them… He had to act quickly…

He ignored the barbs of his cruel maker as he raced through the rays of the steadily rising sun. He had not realised how far he had strayed from his shelter under the trees, but he was extremely grateful that he had had the forethought to build some kind of cover for himself the previous night. It was almost ironic; he had crafted a roof to hide from the oppression of the darkness – but it was actually the light from which he needed to hide.

The pain flowing through his body was like none he had ever felt before in his life. He had been burnt by a flaming torch as a young and stupid boy, and he remembered that pain vividly – but this was different. It was almost spiteful in the way it ravaged the pain receptors in his skin, and he could see himself turning an angry shade of red as he raced back towards his shelter. Eventually, mercifully, he spotted it under the trees and all but dove headlong through the door of his mud and stick hut. He tore off his robe and hung it across the doorway to block out the sun's rays, and finally, he was free of the stinging pain.

A constant in his mind throughout this ordeal was the taunts of the strix. While these taunts angered him, he did his best to ignore them. He picked up his sharpened rock and slashed the throat of the rabbit that he had thankfully maintained hold of during his frantic flight back to shelter, and he simply placed his mouth to the wound on its throat and drank deep. His body guided him to such an action. While he would eat the critter's meat later – it was its blood that his newly changed physiology required – and this blood immediately provided him the healing effects that he required. The cure-all balm for his badly burned skin.

The enhanced emotions brought on by the change

in his system provoked one primal reaction in particular. Anger. Malice. Hate. He hated the accursed monster who had done this to him – though deep down there was also a sense of gratitude for granting him such powers. He hated the town that had rejected him his entire life – none more so than the whoreson, Calvus. Simply thinking his name caused Csanád's blood to boil as he took in his surroundings.

He was hunkered under sticks and mud and thusly trapped to wait for the setting of the sun. It would be a highly uncomfortable day ahead. Meanwhile, he could only picture the shit of a noble going about his day in luxury. He would make sure that Calvus paid for his actions … The only small feeling that lightened the mood for Csanád at this moment was the thought of how Calvus would have reacted to the discovery that he was missing. He could almost picture the blood vessels in his eyes bulging to the point of bursting.

As soon as his mind brought up the concept of blood vessels, his train of thought locked onto one thing and one thing alone. He would make Calvus pay alright … *He would pay in blood!* There was no trace of humanity left for Csanád to cling to. Even before he had been physically turned into a monster, he had already been treated like one simply for being different. He spent the entirety of the daylight hours planning the bloody revenge that he would reap on Ratiaria as soon as the sun set. The sadistic thoughts crossing his mind even managed to surprise the strix that was spying on him from his abode nearby in the Balkan Mountains.

After a day of seething, fantasising, planning – the sun finally hid its painful rays behind the horizon and allowed Csanád to emerge from his makeshift shelter. He knew that he should prioritise a more permanent solution to hiding from the burning orb in the sky – but there was something he simply had to do first. Turning his head in the direction of Ratiaria, a warped smile broke across his face as he set his body in motion towards the town that he had called home since he was a young boy.

Everything combined for Csanád: his skills as a hunter enabled him to move quietly and not draw attention to himself, and his burgeoning grace as a strix provided a deftness to his motions and allowed him to see as clearly in the dark of night as if the sun were still shining overhead. Dressed in the robe that he had stolen the previous day, he was also far less conspicuous than when he was scurrying through the streets in the subligaria alone. The robe was dirty, but it was not enough to draw attention to him.

Finding Calvus's villa took no effort. The pompous noble lived in the largest property in all of Ratiaria. Csanád knew that he maintained a retinue of soldiers to guard his property, but this thought did not dissuade his actions in the slightest. *More blood for him!*

Deftly dealing with two soldiers guarding the back gate of the villa, Csanád gained entry without a single cry piercing the night. He ambushed the poor, unwitting men, snapping the neck of the first man and tossing him to the ground before grasping the throat of the second in his powerful hand and squeezing tight to prevent any outcry. The man's eyes bulged in fear as Csanád choked the life out of him. He dragged both of the bodies out of sight of the alleyway and left them in a pile. The blood now stagnant in their veins was tempting – *oh so tempting* – but he did not want to risk being caught with these nobodies, he had a bigger, juicier target in his mind.

Csanád had no semblance of conscience to hold him back. He had completely embraced the rage and animalistic sense of superiority that came with his affliction. He didn't think anybody would be capable of fighting back against the urges that were pulsating through him.

He continued his assault through the confines of the lavish villa. Along the way he indiscriminately killed any individual that was unfortunate enough to cross his path. Soldiers, house staff, or unwitting slaves – he didn't care. They were nothing more than obstacles in his path. He moved swiftly and silently, and soon found himself at the doorway to Calvus's sleeping chambers.

As he entered the door, Calvus heard his approach but was too slow to react to the reality of the situation. Calvus had been expecting one of his slaves, a whore that he used to gratify himself – the last thing he expected was the face of his would-be killer. Csanád made eye contact with him, and instinctively the mysticism that his newfound affliction had gifted him sprang into action. He held the now-trembling, fat noble in his gaze – subjugating his mind and silencing his overwhelming desires to cry out for help.

Able to sense the panic flowing through Calvus's

mind only served to spur on the cruel urges that Csanád was feeling. He grinned one of those ghastly toothy smiles that he would in future become known for and closed the distance between himself and the petrified standing corpse of Calvus. He moved slowly and taunted the noble with what was soon to be his fate. Csanád grabbed a small dagger that Calvus kept on his nightstand and walked with it towards the statue of his victim.

Raising the blade before Calvus's eyes in much the same fashion that the strix had done to Csanád himself, he then lowered it out of the frozen line of sight of the pompous shit and began rapidly cutting all over his fat body. Csanád was almost getting off on the fact that Calvus was unable to scream for help, but this did not mean he was not screaming internally from the tortures that he was experiencing. Mental screams flowed directly into Csanád's twisted mind, spurring him on even further.

Eventually, he grew tired of mindlessly butchering the noble's body. He decided to put an end to things and brought the blade to Calvus's throat. Having been silent since stepping foot in Calvus's property – Csanád finally spoke for the first time:

'You brought this on yourself, *my lord*. Now die, knowing that your pitiful life held no meaning,' as he traced the sharp edge of the blade across Calvus's throat, opening a thick zipper of red flesh.

He placed his mouth to this wound and drank deep, siphoning the lifeforce of Calvus into himself and feeling the utterly exquisite pleasure with which his body reacted to the taste of human blood.

Csanád was enamoured at his own physiology. He no longer thought with anger or bitterness towards the strix that had turned him. He felt an overwhelming surge of gratitude for the monster that freed him from the tedium of his banal life. But before he could embrace the pleasure of his latest kill, a shrill female scream rang out through the villa. The whore that Calvus had been awaiting had finally arrived, only to see her master lying in a pool of his own blood with a monster sucking on his throat.

The festivities needed to be cut short for Csanád. He knew (and could sense with his mysticism) that this scream had alerted all the remaining soldiers in the villa and that they would be rushing to his position. He was confident that he could probably fight them all on his own too – but it was not something he wished to risk, he needed to learn more about his skills and abilities before throwing himself headlong into such a risky situation. Instead, he fled out the window of the sleeping chamber and raced back towards the gate through which he had gained entry.

Csanád encountered no resistance on his way – he had already killed everybody in this section of the villa during his ingress. He stopped only to steal the swords from the corpses of the guards at the rear gate, and then he fled once more into the night – exiting Ratiaria as he had done just the previous day.

The heightened emotions of a strix combined with the adrenaline coursing through his body granted him the strength to race through the night. He passed by the makeshift shelter that he had crafted for himself, stopping only to grab his spear before continuing to distance himself from the town. He knew that his actions this night would warrant a far greater search effort than when he initially escaped (*had they even searched for him at all?*), so for the next several hours he used his almost limitless energy to carry himself to the mountains in the southwest.

The sun was threatening to rise by the time he found a natural shelter for himself in a cave within the mountains, and it was there that he finally rested after his eventful night. As the sun rose, he finally allowed himself to drift into a deep, dark sleep. It was the sleep that granted him with the Ancestral Memories of the strix who created him.

Twenty-Four

Csanád awoke deep into the night having slept for at least 12 hours. However, sleep might not be the most accurate descriptor for what he had experienced. The Ancestral Memories. Whether that was its true name – whether it even had a name – this was the only way that Csanád could think to describe it. As he slept, he had been whisked through a kaleidoscopic montage of the memories of the strix who had created him.

How such a thing was possible could only be put down to magic, mystical forces beyond his comprehension. But the *why* of the matter seemed fairly clear to Csanád. It was a second education, beyond what was learnt as a (human) child. It was almost akin to a manual that taught freshly changed strix how their fantastical physiology operated – through the memories of their direct predecessor.

Csanád awoke with a fresh sense of wonder and gratitude for the strix who had changed him. What was initially supposed to be a punishment, a form of retribution – had instead backfired and become a great gift. It set Csanád apart and granted him freedom from the banalities of his old life. He could go anywhere, do anything – for all eternity.

This last thought pleased him more than anything else that the change had afforded him. Through the Ancestral Memories in his dreams – he learnt that the strix who changed him was over 750 years old. A Celt named Nechtan who had set up his homeland in the Balkan Mountains to the south and east of Ratiaria. Nechtan had existed throughout all these centuries, growing stronger, taking whatever pleased him. Food, wealth, women – there was nobody who could stand in his way, and he would live forever as long as he continued to feed his monstrous body that one glorious ingredient … fresh, warm, delicious blood.

The thought of living through the centuries at the prime of his physical fitness was an almost erotic thought for Csanád as he stretched his knotted muscles within the cave in which he had been hiding from the sunlight. Something else that Csanád noticed with grim satisfaction was that he had grown immensely during his long sleep. While he previously stood at a respectable six pedes, he estimated that he was now closer to seven pedes – possibly even more …

He could feel the strength rippling through his already muscular body. He felt unstoppable! But one other thing that the Ancestral Memories made abundantly clear in his mind was the sheer scale of his father's strength. No matter how powerful Csanád knew himself to be, after having witnessed flashes through the life of Nechtan, he came to realise the true depth of strength that lay in his future. This understanding was enough to dissuade him from any attempts at retribution against the old strix. Not that he even felt so inclined anymore. If he ever met Nechtan again, he would thank him for this great gift!

Csanád concentrated on Nechtan in his fortified home within the Balkan Mountains to the east. The strange sense of foreboding that he had felt on the periphery of his mind the previous day was now clearly understood in the wake of the Ancestral Memories that had flooded into his mind over the course of his long sleep – it was caused by his mystical connection with the strix who 'fathered' him.

'You have adjusted quickly, my progeny,' the mental voice of Nechtan invaded Csanád's mind across their mystical shared wavelength. *'You are aware that I changed you not as a gift, but a punishment. You have robbed me of this joy – as I robbed you of your friend. Let us call this even. However, be warned. Step no foot in my lands under penalty of death!'*

Nechtan was the only living creature that Csanád would ever respect, even fear. The Ancestral Memories that had washed into his mind painted a vivid picture of the man – the creature – with whom he was dealing.

Csanád replied: *'You have my gratitude, father. Your lands are your own, simply leave me to mine and we shall never cross paths.'*

Csanád received no reply from his father – however, he did believe he sensed satisfaction across the mystical connection that would tether their minds together for all eternity. Or at least until one of them met the unlikely fate of death before their time.

Unbeknownst to Csanád at this moment – the relationship he shared with his 'father' was perhaps the most cordial shared between any striges in the wide world. The changeling almost always harboured a hatred and resentment towards their maker, and the maker held a deep distrust towards their progeny as one of the few threats to their lives. It was for this reason that striges very scarcely continued the bloodline – they possessed a jealous greed and lust for power that they did not wish to share with any other.

Time began to take on an abstract feel for Csanád over the years that followed. He followed the only lead he knew – that of his father, Nechtan – and he crafted a homely fortress for himself in the mountains to the west of the location of his changing – Ratiaria. Unburdened by the human construct of a 'conscience', Csanád preyed on unsuspecting travellers through the mountains that he had jealously declared his domain, taking from them their blood and their wares alike.

Over time, he began to experiment with his powers, and it did not take long before he had mastered the ability to completely enthral the minds of lesser creatures. Having witnessed his father controlling the pack of wolves, Csanád too desired such a family of loyal creatures – and so he would have them. He experimented on all forms of lower life and discovered to his joy that everything that had a mind was susceptible. He added bats and eagles to his list of familiars and through them he consolidated his strength in the region with the ability to scry great distances.

The inevitable progression of his experiments with his abilities led Csanád to attempt to enthral the minds of people too. *Why should this be any different?* Humans were nothing more than lesser lifeforms, after all. To his immense satisfaction – his experiments proved to be a great success. As a result, instead of wildly butchering travellers for sustenance when they passed through his domain – instead he captured a retainer of thralls. Showing restraint that took many years to develop, Csanád had essentially created a 'farm' of fresh blood – keeping these meat-sacks alive and sipping slowly from the nectar coursing through their veins.

It was in this way that almost 80 years passed in what felt like the blink of an eye for Csanád. He had become a recluse from humankind – with the exception of his constantly refreshing retinue of slaves. He had one singular obsession – himself. Throughout these years Csanád had dedicated every moment of his spare time to the development and honing of his abilities. He could craft a mist that rivalled the one his father had called forth the night of his attack on Ratiaria; he could effortlessly scry across his wide domain through the eyes of his countless thralls; and his physical strength had only enhanced in leaps and bounds given his steady and unwavering supply of fresh blood.

He felt like a king. But one thing that set this king apart from all others at the time was that he had no interest whatsoever in the petty squabbles for territory that would pulse throughout greater Europe over the many centuries to come. As long as nothing threatened him directly then he did not care in the slightest who sat in the ornate chair and declared themselves the ruler of arbitrary boundaries. However, this disconnection from the outside world resulted in Csanád being dealt an overwhelming surprise in the year AD 440.

It was in this year that suddenly, inexplicably, the perennial mystical connection that he had felt with his father Nechtan was severed. He might have assumed that Nechtan was trying to hide his presence, that he had sensed how strong Csanád had become and viewed him as a threat – but Csanád knew that this wasn't the case. He could sense the fear and agony in his father's final living moments before his life was snuffed out before its time. He was only 843 years old – his eternity was robbed from him.

Csanád did not particularly care one way or the other that his father was dead. He felt no semblance of grief – but he did feel a pang of fear. Even as strong as he had become, he still viewed his father with a great deal of respect. He knew how strong Nechtan was. *So how on earth had he been killed?* It had happened during daytime. Was it just a coincidence? An accident? Csanád needed answers …

Casting his eagle familiars into the skies, Csanád

scried as they flew into the distant east towards the domain that previously belonged to his father. It was there that he witnessed a great horde of men that had swept down towards the Balkans from the north. The Huns. While Csanád did not care about the goings-on of humanity in the wider world, he had still learnt a great deal from the assorted travellers he had captured and/or killed as they passed through his domain. He was aware of the Hunnic horde, led by their most storied leader – Attila. *Had they somehow found a way to overwhelm Nechtan? Did they know about striges?*

Recalling his familiars, Csanád spent a long while strengthening his foothold in the mountains that he had called home since the time he fled from Ratiaria. Rather than simply keeping a retainer of thralls on which to feed, Csanád also began keeping a separate retainer of thralls to train as guards to protect his realm during daylight hours – just on the off chance that Attila led his mighty horde further west and caused him any trouble.

In a means that was only clear to striges such as himself – the years had a way of washing by with startling rapidity. After having sacked Ratiaria in the same year that he had somehow killed Nechtan, Attila and his Huns continued their march of conquest through the region, but Csanád never found himself bothered in his mountainside lair. By the year 453, Attila was killed before his time and the mighty Huns that he commanded became a pale shadow of the threat that they once presented. By 469, the Hunnic Empire had dwindled to such a point that it found itself absorbed into a new force within the region – the Bulgars.

As the decades marched on, Csanád began to grow bored of his ceaseless life within the mountains that he had called home for over a century at this point. He was stricken with a wanderlust, and despite the ever-present turmoil within the region – he set his mind to exploring the wider world. What was the point of eternal life if one simply hunkered down amongst the rocks all alone …?

The first port of call for Csanád to travel was east. He desired to explore the Balkan Mountains – the mighty homeland of his now-deceased father. There was never a shortage of fresh blood for Csanád in the years that followed. Battles waged throughout the region and he could spirit himself into military encampments under the dark of night – aided by his thick mist – and drink deep of the blood of life. It was the Byzantine Empire that now held sway over the region containing the Balkans, so naturally it was the members of this empire that formed the majority of the victims that Csanád claimed during his travels.

Having discovered the former abode of his father – a veritable eyrie in the heights of the Balkan Mountains – Csanád satisfied his curiosity and found himself inexorably drawn north. He had not crossed the mighty Danube River since he was a young boy travelling south with his parents, when his parents had gotten killed in Ratiaria on the south bank of the mighty river. It was on this south bank that he had remained for the ensuing 170 years.

Exhumed

The year was 538 when Csanád finally achieved this desire, leaving the now-expansive Byzantine Empire and entering the Kingdom of the Gepids to the north. His animal familiars provided him with all the information from afar that they were capable of scrying. While his initial desire to migrate north was driven by his wish to see the homeland of the Visigoths, his parents' kin – he learned that as a people they had been chased far west across Europe and at this time held their domain in a region that would be known as Spain in the distant future.

Csanád held no desire to head west – as he crossed the Danube River and laid his eyes upon the mighty Carpathian Mountains, he knew that he had found a magical land that he desired to call his home. The turmoil beyond the south bank of the Danube was too continual – he desired a more permanent residence away from such conflict. Always present in the back of his mind was the untimely death of his maker, Nechtan, and the fact that it could happen to him too if he were not careful.

The years continued their relentless march, and so too did Csanád continue his inexorable pilgrimage north. He followed the mighty mountainous feature slowly, allowing himself to settle periodically. He would construct strongholds of various complexity and permanency, before continuing his travels. The mighty lifespan of one such as him afforded him no great need of haste in his movements. In such a way, he witnessed the Kingdom of the Gepids fall to the mighty Avar

Khaganate in the year 567. He feasted from a river of blood in the wake of the mighty invading force.

The Avar Khaganate would reign in this region for over two centuries – however this did not leave the land free of turmoil. Csanád decided that he wanted to settle once more, and he did so in a sheltered region of the Carpathian Mountains. It was there that he enacted a plan that had been swirling around his narcissistic mind for many years. He entered the home of a rich noble and slaughtered his entire household … his wife, his children, his guards, his slaves – all washed away in a buffet of blood. He then simply assumed the life and wealth of this respected man, using his mysticism to suppress the minds of anybody who might otherwise dissent to such an overthrow.

Despite his newly acquired wealth, he could not simply live amongst the throng of humanity. It would not be safe if he were to ever be uncovered, and towns also made targets for invading forces. Instead, under the guise of his assumed identity, he crafted a new fortress in the hills of the mighty Carpathians and lived like a lord – quickly rebuilding a new generation of thralls to service his every desire. But something was missing. It had become tedious to constantly replenish his thralls as they died in their pathetic human lifetimes. *What if he created another strix to serve as his eternal slave …?*

★★★

In the year 914, Csanád finally set his plan into motion, scouting the region for the ideal human to change into his eternal son. In a small settlement nearby called

Exhumed

Orăştie, he found a man named Iuliu Dragoş.

Twenty-Five

With centuries of practice and experience under his belt, Csanád had long been capable of passing as a human in times of need. It was not a charade that he enjoyed participating in, as he felt a supreme sense of superiority over their kind and the idea of once again being one of them repulsed him. They were his food. Nothing more than livestock. However, this ability did prove to be an important facet of his repertoire when he was searching for a human (slave) to 'recruit' into his eternal service.

The latest of Csanád's several semi-permanent abodes was located within the southwestern crook of the Carpathian Mountains, so he focused his efforts in the immediate vicinity – scanning the area for human minds with his mysticism. It was very fortunate that his mysticism allowed him a near savant-like ability with varying tongues, as languages and dialects had evolved immensely over the span of his prolonged life. The constant human turmoil in the region led to a shopping list of languages spoken and, with minimal effort, Csanád was capable of understanding all of them.

He left his retinue of familiars behind in his mountainside base, dressed in his finest robes, and entered the town of Orăştie immediately after the sun dipped behind the horizon. This was one town that he had not raided for fresh blood during the long time that he had been living in the region – so the peasants were far less wary towards him as he strode amongst them. Quite the opposite, actually. The sight of his luxurious possessions immediately drew their attention as they desired nothing more than to sell their wares to the travelling noble.

Csanád allowed the farce to play out, drowning his scathing cynicism and hatred in an assumed aura of aloofness. The merchants were used to such treatment from higher-born nobles, so they meekly scampered away when this newcomer did not display interest in their wares. Csanád could hear the bitter thoughts running through their minds behind the forced smiles on their faces. It was this inside knowledge that kept him sane as he had to pass through the throng of humanity. Rather than taking insult at their thoughts, he relished in their negativity.

Orăştie was not the first town that Csanád had entered as such, but it would be the last for quite some time. The night grew late, and the locals all retired to their homes. The expedition had been an abject failure for

Csanád and in his frustration at wasting his time, he was seriously considering summoning his mist and his familiars and pillaging the town in much the same way that his father had done to Ratiaria all those centuries ago. But this kind of indiscriminate attack was something he had steered clear of ever since Nechtan had somehow gotten himself killed by the Huns. He was wary of uprisal.

No, he wouldn't raze the small town to the ground – but he *would* satisfy his hunger. He began seeking a quiet residence where the whole household was asleep so that he could climb in through the window and slash their throats in their sleep. He had done this countless times when he grew bored of his farmed blood and desired the sport of the kill – but before he could set his plan into motion, he was surprised in a way that he had not been for centuries. The biting sting of a blade entered into his back. Once, twice, five times. Someone was trying to kill him!

In a bellow of surprise and fury that no doubt awoke the entire town in its volume, Csanád pivoted his body, turning to witness the man that was attacking him. It was nothing more than an opportunistic scoundrel who was trying to rob the rich noble in the black of night – but he had chosen the wrong 'noble' to mess with. The wounds from the knife posed no serious threat to Csanád, but the bite of the blade did inflict the most severe pain he had experienced since the morning that he had almost burnt to death in the sun 550 years earlier.

The look of surprise on the face of the man attacking Csanád almost made him laugh. With the swiftness and grace only a strix was capable of performing, he spun and slapped the blade out of the intrepid robber's hand. The man stumbled back and fell over in an attempt to scurry away. The entire scenario reminded Csanád of what it must have looked like when he had tried to attack Nechtan back in Ratiaria.

There was one drastic difference however, and in the surprise caused by his aching back it took Csanád some time to realise. *He could not hear this human's thoughts* ... Or to be more clear, he was forced to really concentrate and bolster his mysticism in order to penetrate that skull – something he had never before had to do since coming into his powers as a strix. This intrigued him. After such a long life, finding himself surprised was not a common occurrence. It was this surprise that saved the life of Iuliu Dragoş – be that for better or for worse ...

His untempered roars of pain and outrage had stirred life into the town, and Csanád did not want a throng of people descending on the location before he got to the bottom of this mystery. He could have killed this man in a heartbeat; slashed his throat and dined on the blood as it torrented out – but instead he did something different. Using the full force of his mysticism, he entered the eyes of the scamp who had attacked him and subdued his mind – silencing him, forcing him to obey his desires. He had used this technique countless times, but with Iuliu it was supremely more difficult.

With Iuliu now mesmerised – though fighting it for all his worth – Csanád grasped him by the back of his filthy rag of a robe and began marching him quickly out of town. The pores of Csanád's body began to emit a dense flow of deep white mist that was thickest in his immediate vicinity. It was in this way that he managed to extricate himself from Orăştie and, in the process, kidnap the young man who had attacked him.

After about an hour of swift march through the pitch darkness towards Csanád's mountain fortress – the human that he had stolen out of town finally managed to break free of the mystical hold that was binding his mind. He screamed: 'STRIGOI!', and tried to run – but was immediately captured by the vastly superior specimen that was Csanád.

A rumbling laugh rolled off of Csanád's tongue. *Strigoi*. The term was new to him, but it only served to remind him of the ever-changing, constant evolution of language in the region. It even shared the same etymological roots as the word *strix*. Amazingly, for the first time, Csanád actually stopped to wonder whether there even was one true name for his kind. Beyond 'strix' and 'strigoi', he had also been labelled 'shtriga', 'lamia', and 'vrykolakas', particularly during the time he spent south of the Balkan Mountains. Each culture seemed to have a slightly different myth surrounding blood-sucking monsters. This fact alone allowed him to draw the conclusion that there were more of his kind in the wide world – how else would the myths and rumours begin …?

Returning his mind to the present situation, Csanád was laughing over the frightened man at his feet.

'Count yourself blessed that you yet still live, "boy"! Press me too far and see this blessing disappear! Now MARCH!'

The threat was sufficient to spur Iuliu ever onwards in the direction that Csanád was leading him. He had earlier sent a mental call to his lupine familiars who had now arrived and were flanking the pair as they marched through the steady incline of the countryside towards Csanád's mountainside fortress.

Arriving back at his stronghold about an hour before sunup, Csanád marched Iuliu towards his grim stone dungeon and tossed him bodily inside, before entering himself and closing the door behind them. This would be the worst day in Iuliu's (human) life. Csanád exercised his centuries of practice to exact the most exquisite of tortures in retaliation for the pain that had been inflicted on himself back in Orăștie. The biggest difference between the pair was that Csanád had long since healed from his trivial little stab wounds. Iuliu on the other hand was wavering on the edge of life and death from a combination of blood loss and shock. No human was designed to suffer this much punishment and yet live.

While sport was one of the dominant factors driving Csanád at this moment, taking a perverse pleasure at the suffering of the insignificant human – he also had ulterior motives. He desired to question the man about just how he was capable of fighting back against Csanád's mysticism, a craft he thought he had perfected centuries ago. Iuliu had no idea what he was talking about – and Csanád knew that he was telling the truth since the broken man's mind was now wide open to him. This only served to infuriate him further and spur even greater tortures.

The sun was at its zenith before Csanád finally finished the sickening punishment that he was delivering to Iuliu – however before he performed that final stroke to fell the pitiful worm, effectively putting him out of his misery, he had a better idea. He had gone into town looking for a candidate to be his eternal slave, had he not? In his mind he envisioned such a slave as being a strong hunter, or perhaps a wise scholar – not a scrawny gutter rat like Iuliu … But on a whim, he decided to follow the lead of his own father. He would change Iuliu, and if he failed as a slave then at least he would live as somebody to punish in one of his frequent rages.

Recalling again the method with which his father had changed him all those years ago, Csanád followed suit. It was the most exquisite agony that he had ever felt as he plunged the blade into his own neck. He felt the tip of the dagger graze against his vertebra, which sent a jolt through his nervous system so severe that he almost collapsed – but there was something within his blood that told him he had struck gold. Removing the blade and approaching the barely conscious sack of bloodied meat on the floor before him – he plunged the blade into Iuliu's leg. Not out of mercy, simply because he did not think the man would survive another stab to the chest like Nechtan had done to him.

The days passed rapidly and Csanád ordered his human thralls to tend to Iuliu. 'He is to live!' was his explicit order. Despite how completely these thralls were mesmerised – so much so that they barely even understood the fact that they were still human – the tone of this order managed to penetrate their weak minds and they knew that it carried an implicit threat. *If he dies, then so too do you ...*

Csanád did not step foot within the dungeon again until the tenth day after initiating the change in Iuliu. Over these 10 days he experienced the burgeoning connection between his mind and the swiftly recovering Iuliu's. Gone were the days when Iuliu's mind was a closed book from Csanád, their connection was burgeoning! It was not until the tenth day, when Iuliu finally experienced the Ancestral Memories that Csanád looked upon his newly changed 'son' for the first time.

There was a drastic difference between how Csanád and Iuliu had reacted to the affliction that changed them – that elevated them above the mortality of pathetic humans. Csanád had embraced this nature, he even grew to be thankful to his father for granting him such a gift – but not Iuliu ... After awakening from the Ancestral Memories, disturbed by one of the thralls who had arrived to tend to his (now fully healed) wounds – Iuliu lashed out in a rage. He beat the poor thrall to a bloody pulp, drinking deep of his blood before stealing out of the opened doorway of the dungeon with the intention of fleeing.

Csanád could sense these thoughts and smiled to himself.

'Ever headstrong, my son,' he projected into the mind

of Iuliu as he raced for an exit to the fortress.

Ignoring the bait, Iuliu continued in his mad rush to flee, killing several more thralls who had the misfortune of being in his way. Enough was enough for Csanád. The spectacle had lost its enjoyment. The first thrall was fine – gratis – but losing the rest was a tedium he did not appreciate. Thralls did not simply grow on trees …

The chasm between the power of a newly changed strix (or strigoi …) and that of his father (his master …) was put on eminent display at this moment. Csanád dashed towards Iuliu, like a blur in the deep shadows of the darkened fortress. With one powerful backhanded swipe, he clattered Iuliu to the ground. The blow would have knocked the head clean off an ordinary human, it was only the hardy anatomy of these creatures that allowed Iuliu to live.

Csanád dragged Iuliu to his feet and in his unbridled anger at the situation, he leant in and tore a ravaged chunk out of his throat using his teeth. It was not an act that he often performed. Traditionally Csanád favoured the smooth flow of blood that could be acquired by a gash to the throat with a blade. Strix were not like the folklore suggested. They did not have 'fangs' with which they punctured an artery and supped. This idea simply perpetuated from the fact that they placed their mouths to existing wounds before feeding on the lifeblood of their victims.

With the ragged wound in his throat, Iuliu floundered under the supreme power of his 'father'. It was at this moment that Csanád discovered something completely unexpected ... The blood of another strix was exquisite – it was utterly divine! It took all of his willpower to stop himself from drinking every last drop from Iuliu's body. *Would that kill him?* He realised he did not know the answer to this question, and he did not desire to risk it ...

Twenty-Six

The idea of keeping Iuliu as an enthralled slave changed very quickly for Csanád. For starters, he was unable to dominate the mind of his progeny as he could with his human thralls and animal familiars. Whether it was because Iuliu was in some way different, or simply the fact that a strix could not control another strix – Csanád did not know. But he also no longer cared. Having discovered the sweet nectar coursing through Iuliu's veins, his priorities shifted. He became addicted, and for many years the lot in life for Iuliu was to remain shackled in the depths of Csanád's stronghold as his personal drinking fountain.

Despite Iuliu's stunted existence, the physiology of his species was burgeoning within him. He grew large and strong. The man who was once a scrawny street urchin had become a massive monster like his father – but this did nothing to help his situation. It burnt him up inside that he was seemingly eternally bound to this creature, and there was absolutely nothing he could do about it. He had tried banging his head against the hard stone walls of his dungeon – seeking the freedom of death, but his body would not grant him his wish. After knocking himself unconscious, his inbuilt regenerative abilities would heal him of his wounds and leave him back where he started.

Taking a different approach, Iuliu instead attempted to goad Csanád into killing him himself. One day when Csanád arrived for his daily sustenance Iuliu successfully managed to enrage him by labelling him a coward.

'You are lucky that you have me bound, "Father"! I have grown strong and you would fall before me now!' he said.

He hoped to sufficiently anger Csanád into killing him, but instead it had a different effect. Csanád rose to the bait and instead unshackled him, saying: 'Now is your chance, "boy" – let us see what you are made of …'

Csanád was supremely confident in his skills and power, and for good reason. It had been centuries since he had experienced any sort of true contest and he desired a good fight. Unfortunately for both of them, this was not bound to be a contest at all. Csanád was far too powerful, and the 'fight' was as brief as it was demoralising for Iuliu. It ended with Csanád once more draining him deep, shackling him back into his sturdy restraints, and leaving him to ponder his sorry existence.

Iuliu knew that any attempt to overpower Csanád

was a fool's errand. The monster was unfathomably powerful. He slumped against the wall, manacled in place and unable to so much as walk around and stretch his legs. The despondency that he felt at this moment was remarkable, and he looked back on his life in an attempt to figure out how he had gotten to where he was …

Obviously, he had attacked the wrong person (thing …) that fateful night back in Orăştie, but there was more to it than that. A series of choices throughout his life that he seemed to get wrong at every crossroads. When presented with the opportunity to apprentice under a master carpenter, he spent three weeks on the job before getting fed up with the hard work and never hammering another nail again. When he had a good thing going with a pretty wench from the tavern, he was too rough as he beat her, and she left him. These and a hundred other bad decisions left him as little more than a thieving gutter rat.

Life on the street suited him better. He had guile and animalistic cunning, and these served him well right up until the moment that they backfired when he attacked Csanád. Robbing and even killing people for their spoils had kept him alive, and his eyes lit up with the profit he would make from taking down this new noble casually strolling through the dark streets. How wrong he had been.

Returning to his current position, manacled in the monster's dungeon in the wake of a demoralising beating, he knew that he would never manage to escape his fate through power alone. At least, not for many decades or even centuries. Csanád was simply too old, too powerful, too proud. *But could his pride serve as his downfall?* The cunning and guile that had served Iuliu well throughout his life on the streets might be able to come to his rescue now …

But how? How could he possibly overcome his 'father'? And even if he did miraculously manage to slip his cuffs – *could he chew off his hands? would they regrow?* – then he was still trapped by the accursed mental link shared between two strigoi as a result of the change. Until he could figure out a solution to this final problem, then there would be no point whatsoever even entertaining the idea of escape.

Iuliu was no stranger to falling into melancholy during his long and lonely time spent shackled. Aside from Csanád arriving once daily to sup on his blood and providing him the merest cup of animal's blood with which to regenerate his strength – he would spend the rest of the time in utter solitude. In his latest bout of depression, Iuliu's mind returned to that first night he was unfortunate enough to cross paths with the sadistic monster who now owned his soul.

Csanád was furious about something … He kept asking Iuliu questions about how he was able to close off his mind; but Iuliu did not comprehend what he meant (and was tortured to the brink of death for his ignorance). Now, as a strigoi himself, he had developed a deep comprehension of the mysticism with which his father was raping his mind – but he still was not aware of how he had somehow resisted the mental advances of the creature when he was merely human himself.

Over the span of what would be months – Iuliu latched onto this idea as a potential solution to his final problem. If he could somehow orchestrate an escape from his situation – could he then figure out a way to hide his mind in order for him to stay hidden? His biggest problem, as far as he could see it, was that even if he managed to figure out how to shield his mind sufficiently to sever the link between himself and his 'father' – how would he even know whether it was working or not? It was a massive gamble.

From this moment, each time that Csanád maintained his rigid schedule of sating his bloodlust on the thick juices running through Iuliu's veins – Iuliu would test the control of his mystical 'shields'. He would fire mental barbs into Csanád's head, goading him (and getting beaten to a pulp for his troubles), until one day – it happened …

He hurled a mental insult at Csanád, and his 'father' ignored him – it was as if he didn't hear a thing. Iuliu was certain of this, because the beast was never one to shy away from such a comment and took a sick pleasure in exacting brutal amounts of pain in revenge. *Had he finally found a shield for his mind?* One that prevented even his own projected mysticism from escaping?

Iuliu continued his experiments for many a week – desperate to ensure that he was not falling into a trap of the wily old strigoi – but finally he was certain, he had achieved the impossible – his mind was his own again!

Exhumed

With this step of his plan completed – Iuliu was still left with the more daunting task of finding a way out of his interminable situation. The guile that had served him well as a cutthroat during his human life once more came to his aid now. Over many months, he managed to manipulate Csanád into allowing him to sup from one of his human thralls in order to regain his strength.

'But "Father" …' the meek imprisoned son would say, ' …just think how much better my blood would taste if I were healthy myself! I have not resisted you for many moons, allow me this one small concession …'

Csanád did not possess a single shred of empathy. He could not care less if Iuliu were healthy or happy – but the idea of his blood tasting even better was enough to pique his interest. Fortunately for Iuliu, his gambit bore fruit. Csanád liked the outcome and soon, Iuliu was permitted to feast from his human thralls under the warning that he must drink scarcely – if any thrall were to die then he would be back to rats' blood.

Finally, things began to fall into place for Iuliu. Not only was he able to regain some of the strength that was his right as a strigoi – but he was also able to further his plan of escape. Csanád did not bother supervising the thralls he sent to feed Iuliu – that would be a waste of his time, beneath him – but it would also be the mistake that Iuliu required.

He required the patience of a saint (which he was very much not and would frequently fall into fits of rage when left alone), but he finally managed to overcome the mesmerism holding this human in thrall to his 'father'.

Instead – he would serve only Iuliu …

In the year 927 – after 13 years of imprisonment and servitude to his hateful 'father' – Iuliu was finally ready to enact his grand plan for escape. Night had fallen and for the first time in many a moon, Csanád had left his stronghold in search of the sport of the hunt. His mysticism had detected travellers lost in the mountain passes, and as he had so often done, he would terrorise them before stealing all they had to offer. Their wealth, their blood, their very lives.

Iuliu summoned his one undercover thrall and ordered him to find the key to his shackles. There was no reason for Csanád to jealously carry the key on his person – he was the king, the *God* of his own domain. It was inconceivable that anybody should disobey his desires. This pride worked in Iuliu's favour as he watched his thrall returning with the key in hand.

Freedom, finally, after all these years! Iuliu left the dungeon in which he had been shackled for the first time since the morning after he had awoken from his sleep of Ancestral Memories – and that was the moment all of his plans went out the window. He hadn't taken into account the link of Csanád's other thralls to their master. His other human slaves, the ones that Iuliu had not converted to his side, immediately panicked at the sight of him – and Csanád was able to sense their panic and scry through their eyes, discovering his son's escape in its earliest stage.

Iuliu had to act quick. He raced through the stronghold, brutally murdering all of the thralls that he encountered – drinking deep of their blood to bolster his

Exhumed

strength. He sought the armoury in order to find a weapon with which he might be able to defend himself — and as he progressed through the building, he also upturned all of the oil lamps, burning the lavish furnishings and framework of the structure. Even if he were to die in this attempt, he would make things as inconvenient as possible for Csanád!

He found the armoury just in time. Csanád had made such haste on his return to that it surprised even Iuliu himself. He thought he would be able to grab a weapon and disappear into the night — but he had been foolish and never even managed to make it out of the building itself. He exited the armoury carrying a lavish silver blade that stung to the touch, and when he stepped foot back into the corridor — even he with his supernatural physiology was reduced to a series of coughs from the fire that was spreading throughout the stronghold.

Csanád's furious roar rang through the halls and the sound of his approach grew steadily nearer. Iuliu leapt out of the nearest window, intending to race away into the darkness — but he found himself penned in by a pack of Csanád's strongest wolves. He slashed the silver blade wildly and cut down several of the fine beasts — but they had served to waylay him for long enough that his worst nightmare finally came true. Leaping from the window with an animalistic look of fury on his face, Csanád landed nearby and simply stared at him with such malice in his eyes that even Iuliu was forced to shiver.

'I don't know how you managed to escape,

"boy" – but I promise you that you will regret this mistake for the rest of your life! I am going to take great pleasure in cutting off your arms and your legs and sealing the wounds with a hot brand. Your only sustenance will be your own eyes, your nose, your genitals. I will make you resemble the maggot that you are!'

Iuliu knew that Csanád meant every word that he spoke – and that he was capable of fulfilling his threats. He had two choices ... Stand and fight, and probably lose ... *But he was armed with a silver sword, that should mean something, right?* Or attempt to lop his own head from his shoulders using the same silver blade before Csanád could capture him ... *Was that even possible?*

Csanád did not give him any more time to think – instead he simply leapt into action. The fact that he was unarmed against another strigoi wielding a silver blade was evidently the furthest concern on his mind. He was supremely confident in his own battle skills and the power differential between them – however he was not aware that Iuliu had regained far more of his strength than he let on over the past several months.

Catching Csanád by surprise, Iuliu pivoted from his initial attack and retaliated with a swipe of the silver blade, catching his 'father' across the back of his arm and enraging him into a roar of pain and frustration. Iuliu even began to think that he might stand a chance of surviving this encounter after all. He was much stronger himself now, and he was armed with a fine blade ... but he was mistaken for ever thinking he could compare to Csanád ...

Iuliu landed several more serious wounds on his 'father' before Csanád quickly managed to overwhelm his fledgling son and disarm him of his ornate silver blade. Iuliu glanced around in a panic trying to find any corner in which to flee, but he had no way out. In front of him was the leering and malicious grinning face of Csanád; hemming him in on either side were the remainder of the wolves, each with their hackles raised and a rumbling growl rolling out of their throats, and behind him was the burning ruins of his 'father's' stronghold.

★ ★ ★

Csanád glanced over Iuliu's shoulder at what had become of his home. He had lived in this region for centuries now and its loss hit him hard, but it served to remind him of his former wanderlust. He would need to seek new accommodation and what better reason than this for him to resume his meanderings north along the majesty of the Carpathian Mountains. But he couldn't do that with the burden of such a troublesome child as his constant prisoner. It was all well and good to keep him shackled – he was low effort and out of the way, but not any longer. He would have to forgo the sadistic threats and fantasies he harboured towards making Iuliu suffer – but he was not about to let him get off that easily.

With a thrust of his silver blade so quick that Iuliu did not have the time to so much as react – Csanád stabbed him through the chest and watched him fall immobile to the ground. His aim must have been true, penetrating Iuliu's heart, because his son was no longer capable of any movement. Conscious of the fact that he would need to find shelter before the rise of the sun, Csanád chose not to linger any longer. He parted with the final words to Iuliu:

'Alas but I cannot make you suffer any further, "boy". My parting gift to you is the sun! Live the remainder of your short life with the knowledge that there is no greater suffering for one of our kind than the spiteful glare of its rays …'

With this final taunt – Csanád strode away, leaving Iuliu pinned through the heart and immobilised to await his torturous demise as the sun crept over the horizon. From the enclosed safety of a cave in the mountains nearby – Csanád experienced the suffering and the severance of his connection to his former son as the morning sun arose across the sky.

A melancholic grin broke across his face, reminding him that it was the same fate that his own father Nechtan had intended for him. As night set at the end of this day, he returned to the ashes of his former stronghold to retrieve his fine silver blade and to examine the remains of Iuliu. All that remained was the burnt-out husk of his son lying where Csanád had left him – the blade still pressed through his chest.

★★★

Csanád was not mistaken with his thrust – the aim of his blade was true and Iuliu was destined to live out his remaining hours awaiting the morning sun. At least he would finally be put out of his misery, his 'father' would no longer be able to torment him. However, something that he neither planned nor expected came next. The thrall that he had mesmerised away from Csanád and into his own service yet lived; he had somehow escaped the burning remains of the stronghold and now that the coast was clear he approached Iuliu as he lay impaled through the heart.

This thrall knew only a life of servitude. The instinctive reaction of his broken mind was to remove the blade and free his master. Iuliu could not believe his luck. With the blade removed from his chest he was suddenly free to move once again, he could disappear into the night a free man (strigoi)! But ... if he did that then Csanád would know. His 'father' would hunt him to the ends of the Earth if he knew that he was still alive ... *But how could he convince his 'father' that he was truly dead?*

Glancing towards the thrall – Iuliu grinned as an idea crossed his mind. He grabbed the mesmerised husk of a man and dragged him close, tearing into his throat and draining every last drop of his blood to replenish his own strength. Tossing the corpse to the ground, he picked up the silver blade and meticulously thrust it through the thrall's chest in the exact same way that he himself had been run through. Then he rushed inside the burning remains of the fortress and returned with some lamp oil.

After setting the corpse of his former thrall alight and watching it burn to a shrivelled husk of melting fats and bones – Iuliu stepped back to examine his handiwork. *Would Csanád notice that the corpse was not tall enough?* He couldn't be sure, but he could only hope not. There was one final piece of the plan that he required to do in order to sell the ruse – he needed to 'die'. Knowing his 'father' would sense the turmoil of his mind as the sun rose and would also sense the breaking of their mental connection when he 'died', Iuliu had to give him what he expected.

Nearby, behind a rocky outcrop, Iuliu hurriedly dug a hole and buried himself. He needed a means of avoiding the ravaging glare of the sunlight while keeping his mind where his 'father' expected it to be. Then, as the sun arose, Iuliu perpetuated his farce, feigning the torture that Csanád expected him to be feeling – before finally shielding his mind and severing his mental connection with the creature who made him entirely.

After sensing his 'father' examine 'his' corpse and then disappear into the night, Iuliu spent several more hours hiding in the hole that he had dug for himself. Finally, in a fashion that would later become deeply ingrained in the folklore for members of his kind, Iuliu crawled out from the grave he had dug for himself, emerging into the night a free 'man'.

Twenty-Seven

Csanád grasped the finely crafted silver blade and wrenched it from the chest of the burnt-out husk of his former son. It would be a shame to lose such a fine piece of weaponry – he had already lost so much as it was. Glancing around and taking in the location, he saw the now-gutted remains of his former home. It had fared just about as poorly as Iuliu himself. It took even Csanád by surprise to see the burnt and shrivelled body of what had formerly been a mighty strix lying at his feet. It served as a dreadful warning of what awaited even one as powerful as he if he allowed the bitter rays of the sun to ravage his body for too long. Even still – he never expected that Iuliu's whole body would burst into flames …

As he strode away from the corpse, Csanád fell into an introspective mood. He had lost his finest source of sustenance, as well as his thralls and his home. He would have to start over and it might be quite some time before he found himself as well situated as he had been here. Nevertheless, he was due for a change and the wonders of his physiology allowed him to retain his strength even after many moons without a steady intake of blood – unlike the pitiful humans who would wither and die of starvation.

Another thought that began crossing Csanád's mind as he marched east along the horizontal band of the Carpathian Mountains was the sudden desire to learn more about his affliction. He wanted to learn all there was to know about striges – with the express desire of somehow finding a balm that allowed him to once again feel the rays of the sun against his skin without the risk of self-immolation. That would be the dream …

★★★

Days turned into months turned into years as Csanád slowly traced his path east and then north following the mighty Carpathian Mountains. The eternal lifespan of a strix lent itself to a slow patience and he did not go out of his way to rush as he travelled. A steady supply of blood was never scarce for him, as there were always small towns to raid in the black of night, or travellers on the dangerous roads who would never reach their destination. He simply enjoyed the freedom of roaming and exploring the lands of his ancestral human family – however his biggest frustration was the constant search for shelter as each night drew to a close.

The wanderlust slowly morphed back into a desire to settle down, and in the year 1001 he found the ideal location to once more make his home. A fortification named Castrum Zotmar had been founded in the year 972 as a defensive fort against the perpetual turmoil in the region – but since this time it had drawn a significant number of settlers. In a stroke of serendipity, Csanád learnt this information from the mind of a wealthy travelling Bolyar that he had waylaid and killed on the road.

The noble had a considerable retinue of guards and servants, however they all fell before the mighty strix as he descended upon them from the mountains. Only the Bolyar yet lived as Csanád pilfered his blood and his mind alike. The term 'Bolyar' was not a title that Csanád had encountered in quite some time, not since crossing the mighty Danube River, however it gave him a cunning idea. He was now in possession of the wealth and finery of this noble … he could ride into town and simply declare himself the lord of this domain and force these peasants into serfdom under himself.

But – he could not use the term 'Bolyar', it would not be accepted in these lands. Instead, he settled on the more regionally appropriate term 'Boyar'. Unbeknownst to Csanád at this time – the term would outlive his appropriation in Transylvania. His own strict legacy of violence and dominance would spread and the title of Boyar would take hold throughout the territories of Wallachia and Moldavia in the 14th century and beyond.

Csanád travelled west from the Carpathian Mountains in the direction of Castrum Zotmar, which was now going by the name 'Szatmár'. As he rode on horseback leading his newly acquired wagon of wealth, he found what he considered to be the ideal location for his future fortress: a densely wooded offshoot of mountains within lording distance of the town itself. It would make a fine domain!

He explored these mountains and the woods therein and found some perfect dark shelters to bide his time. From experience, he knew all too well how long it would take for a new fortress to be built – but time was something that he had in abundance. Csanád then rode into Szatmár and simply declared himself their lord.

His finery, combined with his silver tongue and mysticism sufficed to win over the majority of the settlement immediately – however, he revelled in the fact that some pigheaded fools attempted to rebel. It meant that he was gifted an opportunity to provide a first-hand display of his dominance. A display so violent that nobody in town would even think of rebelling against him for generations to come. Before the horrified congregation of peasants, he tore out the throats of these rebels and let their blood wash over his face, drinking deep and showing the town his truly monstrous nature.

He had never before so publicly displayed his true self. At least – not with the intention of letting the witnesses survive. But he was violently proud of his nature, and he hated the fact that he had been hiding it for so many centuries. Now … now he would rule as the strix (or strigoi in their minds …) that he was. He simply needed to be careful and prevent any of these little people from ever leaving his domain and risking reprisal like his father must have done.

For this reason, his ever-present retainer of lupine familiars would be his wardens during the daylight hours. The moment he would sense any minds attempting to flee would be the moment his wolves herded them, before Csanád would arrive after nightfall to deliver their torturous punishment. Fortunately for all involved, these attempts to flee became scarce, as over time, even Csanád's wolves did not favour leaving the shade of his forested domain when the sun still shone.

He was no stranger to the realms of torture, but this latest form of execution he had devised pleased even himself. The looks on the faces of the peasants to see those who had attempted to flee impaled upon stakes told him all that he needed to know. He did not even need the use of his mysticism to read the thoughts going through their minds. They were abjectly terrified, and sufficiently cowed to follow his every command.

He was pleasantly surprised by how quickly he managed to domesticate Szatmár – but it came at a personal price. He could not feed from them. Doing so would weaken their number and also foster an inevitable rebellion - they knew that they were 'safe' as long as they lived by his commands. No, he would simply use them to grow his wealth while feeding off unfortunate folk travelling throughout the region.

Using slave labour populated by enthralled travellers, it took 13 years for construction on Csanád's castle to be completed. After it was finally constructed to his satisfaction, Csanád rode to Szatmár and declared:

'The forest surrounding my castle belongs to me. The penalty for trespassing on my domain shall be a violent death.'

To punctuate this threat, he tossed the heads of two of the enthralled slaves who had worked on the construction of his castle into the midst of the town. He continued: 'Pay me your taxes and you will be granted your lives in peace.'

With this, Csanád rode back to his new stronghold and there he remained. He lived up to his promise that the peasants would be allowed to live their lives so long as they obeyed his commands. Occasionally he was forced to make an example of folks who thought they could flee – but for the most part he simply fell back into legend as the generations passed by and the feeble lifetimes of the humans waned. He became known as 'the Old Wolf' – a moniker that pleased him.

★★★

It had been a great many years at this point since Csanád had tasted the sweet nectar of the blood from another strix. Given how headstrong his former son had been, he knew that it was simply not something that was possible for him to achieve until he was sufficiently settled. But now, finally, he was able to once more inflict the change on one of his unwitting thralls. He no longer cared about finding the 'right' person. It was a foolish concept. Any slave would do.

The intense pain of the blade entering his neck and scraping his spine as he changed his next 'son' was something that he had forgotten. He would have to find a better way of doing this, especially since he intended to change many more people in the years to come in order to experiment and learn about his condition. The names of these slaves did not even register in his memory. Only Iuliu would be remembered – his firstborn. The rest were simply food.

After the change had been completed on the first new strix he had created, Csanád supped deep and drained him completely of his blood. He was unable to restrain himself after having gone so long without the experience – however, it would also serve as an excellent experiment. *Could one such as he regenerate if they had nary a drop of blood flowing through their veins?* Csanád learnt that the answer was no – though it did not fully kill his new changeling. The lack of blood was akin to a staked heart, it immobilised him – but as soon as Csanád poured a cup of animal blood into the changeling's mouth then new life was rekindled within him.

Csanád developed a taste for experimentation after this moment. He crafted a syringe out of the hardened bone of one of his changelings and it was this syringe that he utilised to puncture his neck for the ingredients required to inflict his curse on unwitting victims. In the 11th century, medical 'science' did not exist to inform Csanád that the key ingredient he was working with was cerebrospinal fluid – but he did not need to understand or label his ingredient, all that mattered was that he knew how to extract it. The syringe still caused him pain; however, it was far less severe than pressing a blade all the way to his spine.

As it became more mundane and commonplace for Csanád to change innocent thralls – only ever allowing one changeling to remain alive at a time – he became more enamoured with the idea of how to prevent, or even cure the affliction. He enthralled one particular traveller and imbued his mind with the singular mission of travelling abroad and returning with any and all literature into the occult. His mind was a sponge and he wanted to learn.

These documents, by and large, turned out to be abject failures. After decades of study, he felt that he was making no progress, and in a fit of rage he struck his thrall with such force that his neck snapped and he collapsed to the ground where he was standing. Sending a mental call, his wolves swiftly arrived to dispose of the corpse in a way that only they knew best. The body did not last long ... It was in this way that Csanád disposed of all of his corpses when he was done with them.

★★★

It was not until the year 1097, some 83 years after settling in his new domain, that Csanád would discover a breakthrough in his endless research. He could not even count the number of 'children' that he had created over this time. He did not care to. All that mattered was that finally he had made progress in his studies.

He had collected a wealth of traditional local herbs that were known for their medicinal properties, and after a great deal of trial and error his first success was with Solanaceae plants. He had tried all sorts of local flora, but what he discovered with Solanaceae left him near speechless. It had somehow managed to reverse the change ... *Had he done it right?*

Csanád was so surprised by his findings that he tested them again and again. It was not a foolproof remedy, but it definitely worked occasionally. The entire concept of the plant mimicking the effects of the photochemical manufacture of vitamin D in the skin of the changelings was lost on Csanád. He wouldn't have cared even if he knew. The results were all that mattered.

Following this initial success, Csanád continued testing until such time as he had refined a solution that worked more often than it did not. There was one limiting factor that he discovered during all of this experimentation, however. That was the fact that seemingly *nothing* could cure a fully changed strix, and secondly, as soon as any changeling had consumed so much as a drop of blood, the change was cemented in their system. None of his remedies ever so much as suggested to be working in those instances.

Even more frustrating (and torturously painful for the 'test subjects') was that absolutely nothing he tried would protect a strix from direct sunlight. Many children were tossed out into the burning rays of the sun to face the same fate as his firstborn when the various balms and remedies he had created invariably failed. In a stroke of good fortune for Iuliu – these changelings did eventually self-combust under the rays of the sun. This left Csanád blissfully unaware of the ruse that had been perpetrated against him.

★ ★ ★

Over 100 years later, in the year 1220 – the curious minds of children kicked off a series of events that would eventually lead to the demise of the master strix. David, experiencing these events in vivid detail as he slept the sleep of Ancestral Memories, already understood all that was to come. He saw the children in their curiosity exploring the Boyar's forest. He experienced the sickening glee with which Csanád enjoyed the little girl being devoured by his wolves, and the decision he made later that evening, allowing Andrei's father to sacrifice himself to save his family.

★ ★ ★

The events flickered on kaleidoscopically and 21 more years passed, until the fateful return of Iuliu that would result in the entombment of Csanád. At this point, Csanád had been reigning over Szatmár for 240 years, and he was ready for a change. He had recently killed the latest in his long line of changelings and embraced the idea of continuing his perpetual march north along the lineament of the Carpathian Mountains. *If only he had acted sooner!*

It was thoughts such as these that plagued his mind for centuries in the perennial darkness to which he had been cursed. Never once did a thought of regret cross his mind for any of the actions he had performed. There were rivers of blood in his wake, and if he ever got free from his tomb there would be oceans more to come. Revenge dominated his thought process throughout all those long years. Bitter hatred that could not be understood by a mere human. The amplified emotions of a strix were a world apart, and the hatred he felt for both Iuliu and Andrei Albescu was enough to send shivers down the spine of anybody within proximity of the Carpathian Mountains.

Many times over the long, long years – Csanád could sense the minds of people approaching his vicinity. His mysticism was heavily muted as a result of the accursed spear-tip-cum-stake through his heart, so he was unable to call to them or hear their minds in any great detail. He just knew that they were there, which only served to enhance the torture he was experiencing in his solitude. The human mind is not suited to isolation, and neither for that matter is the mind of a strix. The tenuous grasp with which Csanád could claim 'sanity' even before his entombment was crossed during the eternity he spent alone with his mind. He became more volatile and dangerous. If he were to ever escape this situation then God help anyone who got in his way …

***

Csanád could sense the majesty of his power waning. His body was withering away and he was becoming a desiccated husk of his former self. After almost a millennium of honing his powers, this was a heavy burden to bear – however, it would also be his salvation … Eventually, his powerful muscles and dense bone structure had rotted to such a degree that the stake through his heart had simply fallen loose. It freed him from its hateful hold. He could move again! Whatever good that would do him locked in his casket.

With the feeble power he had left in him, he was

able to sense the mind of a woman hiking in the vicinity of his tomb. He cast his mysticism with the intention of ordering her to free him from his accursed situation, but he could only rage at his own weakness as he sensed her mind departing the area, leaving him to the solitude of his own company once more. Unbeknownst to Csanád at this point, he had sufficiently imprinted upon the mind of the student archaeologist Cristina Grigorcea. He would simply need to remain patient for another 10 years before she was granted permission to set up a dig site in the area.

※※※

With Cristina and her group of students poking around in his vicinity for months, Csanád spent this time studying their language. He didn't need months – but he had nothing better to do as he waited impatiently. The language was very different to the tongue that he had spoken back in the town of Szatmár, which was then part of the Kingdom of Hungary. He knew now that the borders had changed, and he was within a new domain named 'Romania', after which the language he was eavesdropping was named.

The elation felt by Csanád when he felt the jolt of his coffin being lifted out of the cave in which it had been buried was like none other. He had long since managed to free one arm from the vile silver chains that were binding him and once the lid was lifted, he immediately lashed out with the vestiges of his power, using his bony fingers to rake the throat of the closest person. The merest splash of arterial blood fell across his face and the sensation within was like an electric shock as he tasted it for the first time in a very long time.

It would take far longer for him to heal than he had ever experienced before – especially when the fools who had dug him out left his casket lid open for the evil rays of the sun to ravage his body until his mental orders (pleas?) had convinced those nearby to close the lid and save his life. He ravaged a doctor after being flown to the ECDC in another new nation named Sweden, drinking deep of his blood before a strange electrical weapon had rendered him powerless. With this deeper taste of blood, his regeneration finally kicked into effect.

Over the week that followed he slowly manipulated his way to being allowed more blood. He marvelled at the fact that they simply had the magical substance bagged and ready to go. Each fresh meal further bolstered his strength, fighting off an eternity of decay until the moment he finally orchestrated his escape. He was still not at full strength at this point, perhaps only halfway restored – but it was more than enough to handle the assortment of weak humans holding him under guard.

This futuristic world into which he had emerged intrigued him greatly, and he coveted all that it had to offer. Especially the blood doctor ... One such as he might hold the key to many of the mysteries that had remained unsolved for Csanád for his many centuries of existence ...

S.J. Patrick

Interlude 4

Maps of Eastern Europe

Eastern Europe circa 363

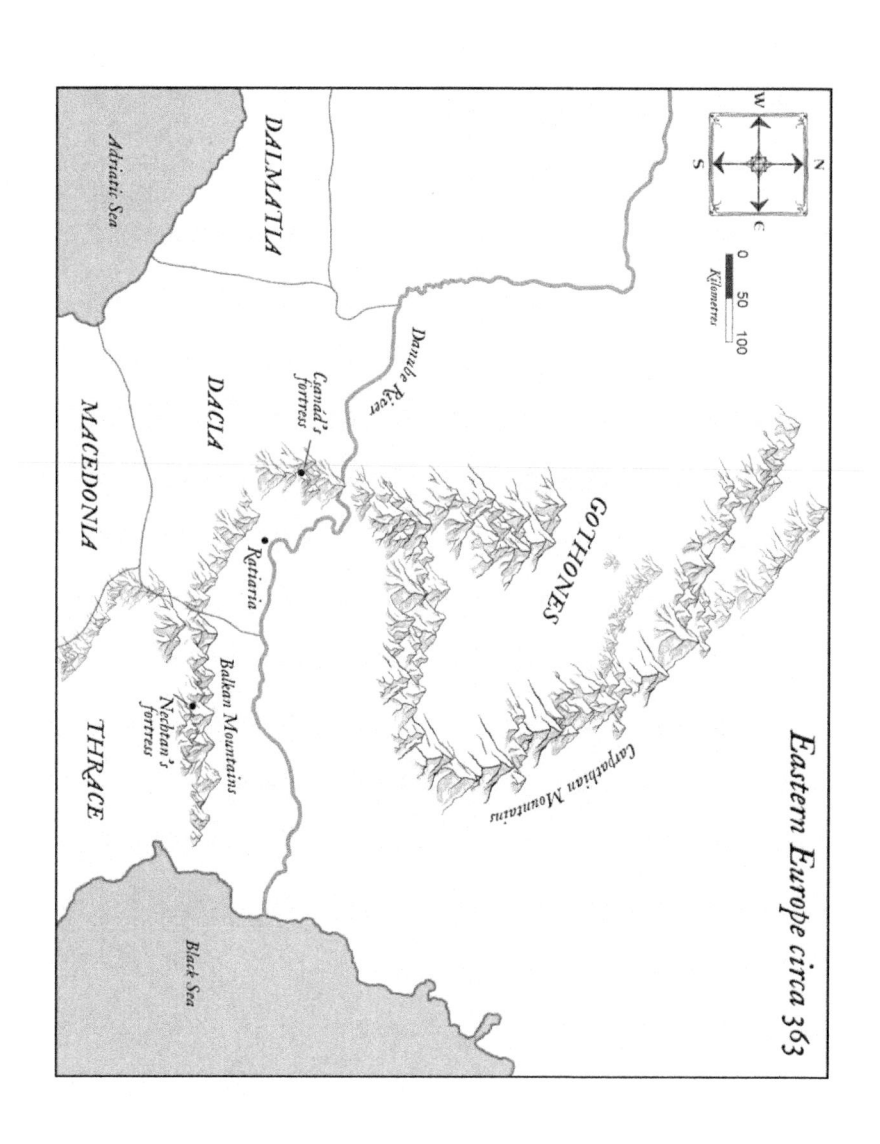

Eastern Europe circa 914

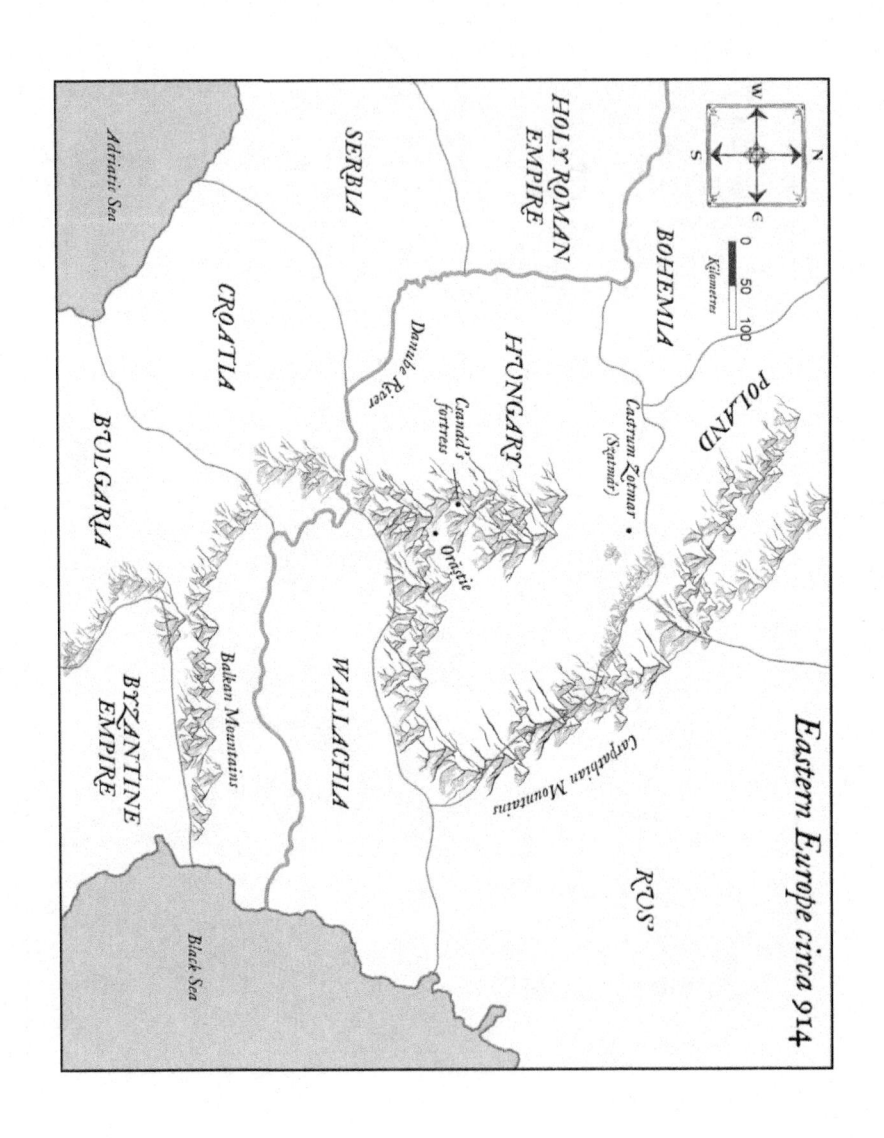

Eastern Europe (present day)

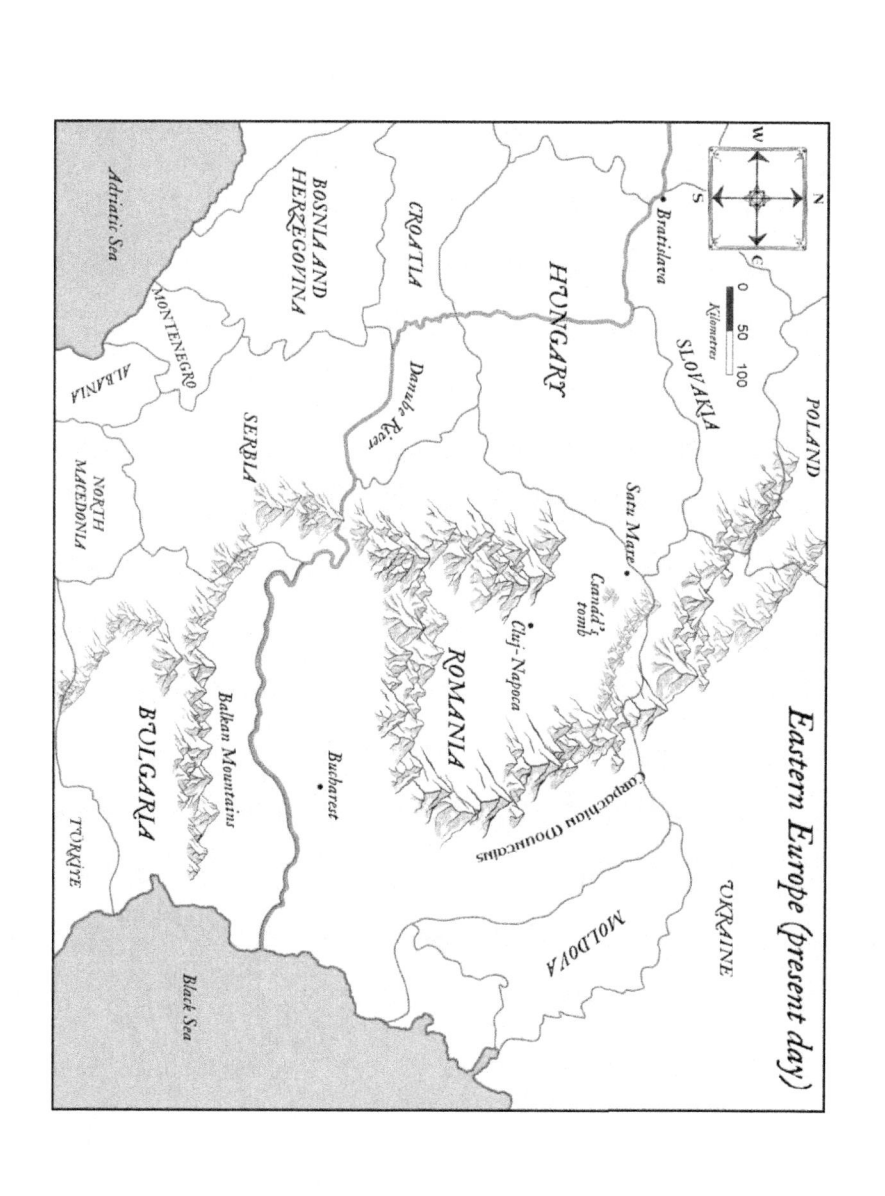

Bucharest

Present Day

Twenty-Eight

David awoke after more than eight hours of unbroken, unmoving sleep. The experience that he now knew as the Ancestral Memories (or at least that's what Csanád called it in his dreams) was one of the most jarring feelings of his life. It was like the soul had been vacuumed out of his body as he slept and transported back through time to live through a montage of the life of his 'father'.

Returning to reality was just as unsettling, when suddenly he found himself rocking softly in the back seat of a modern bus in transit to Bucharest – a city that did not even exist until long after Csanád had been entombed in the Carpathian Mountains. A fitting resting place, given they had been such a profound influence on his life …

Glancing at the little digital clock displaying the time in bright red numbers at the front of the bus, David saw that it was 4:30 in the morning. He should be arriving at Bucharest within about half an hour. As he was leaving Cluj-Napoca, he understood that it was likely a suicide mission to hurtle himself into the path of Csanád – but after experiencing the Ancestral Memories he realised just how true that was. He had *felt* first-hand the immensity of the power surging through his 'father', and it simply defied belief. As a doctor, David would never have even imagined that such levels could be possible in a creature of flesh and blood.

'Avem o scurtă întârziere. Ajungem pe la cinci patruzeci,' a voice announced over the intercom of the bus. The driver clearly didn't care about whether he woke the sleeping passengers.

David understood the words with crystal clarity. The penchant that vampires held with languages served him well. The bus was running about 40 minutes late. The news troubled him briefly. *How did a bus even get delayed 40 minutes when it was driving overnight?* Perhaps one of the scheduled stops took longer than anticipated while he was deeply asleep experiencing the life and times of Csanád. Nevertheless, he should be fine. He knew from the week he had already spent in Romania that the sun rose at around 6:30am. Cutting it close, but he should be fine ...

The situation was out of David's hands, so he could only wait until the bus arrived at its destination. He had plenty of things to think about along the way, none more so than how strongly he could *feel* the presence of Csanád disturbingly close by and getting closer by the minute. The bus's delay might actually prove favourable for him, as he didn't think that Csanád would risk making an attempt against him with the sun so close to creeping over the horizon.

This raised a troublesome point though — despite his drastically improved understanding of his own physiology and how to use some of his various powers, such as producing a mist from his pores — he had learnt that shielding one's mind from their maker was no small feat. It was unlikely he would be able to hide with any great success; he could only run the gamble that Csanád's priorities were focused on Iuliu rather than himself — and he thought that this was a very safe bet to make. Having experienced the literal centuries of malice and hatred as Csanád lamented from within his coffin — David thought he would barely rate a mention in his 'father's' priority list.

Thinking of Iuliu caused David to focus on another blip on his mental radar. In truth it was far more than a mere blip — the ESP signature he was detecting from what could only be Iuliu felt oppressively powerful. It had undertones of seething malice and only served to make David feel even more out of place, having so recently been cast into this supernatural world that he did not know existed until a week ago. He would have been perfectly content to have remained blissfully ignorant.

Unlike Csanád, who always viewed himself as an outsider and immediately embraced the change that coursed through him, gleefully using his power to butcher and feed indiscriminately — David still clung to a shred of his humanity. There had been a couple of close calls before he managed to satisfy the bloodlust within his system with the rancid rat blood, but for now at least, he was doing much better.

He had made it through almost nine hours in an enclosed space with a handful of people and the ever-present urge to tear into their throats was kept at bay. Granted, he slept most of that time, but even now after he awoke, he found himself capable of restraining himself. It wouldn't last forever though – he learnt that abundantly from the Ancestral Memories. He would have to do something about getting more blood into his system before too long – before his humanity faded, only to be replaced by the monster within him. Perhaps he could use his ESP and medical knowledge to bluff his way into a hospital and get his hand on a unit of blood that way …

Time continued to pass and David found his eyes continually drawn towards the little red LED numbers of the clock on the bus. When 5:40am ticked over and they had not yet arrived, he began to feel the pang of nerves charging through his system. Despite the fact that he had survived several minutes in the sunlight after fleeing from Gabriela and the Watchers a couple of days earlier, he was conscious of the fact that his condition had progressed in leaps and bounds since that moment. Feeding himself on the rats' blood and experiencing the sleep of Ancestral Memories had cemented the change in his system.

David felt a wave of great relief as the he finally

spotted the bright lights of the capital city drawing nearer. It was 6:01am when the bus finally arrived at Bucharest train station, and the darkness of night had already faded to the fuzzy morning glow of dawn. The sun had not yet crested the horizon and would not do so for roughly half an hour, so he still had a limited amount of time to find shelter from the coming day.

Moving with purpose, David was the first person (he still considered himself a person) off the bus. He glanced around furtively until he spotted what he was looking for – the bright neon lights that suggested accommodation was available at a budget chain he was abundantly familiar with – Ibis. Racing inside, David felt a surge of relief rush through his body to have a roof over his head before the sun managed to crest any higher. The room itself cost 140 Romanian leu per night. He converted it in his head to the currency he was most familiar with and realised that it was a mere $45 Australian. He had enough money left over from the person he had robbed in Cluj-Napoca for three nights, and he booked them all up front. He could use his ESP to steal more money any time …

After using the cheap plastic key card to let himself into his even cheaper room, David immediately grew impatient. This impatience quickly turned to an anger far more profound than should be possible for such a minor inconvenience. His vampiric emotions only functioned in extremes. *How on earth had Csanád dealt with centuries entombed?* He'd been here for 15 minutes and the prospect of waiting 12 more hours seemed impossible.

To curtail his impatience and boredom, David rushed into the corridor of the hotel when he heard somebody walking outside. He couldn't even tell if it was his ESP or simply his enhanced physical hearing that drew his attention towards them – it didn't matter. The noise was coming from a member of the hotel housekeeping staff pushing a little trolley of assorted items for the rooms. She jumped as David slammed the door open before releasing a nervous laugh as she saw David himself. *She wouldn't be laughing if she knew what I really was ...* David thought.

He made eye contact with her, which allowed him to mesmerise her through his gaze. It was almost horrifying how much power he had over people when he wanted to exert it. For now – all he wanted was her smartphone. He needed to do some research throughout the day so that he had a plan as soon as the sun set and his newfound domain of darkness swept over the city.

Her eyes were dull as she mindlessly reached into the pouch of her apron to fish out her phone in what almost felt like slow motion. David was not watching her movements, but instead found his gaze fixated upon that of her neck. He could see the pulse of her jugular vein, pounding more rapidly as her body experienced the stress of the situation she found herself in. *How easily he could take her by the throat and drag her into his room ...*

David had mesmerised this innocent woman, and she would have no recollection of the encounter or where she lost her mobile phone – but he, too, was mesmerised in return. He realised with crystal clarity just why it had been so easy for Csanád to succumb to his monstrous nature and abandon all semblance of his humanity. It was undeniable – they now stood above humans on the food chain ... Almost without any conscious thought, David's hand reached towards the housekeeper with malicious intent – all of these thoughts occurring in the span of no more than several seconds, but fortunately for her, David regained control of his actions as she reached out to hand him her phone.

That was too close ... He rushed back to his room and closed the door behind him, leaving the poor woman to recover her wits in his absence. In her mind she had simply been away with the fairies. She recalled nothing and would go about her day for several hours before so much as discovering that she had 'misplaced' her phone.

With the door safely closed behind him, David could feel the adrenaline surging through his system. He felt a well of despair build within him as he realised that his good intentions could only go so far – sooner or later he was bound to fall victim to his urges. He had to put an end to this. To somehow wipe out Csanád and Iuliu before simply taking a stroll into the sunlight himself. It was that, or ... No – there was no or. Although something sinister deep in his subconscious mockingly questioned his resolve. *We'll see*, it said.

Almost compulsively, David strode to the curtains and pulled them fully closed. A small sliver of sunlight had crept its way inside and it offended his senses. He then finally slumped into the appallingly uncomfortable couch in his room and pulled out the phone he had just stolen. Fortunately for David, it was not locked, he simply needed to swipe the screen and the phone flitted into life. From there his first port of call was to Google Bucharest for any breaking news. There would be no better way of determining whether Csanád had made any movements yet – and as it turned out, he had ...

In scenes similar to those at Stockholm, when Csanád had assaulted the hospital in an attempt to kill David as he recovered, so too had he launched a violent attack on the Royal Hospital Bucharest. This time, three people were killed as an 'unknown assailant' stormed the hospital and absconded with a cooler filled with multiple units of blood. *The bastard got there first!* However, David wouldn't have gone with the smash-and-grab approach – he had intended to use his ESP for such a mission. Not any longer. The Royal Hospital Bucharest and all others within the city had extensively bolstered security over concern about the ongoing 'terror' threats.

David wondered whether Csanád had been so brazen intentionally in order to screw him over and prevent him from being able to do the same thing. Probably not. He was just like a bull in a china shop and did not possess the patience or ethical concerns about the human lives that he was leaving in his wake. Why would he after centuries and literally thousands of murders in his past? *Was it murder if they were not the same species?*

The news of the hospital turned David's mind back towards Maja in Sweden. He would have dearly loved to be able to contact her right now, but he did not have her mobile number. Calling the ECDC and trying to contact her that way was out of the question because he had no intention of being tracked – it would be too dangerous for all involved if any humans tried to get mixed up in all of this crazy business.

Turning his mind back to the plans he had made while he was still skulking through the sewers of Cluj-Napoca half a country away – David keyed in a new search into the web browser on his stolen phone. He was searching for the nearest universities and was pleased to discover that the most suitable candidate was only a few minutes' walk away from where he was presently located. He was still thinking about the colloidal silver and how he might be able to weaponise it in the fight against Csanád and Iuliu.

After nightfall he would break into the university, using his ESP where necessary to gain access to the chemistry department. From there he should find all that he needed. He just had to somehow make sure that he did not allow himself to fall victim to his own nature in the meantime and attack any innocent humans. *But how could he satisfy his bloodlust now?* Csanád's raid meant that hospitals were not an option, and Google informed him that there were no abattoirs anywhere nearby. His only option if he wanted fresh blood was hunting some kind of animal after night fell …

In the meantime, David ordered room service: Steak, extra blue. He didn't care what the chefs thought about him ordering such a strange meal for breakfast – he simply picked it up with his hands and tore into it like an animal. The taste was actually somewhat bearable unlike most of the normal foods he had eaten back with the Watchers in Cluj-Napoca when his change was still progressing. It even went so far as slightly curbing his bloodlust. He knew better than anyone that the red liquid oozing onto his hands and dripping to the floor was not blood – but he didn't care, his alien body was satisfied and that was all that mattered.

By the time he was done with his 'bloody' breakfast, David glanced at the clock on his stolen phone and saw that it was still only 9:00am, he would have to wait nine whole hours before night fell. It was interminable, and after having slept the sleep of the dead on the bus trip he was in no way tired. Getting through the day would be torture …

Caution gave way to boredom for David as he began experimenting with his ESP. The connection he felt to his father was very strong, and David was even able to sense his dark mood from nearby. The monster had a cooler full of blood – *what did he have to be so annoyed about?* This last thought by David betrayed him. Since he had established a connection with his 'father's' mind, he effectively transmitted those words straight into Csanád's head, unwittingly initiating a dialogue that he was not ready for in the slightest.

'Why have you followed me to Bucharest, my son? If you are so eager to die then I promise you that stepping into the sun right now will be less painful than what I will do if you get in my way!' said Csanád into David's mind.

The Ancestral Memories that David had experienced reassured him that vampires cannot read

Exhumed

each others' minds, even with the bond between maker and progeny. But they could most assuredly empathically sense the emotions coursing through one another. The malice that David felt as these words crept into his mind was like nothing he could have imagined. That crawling feeling told him all that he needed to know. Csanád was here to settle his grudge with Iuliu. David was small fry, but one that would gleefully be squashed if he overstepped his bounds and got in the way.

It was too dangerous to maintain this mental connection, he couldn't risk anymore stray thoughts projecting to his 'father'. Without replying, he concentrated all of his will to severing the connection he had accidentally established, and he breathed a sigh of relief when he felt it break. He was in way over his head here …

For the rest of his daylight hours, David fastidiously avoided all mental contact with Csanád, but instead he set about the task of scrying the location of Iuliu. He was very careful to ensure he did not make the same mistake of accidentally establishing a direct mental contact, and by the time night fell he thought he might finally have some idea where his mysterious 'brother' might be located …

***

Iuliu was the furthest thing from a fool. After he had become aware of the troubling fact that his 'father' had somehow managed to gain freedom from what was supposed to be his eternal tomb – he had bolstered the already extensive security that he maintained to keep him safe during daylight hours. For long centuries, Iuliu had thought himself the sole remaining strigoi within Romania. He was aware of other strigoi in the wider world, having sensed them on the periphery of his mind, but not in his own backyard. Now, however, in addition to his 'father', there was another …

Had his fool of a 'father' produced another child? This thought seemed unlikely to him – he knew better than anybody how distrustful Csanád was of other strigoi, but what else could explain this other blip he could sense? It was so weak. It must be another fledgling creature of the night. He could feel this puny mind poking around at his periphery. The fool must have thought he was being so secretive. After over a millennium, nobody could rival Iuliu when it came to mysticism …

Iuliu smiled knowingly as he summoned a thrall to service his lust for blood.

Exhumed

Twenty-Nine

Watching the ambient light fade from behind the curtains covering his window, David paced back and forth with nervous energy. He had been cooped up in the box of his hotel room all day and he was ready to get back out into the world. There was scarcely anything to keep him occupied all day aside from his own thoughts and the rather terrible Romanian daytime TV.

The phone he had stolen from the poor housekeeper earlier that morning rang a couple of times when she realised it was missing. He didn't answer and very quickly reacted by removing the SIM card from the device. It could still connect to Wi-Fi so that was all he cared about. He also ordered another serving of the ultra-rare steak for a very early 'dinner' in an attempt to curb his monstrous appetites when he finally left his seclusion and re-emerged into a world filled with potential sources of food.

David's first port of call after night fell and he left the hotel was to make a beeline straight for the university that he had scoped out during his time cooped up inside. Though it was only a several-minute walk away, he quickly realised that he had underestimated the sheer hunger of his affliction. It was early evening on a weekend and the streets in the area were filled with life. It took all of his concentration to simply keep his eyes down at his feet and ignore the all-you-can-eat buffet going about their lives in blissful ignorance around him.

The main building of the University of Bucharest loomed ahead as David arrived on campus. It was an imposing structure that was far older than any building he had encountered in his home country of Australia. With his newfound penchant for languages, the signs guided David towards the Faculty of Chemistry, which was his reason for visiting the university in the first place. As with almost any university campus, it was never completely devoid of life and the occasional student walked with purpose across the grounds, so David simply tried his best to act natural until such a time as he could orchestrate a break-in through a secluded window out of sight.

He was nervous of an alarm sounding, but not particularly surprised when no such sirens wailed into the night. Wasting no time, he leapt through the window that he had shattered and scurried through the dark corridors of the building. One of the biggest benefits to his vampirism was that he did not need to turn on any lights to see, his night vision was perfect. It should let him go unnoticed so long as nobody heard the short clatter of broken glass and decided to investigate. He could only hope he would get lucky in that department.

Despite being a medical doctor by profession, David was no stranger to chemistry or chemistry laboratories. The two professions went hand in hand and for the first time since being whisked out of Australia however many days (or lifetimes) ago, he felt at home. Even the time that he had spent 'performing medicine' at the ECDC did not feel natural given the nature of his subject. Well, things had changed now. He was currently breaking and entering a lab in a foreign country with the intention of crafting vampire-killing concoctions – and it just felt right.

It was all going smoothly, too. He had filled a small bag with various ingredients and pieces of equipment and he was almost ready to make his exit when he was surprised by the lights turning on. He had become so enveloped with what he was doing that he had not heard the approaching footsteps or the minds that accompanied them. He turned like a child caught with his hand in the cookie jar and found himself face to face with a pair of campus security guards blocking his path from exiting the lab.

These guards were the typical burly bullying type. A snarl broke out across David's face as they began yelling at him in coarse and angry Romanian. Two puny humans were nothing for him to worry about – however he was now sensing their minds and he could read the level of fear and panic bubbling in the smaller guard's emotions. David made a move towards them and the smaller one reached for his holstered pistol like he was taking part in a Wild West duel. Even with the speed and grace with which David could now move, he was not fast enough and found himself staring down the barrel of a gun.

David knew that gunshots would not be fatal for him – he had already survived and healed from a silver bullet, and it packed far more of a punch than the regular bullets here. But even knowing this – he did not fancy the idea of getting shot again. For starters there was the pain – but most importantly he knew that it would trigger his violent urges and he didn't know if he'd be able to restrain himself from fighting back and killing these men. In addition, he would also need a fresh supply of blood to ensure that he healed in time for his showdown with Csanád.

Acting quickly, David managed to make eye contact with the frantic and panicking guard and the soothing waves of his hypnotic ESP flowed between them. In moments, this guard was silent and still like a statue, and David took the opportunity to close the gap and rush towards them. Seeing David make his move, the other guard also reached for his weapon – but this time David was much too fast. He clattered into the burly guard and sent him flying across the room like a ragdoll. This man, who must have weighed over 100 kilograms, was knocked immediately unconscious and David had the sickening feeling that perhaps he'd been too rough.

Exhumed

Had he killed him?

David grabbed the handguns from the two guards and tossed them into his little bag of goodies. He maintained the trance that he was holding the smaller guard under, keeping him in place as he went to check the pulse of the larger, unconscious guard. David was unsure of the emotions he was feeling when he confirmed that the guard was indeed still alive with a healthy heart rhythm. The human side of him was joyous, but the monster within him seemed almost disappointed and was urging for him to finish the job … Each throb of his pulse served only as a reminder of the fountain of lifeblood coursing through him.

Before he accidentally snapped and did the unthinkable, David somehow managed to repel his violent urges and dragged himself away from the two men. He knew that he needed to exit the university quickly, because he had no idea whether the guards had phoned the police when discovering him or whether they had just gone in guns cocked. It was probably the latter, but he couldn't afford the risk. After David had exited the chemistry lab, the statue of a guard that he had mesmerised was finally freed of his spell. The terror that gripped him removed all function to his legs and he collapsed to the floor with a spreading puddle of urine pooling beneath him.

Despite the setback, David was not altogether unhappy about his trip to the university. He had gotten his hands on everything that he had set out for, and he could take it all back to his room at the hotel where he would have the privacy to perform the somewhat elementary chemistry that he had in mind. It was fortunate that he didn't really need any of the high-tech lab equipment. It would help, of course, but he could make do without.

As David exited the building, now using the door from the inside, he thought he sensed something in the air and it immediately put him on edge. He wasn't sure what exactly it was that he was feeling. Despite having experienced the sleep of Ancestral Memories, there were still many things that were new to him and would take some time to get the feel of. If he had to describe it, he would say that it felt like there was almost an electric buzz in the air around him. It was almost certainly ESP – what his forebears would call 'mysticism' – but it felt different to anything he had experienced in his short life as a vampire.

The reality of the situation soon became abundantly clear to David. He was walking around the main building of the University of Bucharest in the direction of his hotel when he began to hear a clattering din of bats in the sky. He was no stranger to this sound, the bats around his home in Sydney would often fill the night air with cries just like this – but they usually congregated in the treetops rather than flying around the city centre. Something was strange here …

This strange feeling was not limited to just the bats – it was also almost like he was being watched. He was certain that both Csanád and Iuliu were keeping a 'mystical' eye on him, but this was different, it was like he was being physically watched. David felt a small wave of panic at this moment, thinking that perhaps one of the ancient vampires had sought him out to attack him in person – but no, he could still sense them like beacons in his mind and they were not anywhere near him ... *but were they closer to each other?*

In the span of a heartbeat, the chittering of the bats became a fully-fledged cacophony and David suddenly found himself engulfed in a dense black crowd of beating wings and raking claws. He had experienced something just like this one time before – during the Ancestral Memories of Csanád, and it became clear to him just what was happening. Iuliu had launched an attack on him using his vampiric wiles. While David was rooted in modernity, trying to develop scientific weapons – the ancient vampire had relied on a time-tested means of attack, summoning his familiars – *but what could he hope to accomplish with mere bats?*

The cruel bite of silver entering David's chest provided an immediate answer to his question. The bats had been mere distraction while several of Iuliu's human slaves had approached undetected to plunge the blade through his heart. *Had they succeeded?* He felt the bite of numerous blades entering him from the back and side as if he were being attacked in a targeted prison assassination, but to his overwhelming relief he found that he still maintained control over his senses and abilities – the blade had missed his heart, however narrowly.

Only a couple of days previously, David had been

shot in the arm by a silver bullet and had considered the pain to be like none other. He was mistaken. The pain he felt from this coordinated attack left him reeling. Could a mighty vampire like him really be taken down by the surprise attack of a few humans? *No ... he wouldn't let them take him down ... not yet!*

Dimly, David was aware of the screams of normal human bystanders who were watching this sudden and violent attempted murder. He could only imagine what the scene looked like from their perspective as a colony of bats descended on one person while a group of others wearing black and looking almost like ninjas plunged their blades into him repeatedly. *How would Csanád handle this situation?*

Despite that he loathed his 'father' from the bottom of his soul, there was no other choice for David right now than to follow his example. If he didn't, he was going to be killed right here and now without accomplishing anything he had set out to do. The two monsters – or at least whoever prevailed between them – would be allowed free rein over the world and who knows what kind of horror they could orchestrate.

David bellowed a roar that combined his pain and fury into one ear-splitting cry, much as Csanád had done way back in the 13th century when he too was beset by Iuliu's bats. The result now was exactly the same as it had been then. The fragile creatures with their hyper-sensitive hearing simply couldn't withstand the acoustic assault and they collapsed to the ground forming a black carpet around David and his human assailants. The thralls were also stunned into inaction by the power behind David's scream, and he used this to his advantage.

He could now see – and sense – clearly, without the blanket of bats clouding his head. There were four thralls, each armed with gleaming silver blades that had already performed a serious number on David's chest and back. He glanced down his body to see that his clothing was stained a deep and vibrant red – and this was when he knew that he would be left with no choice … he had to feed if he wanted to recover … Despite that he was still a young vampire and the traditional weaknesses applying to his species were less potent against him – nonetheless, this much damage from silver blades would not simply heal itself without a little help.

David reached out and grabbed the shirt of one of the thralls before they could recover and recommence their attack. He pulled the thrall towards him where his face collided with David's clenched fist, shattering his nose and resulting in a torrent of blood. David was not in a position to be picky; he lifted the thrall bodily and allowed the torrent of blood pouring from his nose to wash over his face and into his mouth. The sensation was *divine!* Human blood was like fine wine compared to the animal blood that he had limited himself to until now.

With his back to the wall of the university building, protecting himself from the remaining thralls, David allowed the blood to continue gushing from the first thrall's broken face. It was at this time that the angel of Gabriela re-emerged and prevented him from any further harm. He knew that it was his own subconscious mind talking, but 'Angel' Gabriela said: *'Okay, you've got your blood – now let these men go, they have already had their lives stolen from them once ...'*

The monster within David was sated. The blood was exquisite and he could already feel the wounds in his chest and back beginning to knit back together. It took mere seconds. *Think of the good that could come if scientists could properly study this regeneration ...* the old human side of David thought. The three remaining thralls finally galvanised back into action in a futile attempt to attack him. The angel of Gabriela had shocked David back into some sanity, and he could now see the look of abject terror in their eyes. They did not want to be here; they were like automatons being sent to their deaths by a cruel and capricious overlord.

Taking another page from Csanád's book, David tossed the body of the first thrall, who he was still holding in front of him, in such a way that he clattered against his remaining assailants. As they were distracted, he moved with the typical speed and grace that only one of his species was capable of, bending to grab his bag of chemistry supplies (and guns) and adding the silver blade of the first thrall to his ever-expanding loot.

People were taking pictures and videos – he would be all over the news in no time. He became aware of the sound of sirens growing ever louder. It was time for David to disappear into the night, and thankfully for him this was a skill that his kind were highly adept at doing.

★★★

Events went from bad to worse for Iuliu as he scried on his remote assault against the newcomer. He was still not even aware of David's name, but the fact that another strigoi had set foot in his domain and had been poking around mentally was an insult he would not stand for. As Iuliu scried though the eyes of his thralls, he scoffed at how weak and immature his victim was. It was more of a scouting mission than anything – an attempt to gauge the strength of his new foe. He would never bother sending such a meek force against Csanád – they would be obliterated in seconds.

As David managed to turn the tide, eliminating a whole colony of Iuliu's bats before injuring and immobilising his thralls – Iuliu's mind was suddenly torn back to his present location in the luxurious riverfront mansion in Bucharest's otherwise unassuming Șoseaua Nordului region. He had thought himself perfectly safe in his ultra-modern multi-million-dollar residence, especially since he could sense his 'father' in the distance – not yet making any move. However, his over-confidence was shattered by the sound of breaking glass through a second storey window, accompanied by the rapid spread of flames through his lavish mansion.

Iuliu roared in fury as the insignificant concerns about David vanished in a heartbeat, replaced by far more pressing issues.

Thirty

'Oh my God, that's David!' yelled Gabriela. She had been keeping a very keen eye on all news coming out of Bucharest ever since the story about the theft of blood from Royal Hospital Bucharest the previous night.

'So what ...?' replied Istvan with his typical dour countenance.

He had never liked David to begin with, and his pride had taken a severe hit with how badly he had been manhandled when he attempted to kill him before allowing him to flee.

'We've got to go to Bucharest and help him ...' Gabriela said.

She ended the statement with an upward inflection effectively turning it into a question, pleading her comrades to join her. The second she saw video of David under attack from the wave of bats and knife-wielding people she had already made up her mind that she was leaving – but it was a daunting task and she would feel so much better if her lifelong compatriots joined her. It was selfish and dangerous, but her eyes pleaded for them to join her nonetheless.

'What exactly could we do to help?' asked Marius – as pragmatic as ever.

His piercing question hit Gabriela like a swift blow because she simply didn't have a good answer for him. They had some silver blades, guns with silver bullets, and a meek assortment of other weapons that would mildly inconvenience strigoi – but after seeing even one as young as David overcome silver bullets – they knew how helpless they would find themselves against the ancient monsters that were Csanád and Iuliu.

Helplessly trying to find something to say in return, Gabriela was buoyed to hear the words: 'I'll join you!' from the youngest member of their group, Radu. However, he was immediately shot down by his father Marius who refused to entertain such a thing. Radu and Marius broke into a rapid-fire father–son argument, and Gabriela felt a large amount of guilt when the end result was that Radu would only relent if his father went in his stead. She hated causing such strife, but at the same time she was deeply relieved to have such a stoic ally by her side.

Decebal and Larisa would have nothing to do with it. The situation with David had scared the lives out of them. Gabriela could tell that Istvan was desperately searching for the words that he would stay behind – but his wounded pride eventually caused him to bitterly agree to join them. As it turned out, the same three Watchers who had journeyed north to Stockholm to keep an eye on the ECDC now all piled into the same tiny Dacia Sandero and set off to the south, driving through the night towards Bucharest.

★ ★ ★

David raced away from the University of Bucharest into the dark of night. The problem he faced, however, was that it wasn't overly dark at all. Like any major city, it was awash with lights that stopped him from simply disappearing into the blackness. It wasn't until he made his way into the densely treed Cișmigiu Gardens that he finally found a small amount of privacy from horrified onlooking eyes. He couldn't exactly blame them from staring and running away at the sight of him – he was absolutely soaked in blood. Back in his human days, he would have run away from someone like him too.

The blood coating his lower body was his own – it had flowed freely from the many stab wounds caused by the harsh bite of the silver blades. Fortunately, these wounds had now ceased their bloodletting and they barely even hurt anymore. At the rate he was going, they would be fully healed before he so much as made it back to his hotel. The blood on his upper body, including over his face, did not belong to him. It was the blood that had gushed out of the thrall's nose after David had broken it in self-defence. It was a far better fate than he might have expected from any other vampire in existence. The likes of Csanád would have torn his throat out in a heartbeat.

Exhumed

There had been several close calls up until this point, but David had managed to maintain his humanity. He had tasted his first human blood (*and it was exquisite!*) but he had still yet to cross the line and kill anybody. The angel of Gabriela on his shoulder as his de facto conscience was the only thing that had saved him tonight – and for this he would be eternally grateful. He was fighting the evil that was coursing through his system with all his power, but it was not a fight that any person had ever won before. Vampires, or strigoi, or strix, or lamia, or vrykolakas – whatever you wanted to call them – were by their very nature, evil creatures.

David could hear the sirens behind him back at the university from which he had just escaped. He had no doubt that the crowd of gossiping onlookers would be pointing the police in his general direction, which meant he couldn't afford to dally. It was at this point that he put one of his newly understood vampiric skills to the test. Concentrating deeply, he marvelled at the viscous white ooze of mist that began spilling out of his pores and spreading across the ground of the park in which he was hiding. Even with his profound medical knowledge, he still had no idea how his body was capable of such a feat. He knew it was related to the enlarged adrenal glands – but without a comprehensive study of the phenomenon it would have to remain a mystery to him.

His mist spread far and wide, and from within it he was able to sense the movements of anything the mist touched. He knew about this from 'experiencing' these sensations through Csanád's Ancestral Memories, but feeling it for himself was very surreal. It was like he had a million extensions of his body that were all sensitive to the finest of touches. It almost tickled. But David was not doing this for fun and games, it was vital for his plan to escape.

Sensing a jogger nearby, David scurried through the dark – his massive form obscured by the swirling mist. The jogger was wearing headphones and neither heard nor saw his approach. Once more David relied on the stealth of his mesmerism as opposed to the brute force he knew other members of his species would use. He robbed the unfortunate soul of his jogging clothes in order to replace his own bloodied rags. Thankfully, he had full control over his impulses and was not even tempted by the bare flesh of the man he was accosting. The human blood coursing through his system from earlier had brought him back to an even keel once again – however temporarily.

The loose-fitting jogging shorts and T-shirt actually made David look almost normal for the first time since he had shot up to his giant altitude of seven-feet plus. His final act within the misted park was to wash the dried blood from his face in the flowing stream before he was able to finally stroll back out into the night as if nothing had happened.

The police in Bucharest displayed nowhere near the response time that would have been required to capture David within the five-or-so minutes that he had spent in the forested confines of the park. He made his way back towards his crappy little hotel room and felt a palpable wave of relief wash over him as he shut the door behind him and dropped his bag of goodies to the floor. It had been a chaotic start to the night – but he had made it …

After arriving back to the (relative) safety of his hotel room, the first thing David did was strip out of his new jogging attire and climb into a long, scalding shower. His quick wash in the park had removed most of the visible blood and allowed him to blend into the anonymity of the bustling streets of Bucharest – but as he looked down, he could see a growing pool of pale pink water in the tub of his shower. He examined his wounds to see if the blood belonged to him, but they had long since healed without so much as leaving a scar – the blood had belonged to the thrall with the broken nose.

For a long while David simply allowed the hot water to run over him as he stood there reflecting on all that he'd become. The angel of Gabriela comprising his conscience had saved him again tonight – but how long would she be there to stop him from crossing the line? It was only a matter of time before he killed somebody, even if it happened to be by accident like the security guard he had slammed against the wall at the university. His strength was so great that fighting against humans was akin to a professional boxer pitting themselves against a toddler. The problem he was facing though, was that this same analogy could apply to himself and the two ancient vampires, only he was the toddler.

After what must have been over an hour, the hot water washing over David's skin began to lose its warmth.

He took this as a sign that it was finally time to emerge and begin to set his plans into motion. Before he did anything, however, he decided to check the local news again and see what was being reported about him. It was a shock to the system when he viewed himself from the perspective of the frightened onlookers. Two weeks prior, if he had been shown this picture, he wouldn't have even been able to recognise that it was himself he was looking at.

Strangely though – seeing himself splashed over the news was not the biggest concern on his mind. He spotted another news story that drew his attention – another terrorist attack right here in Bucharest. This time it was being reported as a targeted attack against a wealthy reclusive philanthropist by the name of 'Julius Drago VI'. *Iuliu Dragoş, obviously.*

For the first time, David actually began to wonder how an immortal (?) creature such as himself could manage to live throughout the years without being noticed. In ancient times it would have been easy, but now it would be noticed very quickly if somebody magically lived for centuries without ageing a day. It seemed like Iuliu had latched onto the simplest idea as a solution for this problem. Simply keep to oneself and every generation adopt the identity of his own 'son'. The fact that he was currently on his sixth iteration lined up with the time that public records became more prevalently maintained throughout the modern world.

David drew his mind back to what he was looking at on the news on his stolen phone. The home of this

'Julius Drago' had been firebombed by a concerted attack of Molotov cocktails. The Bucharest fire department had been on the scene for hours and were not optimistic about finding any survivors inside the (formerly) lavish mansion after the intensity of the flames that ravaged the building. These flames had even spread to neighbouring homes and the entire neighbourhood was effectively locked down with emergency services.

At this moment, David was certain of two things. The first was that such a simple plan would never work against one such as Iuliu. He would have remembered the fact that Csanád's peasants from Szatmár had attempted the same plot against him back in the 13th century. Even back then, Csanád had a bolthole to flee to in order to escape the flames. In this age of panic rooms, Iuliu would certainly have a means of escaping a threat such as this. The fact that Iuliu could still be sensed with his ESP only served to confirm his suspicions.

The second thing David was certain of was the fact that it had been Csanád who had orchestrated such an attack. However, Csanád himself had barely moved all night ... David's connection to his 'father' was stronger than ever now that he had the human blood circulating through his system, and he was certain that wherever Csanád was holed up, he had not left the vicinity since night had fallen. It could only mean that he had enthralled slaves to do the dirty work for him. The monster within David actually found it highly entertaining. It was like all the tables had been turned from the last time these two beasts encountered one another. Then, it had been Iuliu arriving into Csanád's domain, fostering unease, before initiating a final conflict.

But what would the final conflict be like this time?

The question troubled David. So much had changed in the world in the last 800 years, and Csanád had absolutely no moral or ethical boundaries. He would do anything and kill anyone in order to satisfy his dark desires. The only question was whether he had acquired enough modern knowledge to understand the sheer destructive capabilities possible in this day and age. The answer David would have rather avoided was that, yes, it was likely that he was abundantly aware of just such things. After all, he had orchestrated the firebombing with Molotov cocktails tonight …

Although he was unable to fully shield his mind from his 'father' like Iuliu had learnt to do (a feat that had taken him over a decade to master …), David did all in his power to minimise the contact between the two of them. The last thing he wanted was for Csanád to learn anything from his own emotions as he worked with the gear that he had stolen from the university's chemistry department. It would be his one and only ace in the hole, and if it failed, he was doomed – it was vital that it remained a secret until the last moment.

★ ★ ★

Unbeknownst to David, a mental conversation was taking place across the wide reaches of Bucharest. This conversation involved his 'father' and his 'brother'. After orchestrating the attack against Iuliu this evening, using several thralls that he had mesmerised into his service –

Csanád gloated: *This is but a taste of what lays in store, "my son" …*

Iuliu was incandescent with rage. He was safely clear of the ashes of his now former home, having escaped using a tunnel he had long ago crafted for just such an occurrence. Until now this contingency plan had almost seemed silly since he thought he was the sole remaining strigoi in Romania – but after the events of this evening he was satisfied at his prior planning. His fury was compounded threefold. First there was his failed attack on the newcomer. Then there was his destroyed mansion and the hateful glee that his father was feeling. Finally, however, there was a deep frustration directed inwardly at himself.

After having sensed Csanád for the first time a couple of days earlier, he had not been idle. He had laid a great many traps in the hope of ensnaring his 'father' if he tried to attack like a mad dog. In truth, that's exactly what Iuliu thought he would do. He had never known Csanád to be as calculating as he was being now. Within his household, Iuliu maintained a retinue of highly trained thralls. These thralls were armed with very high-tech anti-strigoi weapons. Machine-guns with silver bullets and UV laser sights were the centrepiece of the show, but they also had the standard silver blades to finish the job with a stab to the heart before removing the head.

Most of this hit squad had escaped through the emergency tunnel with Iuliu, so he still felt confident in his position. He was just furious at his own miscalculation. Using mysticism to mesmerise humans was trivial — but enthralling them to one's service took no short amount of time. Their minds had to be sufficiently broken. He did not anticipate that Csanád could accomplish it so quickly, but evidently his powers had continued to grow even after his long entombment. He would be as dangerous a foe as ever. Iuliu eventually replied to his 'father's' jibe:

'Do not think you have won, "Father". You know nothing of this world or my power within it. This time I will entomb you in such a way that the centuries you slept previously will seem but the blink of an eye!'

It was a bold threat, but Csanád replied:

'And this time I will make no mistake. I will watch the sun ravage your body until it melts into fat and bone. You will not escape your fate a second time!'

Nothing of any use was achieved in this back and forth. It was nothing more than the bitter and hateful bravado of two ancient monsters with a lifelong vendetta against each other. Neither of them even considered the fact that a third member of their species might play a part in the events that followed.

Thirty-One

The trip to Bucharest was fraught with nerves for Gabriela, Marius and Istvan. Unlike David who had to wait nine hours for the bus to deliver him from Cluj-Napoca to Bucharest, due to its frequent stops along the way – the drive by car only took around six hours. They arrived in Bucharest just as the sun was rising over the horizon, which allowed each of them to breathe a deep sigh of relief. The idea of arriving at a location with no less than three strigoi while it was still nighttime was not a pleasant thought.

Throughout the night they had driven in shifts, allowing the other members to get just a little bit of sleep under their belts. Given the nature of the monsters they were here to chase (and then what?) – it was important that they were as well rested as possible since they had to spend the hours of daylight in an attempt to try and somehow track down David. In one of the rare moments of conversation between them during the drive they had discussed just how this might be possible, but the solutions did not exactly flow freely.

Their plan was to travel to each of the sites where strigoi activity had been reported on the news – under the label of terrorism, of course. This meant visiting the hospital, the university, the district north of town – as well as one other location that had probably escaped the notice of most people. This final location was the site of a single act of murder, a body missing most of its blood … Shocking news in any normal time, but when there were assaults on hospitals and universities and the rich – then something as 'mundane' as this tended to sink out of notice.

It was obvious why this murder had drawn their attention. It was the same MO that they had tracked all the way down from Sweden. Csanád satisfying his hunger, even after all of the blood he had stolen from the hospital. At least they hoped it was Csanád and not David, but given the location on the other side of the city from where they knew David was located – based on seeing him on the news – they were confident it was not him.

The daylight passed with startling rapidity for the Watchers, and despite travelling far and wide across the city, visiting each of the sites that they had planned to do, they found no evidence that would lead them to David other than a general vicinity in which they thought he might be located. They rented a cheap room and hunkered down as the sun began to set and began to discuss their options. The overriding sentiment was 'Why are we here, what good can we achieve?'

To try and allay any further guilt at inaction, Gabriela opened her phone and dialled the police. Her phone was always set to private, so by keeping it short she should be able to provide an anonymous tip without having anything traced back to her. She tried with all of the passion in her soul to explain the fact that none of these attacks that had been occurring were related to 'terrorists', at least not as people thought of them. She blushed as she was laughed at and called a rube when she tried to explain that they were real monsters.

Gabriela hung up the phone in a huff, gracing the moronic person on the other end of the line with some choice Romanian insults before slumping in despondency. They could do nothing for the moment; they could only keep their ear to the ground and wait for something to happen throughout the city before trying to rush to the location ... Having settled on this 'plan', they all fell silent. It felt like the sword of Damocles was hanging over their heads and they were acutely aware that the odds were stacked against them. *What could the three of them possibly even do to help ...?*

★ ★ ★

David's body clock had finally begun to adjust to his new nocturnal lifestyle. He had completed his preparations shortly after getting out of the shower and when he saw that there were still over seven hours of daylight remaining, he decided to lay down and try to get some rest. It had been about 36 hours since he last slept and experienced the sleep of Ancestral Memories, and even though his crazy new physiology wasn't craving sleep — there was still enough of the human memory within him to desire it.

Sleep came quickly for David, drifting into a deep well of darkness — but it was not the wellspring of rest that he was hoping to achieve. Whatever it was within his system that craved blood and violence and death was not being satisfied when David was in charge of his body, so now it would take control while he slept. As a result, his subconscious mind was plagued with a series of violent and gruesome dreams where David was forced to live out all of the bloody fantasies of his vampiric side.

He couldn't even remember the last time he slept when he didn't experience troublesome dreams. It had to be weeks ago when he was still just a normal unknowing person back in Australia. Ever since he had first made eye contact with Csanád at the ECDC it was like his subconscious had been poisoned. It was only now, in his sleeping mind, that some neurons finally snapped in place and he realised why his sleep had been so troubled in those early — still human — days.

It was because Csanád was attempting to enthral him! He now knew that mesmerism was easily achieved — in the short term — but to make such a feat permanent required extensive brainwashing, and that was exactly what Csanád had been attempting to do. His 'father' had identified his skills as a 'blood doctor' and thought that he might be able to use them to his advantage. To continue his vile experimentations with the ultimate goal of discovering a way for one such as them to walk in the sunlight. Csanád wanted his own Doctor Frankenstein.

As David continued to dream, the angel of Gabriela that had accompanied him since he had fled from the Watchers back in Cluj-Napoca finally wound her way into his subconscious state. She was appalled at the actions of his dream self, who was butchering victims indiscriminately. The shock and revulsion that emanated from Gabriela felt so real, it was like she was actually there with him – and that was when he snapped awake from his dreams to realise, he was actually partially right.

'Gabriela …?' David said aloud, looking around his room as if he might find her hiding in the wardrobe or the tiny bathroom. It took several seconds before he was able to understand what he was actually feeling. For whatever reason, his mind had imprinted upon that of Gabriela, and now that she had closed the distance between them he could actually sense her somewhere out there in the city. *But what the hell was she doing here, was she crazy!?*

At the time that David jolted awake, Gabriela and the other Watchers were no more than a few minutes' walk away as they examined the scene of David's attack at the university. He felt an overwhelming urge to race out to meet them – but his accursed tormentor, the sun, was bearing down, which made such a desire impossible.

The enhanced emotions accompanying his affliction sent him into a fit of rage at the frustration he was feeling. She was so close, but here he was, completely helpless to do anything. If only he knew her phone number, but nobody remembers phone numbers anymore, they just get added to contacts lists and that's that. This feeling of utter uselessness during the daylight hours actually brought David to the understanding of just why other vampires use human thralls. *How else were they supposed to get anything done during the damn daytime?*

But therein was the problem for David. He had been refusing the truest nature of his condition by denying his body the satisfaction of an abundance of violence and murder. Imprisoning the minds of innocent victims and using them as slaves was actually worse than the alternative. It would be more merciful to simply kill them, because at least they would be out of their misery rather than in a waking nightmare. He recalled the look in the eyes of the thralls who had attacked him back at the university, and the unbridled fear that they were feeling as their bodies perpetuated the desires of their master.

But what if he could get some humans to help him consensually? The thought was almost nonsensical in its nature – but the small beacon of Gabriela's mind made him question whether it was possible. She had followed him here, even after all he had done back in Cluj-Napoca. *Maybe she was here to kill him?* Somehow, he didn't think this was true. While he did not yet possess the strength or skills to either read human minds or project his own thoughts into them at a distance (excepting his special connection with his 'father') – he could still detect the emotions behind the mind.

The emotions Gabriela felt right now did not

suggest that she was here on a mission of revenge … If only he could somehow get in contact with her, he might be able to guide her to the location of the other vampires and she might be able to burn them out during the daylight hours …

Even as he was thinking of this plan, David sensed the small light of Gabriela dwindling into the distance, clearly driving somewhere based on the speed at which she was moving. It troubled him that he could sense her heading straight towards Csanád. *Had she somehow discovered his location?* He couldn't help but realise the irony of his own concerns. Just moments earlier he was thinking of using her as a tool during the daylight hours, but now that it seemed almost like she was doing exactly what he wanted of her own volition, he was 'worried' about her safety.

But if he could give her the chemical weapons that he had crafted … This last thought cemented in David's mind how imperative it was for him to track down Gabriela as soon as he was freed from his prison of sunlight.

✦ ✦ ✦

Csanád had eventually disconnected his mind from that of Iuliu after growing bored of their back-and-forth of mental insults. He was still riding high on the elation of what he had accomplished, and the destruction of Iuliu's lavish mansion was only the tip of the iceberg. It was the appetiser before what would be the fell swoop that put an end to his 'son' once and for all. It was difficult for him to curtail the urge to race headlong towards Iuliu and ravage him then and there – he had to be smarter than that. For all his hatred of Iuliu, there was one thing he had to acknowledge – his 'son' was no fool.

Iuliu would expect him to act rashly, and would no doubt have countermeasures in place – especially after he had accidentally revealed his mind in his surprise at discovering the ancestor of Andrei Albescu yet living. Instead, Csanád thought it would be more fitting if he approached this more like Iuliu himself. He would take a page out of the history books and flip the scripts – see how Iuliu liked that ...

One thing troubled Csanád slightly, and that was the fact that Iuliu had not even made an attempt at hiding his mind after the destruction of his mansion. Csanád almost hoped he would because it would mean that he was running scared. There was no concern in Csanád's mind that if Iuliu hid himself, he would be lost forever.

Now that he knew about the ability to shield one's mind, and now that he had experimented with such a tool himself – he was confident that it would no longer work against him. That if he truly concentrated, he would be able to peek through the veil and discover the mind of his 'son'. The only reason he had not detected him all those centuries ago was a combination of ignorance and arrogance. He had no reason to suspect that such a thing was possible. Now though, the fact that Iuliu had left his mind open to discovery only told Csanád one thing – that he was laying a trap and waiting for his 'father' to run into it.

Run into it, he would ... But Csanád was not unprepared. He smiled one of his revolting inhuman grins as he considered all that he had accomplished in the short time since his arrival here in Bucharest. The thralls he had sent to firebomb Iuliu's home were just the start. They were expendable. His true strength lay in the fact that he had infiltrated the night shift of one of the offshoot police stations in the south of the city. These policemen would not answer any calls – they were undergoing the strictest of brainwashing by Csanád as he managed to completely enthral them in the span of a single night – a feat unheard of by any strix to Csanád's knowledge …

With these thralls also came access to weapons and armour. They would be his personal hit squad when he launched an attack on Iuliu. He would have liked a retainer of wolves like the old days, but finding such beasts was out of the question in the thrum of the city. He had something better than wolves, however. Having gleaned the scale of destruction capable in this modern world from the minds of his thralls – Csanád had ordered one of his policemen to visit the demolitions centre and abscond with explosive devices. He would live up to the title of 'terrorist' that he had been labelled in the news …

As the seedy pits of Csanád's mind swirled over his malevolent plans, he suddenly found himself distracted. Much like David before him, Csanád now sensed the arrival of Gabriela into his vicinity. The rage flared within him as he recalled the look on Andrei's face as he closed the coffin and condemned him to centuries of starvation and blackness – but this rage gave way to a twisted smile. If this woman wanted to die so badly, then who was he to deny her!

He considered sending his hit squad after her right then and there, but for now he needed them to maintain their cover. They were going about their everyday lives as normal people, many of whom were sleeping in preparation for what would likely be the final night of their lives. He decided that it was not worth risking them. This Albescu would be ripe for the picking after he had finished dealing with his errant son. No, his errant 'children'.

Csanád had learnt that blood doctors like David were a dime a dozen in this modern world. While David might be at the top of his field, he was still expendable. He would find another – one that had not been changed into a strix through a twist of fate – and using them he would continue his mad experiments in an attempt to reclaim the day. But that could all wait just one more night ... One violent, bloody night where he eliminated all that stood in his path ...

★ ★ ★

After the disconnection from the battle of insults with his 'father', Iuliu felt explosively angry. He had not experienced rage of this magnitude in many, many years. He had thought that this human world was his to feed upon. His and his alone. He had laid his roots so deep that he was able to sup on a limitless supply of fresh blood without raising even a shred of suspicion. As a result, the darkest side of his nature as a strigoi had been held in check. The blood had pacified him.

Now, with Csanád back in town, as well as

another interloper (who he was still unsure how they fit into the picture) — it was like everything he had worked a lifetime (many lifetimes …) to build was crumbling away. There was one thing he was certain of, however, and that was that he would not back down. He was not the mewling little baby of a strigoi that his 'father' had humiliated so badly all those centuries earlier. He was over 1000 years old himself! He could never face himself again if he turned tail and ran away, and he would always be looking over his shoulder and waiting for Csanád to somehow find him.

No … Csanád wanted his final showdown, and he would have it … Iuliu would make him live to regret the curse of fortune that had somehow allowed him to escape his bondage. What better location for their final showdown than right here in his bolthole. In truth, it was far more than a bolthole. It was a large factory warehouse in the industrial area of town, which Iuliu owned under a shell company — and it would forever hold a special place in his memory as the place that he eliminated his hated 'father' once and for all …

Thirty-Two

David glanced down at the ugly carpet in his hotel room, almost certain that he would see a path worn into it from his furious pacing back and forth. Ever since he had sensed Gabriela in the vicinity it was like time had slowed and the daylight hours had lasted an eternity. Throughout the day he had nervously traced her movements across the city of Bucharest, always anxious that he would feel a sudden pang of fear emanating from her if she got herself into trouble with Csanád or Iuliu – but thankfully no such occurrence ever eventuated.

After a few hours of circling the city, Gabriela finally settled in one place, and it was there that she remained. It could only be where she was planning to spend the night. After the beacon of her mind had remained stationary, and David was able to focus his attention towards her more easily, he was also able to discern the fact that there were two other minds present with her. Even though he hadn't imprinted upon them as he had done with Gabriela, David was reasonably confident that they were the minds of Marius and Istvan.

Thinking about Istvan raised David's blood pressure and threatened to send him into a fit of rage. The last time he had seen the little shit was when he was on the verge of tearing into his throat after Istvan had shot him in the arm with a silver bullet. David had suffered immeasurably from that bullet; he would love a bit of retribution … No … stop it … He had to free his mind from the destructive grip of the monster within him and focus on Gabriela. He would track them down as soon as night fell – and not for revenge, but for help …

There was a feeling pervading the ether within Bucharest. The calm before the storm. None of the humans would be any the wiser about it, but for David, he could feel it like an electric charge. Whatever conflict was going to happen between Csanád and Iuliu was going to take place sometime tonight. He had to make sure that he was there too, he couldn't allow for either of the ancient vampires to walk out of this. *But what would he do if his own plans failed?*

For the thousandth time, David checked his bag of goodies. He had liberated several bottles of silver nitrate from the university's chemistry department. The substance was a white powder that he had dissolved in water, forming his own solution of colloidal silver. It was not the same formula that was sold to gullible people in 'health' shops – it should be far more potent!

David had tested a few drops of the solution on his own skin and it had caused him a great deal of pain until he raced into the bathroom to wash himself clean. It was a promising sign. In his short life as a vampire, David had learnt that the severity of their weaknesses was intrinsically linked to their age. Whatever he experienced as side effects – they should be enhanced exponentially for creatures as old as Csanád and Iuliu. Even still – he felt anxious about his solution. It would effectively boil down to an 'acid' attack.

Aqueous silver nitrate had the benefit of being targeted to vampires too. While it wouldn't be a good idea for a human to bathe in the solution, it wouldn't react with their skin like other more potent acids – but it would when it came to vampires. It should completely debilitate them in agony, and the silver should sap them of their strength. Maybe – just maybe – this would craft enough of an opportunity for him to swoop in with his stolen silver blade and apply the finishing touches …

The sun finally dipped below the horizon and David wasted no time as he sprinted out of the lobby of his budget hotel. He got some weird looks from the reception staff, but he did not care in the slightest. He was wearing the jogger's gear that he had stolen the previous day, so they could just assume he was getting out for some vigorous nighttime exercise.

Using his ESP, David followed the beacon in his mind that was Gabriela. Running at a near superhuman speed, he found her location no more than 15 minutes later. His assumptions were correct, and she (they) were holed up in another crappy hotel chain just like he himself. Not bothering with reception, he let his senses guide him as he raced upstairs until eventually, he found himself standing in a bland hallway in front of room number 217. Stifling his nerves, he rapped against the door loudly.

From inside the room, a wave of nervous tension washed over David and he could physically hear the rapid-fire Romanian as the three Watchers looked around nervously.

'Gabriela, it's David!' he called through the door.

'DAVID!?' returned the female voice.

He could hear footsteps rushing towards him, but before she managed to open the door Istvan had grabbed her by the hand to hold her back. They broke out into a fierce discussion about whether it was safe or not and in his growing impatience, David called out:

'Please … if I meant you harm then this flimsy door would not stop me … I need your help …'

More rapid, hushed Romanian from the other side of the door. Why they bothered whispering was beyond David – he could hear their every word, but he forced himself to let the charade play out. If he did anything volatile, he could lose his only opportunity with them. Eventually the voice of Gabriela came back to him:

'Okay, I'm opening the door …' and from the background there was Istvan:

'Don't try anything, arsehole!'

The door cracked open, still connected to the flimsy little chain as Gabriela peeked out to see him. She then unhooked the chain from its housing and allowed the door to open fully. Seeing her face felt like a wave of comfort washing over him. It was bizarre how important she had become to him in the very short amount of time that he had known her. It could only be put down to the crazy emotions of vampires.

Meanwhile, on the other side of the door, David took in the faces of the three Watchers as they laid their eyes on him. A mixture of relief and awe from Gabriela, shock and caution from Marius, and fear and anger from Istvan. David could see that Istvan held a pistol in his hand, though wisely he was pointing it at the ground. David was unsure just how he might have reacted if he saw the little shit pointing the gun at him once more …

It was an awkward encounter to begin with – but thankfully the unflappable cheer of Gabriela was enough to sooth the tensions. To the horror of Istvan and Marius, she leapt forward and hugged David, looking almost like a child next to his massive height. Even David himself was taken aback, but after a second, he wrapped his arms around her in return. It was the first semblance of positivity that he had experienced in his life as a vampire – and it felt bloody good.

After she broke away from the hug, Gabriela looked David up and down, taking in his outfit and breaking out into a giggle.

'What on Earth are you wearing …?' she teased.

Istvan almost squealed: 'Gabriela!' in a panic at the fact that she might trigger David into a rage.

But at this moment his perennially bubbling anger

had seemingly dissipated into the ether. He felt the warm rush of tears falling down his cheeks, and this act of emotion was sufficient to convince Istvan and Marius that just maybe he wasn't as bad as they had expected.

Gabriela grabbed David by the hand and dragged him inside from the corridor. He sat on the edge of the bed and began explaining all that he had been through since he had seen them last. He could have talked for days, especially recounting the Ancestral Memories – but he was ever conscious of the imminent battle that was due to break out in Bucharest at any moment, so he kept his story as concise as possible. Most important was for him to convey his plans for dealing with the ancient vampires – and the possibility that they could help if the battle was delayed for another day.

They marvelled at his ingenuity with the chemical weaponry he had crafted.

He also explained to them just how difficult it was for him to control his urges, and even that he had been using an avatar of Gabriela herself to serve as his conscience. It was this conscience that had thus far prevented him from killing any person – though he had caused more injuries than he liked to admit. He also explained to them the irony behind his bloodlust. The fact that feasting on fresh blood allowed him to retain his sanity and strength, whereas when he was injured or hungry then the monster within him bared its teeth and left him teetering on the edge of violence.

Gabriela asked David when the last time he fed was, and he explained that it was the blood of Iuliu's thrall around 24 hours ago. Upon hearing this, Gabriela leapt to her feet without saying anything and rushed into the tiny bathroom of their accommodation. She emerged carrying a red first-aid kit that they had brought along with them, and to the shock of everyone in the room – none less so than David, she emerged with a needle and syringe from the bag.

'Drink my blood!'

Another fierce debate broke out between Gabriela and Istvan while Marius looked on in indecision. David just sat stunned. The logic was all there. If he could drink Gabriela's blood – consensually – without causing her any harm, then it would make him less likely to fall victim to his impulses and hurt anybody else. He would also be more fit for the conflict that was threatening to kick off at any moment.

While Gabriela and Istvan continued their back and forth, David leant down and rummaged through his bag of supplies. He cut their conversation short when he pulled out the silver blade he had stolen from Iuliu's thrall and turned it so that he was passing the handle to Gabriela.

'Press the blade to my chest. Right here …' he placed his finger over his heart. 'That way if I lose control, you can plunge the blade in and stop me dead …'

Even Istvan couldn't argue against that. David knew that deep down he was considering how he might be able to orchestrate the blade plunging in regardless of whether he lost control or not – but he trusted Gabriela implicitly. With this gesture seemingly settling the matter,

Exhumed

David traded the blade for the syringe. He was the doctor; he knew how to handle such equipment.

Some old habits die hard. David rummaged through the first-aid kit for disinfectant which he wiped across the skin covering the basilic vein in the crook of her elbow. He then removed the plunger from the syringe and asked her one final time: 'Are you sure about this …?'

'Yes, yes, get on with it!' she replied in mock impatience.

David sat across from her, guiding her spare arm holding the blade and placing its tip against his chest. With her insurance policy in place, and Istvan and Marius looking on in silent horror at the ridiculous spectacle playing out before them, David began working on the syringe. He tucked the plunger into his pocket, then he placed his thumb over the open chamber to form a seal. With a (former) lifetime of experience he pressed the metal tip of the needle through Gabriela's skin and into her pulsing vein.

Throughout this whole operation, David's vampiric mind was racing in overdrive. Seeing her vein pressing through her skin, hearing (feeling) her pulse, knowing that a fountain of blood was hidden behind such a thin protection of weak flesh – it was almost too much to bear. But he absolutely refused to allow himself to betray her trust. He didn't need her 'angel' on his shoulder – he had the real thing right in front of him.

The thumb with which David was forming a seal on the syringe prevented Gabriela's blood from spurting free, but as he guided his mouth to the end of the syringe, he broke the seal and allowed the pulse of her heart to gush a steady stream of warm, life-giving blood into his mouth. It was enough to cause even Marius to turn away in disgust, barely concealing a gag. Meanwhile Istvan simply looked on with a burning seriousness in his eyes, never tearing his gaze away from David and ready to grab the gun sitting just within his reach – almost desperate for an excuse to use it.

The previous day when David had tasted the blood gushing from the nose of Iuliu's thrall, he had experienced what could only be described as ecstasy for his vampiric nature. Despite that the blood had been flowing freely from the broken nose of this individual, David of all people knew how misleading it could be. A broken nose might gush forth about 30 mL of blood, but this was more than enough to make it look like a massacre had occurred. With the controlled bloodletting from Gabriela – David was receiving far more blood than he had ever tasted before.

A typical blood donation at the Red Cross would take around 470 mL of blood – around about 10 per cent of what the body had to offer. Here, David would try to match this amount, but he was left with the problem of gauging just how much he had drained with no quantitative measures like a set of scales to weigh it as it left the body. He immediately regretted the arcane method that they were using and realised that he simply should have allowed the blood to drain into a cup or a bottle which he could drink later. Too late now …

While the logical side of David's brain may have

been berating him for making such a bad decision – he understood just why he had allowed this charade to play out as it had. It was the monster within him. It wanted to sup directly from the source – something he had denied it for all this time. All these thoughts crossed David's mind in an instant as he concentrated profusely on Gabriela's mind. He looked up into her beautiful brown eyes as she looked down into his. It would have been so easy to mesmerise her and drain her dry – remove her ability to stop him with the blade, but that was not something he would allow himself to do.

Using his ESP to monitor her thoughts, David reached a point where he felt her becoming slightly fuzzy and light-headed from the blood loss. It was perfectly normal and that was why the Red Cross made you wait for a little while and eat a snack before they let you leave. Using a monumental amount of willpower – more than he thought possible – David allowed one last pulse of blood to flow out of the syringe before he placed his thumb over its tip once more and plugged the seal.

He grabbed a little ball of cotton wool from the first-aid kit and placed it against the needle that was still in her arm, then he slowly slid it out and pressed down to stem the blood flow. Like a kid playing with a straw, David couldn't help himself but suck the remainder of Gabriela's blood from the syringe as he stepped away from her and allowed Marius and Istvan to rush to her side in order to make sure that she was okay.

Her sunny disposition had not disappeared. In truth she had done little more than 'donate' blood – they really didn't need to worry about her. David's disposition was uncharacteristically sunny also. A chemical reaction within his body reacting to the first real meal he had fed it since he'd become a vampire. Endorphins, most likely.

Gabriela needed a little rest and some calories to kickstart her body into the production of more blood to replace that which she had lost. David crossed the room to the cheap packaged biscuits that can be found in any hotel room in the world and was in the process of tossing them to Gabriela when he suddenly sensed the moment he was dreading. The beacon of Csanád in his mind was on the move and was heading right for the beacon of Iuliu …

There was no need for ESP for Gabriela to realise that something was wrong. Even as she spoke to Istvan and Marius and confirmed to them that there was nothing to worry about, she had not taken her eyes off David and she could see the change in his demeanour immediately.

'David, what's happening?' she asked.

'It's started …' he said, looking around the room frantically.

He had no time to sit back and savour the meal he had just had or the reunion with the closest thing he could consider 'friends'. He rushed and grabbed his bag of goodies, taking the blade from Gabriela and placing it back inside. He then said:

'Please tell me your silver bullets will work in these guns?' he said, as he pulled out the weapons that he had taken from the security guards at the university.

Marius stepped forward to examine the guns

David was holding and saw that they were Beretta Px4s – standard issue here in Romania. Whether it was dumb luck or a stroke of fate, David didn't care, but he rejoiced internally to find that they were the exact same guns that the Watchers had in their possession.

Marius reached into their supply bag and emerged with two pre-loaded clips, handing them to David. Istvan almost had a haemorrhage, unable to stand working with a 'strigoi' as such – but his anger turned to bemusement when David did not even know how to remove the existing clips and replace them with the fresh ones. Marius was more patient and showed him, explaining that each weapon carried 20 rounds. *Would that be enough?*

David looked him in the eyes and thanked him for his help, he then walked to Gabriela and hugged her once more, kissing her softly on the cheek and whispering that he was sorry.

'Sorry? What for?' Gabriela asked.

In response, David simply raced out of the room in possession of the keys to their Dacia Sandero. He couldn't allow them to be part of this – it was far too dangerous, and he cared about Gabriela far too much …

Thirty-Three

'David!? Wait!' Gabriela cried. She leapt to her feet and made to race after him but stumbled and had to steady herself against the wall. The blood she had donated would not allow her to move so strenuously just yet.

'I'll kill the bastard!' growled Istvan, who, as usual, misread the situation.

Marius understood David's actions, however, and deep down he felt a large surge of relief. David had run in order to protect them. They had no place in a conflict such as this, they'd only get themselves killed.

Marius rushed over to Gabriela and put his arm around her to guide her back to the bed. There were tears falling down her face, but he tried to ignore her emotions as he opened the biscuits that David had tossed over earlier and encouraged her to eat them. While she was sullenly nibbling away at the snacks, he also walked to the room's obnoxiously noisy little bar fridge and examined inside. He returned with a little bottle of juice and handed it to Gabriela – she needed to recover her strength.

'He's going to get himself killed …' Gabriela sobbed through the snacks she was eating.

She felt so helpless and would have given anything to be with him. Somewhere in the background Istvan quietly mumbled 'Good', before the fierce glare of Marius caused him to turn his eyes to his feet in shame.

It was at this point that Marius remembered something – but he was loathe to bring it up. For what felt like an eternity in his mind, he wrestled with the arguments to and fro. Something about his demeanour must have changed as he sat by Gabriela's side with his arm around her, because she turned to look at him inquisitively and asked:

'What is it, Marius?'

He winced like he had been struck. Caught red-handed. Looking into the emotion-filled eyes of Gabriela, he was powerless and unable to lie to her:

'…the keys. Remember …?'

For a second the pieces didn't click together for Gabriela, but when they did, she almost shot off the bed in excitement. She raced over to her mobile phone, which was sitting on the desk across the room. Whether it could be attributed to the sudden burst of adrenaline or the calories she had fed her body, she was far steadier on her feet already. *How could she be so stupid!* The key fob for their little Dacia had an Apple Air Tag attached to it: a tiny GPS tracking device so that items just like car keys could be found if they got lost.

Gabriela loaded the tracking app on her phone and after a few seconds of buffering the map of Bucharest in the background, suddenly there it was. The little red beacon that guided her straight to David as he was driving north through the city. She wondered with mild awe whether this was what it was like in his head, given how he had described the 'beacons' pointing him towards Csanád and Iuliu in his mind. For now though, she didn't care – they could see where he was going and they could follow him!

'Come on! Pack the gear and let's get moving!' she cried as she turned the phone to show Marius and Istvan the red dot on the map.

'Why should we?' Istvan said bitterly, before following up with: 'Besides – we don't even have a car anymore, so how could we anyway?'

Gabriela crossed the room to Istvan without saying anything and then slapped him so hard across the face that his ears would ring for hours. He deserved it for a number of reasons, none more so than the fact that he was the one who had escalated things with David back in Cluj-Napoca and caused him to race off into the world. His attitude and insults towards Gabriela had not been forgotten either.

'We owe him. *YOU* owe him. Now come on …'

She didn't answer his last question, but Marius already knew the answer. It was him; he was the answer. In his youth he had been a petty thief, before giving up that life to join the Watchers. Gabriela knew that he could steal them a car from the parking garage. He sighed deeply, knowing he would be incapable of denying Gabriela her wishes – but his stomach was fluttering like a pit of vipers with nerves knowing what they'd be running into.

★ ★ ★

David struggled with his emotions as he drove away in his stolen car. After such a filling meal of divine human blood, his conscience was at an all-time high, suppressing the urges of the monster within him. He felt awful for betraying Gabriela like this – even if it was for good reason. As he had fled from the hotel room, he had cast one forlorn look back towards her and seen the tell-tale signs of confusion breaking across her face as she watched him flee – it did not feel good.

Meanwhile, there was a part of him that actually rejoiced in his own guilt. Feelings like this had been lost to him since the affliction had started taking hold. He thought of himself as completely soulless. *Could he actually live with this condition if he had a steady supply of blood?* It would be dangerous though – because what would happen if extenuating circumstances prevented him from getting his daily dose and he was then unable to control himself …

David tried to turn his mind away from such thoughts and concentrate on what lay ahead for him. Thinking like this was the definition of putting the cart before the horse. There were two ancient creatures who absolutely dwarfed him when it came to power and abilities – yet here was he trying to stand in their path.

Some nobody haematologist from Australia racing through the streets of Bucharest with what equated to jars of vampire acid and a few silver bullets. *How had any of this even happened ...?*

Oh no ...

As his mind was distracted on other matters, David finally realised that the two beacons in his head representing Csanád and Iuliu had finally converged in one location. Or, more accurately, Csanád had finally made his move on Iuliu who had patiently waited – no doubt with a trap in which to ensnare his much-hated 'father'.

The electric charge that David could feel in the air had risen to fever pitch. It was fortunate that the normal people in Bucharest could not sense it because he was certain that widespread panic would ensue if such a feeling was present in everyone's minds. He took stock of how far away he was from the action and his best guess was that it would still be a few minutes before he arrived. The fact that he was drawing ever nearer left him questioning his own sanity: *why would he want to race towards them?* But deep down he knew that this was the only path forward. Whoever won this battle would not rest until David was killed in the aftermath.

What was that? David thought he could hear fireworks going off in the distance. He wound down the window of his car and he could definitely hear the trademark explosive pops – but there were no pretty lights in the sky (nor was there any reason for fireworks at this time of the year). This wasn't a lightshow ... *this*

Exhumed

was gunfire …

'Shit, *shitshitshit* …' David mumbled to himself as he pressed down harder on the accelerator. The battle had begun, and it sounded like he was heading towards a war zone.

David's ESP was buzzing past a sea of minds as he drove at high speed. He could sense fear and confusion as the dominant emotions. Gunfire was not a common occurrence in Bucharest due to Romania having some of the strictest gun laws in Eastern Europe. Given the fact that it was (obviously) noticed so early, David wondered what would happen when the police showed up to such a scene … it wouldn't be pretty … but fortunately (?) both Iuliu and Csanád had taken measures that would allow them privacy – at least for a while.

Iuliu, as an influential, rich 'philanthropist', had easily been able to bribe the police commissioner with the request for privacy in the industrial district. Csanád instead had simply created his hit squad out of a group of policemen who had mysteriously gone AWOL from their posts when summoned by their master. The end result was an all-out war that would go uninterrupted until a victor was crowned.

David could feel the distance rapidly diminishing between himself and the scene of the fight. As he was driving there were innocent civilians racing away on foot with terror in their eyes. After having been labelled as 'terrorists' for the past couple of weeks – now these vampires were finally living up to the title.

A white mist that started off thin on its periphery

and grew ever thicker became present and this, more than anything, confirmed for David that he was approaching the epicentre. He decided to park the car and race the rest of the way on foot in an attempt to remain incognito and hope that he could add the element of surprise to his very thin bag of tricks. It was a naïve hope when the likes of Csanád and Iuliu were concerned. Their mysticism had felt every moment of his approach – he was simply left unaccosted due to his perceived insignificance. They had bigger fish to fry – namely, each other ...

David released mist of his own. Not only as a means of hiding, but also so that he could use it to scout his immediate area. Having gotten a feel for how it worked the other night in the park, he knew what a useful tool it could be.

The gunfire was relentless. Hundreds ... thousands of angry slugs of metal (probably silver) flying through the air. But for the moment, the two generals were not the target of these bullets. It was an entirely human conflict. Iuliu had his enthralled forces to defend himself, and Csanád had been prepared enough to bring his own hit squad to clear the hurdles so that he could fight Iuliu man-to-man (monster-to-monster).

With David's mist now having sufficiently spread and mingled with the mist of the other vampires, he had the same overview of the battlefield as they did. He could sense the numbers of humans dwindling as they were picking each other off with angry waves of gunfire. It became clear very quickly that Iuliu was winning this battle hands down. It should come as no surprise. He'd had centuries to build his power whereas Csanád had only been in town for several days – it was a wonder that he'd grown such a force in such a short amount of time. It really cemented to David how much of a threat he'd be to the wider world if he walked away from this battle tonight.

'YOUR THRALLS ARE ABOUT TO BE OVERWHELMED, "FATHER". DON'T YOU THINK YOU SHOULD TURN TAIL AND FLEE!?'

The booming voice of Iuliu bellowed into the night, so loud it was able to be heard clearly even over the sputtering of automatic gunfire.

A gurgling, sinister laughter permeated across the battlefield comprising the streets outside Iuliu's factory.

'MY POOR, NAÏVE CHILD – THIS HAS ALWAYS BEEN YOUR FATAL FLAW. YOU OVERESTIMATE YOUR OWN ABILITIES. FLEE ...? WHEN I AM SO CLOSE TO MY REVENGE? I THINK NOT!' roared the voice of Csanád in reply.

While he could not read the thoughts of these vampires with his ESP, David could sense the emotions emanating from them. Iuliu had begun with such confidence, but upon receiving the reply from Csanád his confidence had turned to doubt. The implication was obvious – he was wondering why Csanád was so sure of himself – *what did he know?*

A giant fireball lit up the night sky. The heat and pressure of its shockwave was enough to cause even David to duck behind the cover of a nearby building.

What the fuck was that? The sinister laughter of Csanád provided the answer. It was his ace in the hole.

The gunfire had ceased completely. One of Csanád's thralls had detonated a vest of high explosives in a suicide attack that had allowed him to wipe out the remainder of Iuliu's hit squad (as well as his own comrades) – he was the equaliser. Suddenly David realised the implications of such an event. Csanád had brought this conflict to its final stage. No thralls remained as buffers – the real battle was about to begin ...

Emerging from the mist almost like a magic trick, Csanád stepped into the open amidst the smouldering rubble and raised his arms in a taunting gesture. David's mist then alerted him to movement elsewhere and he turned his head to see Iuliu also emerging from his cover to stare down his 'father'. *Holy shit, it's about to happen ...* was all David's dazed mind could think. Forget Ali-Frazier and the 'fight of the century' – this would be the fight of the millennium ...

Without words, and almost as if it were a coordinated action sequence from a movie, David watched on as each of these monsters suddenly raised their weapons and fired them at one another. Their aims were both true, with each vampire taking (presumably silver) bullets to the chest. *Would it really be this easy?* But something was wrong – neither one of them displayed the slightest emotion of pain. *They were wearing bulletproof vests!*

Shit! David thought. If they had Kevlar protecting their chests, then perpetrating a sneak attack to pierce

Exhumed

their hearts would be out of the question. It was obvious they had both learnt a lesson from the last time they had faced off, when Csanád, in his distraction, had allowed Andrei Albescu to spear him through the heart from behind – a mistake he had paid for for centuries.

Csanád was the first to make a move following this initial spray of gunfire. He began an erratic zigzag motion to close the distance between himself and Iuliu. The speed at which he moved beggared belief – it looked almost like something out of *The Flash*, a blur of motion. But Iuliu's eyes were not deceived – he stood his ground and raised his weapon to fire upon Csanád as he approached.

David could feel the emotions coursing through Csanád when at least one of the bullets hit its target, tearing through some part of his exposed flesh. But he was not alone in taking damage, he had swung his own weapon up and returned fire on Iuliu. The roar of pain from the stationary vampire was evidence enough that he, too, had been hit.

The distance between them disappeared as Csanád clattered against Iuliu with great speed. With a mighty backhanded swing of his arm, Csanád sent Iuliu's gun flying. Iuliu returned the favour with a flat-footed kick to the solar plexus causing Csanád to drop his own gun, which Iuliu promptly kicked out of reach. Iuliu then reached behind his back and drew the very same silver blade that David recognised from the Ancestral Memories of the pair's previous fight in Szatmár all those years ago. Csanád only possessed a small silver dagger that he had stolen from one of Iuliu's thralls — he was at a disadvantage.

Iuliu, holding the sword defensively to parry any attacks, began slowly retreating into the building. It was the same ploy that he had used in Szatmár to lure Csanád into a trap. Csanád paused briefly, considering his options, before he smiled one of his sadistic grins and began following Iuliu into the building. Just before he disappeared inside, he stopped and turned his head towards David. In his mind, David heard the taunt: *'Well, are you coming, "boy"?'* — and then Csanád was gone from his sight.

It rattled David. Until now he thought he had gone undetected, but evidently not. And what other choice did he have? He *had* to follow them ... David rummaged through his bag of supplies, carefully contemplating the plan he had been formulating in his mind.

It was now or never ...

Thirty-Four

Csanád was no fool – he understood the bottomless well of deceit through which Iuliu operated. Nor was it lost on him that Iuliu's retreat into the cover of the building was exactly the same strategy he had used back in Szatmár when Csanád gained the upper hand in their battle. Back then, it had been a thrall armed with silver-tipped arrows; now, it was certain to be far more potent.

Iuliu was banking on Csanád racing headlong towards his goal and ignoring his senses – but that was not a mistake the older strigoi would make again. Even before Iuliu had disappeared into the building, he had detected the mind of the thrall hiding somewhere on the second level of the large factory. In the seething pits of his mind, he revelled at the shock that Iuliu would experience when he learnt just what Csanád was capable of – a little trick he had been honing ever since he began his pilgrimage south from Stockholm.

Before he allowed himself to 'fall into' his firstborn son's trap, Csanád turned towards his latest progeny to fire off a quick mental barb. It infuriated him that the blood doctor thought he was being so secretive – he just had to ruin that for him. He was no threat and having him here would only save him from having to hunt him down later. Plus, he had a morbid curiosity to see just what David had planned in the first place – he would take great pleasure in watching it fail …

With that, Csanád slowly stepped inside the building – ever-conscious of the location of the 'trap' into which he was walking. In an act of showmanship, Csanád made it seem like he would blindly stumble into the open. He wanted Iuliu to experience the hope of winning before he snatched it away. So, just as he was on the verge of stepping into the line of sight for the sniper with the high-calibre explosive silver rounds, Csanád stopped.

A malevolent grin broke across his face as he flexed the true majesty of his mind – unleashing a skill that even Iuliu thought to be impossible. The tinny pop of a gunshot echoed through the factory as the thrall unholstered a handgun from his hip, turned it to his own head and pulled the trigger.

'HOW!?' bellowed Iuliu as he stepped out from the cover he had taken to stare down his evil 'father'. Back when Iuliu had faked his own death it had taken him an eternity to undo the hypnotic hold that his 'father' held over his thrall's mind. Here, Csanád had done it in moments. It was impossible.

Exhumed

'You should have killed me in Szatmár ...' Csanád declared honestly. 'Staked through the heart and bound in silver – you gifted me nothing but time. Time to discover the true depths of the powers of a strix. You think you have grown strong – but really you have grown stagnant!'

Csanád would have happily continued to gloat – he was revelling in a situation that he believed he had already won. He was older, he was stronger. The burning ache of the silver slug that had embedded in his forearm as he raced towards Iuliu outside was barely even an inconvenience for him. He saw Iuliu walking with a limp and knew that his own silver bullet was clearly causing more discomfort.

Iuliu was in no mood to listen to any more of Csanád's taunts. Nor did he share Csanád's outlook that the battle was already decided. His 'father' was forgetting the fact that he had lived for these last 800 years amidst an ocean of blood. He had grown far stronger – more than he had yet let on. Csanád would be unpleasantly surprised to see the tables turned. With this thought, Iuliu raised his silver blade and began rapidly closing the distance. He would once more stake his 'father' through the heart and put an end to this once and for all.

⋆ ⋆ ⋆

David was conscious of how ridiculous he must have looked from an outsider's point of view. He had pistols wedged into the loose pockets of his jogger's shorts, a silver blade tucked into the back of his waistband, and within each hand he carefully carried glass bottles containing a clear liquid. He stumbled a little as he approached the entrance to the building and forced himself to regain steady footing before continuing inside. If he fell now and broke the glass bottles then he was done for. The pig sticker and pistols would never be enough to win this fight, regardless of the fact that they were silver.

David heard the short conversation between Csanád and Iuliu before he could see them, but then he could sense the bloodlust within the air amplify a thousandfold. The climactic battle had kicked off, and there was something inside him that wanted to watch. His vampiric mind was fascinated – but his human mind also urged him on as he didn't want to miss any opportunity to strike.

Glancing through the doorway, he saw Iuliu rushing towards Csanád with his sword wielded in what appeared to be a highly trained fashion. It should be no surprise that in a lifetime spanning 1100 years, he would hone his skills to a fine edge. Csanád was not one to be cowed by such an advance, however. He may have only carried a small dagger just like David, but he deftly parried each advance from Iuliu. His speed and reflexes were godly and Iuliu could not find an opening. The same could be said in reverse though, nor could Csanád find a weak point in Iuliu's defences.

Beginning to feel a little concerned that the fight was taking too long, David crept inside to get closer to the action. It was then that somebody finally broke through and caused some real harm – punctuated by a roar of agony echoing throughout the giant room. *Who had it been?*

Retraining his eyes on the vampires from his new vantage point closer to the action, David realised that the answer was that both of them had struck a blow. The tip of the sword wielded by Iuliu had run right through Csanád's shoulder, but at the same time Csanád's dagger was plunged to the hilt into Iuliu's thigh.

The two monsters withdrew their blades and stumbled slightly away from each other, reeling from the wounds that had been inflicted. There was no time for rest though, as Iuliu attempted to press his advantage by charging again at Csanád – swinging wildly. The perfectly trained technique that he had displayed earlier looked sloppy now. Fatigue from his wounds was holding him back, and the same could be said about Csanád in return. His vampiric grace almost failed him and he stumbled to retain his footing as he retreated away from the wildly swinging blade.

What came next took David by complete surprise. Iuliu was only feigning his fatigue to lull Csanád into a false sense of complacency. He suddenly resumed his stature as a world-class swordsman and with a trained swipe he tore a deep groove through the hip of Csanád, which was met by a resounding roar of agony. In an attempt to keep the upper hand, he pressed on – but Csanád was not ready to give in just yet. He dodged the blade deftly before unleashing a brutally powerful sweeping kick to Iuliu's leg – the same leg that had been both shot and stabbed previously.

Iuliu collapsed to his knees and Csanád pounced with his dagger, landing on top of Iuliu and plunging it deep into the shoulder of his sword arm. The wound was enough to cause Iuliu to lose his grip on the blade. He had lost. The sheer power and desperation of Csanád had overwhelmed him, and they both knew it. Csanád unleashed psychotic laughter as he made to withdraw his blade and deal the final blow — a slash to the neck so violent that it would lop the head clean off. However — before he could manage such a finishing blow — the sound of shattering glass interrupted his revelry.

David had finally launched into action. The two bottles of aqueous silver nitrate had hit their targets. The first shattered on the floor next to the two vampires and splashed them with its deadly contents. The second hit Csanád directly in the chest and broke against his Kevlar armour — this strike was the one that caused the most damage as it soaked through both his and Iuliu's clothing and began to ravage their bodies.

Csanád rolled free from Iuliu, flailing around like a man on fire. Iuliu too leapt to his feet and performed similar mad motions. It would have been funny to see if not for what was at stake here. David didn't just stop to watch the scene though — he pulled the two pistols out of his pockets and began unloading the 40 silver bullets towards the two dancing vampires. One thing he hadn't expected was how bad of a shot he would be ... shooting pistols at moving targets wasn't as easy as the movies made it seem ... but he still managed to land a number of hits to their exposed flesh — each shot punctuated by a fresh roar of pain.

Holy shit, this is actually going to work!

The guns ran dry within moments and he was down to his final weapon – the little silver dagger tucked into his waistband. He launched himself headlong into the fray now – but this was where all of his plans went out the window. He was still just a baby. Even the Ancestral Memories were insufficient when it came to educating him about the sheer tenacity of creatures such as these.

Not just one, but both of the vampires reacted to his proximity. Csanád and Iuliu worked together for the first and only time in their lives in order to take care of their common enemy. The melting pink flesh of their bodies and the holes plugged with silver had weakened them dramatically – but they were still too strong for David. The first swing of his silver blade was aimed at the throat of Csanád – but his arm was blocked by his furious father.

He stood, stunned, looking at the face of the devil himself, and his heart sank. He did not even have the time to realise the trouble he found himself in, because from behind he felt the agony of the bite of Iuliu's blade enter his back. He looked down and saw the tip had emerged from his chest – it was the most surreal thing he would ever see.

Slumping to his knees, David could only watch as the two vampires suddenly stalked him like hungry lions. The enmity between them temporarily forgotten in their overwhelming desire for revenge against the one who had disfigured them as such. The skin was sloughing off their bodies – they *needed* to feed, and soon, or else they would both be dead regardless of who won this final bout.

With an unspoken agreement, they each approached David. *He* would be their sustenance. Nothing better than vampire blood to rejuvenate their wounds – and with David taken care of then they would be free to resume their grudge match spanning the millennia.

Csanád was already holding back one of David's hands – the one he had blocked from swinging the blade aimed at his own throat. He pulled it to his own mouth and tore a crude chunk of flesh out of David's wrist with his teeth. The blood pulsed through his superficial radial artery, and Csanád roared in triumph as the sensation flooded his mouth and entered his system. Meanwhile, from behind, Iuliu performed the exact same ritual by latching onto his throat and drinking deep of his lifeblood.

★★★

Gabriela had driven their stolen car like a bat out of hell in pursuit of the red blip on the map marking the location of where David had stopped in the north of Bucharest. Even with her flagrant disregard for the speed limit, they still arrived at the scene of the conflict about 10 minutes after David had. By the time they found their little Dacia Sandero, with the keys still in its ignition, the battle had long since moved indoors.

Stepping out of the car, the Watchers were astounded by the apocalyptic levels of destruction and bloodshed laid out before them. Many small spot fires continued to burn in the aftermath of Csanád's suicide-bombing thrall. Bodies (and body parts) littered the ground all around them. It was obvious just why David had tried to leave them behind ...

'Quickly, come on!' called Gabriela as she raced towards the door of the factory.

She was acting rashly and guided by her emotions, but there was no force in the world that could have stopped her. Istvan and Marius shared a look of despondency, but they couldn't allow her to run off on her own so they quickly followed behind. Each of the three were carrying one of their handguns with the silver bullets – for whatever good that would do them against their near invincible enemy.

'DAVID, NOOO!' the shrill scream of Gabriela pierced the night as she finally witnessed the scenes inside the factory.

She had walked in at the exact moment to see David with a sword through his chest and two monsters latched onto him, draining him of his blood. She lifted her gun but was unable to bring herself to fire. The distance was too great, and she would risk shooting David in the process.

Iuliu did not recognise the significance of Gabriela arriving at the scene, but Csanád did. Their whole story had gone full circle. He would take care of the Albescu next, and all of his enemies would be felled in one bloody night. With his mouth still latched firmly to David's wrist, Csanád flexed those same mystical muscles against Gabriela that he had used to force Iuliu's thrall to commit suicide earlier. He watched with a smug satisfaction to see the confused look across her face as she tried to fight against her hand as it began to raise the gun towards her own head.

Istvan, faster than Marius, arrived at the scene just in time to prevent tragedy. He crash-tackled Gabriela to the floor, sending her gun flying and saving her from the mysticism that was assailing her. Csanád growled in frustration, before finally detaching from David and roaring for them to wait their turn. Iuliu also detached from David's neck and withdrew his blade from David's back. It was time for them to conclude their battle. These humans would allow him to heal his wounds after he was done with Csanád.

With their newfound audience watching on with horrified awe, Csanád and Iuliu once more faced off and prepared to resume their battle – but before so much as a single blade was swung something else drew everyone's attention ...

David was laughing ...

This was an insult beyond which Csanád was in the mood to bear. He would remove David's head from his body and revel in the screams of the Albescu girl ... but ...

Suddenly he felt ill in such a way he had never experienced before. His gorge began to rise and he experienced a violent eruption of dark red vomit. Gabriela watched on in shock to see Iuliu reacting the same way. *What the hell was going on here?* Meanwhile David was still laughing at their feet.

Within her head, Gabriela heard the faint mental contact from David. He was very weak from the blood loss, but using his ESP he said to her: *'Act now! Remove their heads!'*

She trusted David implicitly, and she did not need to be told twice. She lunged headlong into action, paying no heed to the desperate cries of panic from Istvan and Marius who missed in their attempts at holding her back.

★ ★ ★

David was weak. He did not have long left. The silver nitrate that he had injected into his bloodstream before entering the factory building had been taking a toll on his insides – and the blood loss he had experienced from Csanád and Iuliu alike left him almost at the point of expiry. Despite realising that this would be the end, he was happy. He continued his taunting laughter, elated that his gamble had worked in his favour.

In his short time as a vampire, there was one observation that had stuck with David. While strength increased immeasurably as a vampire aged, so too did the potency of their weaknesses. The idea to inject himself with silver nitrate was something he only thought of on the spur of the moment – his initial plan was to simply attack the monsters as he had done. However, as he reached into his bag of supplies before entering the building, he had felt the bite of the needle still in his pocket. The same needle and syringe that he had used to feed from Gabriela.

This victory was her doing. If not for her

selflessness and trust, allowing him to feed from her blood earlier and delivering the needle into his possession then he would have lost. The gamble with the silver nitrate was his silver bullet – so to speak.

Before the light left his eyes, David watched on as Gabriela lifted the silver sword that Iuliu had dropped during his violent sickness. She moved with such grace and displayed more strength that should be possible for one such as her stature. The final sight that David saw before his vision faded into black were the heads of Csanád and Iuliu removed from their bodies.

Epilogue

The eclectic collective of professionals gathered at the ECDC in Stockholm to examine the vampire locked in the quarantined room. This time, however, the situation was very different. The vampire was no longer an emaciated corpse freshy dug out of the Carpathian Mountains in Romania; nor was he being held against his will. David had suggested this idea of his own volition.

★★★

After David had lost consciousness during the fateful battle in Bucharest, a lot had happened in a short amount of time. With the heads of the strigoi removed, Gabriela took charge of the situation like a seasoned general. She ordered Marius to race to the car and return with fuel. It was easy, they always kept a couple of spare jerry cans in the boot of their Sandero. With this in hand, they doused the remains of Csanád and Iuliu, melting their bodies down right there on the floor of the factory. No power in Heaven or on Earth would be capable of bringing them back from this destruction – they were truly, *finally* dead.

While she watched this bonfire play out before her eyes, Gabriela rushed towards David's body on the floor and cradled his head in her arms. She thought he was dead, until … a slight sputter of a cough alerted her that he yet clung to life. In an emotion-driven panic, she grabbed one of the silver blades from the floor and was on the verge of slicing her own wrist to deliver the life-saving blood for David to recover.

For the second time in the span of minutes – Istvan saved her life. She had already lost a lot of blood tonight and she couldn't afford to be so reckless. She argued and fought against him bitterly, but Istvan overpowered her and took her by surprise when he told her to let *him* do it. She watched on with a sense of distrust lingering inside, thinking perhaps this was all a ploy to allow him to finish off David once and for all – but she felt a tremendous surge of guilt for these thoughts when she saw him slice his wrist and pour the blood into David's mouth.

The reaction was almost instantaneous. The wonders of the strigoi never ceased. Something else that played strongly in David's favour was that the poison he had introduced to his bloodstream was almost entirely sucked free by the leeches of Csanád and Iuliu. Now, he just needed a little blood to kick off his regeneration and he would be as good as new …

Exhumed

It took David several seconds to understand what was happening, but when a semblance of clarity restored within his mind, he found himself assaulted by the violent hug of Gabriela. He gasped in pain from the sword wound through his chest. It would take a little longer and a little more blood to return to full health. Gabriela broke the tension by giggling like a schoolgirl who had just punched a boy in the shoulder.

'Come on, tough guy, you gonna let a little scratch like this hold you back?'

After a short while, David thanked Istvan for his blood and instructed him how to administer first aid for his wound. It was a risky manoeuvre – but he would be fine as long as David was able to properly tend to it later. For that, though, they would have to get out of this filthy factory. The influence of the vampires could not last forever – certainly they would find themselves accosted by the police sooner or later …

Things moved quickly after this. All piled into the Sandero, they returned to the hotel where the Watchers had been holed up. David took care of Istvan's wound, and between the three of the Watchers they donated enough blood for David to return to full health. But there was one problem that was insurmountable – they simply couldn't continue like this forever … It was then that David came up with the solution to all of their problems.

He explained his plan to the Watchers, and though Gabriela especially did not like it, she trusted David and allowed him to go through with it. Using Gabriela's phone, he dialled the ECDC and after waiting an eternity on hold and being transferred to several different people, he finally got Dr Maja Nilsson on the other end of the line. Their conversation lasted for almost three hours as David explained what had happened since the last time they had seen each other at Stockholm Hospital – as well as the plan he had in mind.

Maja immediately agreed to David's idea, and within two days he was back in the sterile security of the ECDC facility – only this time, on the other side of the glass looking out. It was a win-win situation for everyone involved. Even though David had managed to go this far without crossing the unthinkable line and taking a human life, he couldn't trust this luck to continue. If he were left alone in the wide world then it was only a matter of time before he followed the same path as his hated 'father' and 'brother'. Seclusion was the only option short of death.

It wasn't all bad though – from his quarantined room, David was delivered fresh blood daily and this allowed him to maintain his humanity. It also allowed him to not only contribute, but to lead the scientific study of his own affliction. In the span of only two short weeks, he had already learnt so much and he was confident that some good could come out of this after all. A cure for cancer, perhaps? *What good was blood that could heal any wound if it couldn't be shared?*

Only one person had the nerve to enter the quarantined cell with David. Gabriela was his constant companion. She visited on a daily basis, even when David told her that she did not have to. Her nature was unquenchable, and she would only ever reply to him that she was a Watcher – it was her job to keep an eye on the big bad vampire (she even used the term 'vampire' now, since that was how David considered himself).

★ ★ ★

Staring through the window at David and Gabriela, stunned by the bizarre stroke of fate, were several of the same members that had accompanied David when they were originally gathered to study Csanád.

Janik Schuler, the Swiss linguist; Ana Vida, the Hungarian historian; and Cristina Grigorcea, the Romanian archaeologist responsible for uncovering Csanád in the first place formed a team of social scientists. They studied from David and his Ancestral Memories and learnt a massive wealth of knowledge that had been previously lost to the winds of time. The German historian, Jürgen Albrecht chose not to reprise his invite to the ECDC, still understandably shaken from his first visit.

On the medical side: Drs Maja Nilsson, Director of the ECDC; Eva Björklund, the Swedish general practitioner; and Barbara Wood, the British biologist (who had backflipped on her decision not to join the taskforce when she learnt that it was David) all fell into line with David himself to study his alien physiology …when Gabriela let them get near him that was.

S.J. Patrick

Postlude

Sânge de Argint

$$\overset{+}{Ag}\overset{-}{NO_3} + H_2O \rightarrow Ag^+_{(aq)} + \overset{-}{NO}_{3(aq)}$$

Silver Nitrate   Water   Aqueous Silver   Aqueous Nitrate

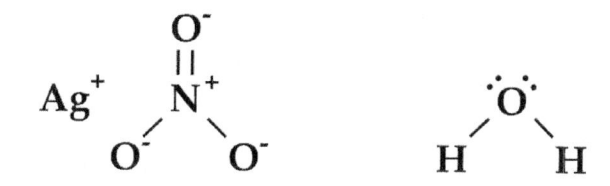

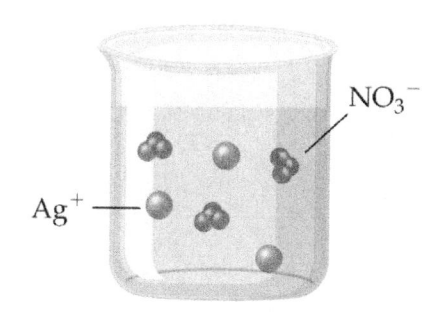

Read on for a sneak peek of the sequel to *Exhumed* – *Siren* – coming soon!

Siren

S.J. Patrick

S.J. Patrick

Prologue

The night was young when Patrice Laurent entered the VIP 21 Club. One of Dijon's classier establishments, it was a favourite haunt for Patrice whenever he could find time away from his busy schedule. In his late twenties, he was already a successful businessman; and this, combined with his pronounced good looks, was enough to make him a highly eligible bachelor. Patrice was Afro-French, born to Cameroonian parents. He shared more than a passing resemblance to one of the most famous members of the French national football team – Kylian Mbappe – which went a long way towards earning him attention from the ladies.

That was his goal for the evening. Attention from the ladies.

Rarely would a night go by where Patrice didn't leave the club with a gorgeous woman on his arm and a story to tell his friends and colleagues. Tonight, it seemed, would be no different. Sitting at the bar, Patrice quickly struck up conversation with a pretty young woman. Her name was Manon and Patrice was already envisioning the look and feel of her body beneath the already revealing black dress that barely left anything to the imagination. However, as Patrice was on the verge of propositioning Manon to leave the club, that was when, from across the bar, he caught the eye of the most beautiful woman he had ever seen.

Manon, tipsy and overly conversational, was chatting away in Patrice's ear – but he wasn't listening to a word she was saying. All of his concentration was on the goddess making eyes at him. He wasn't even sure exactly what it was about her that entranced him so – he had seen (and slept with) many beautiful women before – but there was just something otherworldly about this one. She was strikingly tall, probably rivalling his own 185 cm. Her skin was pale as porcelain, which contrasted against her flowing auburn hair. Her face was symmetrical, with full-bodied lips curled into an almost teasing smile – but it was her eyes that were the most enchanting feature. A deep black that looked out of place against the ivory of her skin.

Patrice found himself rising from the barstool and walking towards this new woman. Gone were any thoughts of Manon. He didn't even pay attention to her offended protestations as he glided towards the redhead who had not ceased her eye contact with him since the moment he noticed her. Narcissistic by nature, Patrice considered himself the equal of anybody in terms of his looks, so he tried to play it cool as he sidled up close to the porcelain goddess and introduced himself. For her part, she didn't say a word – she simply interlaced her fingers between his own and began to lead him away from the bar.

Not used to finding himself on the backfoot in situations such as these, Patrice simply allowed himself to be dragged along like a schoolboy being escorted to the principal's office. Not that he would have minded in the slightest if the principal looked like her and wanted to administer discipline to him. His mind began to conjure sordid imagery of the events he just knew were going to come later, and a smile broke out on his face as he was led through the VIP area of the club. He thought that she was taking him some place quieter so that they could talk, and he was right – just not in the fashion he expected. She led him through a private exit of the club, where he immediately spotted an impressive black limousine awaiting them right outside the door.

Just who is this woman? – Patrice was thinking. It felt like he had stepped into Wonderland, and little did he realise how apt a thought this would turn out to be. He watched as the woman – still without having spoken a single word to him – climbed into the backseat of the limo. Her stunningly short dress rode up, exposing enough skin for Patrice to almost lose his composure before he too climbed into the vehicle after her. Once inside – she pounced onto him, her lips latching around his own, kissing him with such passion that he suddenly felt decidedly inexperienced in contrast – a feeling that he was far from used to.

He matched her kiss with his own, his hands naturally moving to roam over her body as hers began to do the same over his own. He was vaguely cognisant of the fact that there must be a driver at the front of the vehicle who was able to see all of this, but he really didn't care. The pair continued to kiss for what felt like an eternity, becoming ever more passionate until such a moment that Patrice's inner monologue exclaimed *'Mon dieu!'*. The mysterious woman, in the throes of passion, had bitten him on the lip.

Something snapped in Patrice's mind, which broke him away from the trance that he had been in, and he tried to pull away from her kiss to explore the damage to his lip. He could already taste the blood in his mouth, however — the woman's hand shot out and grasped him by the back of his head, holding him to her as she continued to kiss (suck?) his lips. Her grip on his head was not violent, but it was unrelenting — it conveyed such a power that did not seem possible for such a delicate woman as she. In his mind, Patrice was left with the decision: go along with the kinks of this crazy woman, or put his foot down and head back inside to Manon. The throb of pain through his ruptured lip eventually decided for him — he had had enough here …

Fighting harder to break the iron grip of this woman, Patrice eventually managed to escape her grasp. No, not quite — she relented her hold. He could tell that if she wanted to keep him then she was evidently more powerful than him. It was a marked hit to his pride. After breaking free from her kiss, his lip swollen and throbbing, the taste of his own blood in his mouth, he reached for the door handle to exit back into the alley. The door was locked. Turning to face her, a new indignation building inside him, Patrice saw her mouth turned upward into a sneer. All of a sudden, she was no longer beautiful, it was like some kind of a spell had worn off and he was seeing her for what she truly was.

A flash of movement and a glimmer of something shiny caught Patrice's eye. Then came the pain — and finally his mind caught up to what had occurred. Looking down, Patrice's stylish pink shirt was somehow soaked with blood, becoming redder and redder by the instant. The warmth he felt through his shirt was unable to offset the chill of ice that he could feel through his veins as he felt his own life draining away.

The last thing that Patrice witnessed was the ghoul sitting next to him as she leapt towards him, placing her mouth back onto his body — drinking deep from the blood that spilled from the gash in his throat.

★★★

It was the thrill of the hunt that excited Aalis. She had a well-developed network of blood slaves under her command, but there was nothing quite like the sensation of satisfying her urges on an unsuspecting victim. Her mysticism was second to none, allowing her an all-access pass to the minds of pitiful humans such as 'Patrice'. This was something that was lacking with her blood slaves; they were enthralled and under her total control — they didn't experience the same levels of incomprehension and fear. They didn't think that they were the ones in control, completely unaware of their imminent demise. God – it was sexual.

Upon satisfying her bloody urges, Patrice was long since dead – his corpse, now devoid of blood, was beginning to lose its warmth. Aalis was not squeamish by any means – how could any creature like her ever be so – but she soon found herself disgusted by the husk slumped beside her. She would have preferred nothing more than to simply open the door to the limousine and toss him out next to the dumpsters – but she knew better. You didn't live for centuries amongst the humans by being so careless. Aalis used her mentalism to instruct her enthralled driver to set a course back to her lavish mansion where Patrice would be disposed of in such a way that he would never be seen again.

A sudden chill struck Aalis.

A sensation she thought she had closed herself off from.

Iuliu …?

That name stirred a mixture of emotions through her. The first such emotion to rise to the surface was rage, recalling the last time she had seen his hateful face – but this was quickly followed by a loneliness and longing. She had purged him from her life centuries earlier, and she had shut her vast mind away, locking the feeling of him out of her life. But now … something had happened …

Opening her mind, Aalis flexed her mentalism for all it was worth, casting her mind across the mental ether and hundreds of kilometres east to Romania. It surprised her where she was drawn – having last seen her lover in Spain – however it did not surprise her that he had followed her lead and returned to the place of his birth. There was something about their species that was ever protective and jealous of their own lands.

Aalis quickly discovered far more than she ever would have expected. Not just Iuliu, but the minds of two additional creatures of the night. It was difficult for her to come to terms with what she was feeling. As with all vampires, her connection was strongest with that of her maker, and it was through this connection that Aalis experienced a level of suffering emanating from Iuliu that she did not believe possible. Touching the minds of the other vampires nearby, she experienced the same sensation from one other creature – such power he possessed! The final of the trio was easily the most feeble of the bunch, and his mind felt like it was about to blip out of existence – however what came next took Aalis's breath away completely.

Iuliu was gone.

This was different to when she had closed her mind to him.

Aalis knew, beyond a shadow of a doubt, that she had just experienced the death of her creator, her father – her lover …

She suddenly felt hollow inside, but this emotion did not last for long – it was replaced with a roiling, burning rage. Her vastly powerful mind continued to scry afar, sensing the demise of the mysterious and powerful vampire alongside Iuliu – yet one blip remained. The weakest of the bunch yet lived, and somehow, he was growing stronger once more. He must be drinking the blood of her lover!

The limousine drew to a halt and Aalis's thrall raced to open the door for her to exit. Her rage exploded out of the vehicle; the blade that she had used to slice Patrice's throat was lodged into the side of her driver's head, dropping him to the ground immediately. A waste of good blood – but the only outlet for Aalis's burning fury.

She would never forget the feeling of the pitifully weak mind that had somehow managed to kill her lover. She would make him suffer beyond anything he could ever comprehend …

Printed in Great Britain
by Amazon